Brotherhood of the Times

To Jeanne + Tom,
Thanks for all your
love and support -
best wishes always

love, Steve

Brotherhood
of the Times

STEPHEN BIRCHAK

To order additional copies of this book, contact:
Xlibris Corporation
1-888-795-4274
www.Xlibris.com
Orders@Xlibris.com

45005

Contents

For Annie

ACKNOWLEDGEMENTS

IT IS IMPORTANT to acknowledge history – for history generated the headlines we delivered. The main characters in this book are fictional, but the emotions from 1968 were real. Our mothers cried for the Kennedy and King families, and we grieved Viet Nam, from which I lost a cousin. However, we celebrated good history – in box scores and ball cards. With great reverence and respect, I write about 1968 using this history.

Special thanks to Schenectady Literary Consultants – Bresch, Mac, Karen, "Uncle" Corbett, and Annie. Your encouragement made me a better writer. Thanks to Apollo Art Studios for your incredible artwork.

PROLOGUE

Final Journal

We were the last generation of American men to grow up in a world without Internet, video games, cell phones, terrorist invasions, or cable TV. We didn't have character education, attention deficit disorders, or social skills curriculum. We made money delivering papers, mowing lawns, and cashing in soda bottles. It was a time when one sport hovered above all others, and it was played with a bat and a ball. Expertise didn't come from cable sport channels; it was found on the back of baseball cards. We may have been the last generation to actually read those cards – before carefully placing them in the spokes of our bicycles. We learned all about life on the vast sandlots which now are nearly extinct.

Autumn is on its way. I was unsure for so many years whether I ever wanted to go back. In the summer of 1968, I learned lessons that changed my life. During those sun-filled months, I found love for the first time and felt the joy of a first kiss. Golden sunbeams, the greenest grass I ever played on, and the carefree relationships allowed me to drink in deep breaths of air.

It was the last true summer of freedom before high school. We delivered the Rocky Mountain Times *newspaper in the predawn hours. We spent our days in confident moments playing baseball or in awkward moments with girls at the local pool. Nighttime found us lying on our sleeping bags and staring at the heavens above Denver. Our future and our dreams were shared with the stars that twinkled in perfect harmony with the sounds of crickets.*

For the first time, I understand the moment of passage. Today I am Daniel, but I can crisply recall the feeling of being Danny. My best friend, Michael Terrence Hannigan, I'm sure looks likewise in his mirror as Mickey again. The world was right in one glorious summer when Danny, Mickey, Mags, and Sanners rode through the streets of Denver in the predawn hours and delivered newspapers. We were comrades in mischief, determination, and purpose. Life is good when you have friends consumed in the same three things day after day: paper routes, girls, and baseball. What else could anyone ever hope for in life?

With all our love, potential, and spirit, I wonder still how a deranged force could wander into our path and steal everything life had to offer. I may never understand, but I am glad I returned to 1968. I am reminded of a true brotherhood. Yes, it was a brotherhood of the times.

1

The Apartment

TERRENCE CAUGHT HIS balance in just enough time to avoid stumbling headfirst into the picture window. The living room was small but average size for apartments in downtown Denver. Located on the third floor, unit 31-A overlooked the parking lot below. In this moment, Terrence was content to stand in the window and stare blankly into the world outside. He glanced at his brown Chevy parked two stories below. The car looked out of place. It was parked over the lines, selfishly taking up two spaces.

In one slow motion, Terrence raised the bottle to his lips. Two hours ago, the bourbon stood proud in its black-and-brown label among other bottles on a liquor store shelf. Now, only a few reluctant swallows swished helplessly in the bottom. The bottle purged itself of its duty to contribute to a depressed man.

In his finest three-piece suit, Terrence continued to stagger from side to side, trying to catch his balance. He reached up, rubbed his eyes, then stroked his cheeks. The smoothness reminded him that it was the first time he had been clean shaven in over a week. Red tracks in his eyes and the bags that puffed beneath them were nothing more than a cover on a tattered book. The pages beneath held no mystery, suspense, or excitement, just another tale about life that no one wants to hear.

Terrence Hannigan had finished crying; there was nothing left to give and nothing left to feel. The burn in his throat from the whiskey matched the pain in his heart from the isolation he felt. He endured loneliness most of his life but never imagined that it could feel worse. It did now. Two hours earlier, he watched his mother being lowered into the ground. Fate's cruelty forced him to witness the pancreatic cancer as it slowly drained the life out of her over the past year. Terrence stood by her side daily and watched her whither away through slow and senseless pain. With each of her dying breaths, he felt his sense of isolation grow more profound; she was just one more person whom he couldn't keep from death. Along with relationship problems and career difficulties, he had never felt more hopeless and inept in his pathetic life.

He turned and lost his balance before stumbling into the kitchen. He sidestepped the scattered evidence of his solitary life that was spread throughout the apartment. The trash, junk, and clutter reminded him of how ineffective he had become in his futile attempt to manage his life. Piles of clothes had been carelessly flung over the backs of chairs, and the dishes in the sink displayed fossilized specks of cereal – the remnants of meals mindlessly devoured earlier in the week. Pizza boxes topped the garbage pail, and bags from fast-food restaurants had been crumpled and stuffed between them.

His trembling hand picked up the phone. The wayward shaky fingers gave up on dialing and dropped the phone on the kitchen table. The heart wanted to cry, but the body had no tears left to give. He felt the coolness of the table as he rested his forehead on the smooth surface. Pulling his hands behind his head, he ran them through his hair, then lurched with each futile attempt at dry tears. Clenching his fists, he pounded the table – each thump growing softer until his hands came to a rest. He felt his strength and his will to live slowly drain from his body.

Terrence raised his head, then tilted the bottle for its final contribution to a beaten man. He attempted to place it back on the table, but it wavered and fell to its side. It rolled slowly to the edge of the table before crashing to the ground. Terrence stood up as his shoes crunched over some of the newly broken shards of glass. He walked to a small drawer of junk next to the sink and shuffled through tape dispensers, screwdrivers, and assorted pens and pencils. His hand finally found what it was looking for as he pulled it from the drawer. His feet shuffled on the broken glass as he placed his thumb on the side of the utility knife and pushed the blade outward. The dull blade revealed the remnants of tar. For a moment, he recalled its last duty in cutting roofing shingles over the weekend. He helped Jessica, his ten-year-old daughter build a small doghouse for her new puppy she named Marky.

Terrence clicked on the lock, then gripped it in his right hand. Lowering it to his left wrist, he turned the sharp edge toward his skin. With his quivering right hand, he pressed down, and in a methodical deliberate motion, he pulled the dull blade across his wrist. For a moment, it seemed odd to him as he heard what sounded like the muffled sound of a piece of paper being torn as he dragged the blade across his skin. The blood immediately gushed from the wound and ran down his arm. At once, the red pool began soaking into the pale dress shirt. Transferring the knife to his left hand, he gripped the handle. The tightening of the muscles of the injured wrist shot pain up his arm and caused the blood to stream out quickly. Turning the blade to his right arm, the second incision was much quicker. He pulled down hard to cut deeper than the gash on his other arm.

Terrence closed his eyes, inhaled, and clenched his fists as he began to feel faint. The colors of his world faded into darkness. His feeling – his grip on reality – faded into numbness.

I'll be free . . . Finally . . .

Mickey . . .

Terrence fell to his knees, unaware of the glass shards cutting into his knees. "No!" he screamed.

A voice mixed into his thoughts again. *Mickey . . .* He pulled his ravaged arms to the side of his head as the streams of crimson ran down his face. "No! No! No! Never call me Mickey again!"

Terrence fell forward to his face, then propped himself up on his elbows in a futile attempt to find his feet beneath him. "I'm Terrence, don't ever call me Mickey again!"

Mickey . . .

His voice quivered as it became softer and gentle, "I'm not Mickey, please don't call me Mickey . . . Mickey was just a boy . . . just a boy . . ."

In the apartment next door, a young man kissed his wife on her cheek and headed out the door to find his truck. In the apartment below, a mother cradled her newborn. Behind the apartments, a pair of seven-year-old twins competed to see who could go the highest on the swings. Their laughter was lost on apartment 31-A, where a man lay dying. The world, indifferent to its inhabitants, kept on turning.

2

May 4, 1968
Uncle Bud's

DANNY GLANCED AT his wristwatch, 5:55 a.m. He smiled, knowing his paper route would be finished by 6:00. The sun began to rise exactly seven minutes ago, and it will set at 7:56 p.m., and by the end of the week, the days will end later than eight in the evening. It's easy to know this if you monitor the sunrise and sunset times every morning in the *Rocky Mountain Times* newspaper. That other paper, the *Denver Gazette*, has the same information, but it would be sacrilegious to read it. The *Gazette* is inferior, but its greatest fault is merely the fact that it is the competition.

The knobby tires of the newspaper bike ground with the asphalt to create a soft buzz in the still morning air. The only other sounds were that of a nimble gallop and huffing that came from twenty feet behind the bicycle in the form of a forty-five-pound brown mutt. Scooter had no trouble keeping stride, but if he fell behind, it was purposeful. While the big kid attended to his serious duty of throwing papers, Scooter also had his responsibilities; this was his early-morning kingdom as well. The loyal companion stopped at least two or three times on each block to attend to his duty of smelling mailboxes and bushes for scents of other animals and marking them when necessary. The beagle-sized mutt was affectionately named after the former New York Yankee shortstop Phil "The Scooter" Rizzuto. The former orphan had no recollection of four years ago when his sad puppy eyes peered from behind a cage at the pound. He figured he must have grown up from the beginning with this kid.

Three houses to go. Danny glanced over the edge of the handlebars to see four papers. Two papers remained in each of the two bags that were hooked to both sides of the wide handlebars. Precisely, like clockwork. He would finish before 6:00 with exactly one extra paper. All *Times* carriers were required to finish their routes by 6:30. The advertisements boasted, "We guarantee the *Times* on your doorstep by 6:30 every morning." Danny liked to be done ahead of time, and he didn't like to take chances. He could guarantee 6:30, but the "on your doorstep" was the tricky part. Like most carriers, it was a matter of getting it as close as he could.

For a ninth grader, Danny had a powerful arm that consistently propelled a two-hundred-page Sunday paper well past the average front porch of most houses. He had delivered the same route for three years, and his body had gone through dramatic changes during that time. When he started this business in the sixth grade, he knew he was just a kid, but now things were different, and he was an old hand at this. His legs and arms were much more powerful than they had been a few years ago, and his voice and reflexes had matched the change. Danny's black hair now grew in more places than just on his head, another indicator that he was not a kid anymore. His body grew stronger with each day, each throw, and each pump of the pedals; and he liked it.

Throwing a paper a considerable distance is only one of the many skills found in veteran paper carriers. The trick is to not bash a door and make a racket or to roof it (which meant you would come up one paper short). Or, on occasion, if the papers were packed too tightly in the bag, the rubber band might come off. The result was what the carriers referred to as a "boosh." This is the sound when the paper leaves your hand. It comes flying apart with a noise that is a cross between a small sonic boom and a whoosh, hence the name "boosh." What follows is at least a five-minute delay, where you have to get off your bike, gather, and reassemble the newspaper.

The worst casualty of all could set a carrier back nearly a month's pay – the dreaded "glasher." Whenever a carrier shares with his comrades that he had a glasher, it meant he sent one through the glass on a screen door. Just hearing, "I had a glasher this morning," sinks a fellow carrier's heart in a hurry. Danny had only one glasher in the past year, but he felt lucky beyond his own belief. The owner of the house came flying out in a half-panicked sprint. When you are asleep or sipping your morning coffee, the quickest way to a cardiac arrest is the sound of a window in your house shattering in a violent explosion. Older paper carriers usually prepare the younger carriers for this terrible occurrence with words of wisdom. "Just wait for a minute. They will usually come out screaming because it scares the daylights out of them. Remain calm and offer to pay, try to make them feel sorry for you."

In Danny's case, he didn't have to fake remorse, he knew the customer for years, and felt his heart leave him immediately. When the customer came charging out in his robe and slippers, Danny could barely pick up his head. He had known Mr. Snider for two years of deliveries. This made Danny feel even worse because the homeowner was one of the less demanding and better-tipping customers. When his racing heart finally slowed down, he said, "That's okay. Son, I know you didn't do it on purpose. I used to carry papers too. This one's on me, just be careful next time." Danny even got a tip when he collected the next month; a carrier doesn't get any luckier than that.

Left side, right side, left side. Danny's last three deliveries were at the bottom of the block, by design. He set up his route to finish on a downhill street. Danny started narrating to the quiet street with his play-by-play account of the end of his route. "It's the bottom of the ninth, two outs, a three-two count . . . the pitch . . ." Danny aimed for the porch on his left, but the paper fell two feet short of the porch. "Oh, he walked him!" With the precision of an old crop duster, he swung his bike to the other side of the street. "Man on first and second . . . the pitch . . ." Danny backhanded the paper to his right. It was headed straight for a bush, a certain third out, but veered at the last second to land in front of the porch. "He lined a single up the gap. The bases are loaded!"

"Oh my goodness, Grizzly fans, have we got a game! The outfield has shifted to the left. Big Dan digs into the box!"

Danny cocked his arm back. The last house on Shoshone Street was a tough uphill throw from the street. It needed a looper to get over a railing but not too high, or he would get a glasher.

"Bases loaded, the crowd at One-Mile Park is on its feet, the piiiitch!" Danny let it rip. "Oh, it looks like a hard shot to center field! It is far! It is deep! BINGO! And quadruple bingo! A grand slam! Ball game over, the Grizzlies win!"

Pulling the bike around the corner, Danny looked at his newsprint-stained fingers. Without thought, he stuck two of them in his mouth and whistled. Scooter caught up.

Danny felt the usual pride of a finished job. Ninety houses – ninety deliveries. Mornings like this are even better because they are the good months. Pushing a bike through a foot of Colorado snow in December is a nightmare, and the only good thing about winter is the Christmas tips. Carriers never complain in the summer; this part of the job is cake.

In one canvas bag, he carried his sole remaining paper, and in the other was the sweatshirt he removed earlier as the morning sunrise began to warm him. The feel of the machine under him and the morning breeze on his face and arms combined for perfect harmony.

The bike wove through four residential blocks before turning down Iowa Street. A half-block away, Danny spotted two bundles of papers sitting in a driveway. "Shit!" he shouted to no one in particular. His powerful legs pumped at full speed ahead as he flew down the driveway. In one quick motion, he laid his bike down without the help of a kickstand. Immediately he ran toward the bundles, picking up one up in each hand. Hauling the bundles behind the house, he then scooped a handful of dirt from the garden and threw it at a second-story window. The house was a modest two-level, three-bedroom home. Like most houses in southwest Denver, they were simple middle-class homes built for economy, not style. Sprinting back from a wooden shed, he emerged with a wire cutter in one hand and a box of rubber bands in the other.

Danny cut the wire on the bundles, then grabbed another handful of dirt, this time a bigger one. He hurled it at the window again, and it made a swishing wave sound as it connected. Danny knelt down and began folding and banding the papers from the stack. He had already folded ninety of his own papers. By the time you finish a stack, you've already got the headlines memorized: Kennedy and Nixon Win Primaries in Indiana. Mortgage Rates Up to 6 ¾ %.

The window squeaked above him, and an adolescent head poked through. One eye drooped, and the blonde hair went in three directions. "Oh shit, my alarm didn't go off," said the voice.

The "alarm didn't go off" was a familiar tune to Danny. He heard this from Mickey about once a month. He wasn't irresponsible; he just forgot to set it once in a while.

Another carrier and good friend, who went by the nickname Mags, once called their situation "a brotherhood." It was buddies checking up on buddies in case help was needed with each other's routes in the morning. Of course, no one ever had to check on Thomas "Mags" Magliano. He compulsively set two alarm clocks, woke up a half hour before all the other carriers, and porched 99 percent of his papers.

The screen door opened, and Mickey stepped out in his white T-shirt and jeans. A red baseball cap with a Falcon emblem concealed the wayward hair. "Hey buddy, thanks," he said. He then skipped to his left as a white terrier barreled past him and leaped on Scooter. At once, the two dogs began rolling around in a mock-wrestling match. It was easy to see that they were old friends. The smaller dog barked as he played with Scooter.

"Dodger! Get down! Quiet!" yelled Mickey to no avail. They continued to wrestle as Mickey knelt next to the other bundle. He began to fold and band papers with frantic efficiency. "Can you get the Sunnyside for me?" Sunnyside was a seventy-five-unit retirement complex that took up about a third of his route.

Danny didn't look up as he continued to fold papers. "No prob, then I'll meet you at Uncle Bud's."

Most mornings of the week, Danny and Mickey would join Mags and another carrier named Vic Sanners at Bud's Coffee Shop on Federal Boulevard after they finished their routes. Federal was the busiest north-south street on the west side of Denver and was also home to Buds, who made the best donuts in the city of Denver.

When they finished folding, Danny counted out thirty papers and loaded them in his bag. He then went to the shed and studied a small clipboard. "Are these up-to-date?"

Mickey looked at the addresses on the sheets. "Yep, all but 221. You can cross that one out. She moved out last month and add 114 and 316, better take one more." He handed him another paper. "Thanks a bunch, buddy, I owe you."

Danny paged through the small clipboard as he rode along. The clipboard was another one of Mags's compulsive ideas. He convinced the other three carriers to create the small clipboards in the event that someone was sick or on vacation or if you needed help one morning, you could deliver the route from a small handy clipboard that attached to the handlebars of the carrier's bike. As much as the boys hated taking time to keep the lists updated, they knew Mags was right, and the lists were useful.

Danny glanced at his watch. A quarter after six. He figured he could make it to Bud's by 6:45. The retirement unit was a piece of cake.

"Hey, Bud!" Danny waved a newspaper in the air as the squeaky screen door slammed behind him. The slight breeze behind him wasn't enough to remove the blanket of warm air in Bud's Coffee Shop. The smell of rich coffee and fresh donuts wrapped a warm welcome around all who entered Bud's. The wave of the paper was a signal to Uncle Bud, who had an arrangement with the boys. If each boy brought in an extra paper, he would serve him a donut and a drink every morning. Uncle Bud figured it was a cheap way to have extra newspapers delivered for his customers; at least this is what he told the boys. In reality, it was his fondness for the boys that gave him the motivation for the arrangement.

Uncle Bud also held four stools at the end of the counter for them each morning. As they walked in, it only took a nod, a wave of the newspaper, and he brought them "the usual." To the boys, it wasn't just a donut and a glass of orange juice. It was veteran officers winding down at the canteen. This is what life is all about. You've got your wheels to get around town. You've got money from your route, *and* you've got respect.

To strangers, the place may have felt busy and stuffy. To regulars, Bud's Coffee Shop was a second home. The place bustled mostly with men, and the conversation was friendly. Above the sounds, the snap of Bud's voice was clear and loud. He had the uncanny ability to talk to and pay attention to everyone in the place all at the same time. Hearing his voice felt like having a friend throw an arm over your shoulder.

"You're set, sir!" Bud slapped the polished counter next to Mags and Sanners, who had arrived a few minutes before. As Danny sauntered to the far end of the counter, he failed to notice the six weathered booths that held stories, chuckles, and appetites seven days a week. He could only see his usual chocolate donut with sprinkles and a cold glass of orange juice.

The lack of etiquette in this establishment was one of its most endearing qualities. If your hand went in the air or you hollered, it meant you were ready for a refill or another donut. The place wasn't pretty, but it could have been the most efficient coffee shop on earth.

Bud only wrote table checks for strangers that might have entered his mess hall. Fewer table checks saved him a lot of time. The rest of the regulars simply gesture with a nod when they are leaving and ask, "What do I owe you?" The booming voice and a firm point to each member of the group combined to resemble a master sergeant's bark to lowly privates. "One buck! Seventy-five! Buck and a quarter!" The old-timers often chuckled as they left their money on the counter. On a given day, a couple of cinnamon rolls and coffee might be seventy-five cents; on another day, it might be fifty cents. No one ever complained; as a matter of fact, it was worth the price of admission to the show.

At this juncture in life, meaning and purpose is clear-cut. When you are in ninth grade, hell, you are an adult. Just figure what's important and go after it. Every morning, they talked about the three things in life that mattered. The paper routes were their duty, baseball was their lifeblood, and girls . . . well, girls were the greatest thing since roller coasters.

Sanners and Mags were already halfway through their chow when Danny found his stool. He knew it would be another fifteen minutes before Mickey would show up. Sanners was Mags's alter ego and best friend. They fought like an old married couple and were as different as night and day. Mags was compulsive, neat, and on time. Sanners didn't give a rat's ass if the papers were early or late. Sanners received a complaint or two each month for a missed delivery or a paper thrown in a tree or bush. Mags won a new bicycle last year as Capital District Carrier of the Year for numerous nominations by his customers and not having a single complaint over a twelve-month period. Mags had a Santa Claus body that jiggled when he walked or laughed. Sanners was like a rock. He read Charles Atlas books and lifted weights. Mags was just beginning puberty; Sanners was starting to grow sideburns. Mags tried to make his brown mop top of hair like that of Mickey Dolenz, from the music group the Monkees. Sanners went for the Green Beret crew cut. Mags had milk with his donut; Sanners had coffee, black of course. Mags had a squeaky voice; Sanners had the deepest voice in the Kepner Junior High choir.

Sanners was the only guy the boys knew who drank coffee at the age of fifteen. It seemed to fit for Sanners; he looked much older than the other boys did. He was also huge. His 190 pounds of muscle made the high school football coaches' mouths water. They can't wait to get their hands on this prize next year. If Sanners collided with a train, the train would lose.

Unfortunately, Sanners also had a bad reputation. To the boys, he was simply misunderstood. To the adults, "That Sanners is just a short-fuse kid from a short-fuse family." It was common knowledge that he had a renegade brother and an alcoholic father. This is where Mags was also different. He came from a caring family, where laughing was nearly as important as breathing. No booze either. This was the primary reason that Sanners spent most of his waking hours at Mags's house.

Mags inherited his dark skin from his mother, who was a second-generation descendant of Old Mexico. Juanita Martinez married Robert Magliano, who had a fondness for his Italian food. Consequently, Mags inherited the extra weight from both parents.

Vic Sanners seemed to have no particular cultural heritage. He came from a white family that drank a lot and fought a lot. Stories of tattoos, beer, cigarettes, and fighting were the only family history he knew; and most of those tales came from his uncles.

Vic got his huge biceps from his older brother. John and Vic were often locked in a bedroom with a padlock when their father, Ernie Sanners, was mad at them. "I'll show you boys to sass me, how do like your room?" He would shove them in and let them out when he felt damn good and ready.

John was three years older than Vic and was his hero as long as he could remember. John was a self-taught motorcycle mechanic genius. He could take apart a Harley

Davidson with his eyes closed. Over time, he also added an art gallery of blue tattoos now scattered over his body. When Ernie locked them away, it was smoke dope and pump iron. Vic pumped iron but couldn't do the dope; it made him puke.

The brothers grew massive muscles and bonded over dreams of a day in the future when they would open a motorcycle shop, work side by side, and finally achieve a successful life. It didn't take more than a couple of years of the lockups to create massive biceps on both of them. The punishing father never dreamed it would backfire when John would use those human hammers on a violent night during his senior year. The result was a hospitalized father who caught the wrong end of four punches. Unfortunately, they weren't just your average arms swinging. They were fueled with eighteen years of resentment. The family court judge had been following John's fights for years and gave him the option of joining the army.

Vic was impressed with John's crisp, clean appearance after boot camp. Vic squeezed him tight and felt his eyes become misty. "Dry 'em up, brother. When I get through my tour of duty, you and I are going to open that shop. Stay out of trouble and take care of Ma."

It was the last time Vic saw him, but he heard John's voice in his head every time a motorcycle buzzed past him. He was reported missing in action in Viet Nam nine months ago.

"Hey, guys!" Danny started in on his donut. "How'd the Yanks do?" he asked Sanners.

Sanners already had his nose buried in the box scores and was searching through the important data. He was oblivious to the fact that something was different about Mags today. Mags's donut sat half finished on his plate. By this time most mornings, he was already counting the change in his pocket to see if he could buy another. Today there was no jiggling, reading the comics aloud, or laughter coming from his end of the counter. Silence filled his end of the counter today while he compulsively arranged the sugar, cream, and shakers while staring blankly into space.

Mickey walked in ten minutes later and nodded for his cinnamon role and grape juice. Even though he had been there for only a couple of minutes, he sensed that something was out of place. "Hey, Mags, could you show me how that oiler on your bike works? I'm thinking about buying one for mine."

Mags took pride in the self-oiling unit attached to his chain guard. When he won his bike, he glowed with pride over what the pamphlet described as the "world's first self-oiling chain." It made an obnoxious grinding sound with each rotation of the pedals, and Sanners was so annoyed by the sound that he threatened to cut the damn thing off. To his husky friend, it was nothing more than a heavy piece of oil-soaked felt attached to a bracket.

Mags and Mickey stepped into the morning sun as the other two were still arguing over whether Denny McClain would continue to pitch well for the Tigers. Behind Bud's shop, Mickey motioned for him to sit on the rear step. "What's up, Mags?"

Mags dropped his chin to his chest as a tear rolled down his cheek. He couldn't force the words into his mouth. Mickey put a hand on his shoulder and sat down next to him, knowing at once that his senses were right. Mags was one of those fluffy-stuffed animals. Every time you pull the string, he laughs or tells a corny joke. This morning was different.

Mags pulled a trembling fist out of his blue jeans' pocket and held it in front of him. He sniffed as another tear ran down his other cheek. Crying was definitely not cool, but all things were okay in front of Mickey; nothing would ever be held against you.

"Open up." Mickey sensed that whatever was in his hand was attached to his sadness. After another few seconds, the shaking hand slowly opened to reveal a shiny ring. Mags spent his route money to buy the ring from his cousin, Johnny. After Johnny broke up with his girlfriend, he had no use for it and sold it to Mags for eight-fifty, much less than the ten bucks you would pay for it in the store.

The last two weeks had been big ones for the Mags as the guys helped him with his hemming and hawing over the purchase of the "going steady" ring for Jennifer. The two of them had been holding hands at school for the past three months, and exactly one month and two days ago, Mags worked up the nerve to kiss her. This was an event that sent him to seventh heaven, and he giddily shared all the details with the guys. They all knew that sooner or later he would ask her to go steady. He did last week, and he gave her the ring.

"What happened?"

Mags's shaking hand closed around the ring as he wiped the tears away. "Her mother is sending her to Holy Names Catholic High next year and told her she needed to give it back." Mags began rambling, and Mickey knew it was best not to interrupt. "It's like she said she was going to go to these mixers, these dances where the Holy Names girls meet other guys like from Notre Dame High School and her mother said, 'You don't need to be going steady with some other boy from some other school. You'll have no social life, and then you'll be sorry,' and I don't think her mother likes me anyway because I'm not some pretty boy from some other private high school and that maybe I'm just too fat, but Jennifer don't care that . . . that . . . shit, I don't know." Mags's head fell to his chest as another tear ran down his cheek.

Mickey allowed for a moment of silence before offering a gentle slap to his shoulder. "So what's your plan, man?"

Mags didn't look up. "What plan?"

"Your plan, man? You know, all problems can be solved with the right plan. What's your plan, man?"

Ten minutes later, the two came back into the coffee shop. It was enough time for Mickey to go over the facts that Mags and Jennifer still had a month together in school before the end of their ninth-grade year, and a ring didn't mean anything if they were still going steady in their hearts. They also concluded that no mother could get in the way of true love, and he could call her on the telephone (on the sly, of course) when he figured out when Jennifer's mother would not be home, and Jennifer really did care for him, and she was worth all the trouble. In a few short minutes, Mags was back to his old self. He had confidence, he wasn't giving up on Jennifer, he was laughing again, and he was jolly. Another pat on the back and the plan was sealed. Mags, like most guys, felt better when they were around Mickey. He made you feel like a man.

Uncle Bud was refilling Sanners's coffee as Mickey caught part of the conversation. "I'm sorry, Uncle Bud, I'll bring it tomorrow."

"That's the third time this week you've told me that." Uncle Bud set the coffeepot on the counter and stood in front of him with his hands on his hips. He looked everyone square in the eye when he talked, and no one could recollect when he had served without a smile.

You didn't have to wonder if Uncle Bud loved his life. When you walked into this worker's domain, you also didn't have to wonder if he had been earning his keep. His blue apron had grease stains from this morning's batch of donuts. The brown splotches on his shirt and apron were the evidence that he wasn't afraid of hard work. He would earn no fashion awards, but the baggy pants and shirt were meant for movement, not beauty.

Uncle Bud's shop was mostly filled with older men who were either retired or on their way to work. The reason you come back to Bud's is because he never forgot a name. Thousands of names were stored in that head of his, along with numerous baseball facts and figures. This made him, in the boys' eyes, an outright genius.

Uncle Bud pointed his finger in a warning, "All right, don't forget, I want that schedule. So when do you play St. Augie's?" Everyone referred to St. Augustine's Parish as St. Augie's.

"Last game of the season, as usual," said Sanners.

"Are you gonna whip their asses this year?"

"I hope so."

The ninth-grade year was the final year of play for the boys in the Denver Catholic Youth Baseball Association. The DCYBA was like the poor man's version of Little League baseball in Denver. The boys played for St. Anthony's team. Archbishop Rogers, who was a well-known sponsor of youth athletics in Denver, created the league. The Denver Catholic Youth Baseball Association had twelve teams, and there was no fee. Anyone could play in the league whether you were Catholic or not. All of the boys were issued a hat and a T-shirt with their parish name imprinted on the front. There were no cleats or baseball pants. You wore your shirt, hat, blue jeans, and sneakers.

The boys assured Uncle Bud that the schedule was forthcoming, then went through their normal routine of paging through the sports and spouting out important issues. *The world was not right. The Yankees are in seventh place. Mantle's average is down to .233. He hit his 522nd homer this week to pass Ted Williams and move into fourth place on the all-time home run list. Can he last long enough to pass up Babe Ruth at 714 homers? There should be a heavy paper tomorrow, lots of inserts. Damn, those Sunday editions. The*

Orioles are in first place. Frank Robinson drove in two runs. McClain is 4-0 and getting stronger with every game. Mickey's cousin, Lisa, is bringing another ninth-grade friend to a dance at the Y tonight; she's supposed to be cute. Catfish Hunter threw the first perfect game in the American League since 1922. There's a new movie, Planet of the Apes. *It looks cool. Are you going to watch* Laugh-In *on TV tonight?*

Most of the conversation wafted among the smells of donuts and coffee, and like the boys' attention, the talk changed with every fleeting thought. Sanners spotted a third-page headline: Enemy Mortars Assault Saigon. He wondered how John was doing. His sorrow would remain like most of his emotions – silent and checked at the door. Mags studied the movie times at the Brentwood Theater for *Planet of the Apes.* Danny wondered what Lisa's friend would look like.

On a Saturday morning, the boys didn't have to be in too big of a rush. Eventually, they had to get home and do the chores. Danny's mom had already gone to work. No rush.

Mags and Sanners went their separate ways, and Danny stopped with Mickey in front of his house. "So what do you think? Should we go to the noon *Ape* show?" asked Mickey.

"Sure, my mom won't care as long as I vacuum and do the dishes," said Danny. "Then we can still make it to the dance tonight. Are you sure Lisa's friend is cute?"

"She says she is, but you know how – "

"Terrence Michael Hannigan?" The morning conversation was pierced by a voice coming from Mickey's front step. A slim woman stepped out of the front door. Dressed for work with a bandanna wrapped around her head, she appeared to be in her late thirties. "I need that room and the garage cleaned this morning, let's go!"

"Okay, Mom, on my way." Mickey turned back to Danny. "I hate it when she calls me by my full name. It usually means I'm in dutch. I'll give you a call when I get done. See ya."

"Ya, I'll see you, Terrence," said Danny in a sarcastic tone. "Get that room cleaned, Terrence. Do the dishes, Terrence. Feed the dog, Terrence!"

Mickey stopped and turned halfway around. His eyes squinted as he revealed a purse-lipped smile. He then extended his arm and shook his finger in a warning. "Shut up, Daniel, or I'll pin your scrawny ass later."

Danny held up is fingers and fluttered them in the air. "Oooo, I'm scared, Terrence!"

Mickey shook his head, laughed, and continued toward the house.

Danny rode off with a smile pasted across his face. In many ways, he was well aware of his own insecurity, and he knew he would be just another starving animal without Mickey; but with him – *that was another story.* He always felt full of life, smarter, confident, and on top of the world. *That's what friends are for,* he thought.

3

Group Screening

TAKING TWO STEPS to his left, he stepped into the line of danger and held his arms out from his side. He turned his palms up and moved toward the gun. His eyes closed as a gentle request flowed from his lips, "Now . . . please . . ." The bullet exploded into his chest, sending him flying backward. Clutching his fists to his chest, he staggered to his feet and smiled. A tiny voice came from behind him, "Thank you, Mickey . . . thank you . . ."

Terrence bolted up in bed and put his hands over his heart. He shook his head and drew in a huge breath of air as his heart pounded through his chest. His breathing matched the state of his body as his bulging eyes stared at the empty wall ahead. He looked down at his wrists to see them wrapped with tape and gauze. As his breathing slowed, he wondered how many more times he would have this same dream. Over and over, night after night, he had relived the scene. Some dreams were more vivid than others. Sometimes, he took a bullet; other times, he did not.

Terrence held palms to his cheeks and peered through his fingers. He whispered to himself, "Just once, I'd like to die right."

The wounds were two weeks old, but they were deep enough to still hurt when he moved them. As Terrence dipped his head forward, he moved the palms of his hands over his eyes and tried to hold himself still. He wasn't sure whether it was a nightmare or a dream. He was convinced that the advantages of death exceeded the advantages of life, and he could not imagine the pain ever ending. The only difference now was that his head was clear. His head pounded with the torment of his physical withdrawal from the drug of alcohol, but at least it was clear.

Terrence's head had not been this clear in years, and for this he felt thankful. Downstairs in this building, he knew that there were people who were interested in helping him. He wondered whether he would be thankful for that too.

"No . . . It's too much of a risk." Dr. Ferron looked across the table at Meg and waited for her reply.

"It really isn't." With a slight tilt from her head, she tried to make eye contact with him. "To borrow an expression from Shaw, he's really more of a 'normal neurotic.'"

"Normal neurotics aren't clinically depressed, Meg, and normal neurotics don't go around slashing their wrists every day. For God's sake, Meg, Terrence Hannigan was hospitalized for a month in Denver General's psych ward, then went right back to the bottle. Here we are five months later, and I know he would be dead if he weren't in here. For the sake of group, he's a risk."

Megan held back on her response as she allowed for silence. She knew that patience and time were the best tools for working with Ferron. He was thorough and fair.

The room was at a standstill to the point of dead silence, but to Meg, it screamed with body language. Dr. Walter Ferron was the director of the Shiler Alcohol and Substance Treatment Center and had a knack of saying a lot of things without ever speaking. He continued to page through the file, sigh, and throw out a few "hmms."

Meg tried not to grin as she looked around the table. In private, she often claimed that it was impossible to become bored in any setting, especially meetings. All she had to do was watch other people's body and facial expressions. It was a skill that made her an excellent group therapist. This meeting was like all others, where they had to decide who would be in group therapy and who would be excluded; the final decision rested with Dr. Ferron.

Across from her sat Shawnon Durneck, her good friend and a part-time practitioner. No one called him by his given name in years – he simply went by "Shaw." He was a full-time associate professor at Denver State University and put in ten to fifteen hours a week at the center. His finger on the side of his temple indicated he was deep in thought, a rare place for someone who had a tendency to be more emotional than logical.

To her right sat Dr. Darion Walsh, a full-time psychiatrist at the center. Darion was always dressed to the hilt in fashionable suits. *A facade,* Megan thought. Darion attempted to take his best analytical poise with his hands steepled in front of him on the table. He was tall, dark, and well groomed. He could pass as a model for the cover of *GQ* magazine, but to Megan, he was the most unattractive person in the room.

On first examination, it would seem that the four professionals who sat in the meeting were incompatible. Megan was the only one who did not wear a tie. Her dusty brown hair rested softly on her shoulders; her only other style was to pull it back into a scrunchie tie. This day would not entertain that style. Other than the few gray wisps of hair and a few smile wrinkles around her eyes, there were no other signs that revealed her midforties age. She generally looked younger than others her age. This was due in part to her love for running. Her cheeks and nose also displayed a scattering of freckles. Combined with a genuine smile, she exuded a young-at-heart appearance that easily connected her to the more fragile clients at the center. Practical and casual in appearance, she never underdressed or overdressed for any occasion. In the usually extended autumn and winters of Denver, she most often wore sweaters with khakis, but now it was summer, and lighter shirts were the style of the day.

Megan scanned the faces and waited for someone to break the silence although she knew that Dr. Ferron would be the only one who would accomplish that minor feat. Darion never had an opinion of his own when Ferron was around. Megan thought of him as spineless and gutless and believed he was often capable of doing more harm than good for his patients. Ferron intimidated the hell out of him, and everyone in the center knew it. Darion maintained a *holier-than-thou* attitude because most of the staff was either licensed professional counselors or licensed psychologists. Darion believed they were a step below his psychiatrist stature.

Ferron was a seasoned psychologist but became much more cautious after taking on the position of the director two years ago. When it came to screening for many of the services at the center, he played a careful role as though the client's life depended on it. Sometimes it did.

Darion scratched notes on his pad to make it look like he was analyzing something. Megan could tell he was bored and thought, *He's probably making a list of single bars that he can sneak into before he goes home to his wife.* Megan put forth a great deal of effort to be professional with him, but it was no secret she despised him. Not only did they often disagree on the treatment of clients, she saw him as pompous and self-centered.

She looked back at Shaw as he grinned and sent her a wink. Shaw and Meg co-facilitated about half of the group therapy at Shiler. The chemistry between them enhanced their effectiveness as professionals.

Megan couldn't help but smile as she looked at Shaw. She wondered, *How in the hell do you get creases in a tie?* Shaw had been divorced from his wife for six months, and since then his clothes became progressively more crumpled. For the past two months, he also grew his beard back. *It probably saves him shaving time in the morning,* Megan thought. The clothes and the disheveled appearance were the result of fewer financial means, and he wasn't getting his shirts professionally laundered anymore.

Shaw was idealistic and often impulsive. He met his wife at a concert in a park in Denver and married her a month later. The whirlwind romance quickly revealed they had nothing in common, and here he sat two years later suffering the post divorce blues. His lifestyle also reflected his appearance. Even though he and Meg were the same age, he looked five years older. He had a contagious Kris Kringle smile, a round face that showed his extra twenty pounds, and a slight recession of his curly brown hair.

Shaw held two fingers over his mouth and stared with Megan in the direction of Ferron. Megan knew she had a chance because Ferron was stroking his chin; it usually meant that he was on the verge of a decision. His mannerisms revealed that the decision wasn't without contemplation. When he rubbed his temples, it meant he was stressing. Finally, with his head tilted forward, he rolled his eyes up and looked at Megan. "As usual, I will say that I have confidence in your professional ability and will trust your professional judgment. In this case, however, I continue to maintain strong reservations." Ferron looked down at the table and brought his head up. "I haven't heard from everyone, gentlemen?"

Shaw waited because he knew Darion would want to speak first. Darion sat erect in his chair as he leaned toward Ferron. "I definitely have to agree with you. I also have strong reservations."

As Shaw heard Darion speak, he jotted several notes on his pad, looking downward and pausing as though he was in heavy thought, he wrote, "Is there a parrot in here, or is the butt sniffer speaking again?" Shaw glanced up again and grunted a "hmmm," then started to write again, "Why I do believe I see brown specks of spit coming from your mouth. Dr. Darion, are we getting a little too close when sniffing these days?" Shaw shared Meg's contempt for Darion, and in his private sarcasm, he would often doodle thoughts he had about other people in his notes. Shaw was a classic attention-deficit adult. At a typical boring faculty meeting at the college, he could fill up three pages of doodles and comments in a spiral notebook.

Shaw brought his elbow up to the table and held his palm open. "I disagree with Darion. I've seen Meg work with much tougher cookies than him, and I don't have a problem with it. I think things will go just fine."

Ferron began to put the papers back in the manila folder, "All right, give it a shot. Overall, it sounds like a good group. I hope things go well for you. I want you to staff with Darion once a week and to see how Mr. Hannigan's progress is going in individual counseling."

Darion had been counseling Terrence in individual sessions for the past month. "Anything else?" asked Ferron.

"No, I just need to meet with Shaw, but I have nothing else," said Meg.

"I don't have anything else," said Darion as his body leaned out of his chair ready to leap for the door.

Ferron stood. "I'll see you on Monday then . . ." He hardly finished his words, and Darion had bolted halfway out the door.

After Ferron walked out, Meg reached across the table, and in one quick motion she snatched Shaw's notepad. Hiding behind his devilish smirk, Shaw yelled, "Give me that!"

Megan turned around and laughed, "One of these days, you're going to get caught making these stupid notes. Parrot or Butt Sniffer? Is that a DSM technical term you use to describe Darion? I thought you said he was JPN?"

Megan was referring to the DSM-IV, the abbreviation for the "*Diagnostic and Statistical Manual of Mental Disorders* – Fourth Edition," from which they made all of their diagnoses in the center. She didn't like making a lot of diagnoses, but she needed them, like all other practitioners, for insurance reimbursements. Meg was also alluding to Shaw's unique set of terms that he used in private to describe people. Therapists often used acronyms such as GAD (generalized anxiety disorder), OCD (obsessive compulsive disorder), and PTSD (posttraumatic stress disorder). Shaw used them, like any other therapist, but also took the opportunity to create some of his own. Sometimes he would refer to people like Darion as JPN (just plain nuts). Other times, he would say, "Yes, he definitely has GAH syndrome," (goofy as hell). Megan enjoyed Shaw's company as a fellow psychologist as he found humor in most situations.

She handed back his notepad. "So what do you think? Am I taking on too much?"

"Well . . . to tell you the truth, I wouldn't have put him in the group, but I don't think it's a big deal. We'll all survive."

Meg sighed again, "I think he really needs a group. I know for damn sure he's not getting his needs met in individual." She had her reservations about Darion's ability to be of value in individual therapy. "I suppose we'll see next week."

4

May 11, 1968
The Dance

DANNY'S THOUGHTS DRIFTED as he pushed extra hard to get the vacuum sweeper over a buckle in the carpet. It then easily glided over the area that was worn down. He fantasized about a lavish new home with a new car. He could see his mother's face light up. *If I had a million dollars.* Pats was the hardworking mom who deserved it.

Pats was a single mom who put all of her life energy into her kids. Her appearance and lifestyle often reflected her priorities. She maintained a short dark black haircut that was styled and highlighted in her sister's kitchen about once a month. It was as close as she had been to beauty shop in years. Even the purchase of a do-it-yourself hair-coloring kit was enough to make her feel guilty. Her husky pear-shaped body on its five-feet-four-inches frame didn't resemble its once-youthful appearance, but it served her well, and besides, she didn't have the energy to diet at this point in her life.

Danny often dreamt of what it could be like to give her everything in the world. On Saturday mornings when he cleaned the house, he felt helpless and useless. Their financial situation was always on the edge of a tightwire, and the old carpet and furniture reminded him that only people in the movies lived like kings. Certainly no one in southwest Denver did.

Danny's thoughts wandered to three months ago when she left for work. She squeezed him extra hard and extra long. When she finally pulled away, a tear ran down her cheek. She said, "I'm sorry, I'll never ask again." She borrowed $40 from

Danny's route money. Extra bills, doctor's expenses, school clothes, and sneakers for the two boys all caught up at once. *If only I had a million dollars, I would give it all to her.* Ever since then, he tried to offer money to her after his monthly paper-route collections, and each time she refused. It only made her feel guiltier for the time she asked. Somehow, it wasn't fair. Danny felt rich "for a kid" but poor because of the house he lived in.

Everyone in the neighborhood knew the family's story. When he was two, Danny's father left without warning, and Pats worked like a driven soul to support her two boys. Aaron was five years old at the time, and he remembered his father, but Danny only knew him by his faded pictures.

Even Pats was surprised when the neighborhood came to her aid and didn't look the other way. She found cheap babysitting in the neighborhood until the kids were old enough to go to school and landed a job as a forklift operator at Yates Rubber Company through the recommendation of another neighbor.

Pats was informally regarded as the go-to person in the neighborhood, a quality that everyone appreciated. Last summer when Jerry Brannan ran through a glass door a half-block away and needed a doctor, it wasn't one of the dads who were sought out to rescue him. The older kids screamed, "Go get Pats, now!"

Since her youth, Pats disliked her given name of "Patricia." "Patsy" sounded too damn girly, and she often thought that "Pat" sounded like a guy's name. Thus, it was "Pats" she settled on at an early age, and in this neighborhood, it was "Pats" that was synonymous with the Rock of Gibraltar. She fixed bikes, bruises, skateboards, cuts, and hurt feelings. She could hug a grieving neighbor with the softness of grandmother, heal a skinned knee with a kiss, or send a two-hundred-pound bully on his way with a snap of her fingers and prizefighter's stare.

Danny was regarded as a good kid by most people's standards; he got into just enough mischief that he didn't get into trouble with authority. He kept on the straight and narrow mainly for Pats, and he didn't want to let her down. In his heart, he felt like he owed her something for all of the tireless overtime hours she put in on Saturdays.

Aaron, on the other hand, just hung out. He was graduating next month and would probably take a minimum-wage job. Spending time with guys who were a few years older than him often resulted in trouble. Most of it was related to 3.2 beer. He turned eighteen early in the spring and could buy the watered-down version of 3.2 percent beer that could be legally purchased at that age. He couldn't wait to turn twenty-one so he could buy the hard stuff.

Danny could expect the threats every Saturday morning when the vacuum woke him from his 3.2 hangovers. In most cases, he paid no attention to his brother's mood and finished his job.

"Hey, pal," said Danny as he wandered through Mickey's door. "Hello, Mrs. Hannigan."

"Hi, Danny, do me a favor, will ya? Keep Mickey out of trouble tonight, okay?" Mrs. Hannigan reached out and planted a kiss on the cheek and a friendly tap on Danny's shoulder. Marilyn Hannigan treated Danny like one of her own.

Danny felt jealous of Mickey's family life in a guilty sort of way. The guy had everything. He was undoubtedly the most talented ball player on earth, every girl adored him, he was blonde, good-looking, and . . . he had the perfect family. Danny knew he had the mom that most kids only dreamed of. Everyone knew that Pats could do it all. But Mickey, he had everything. His setup was perfect. He had a little brother who idolized him and a father that every kid idolized. Being in the middle of that combination was enough to tell a kid that they were important and needed.

Spikes turned five last month. Mark Hannigan was nicknamed Spikes because at the age of three, he kept trying to wear his dad's baseball cleats. They were ten sizes too big, but it was his fantasy world. One day when Joe came home from the station, he spotted Mark running around the trees in the backyard in his own fantasy game of baseball while wearing his father's spikes on his feet. Joe grabbed a beer, quietly watched through the bedroom window, and laughed until he literally couldn't move. For the next week, he started calling him Spikes, and the name seemed to stick with him.

As fathers go, Joe Hannigan was the envy of most families. Joe was a man's man. A fireman, his two-hundred-pound, thirty-seven-year-old body was taut, and living evidence of his love for sports. His status was further escalated by the fact that he was the kingpin of the fire department's softball team. His love for kids and a deep devotion to Marilyn seemed to complete the package. Last fall, they celebrated their eighteenth anniversary.

The combination of having a live-in idol and a live-in idolizer made Mickey's situation perfect. Danny knew he had the best mother in the world, but all he had for a brother was a graduating senior in high school who would probably end up with a factory job.

Mickey and Danny had been best friends since the fourth grade, and Joe filled the role as a surrogate father in Danny's life. He taught them baseball, football, and basketball. His heart never relinquished its kid status. Playing with the boys and teaching them sports gave him another crack at his youth.

Danny never complained about the lack of a father in his life. It could be worse, it could be a life without Joe, or it could be a family like Sanners's. Mags's family was great if you were hungry. They specialized in food, laughter, and board games at the dining-room table. But nobody had what Mickey had.

Spikes had the best of all worlds; he had four guys who treated him like a younger brother. He wasn't just happy to be their mascot; he was surrounded by his heroes when they were around. He never had to think about getting a new bat, ball, hat, or ball cards because the four boys showered him with their leftovers. To Spikes, these were the artifacts of giants; and he proudly hung or stacked his pennants, posters, and sportswear throughout his room. This year, life couldn't be more perfect; in fact, it was special, and his dad said he could be a ball boy for the senior's team.

"So you know Lisa?" Danny's voice cracked. *What kind of a stupid question was that? Of course, she knows Lisa. She was introduced as Lisa's friend.*

Danny stood on the large outdoor pool deck at the YMCA. The DJ had been spinning records for only a half hour when Lisa showed up with her friend.

In one smooth gesture, he slid his hands into the pockets of his blue jeans. Any guy knows that you have to be cool when you talk to girls, and Danny realized he wasn't. *What do you say when you've just met the most beautiful girl on the planet?* She was striking, radiant, and everything about her was perfect. The voice, the smell, the long auburn hair, and the blue eyes were intoxicating.

Danny summoned all of his power to look like he was in control, but the hands were being stored in the pockets to cover up the shaking. Unfortunately, you can't slide your voice into your pocket. It will just have to shake until it cools down.

"Yes, we've been friends since I moved in down the block two weeks ago," said Jean. Her soft smile indicated that she was much calmer than Danny.

Danny waited for the song to end. *Just one opportunity – a guy has to know when it's just right. You can't make a wrong first impression. Okay, after the next one I'll ask her to dance. Just wait, just be cool, it's not cool to ask in the middle of the song. What if she turns me down? She won't. She smiled at me. But what if she does?*

Sanners walked toward them; he slapped Danny on the back with a "hi, buddy!" gesture. His brutal intrusion of their space was capped off with seven dreaded words, "Hey, Jean, would you like to dance?"

"Sure!" she answered as they walked off to the dance floor.

You jerk! You ass! You should have seen me working here! What the hell kind of a guy would do that to his buddy? For crying out loud, it's in the middle of the song! Thanks, Sanners, you numbskull.

Danny knew he would have to wait and work up the energy. "Hey, Danny!" It was the familiar voice of Mickey with his cousin, Lisa.

"Hey, Danny, looks like you've got your eye on Jean," said Lisa. Danny immediately blushed. He didn't just have his eye on her – he was in love.

A best friend to all four boys, Lisa was every bit as athletic as they were, but there were only limited opportunities for girls in sports. Growing up with Mickey, the two watched each other develop into their adolescent bodies. Lisa provided a buffer between the boys and their connection with girls in this emotional world of puberty. *A guy could actually talk to Lisa and not have to stammer or act goofy.*

She provided that safe link between them and the many girls she had introduced to them over the past few years. This included the relationship between Mags and Jennifer, who were now twisting to a song on the dance floor. It was sort of a sweat-covered jiggling version of the twist.

"I think she's nice," replied Danny.

Mickey chimed in, "I think you think she's more than nice. How come you haven't asked her to dance?"

"I'm not in the mood to dance," said Danny in an unconvincing lie. He was dying to dance with the goddess, and he would have if it wasn't for that ass Sanners.

Danny envied Mickey's smooth, cool strut. On the dance floor, his goal was to simply attempt to be as much like Mickey as he could. Mickey would usually dance half the night with Lisa while other girls would stand by hoping he would ask them to dance. Lisa was unafraid to grab any of the boys and drag them out there. If a guy was shy, at least he could count on a couple of dances with Lisa.

Danny's plans continued to fall apart. He waited until Sanners was done and struck up the conversation again with Jean. Then, tragedy struck again when Lisa grabbed Danny for a dance and motioned to Mickey. "You two need to dance," she said as she pushed Mickey and Jean out on the floor. *Drats.* Danny positioned himself so he could watch Lisa with Mickey. *A good set of songs, damn, she'll be too tired to dance with me. Damn.*

When the set finally finished, Danny had to strategize again. *This time I won't wait for two songs to go by. Wait, be patient.* The courage grew. *Now, do it now, go now.* The song ended. *Now – make your move!*

"Um, Jean, um . . . so . . . do you go to school?" *What the hell kind of a question is that? Of course, she goes to school. Idiot! Idiot!*

"I went to Kunsmiller last year, but I'll be at Roosevelt next fall."

"Cool, me too." *Oh gawd, what a stupid idiot I am. Crap, here comes Sanners again.* Danny swallowed hard. *Find the words, now!* He tried to open his mouth, then gulped. A song was starting. *Oh shit, it's a slow one. Never ask for a first dance on a slow one! Crap!*

Jean reached out and touched his arm. Danny thought his heart would stop. He couldn't breathe. He couldn't speak.

"Would you like to dance?" Jean said. Danny couldn't stop staring at her smile. It was a smile fully capable of producing world peace.

"Uh . . . um . . . ya," Danny said in a faint whisper, heart-attack reply. Pulling his shaking hands out of his pockets, he followed her out on the floor. Reaching out with his left hand, he gently took her hand. He shook so badly he was afraid that his right hand would begin beating her back like a sick woodpecker.

Jean looked up at him with a smile that melted him like a candle. "Do you like this song?" she asked.

"Um . . . ya, a real lot." He also loved heaven.

For the next two minutes, Danny wondered if his heart would ever slow down. *What if I faint? What if they have to bring in an ambulance? For sure she'll never dance with me again.* He smiled. *Just let heaven happen.*

Danny felt a sudden jolt on his left arm. Someone was trying to pull him back. *If that damn Sanners is trying to butt in, I'll kill that son of a – "* Danny stopped. The greasy long hair didn't register at first. It was Rob, his brother's best friend. He had a panicked look on his face, and he was clearly out of place at this dance.

"Danny, it's your brother. You've got to come with me now."

Danny was too stunned to reply. *Why would anyone interrupt heaven?*

"Aaron's all screwed up, really, man, come on. He's a mess."

Mags and Mickey stayed behind at the dance while Sanners graciously offered to go with Danny. Their legs pumped hard on their bike pedals to keep up with Rob's car. Rob drove slowly so they wouldn't fall far behind. Danny could see the taillights weave. *They've been drinking.*

Rob graduated last year and now lived in an apartment six blocks away. He called Pats a half hour ago to ask Danny's whereabouts without revealing the reason.

When Danny and Sanners entered the apartment, they were overcome by the pungent smell of vomit. It made his skin shrink. Aaron sat propped against a kitchen cabinet and was covered in his own vomit. His head slid from side to side as he made feeble attempts to sit forward.

Danny shook his head. "What did he drink?"

"He smoked a few doobies, had a few shots, some wine, and about a twelve-pack. We thought he was dead for a while. He just wouldn't stop."

Danny bent down and picked up his chin. "Aaron, look at me."

Aaron's half-drooped eyes looked up. "Wuut the hell are yo babees doin' here?" The spit ran down his chin. His intentional insult lost its effectiveness in his pathetic state. Danny pulled his sticky fingers away and wiped them on his jeans. He was used to this. It wasn't the first time. Aaron never knew when to stop.

Danny's mind went to work, forming a list in his head. He would have to make all the arrangements: sneak some clothes out, lie to Pats, help Rob clean him up, get him to bed, tell Pats he was sleeping over at Mags, lie to Pats with a story that Aaron and Rob had gone to a drive-in, and he would sleep over at Rob's, stay up with Aaron all night so he doesn't drown in his puke. Danny had a gut-wrenching feeling every time he had to cover for Aaron. He hated lying to Pats. When it came to Aaron, he felt that Pats deserved better. What a great night. *Craps.*

Two hours later, Danny sat on the floor in Rob's apartment next to his brother on the bed. What a rotten night. *First, I ask the world's dumbest questions to the world's most beautiful angel. Then Rob hauls me out. I hope Mickey didn't tell her about Aaron's drunken habits. She must think I'm a knucklehead. She'll never dance with me again. I'll probably never see her again. And all I got out of it was half of a song to dance with her. But what a dance. What a dance. What a dance. At least there was one bright moment in the night.* Danny sat back, closed his eyes, and smiled. *What a dance.*

Louis Garrison paced his cell. The parole hearing was only hours away. He looked in the mirror and adjusted the collar on his shirt to hide the tattoo on his neck. Third time's a charm. *This time I'll be paroled, I just know it.*

5

The Shiler Center

MEGAN LEANED BACK in her office chair and rubbed her eyes. Her office door opened to the empty and quiet hallway. On many nights when most of the therapists went home, Megan would sit and stare at her files in preparation for individual and group counseling. Tonight was one of those nights – she was readying herself for her new group. She closed her eyes and imagined them in front of her right down to minute details. *Where will I place them for seating? Who should be across from whom? Who will shut down? Speak up? Overdisclose? Underdisclose? Narcissism? Distrust? Suspiciousness?*

Meg took pride in her reputation as a skilled group therapist. She was attracted to group work because it could be the most challenging and unpredictable form of therapy. At one time, she considered specializing in marriage and family therapy, but her love for group work kept her at Shiler.

The Shiler Center was a two-story facility that serviced a combination of inpatient and outpatient clientele. Located on Federal Boulevard in Denver six blocks south of Mile High Stadium, the center overlooked the tall buildings of downtown to the east and the Rockies to the west. Allen Shiler, a wealthy real-estate investor in Denver, founded the center during the early sixties. After recovering from his own alcohol addiction in the late fifties, he became interested in the field of addictions and recovery and decided to open a nonprofit facility. When he died in 1985, a sizable portion of his estate went to the center, and it continued to thrive under the direction of a board of trustees. Up until that time, the unit was called the Denver Alcoholism Recovery Center, and the board renamed it the Shiler Alcohol and Substance Treatment Center a year after his death.

Most of the work was for the hard-core problems that required abstinence, but the center did not rule out the possibility of recommending *controlled drinking* for some people with abusive patterns.

Megan facilitated her groups with a nontraditional approach. Her primary focus was on each member's personal growth and consideration for the addictive substance was secondary. She discouraged excessive advice and asked no questions. Rather, she challenged the members to stay in the present moment and address the interpersonal dynamics of how they interacted with others. She believed, like many other theorists, that most of life's problems are rooted in relationships or lack thereof. To her, groups are a social microcosm where all the good as well as the ugly parts of people seem to poke their heads out when they are pressured.

Megan picked up the file for her couples and thumbed the pages. She made some initial observations based on her screening interviews, a process she believed was critical to the success of the group. For this group, she interviewed seven couples and rejected two, leaving her with ten members and herself and Shaw. Each couple had at least one member who had received treatment at the center from inpatient or outpatient services. The patient was required to identify a support person who would accompany them to the group. Most often, it was a spouse; but on occasions it was a friend, parent, or sibling. The only stipulation is that each person agrees to engage in his or her own issues.

Megan took extra preparation for her "couples" groups. The interpersonal dynamics were different from other groups because each couple already had a history and an established style of dealing with each other. Other groups – such as men's, women's, mixed, or thematic groups (such as anger management or grieving) – were generally easier. The couples groups served two purposes: to foster supporting relationships, and to deal with relationship issues that may affect relapse.

In group therapy, she was constantly looking for clues to the origin of each person's style of relating. Meg developed a sensitivity to persons who were violated or traumatized in earlier relationships knowing that they would carry those patterns into group relationships.

In the past, she experienced members of couples who would unknowingly poison their relationships in a reaction to their inability to move toward intimacy. In the groups, Megan's goal was to offer a safe place where the deficits could be understood and replaced with intimacy.

She closed her eyes in contemplation. *Clues, history, love, nurturing, and interests.* She would try to paint a profile from her screening interviews and think about how she would create the norms starting in the first session.

The group consisted of Janice and Donald Simper, an educated couple who had been married for eighteen years. They had dated in college and were married shortly after their graduation. Both had problems with alcohol in the past, but most recently it was Donald who received individual counseling for his binge drinking.

The second couple was Lisa Cammon and Gerri Adnoski, a lesbian couple in their late twenties who had been living together in Boulder for the past four years. Three years ago, they went through a union ceremony among friends in the Boulder Canyon. Their relationship had been strained by Gerri's drinking in response to the stress in her career. She was receiving inpatient care at Shiler.

The third couple was Tony and Rose Hernandez, a late-thirties Hispanic couple with three children. Tony was a tree trimmer work hand, and Rose had been a minimum-wage cashier for various stores since high school. They had been married for fifteen years. Rose had been addicted to her wine for many years. When the drinking started to upset the children, they sought therapy together.

The fourth couple was Doris and Earl Fitzgibbons, a couple in their early forties. Earl was an accountant, and Doris was a part-time hairdresser. They recently sent their only child off to college, and Earl began drinking heavily in response to his depression.

The fifth couple was Terrence and Daniel. When Meg interviewed Terrence, she assumed that Daniel was a trusted friend. She had no idea that they hadn't seen each other in years. She also had no idea that beneath the surface of Terrence and Daniel was a soul mate connection. She had no idea of the bond that went back to earlier years when innocence prevailed, and two boys named Mickey and Danny were full of life and potential.

6

May 31, 1968
Practice

BILLY EGGLER PARKED his 1960 Corvair at the edge of Harvey Park and walked around to the front trunk of his car. The car cost him $185 three weeks ago, a real bargain, and they were getting cheaper every day. Ever since Ralph Nader published his report, "Unsafe at Any Speed," the cars were practically giveaways on the used-car market. He, like most other lower-income workers, only dreamed of spending $3,150 on a brand-new 1968 Galaxy 500.

A strong left arm reached inside and pulled out a large canvas bag filled with balls, bats, and catcher's gear. This was Coach Eggs's third year of guiding the senior boys' team for St. Anthony's, and merely arriving at the practice field was enough to put a smile on his face. The afternoon sun, the grass underfoot, the smell of leather gloves, and the sounds of clinking wooden bats in the bag combined in harmony to sing the real songs of spring and summer. If you can't play the game, the next best thing is to coach it.

As Coach Eggs approached the practice field, he watched a dozen teenage boys laughing hysterically. Half of them watched, and the other half rolled on the ground caught up in hysterics. He immediately figured out who was entertaining them, and it caused him to grin. It was Mags in full form as he was putting on the final touches of his personal show before practice. For the last ten minutes, he and Sanners entertained the troops with their rendition of the *Planet of the Apes* movie. Sanners had played the part of Cornelius, the ape, and now Mags was doing his Charlton Heston impression.

Mags skipped along on a gallop toward the backstop while his baseball bat filled in as a pretend horse between his legs. He suddenly dropped the bat and fell to his knees at home plate and stared up at the fence. Mags then slumped to the ground in a passionate display of emotion. He then grabbed two handfuls of gravel and pounded the ground. "You bastards! How could you? You bastards!"

By now the entire team was screaming with laughter. Most of them had seen the movie and were out of control as they watched Mags's moment of improvisational hilarity. In the final scene of the movie, Charlton Heston finds the half-buried Statue of Liberty and falls to his knees realizing he was back on earth in the future.

Coach Eggs had not seen the movie but chuckled as he caught the trail end of the scene with "you bastards!" coming from Mags.

"Gentlemen!" shouted Eggs. "Let's get in one lap to get warmed up." The boys threw down their gloves and started to jog around the Harvey Park pond. Most were still laughing at Mags.

To the senior boys' team at St. Anthony's, Billy Eggler was perhaps the greatest coach that ever lived. He was a baseball god, and the boys treasured every moment in his presence. They felt a sense of honor to be coached by him. Coach Eggs was a legend in southwest Denver. Six years earlier, he was a star with the Denver Grizzlies, a triple A minor-league team. The team played at One-Mile Park, and all of the boys had seen him play. Mags, Sanners, Danny, and Mickey had seen him play dozens of times. With the advent of transistor radios, the boys often listened to the games on a local station as they fell asleep at nighttime.

The city of Denver never had a star as promising as Eggs. He commanded the field with catches and throws that had the local newspapers making comparisons to Joe DiMaggio. His flattop haircut gave the blonde-haired, blue-eyed prospect the look of an all-American kid. His six-foot, two-hundred-pound frame also provided power for home runs that couldn't be contained by a mere minor-league park.

Carl Beber was the well-known local radio announcer who first started the wave of interest in Eggs. The glee and excitement of eight- and nine-year-old radio fans would reach a pinnacle when Carl would dream up new and creative ways to describe Eggs's plays and home runs. Even as the boys grew older, they would replicate the lines they heard on the radio to describe a Billy Eggler home run. Mags was especially good at replicating Beber's voice while playing sandlot ball with, "Eggs overeasy! That's another one that left the frying pan, boys!"

Eggs was the talk of the town for two and one-half seasons in Denver. The citizens of Denver knew it was only a matter of time before this young star was gone. He was simply too good, too flashy, and too big for this minor-league town.

Billy Eggler bent down, pulled the wooden bats out of the canvas bag, and began leaning them on the backstop. The bats were carefully moved one by one with his left arm. The right arm still had strength in its biceps, but the hand could no longer grip and hold anything more than a couple of pounds. This was an arm that once could throw a strike from center field to nail a base runner at the plate.

In 1962, Eggs's third year in Denver, his popularity was moving toward an expected crescendo. He was on track to blast at least fifty homers, he married a local girl, and the big leagues would call him up any day. The *Gazette* and *Times* sportswriters competed daily for newer and more imaginative ways to describe his feats. The headlines used the standard "Eggs overeasy!" to describe a game-winning homer here and there but also threw in "scrambled, hard-boiled, soft-boiled, or sunny-side-up" descriptions. One writer even quipped, "Can't stop those runny Eggs!" to describe his base stealing.

On August 20, 1962, it all ended. Eggs had just hit two homers the night before to beat the Iowa Ravens. He arrived at the ballpark an hour early to take additional batting practice. He got caught up in a game of catch with one of his teammates who was hitting fly balls to him in the deep part of center field. At the farthest part of center field was also a gate that opened to bring pregame deliveries into the park. As Eggs chased down a long fly ball and didn't see four popcorn makers with large glass enclosures. As he dove to catch a ball, his right arm went through the glass. In one leap, his future was shattered as well as the dreams of thousands of baseball fans in Denver.

Eggs took up residence in Denver and faded into obscurity. After seven operations, hope was given up on whether he would ever throw again. He resigned himself to never play again. The boys always wondered why Eggs wasn't a minor league, college, or high school coach but felt honored to be under his tutelage nonetheless.

As the boys finished running their laps and approached the backstop, Mickey was twenty feet ahead of everyone. He led by example. Mags was thirty feet behind everyone else. He had to lead the team in other ways.

"If it wasn't for me, somebody else would always have to finish last," puffed Mags as he stumbled to catch up with the rest of the crew. If he had to finish last, at least he could provide a chuckle for the team.

Eggs split the team and had Danny hit fly balls to the outfielders. He assembled the remaining players for infield practice. The location where the St. Anthony team practiced was hardly a field. It was a large gravel area behind an elementary school. The DCYBA didn't have fancy ballparks. The bases had to be placed loosely on the ground, and if you weren't careful, you could sustain some nasty groin injuries if it slid out from under you on a dead run. The only bonus was that the field backed up to Harvey Park. To the boys, the park was one of the two best recreation sites in the city. The other was Ruby Hill that overlooked downtown Denver from the southwest suburbs.

Mickey was the best starting pitcher in the league, and he knew the season would depend on his talents. He could start every game since they played only once a week. None of the other guys on the team balked since they all knew they were a few steps behind his talent. The infield was rounded out with Mags at the plate, Sanners on third, Joey Pelloman at first, Tom Dunlap at second, and Kevin Burke at shortstop.

Eggs brought the team from perennial losers to one of the best teams in the league. They knew they had a shot at the title this year, but it would come down to St. Augie's in the end, and everyone knew it.

St. Augustine was not only their biggest rival – they were the enemy. They won the last four senior boys' titles in a row, and St. Anthony had finished runner-up to them for the past two. They also had another reason to hate them. Three of their players delivered the Denver *Gazette*, and Mags had a crossover route with one of their team members, Johnny Gonzales.

Chet Anderson was also one of their talents, and he nearly rivaled the size of Sanners but had the skill of a Mickey. He was a true prodigy but unquestionably a sinister entity; he also delivered the *Gazette*.

From a *Times* perspective, these guys were jerks. Gonzales had also beaten up Mags on two occasions during their junior-high years. If there was ever a haunting figure in Mag's life, it was Gonzales.

When practice was over, Mickey, Mags, Sanners, and Danny were always the last to leave. Each one of the boys appreciated every practice with the team in a different way. For Sanners, it was a chance to throw hard, run hard, and play hard. Be the beast.

For Mickey, it was a matter of pride. Every throw and every swing of the bat was an effort to practice perfection. It was second nature to him.

When Danny practiced, he often drifted off in fantasy, imagining he was Willie Mays – his favorite fielder – or Ernie Banks, his favorite hitter.

For Mags, it was social time, fun time, playtime. *What's the use in being here if you can't laugh and have fun?*

The boys devoured the small world that insulated them from the rest of human existence. As *Times* carriers, they read the news every day. Sometimes ninety times over if it was on the front page. They were aware that thirty-nine students were suspended from Denver State University this week because it was on the front page of the *Times*. The students staged a sit-in protest and had to pay the consequences. They also knew that roast beef went for thirty-five cents a pound and that hamburger buns went for fifteen cents a dozen because it was advertised on the back page. Most of the current events, however, were lost to the important things in life.

The postpractice ritual was meant for those important things. This was the place to hang out, talk baseball, and trade cards, think about girls, and dream about new ten-speed bikes. Harvey Park provided a nice pond, a thick shag carpet of generic grass, and a lot of trees. Some of the nice three-bedroom brick homes nearby went for as much as $19,900. Advertised in the *Times*, of course.

The boys had a customary tree they camped under after practice. It was their player's clubhouse to wind down after each practice. There was plenty of time. The sun would not be setting until exactly 8:20, according to the second page of the *Times*.

"I don't like them." Sanners was scrutinizing the new design for the 1968 baseball cards. He leaned against the tree. The boys were getting their first look at the newly released cards. Each of them picked up a new pack before practice.

"I like 'em. The border is kind of cool," said Mags.

"It's boring," replied Sanners. He disagreed in an attempt to get a response from Mags. "I like the 67's and 66's better."

"Hey, I got a Mickey Mantle!" Mags's voice muffled as he spoke from behind his glove. Mags smelled everything he touched. He especially loved the leather smell of his glove and would often hold it over his nose when he spoke.

"Lemme see!" Mickey reached over and immediately looked at the back of the card. "Wow, his average went down again. It's kind of sad. If he's not careful, it may go below a lifetime three hundred."

Conversation followed the other significant issues in life. *The Yanks dropped nine out of their last ten games. Did you watch Bonanza last night?* Voyage to the Bottom of the Sea *was cool last week.* 2001: A Space Odyssey *is at the Cooper Theater. Koosman is 4-1, and he's a rookie. The rookie baseball cards are dumb. They have two guys on a card. Koosman is on the same card as a guy named Nolan Ryan. He'll probably never make it in the majors. Will you see Lisa again? What about her friend Jean? The pool opens in a week. There's a new show on TV called* Second Hundred Years *about some guy who was frozen in an iceberg one hundred years ago and comes back to life.*

Danny fell on his back and looked at the stats on Willie Mays's card. He sighed and stared at the clouds. The feeling of grass on your back is the lifeblood of summers. It doesn't matter how long it is. It doesn't matter if it's crabgrass or golf-course quality. Grass is grass. When it's freshly cut, the aroma is therapeutic. It's what you pray for through the long Denver winters, and when you reach spring, it becomes a retreat from life's busy demands. Danny dreamed of dancing with Jean one more time.

Louis Garrison was summoned from the waiting room. He was given the news. He would be paroled. With pocket change and his old clothes, he bought a bus ticket for Denver, only a few hours away from Canon City, the state pen. With a sigh, he vowed to never return; he had done his time. Armed robbery, it will be different this time. No mistakes.

7

Daniel

DANIEL STARED OUT his kitchen window. For the moment, he was preoccupied with thoughts about the lawn. He could only see the dead spots on his grass. *I'll need to pick up some extra seed, some fertilizer. Having a good lawn is such a chore sometimes.* His thoughts were broken by the chattering glee that came from behind him.

He whirled around and smiled. "And . . . where are my . . . little . . . girls . . . going . . . TODAY?!"

The four- and five-year-old girls giggled in their chairs at the breakfast table before the older one screamed, "TO THE CIRCUS PLAYLAND!"

"HOORAY!" shouted Daniel. "And what will my little girls do there?"

"We will play!" shouted the four-year-old. The two girls could hardly finish their bowls of oatmeal as they fidgeted in their chairs. The Circus Playland was their favorite place to spend a summer afternoon. They had slides, games, climbing nets, tunnels, and other assorted wonders that Sarah and Christina loved.

The summers were special for Daniel and Monica. Both were teachers and loved to spend all of their time with the children. Their third child, Marcus, was already out on his bicycle. Marcus was a typical twelve-year-old and spent most of his days outdoors. Daniel taught physical education at Arvada East High School in a suburb of Denver, and Monica taught elementary school in the Wheat Ridge suburban school district. While teachers are not rich, they were both committed to education. As a bonus, they loved the flexibility, the freedom, and the summers that came with their jobs.

Between bites on her toast, Monica mumbled, "How many times did you talk to him?"

Daniel sipped his coffee. "Only about three times." He stirred the cream into the cup. "To tell you the truth, I have very little idea of what this thing is all about, and I really don't know why he wants me to do this."

"Did he ask anyone else?" asked Monica.

"No, I don't think so," Daniel replied. "It's my understanding that ever since the separation and the funeral, he hasn't talked to a soul."

"But why you? Up until about a month ago, you hardly ever heard from him. And then he tries to kill himself, gets bounced in and out of the hospital, and then calls you." Monica stopped and took in a deep breath. "I can't help feeling sorry for Maggie and Jessica. She's only ten and may not know much, but I know Maggie still loves him so much, and it's killing her."

Daniel felt on edge. He didn't know if it was too many cups of coffee and no breakfast or the exchange he was having with Monica. Daniel rubbed his eyes, then folded his hands on the table over the sports page. He sighed and thought, *This is all I need to get the summer off to a great start.*

"I don't know," he said with a pause and another sigh. "I'd like to help him any way I can, but sometimes I feel like I'll be like this guy in this gerrrooop uh therapeee" – there was sarcasm in his voice – "talking to all of these former drunks."

Monica looked up and laughed, "You know it's not *that* bad. My mother was in rehab."

"Oh ya, wasn't she the poster child for sobriety?" he said with a cynical laugh. She had quit drinking eight times and quit smoking ten times since Daniel and Monica had been married. Daniel became more serious and stared down at his coffee. "I want to help him, but I don't know if I belong there."

Monica looked at the oatmeal spilled on the table. "Now you girls put your bowls on the counter and brush your teeth." The younger one dismounted from her chair and ran to the sink singing, "Weeeer'e goooooooing to Circus Playlaaaaaand."

Monica sat down across from Daniel and tried to make eye contact with him. "You ought to call Maggie and see what she thinks. Did you know that she was the one who found him? He called and hung up the day of the funeral. Maggie kept trying to call back and got no answer. She rushed over there with Jessica, and they found him on the kitchen floor in a pool of blood. God, I feel sorry for them. Maggie's such a sweet person."

Monica could sense that the conversation was getting too serious too early in the morning. She cleaned the rest of the table in silence and took the last bite of her toast. She tried to lighten things up. "So, group therapy boy, how was your meeting with doctor . . . what's her name?"

Daniel smiled. "It wasn't a meeting, dear. It was a *screening.*" He rolled his eyes as he said the word "screening." He was being sarcastic again.

"Do I detect a bit of skepticism?" asked Monica as she ran a washrag over the oatmeal-spattered table.

"I suppose a little, it just seems so damn hokeypokey sometimes. I feel like someone's going analyze my gray matter."

Monica laughed, "Better watch out, or they might not let you come home, dear!"

Not amused with her comment, Daniel tilted his head in a mocking pompous stance. "Her name is Dr. Megan Talden, and of course, like all cosmic shrinks, she says, 'Pleeeease call me Meg,' like okay, yes, we're close already." Daniel's obvious tension was coming through. He was aware that when he was nervous about something or stressing, he often reverted to sarcasm.

Monica moved behind him as he hunched over his coffee and sports page. She sensed his stress and began to rub the back of his neck. "Soo . . . sounds like our big Danny might meet his match with a woman psychologist."

"No," he said as he laughed. He allowed only a few people in his life to call him Danny. They were his mother (which he hated because she used it for the sole purpose of sounding motherly), Monica, and the guys on his softball team. "So you think I'm intimidated by her? Well, I'm not. I just don't like this psych crap."

Monica put her arms around his neck and kissed him on his cheek. "I don't see how it could be that bad. It won't mess up our summer, and actually you might learn a few things. Maybe we can psychoanalyze my mother a little better!"

Daniel laughed with her. He knew he needed to relax a little about this whole thing. Pondering his newly volunteered status he thought to himself, *Okay, so it will be ten weeks. We will meet once a week, and it won't ruin my summer, but Jesus, what a mess Terrence is, the poor son of a bitch.*

8

June 6, 1968
The Phone Number

THE SILENCE AT Bud's Coffee Shop hung like thick cloud over its customers. There was no snapping of the drill sergeant's voice today. Bud quietly went about his work.

This is too silent. It's too eerie, thought Mickey. He suggested to the other boys that they get out into the fresh air. They rode their bikes to Ruby Hill Park, then sat on the knoll, and stared out at the tall buildings in downtown Denver. Ruby Hill Park was an oasis on the edge of the city. The mountains in the west were visible from the top of the hill every day of the year. It was a popular place for sunrises, sunsets, or just pondering in the midday.

Danny's eyes welled up when he thought of Pats. Normally, he wouldn't see her in the mornings when she gathered her lunch box and headed off to the factory. This morning he finished his route as quick as possible so he could see her before she left for work.

Every morning before Danny delivered his route, he would leave a newspaper on the table and turn on the percolator for Pats's morning cup of coffee. The two small gestures were his way of saying that he cared about her.

This morning, it felt too awkward. He couldn't bear to leave the paper facing up, so when he went out to deliver his route he turned the paper over, headlines down. It was as though he believed it would somehow soften the news.

When Danny came through the door at 6:00, he saw the paper turned over and realized she'd read it. All the *Times* carriers had read the headline at least ninety times with each paper they folded. After a while, it became a numbing, depressing task. With each folding and banding of the paper, it didn't get any easier. Today the *Times* carriers would be the bearers of devastating news.

> Robert Francis Kennedy
> November 20, 1925-June 6, 1968

Pats heard him come in but didn't turn around. She hunched over her lunch box at the counter and stared out the kitchen window. She loved the Kennedys and all they stood for. In her heart, she knew that Robert would be our next president.

"Mom?"

Pats slowly turned around and revealed a tear-streaked face. This was Pats the Strong, Pats the Invincible, and now it was Pats – the Grieving Mother. She had the same look two months ago when Martin Luther King died. Danny felt guilty as if his delivery of the paper was somehow responsible for the events. In some strange way, he believed it was his action that made Pats sad.

She reached out and pulled Danny close in a tight hug. He could hear her sniff as they hugged in silence. When she first heard the news yesterday that he had been shot, she immediately went to St. Anthony's to light candles and pray. She lit one for him and another for his family. Yesterday, Danny had to deliver that front page as well: RFK Fights for His Life.

Her voice cracked as each word seemed to drift out, "What's this world coming to, Danny?" When she heard of his death, all she could think was, *Oh . . . that family, that poor wife, Ethel, and oh those kids . . . only thirteen and sixteen – nearly the same age as my own, and oh . . . how could that mother survive any of this nightmare.* When Martin Luther King died two months before, the kids again were all she could think about.

Pats gently pulled away to see Danny with tears in his eyes. She reached up and took his face in her hands. "I have to go now. You boys stay out of trouble and be sure to get Aaron out of bed." Pats pulled him close and kissed him on the forehead.

As he watched her drive away in her pickup truck, he couldn't help but feel guilty, but he didn't know why.

The boys sat on the top of Ruby Hill and stared straight ahead. "The first thing my dad said was, 'I'll be damned if I'm voting for Nixon,'" said Mickey. The Hannigans were devastated. Their Irish Catholic blood made them feel connected to the Kennedys.

Mags forwarded his family views. "My mom said she couldn't believe what kind of a country we are living in. You know, when our leaders are getting shot. It's crazy. My dad said the damn NRA keeps fighting against gun control, he said things will change now, and finally it will be hard to buy a gun. There was an article in this morning's paper on that, you know."

Sanners sat in silence. He wondered if his mom and dad had ever even voted. He didn't have a family perspective to offer.

"My mom was really busted up this morning," said Danny. "Yesterday, when he was shot, she said, 'I just know he's going to make it and be our next president.'"

Mickey interjected, "No way, man, not when you get shot in the head. Did you hear about the guy with the gun? He got tackled by Rosie Grier – the football player, and Rafer Johnson – the Olympic Gold Medal winner. The guy who shot him was named Sirhan Sirhan. What kind of a name is that where your first name is the same as your last name?"

Sanners spoke his first words, "Hey, I've got an idea. Let's start calling Mags by two names. Hey, Mags Mags!"

The guys started laughing. Mickey, then Danny both repeated it, "Hey, Mags Mags!" "Hey, Mags Mags!"

Danny started to laugh, "It sounds like you are calling your pet poodle. Come here, Mags Mags!"

Mags started to laugh with them before jumping on Danny in a wrestling match. Danny seemed to be the easiest to attack; he certainly didn't want to jump on Sanners.

As they wrestled around, Sanners was calling out in a half-laugh, half-scream voice, "Get down, Mags Mags! Bad boy! Don't bite, Mags Mags!"

Mickey joined in, "Watch out, Danny, or Mags Mags might try to smell your crack!" The boys howled. Danny was so weak from laughing that it was easy for Mags to pin him. After a half hour of laughing and wrestling, the boys made plans for their day and disbanded. They were ready to get their lives back on track. There's no better place to do it than from the edge of the swimming pool deck at the Y.

"Is Lisa coming?" asked Danny as they sat on the edge of the pool. The four boys sat on the edge of the "baby pool" at the YMCA. It was opening weekend at the Y, and the lifeguards were still cleaning the main pool. Mickey was given the assignment of watching Spikes for the day. The four boys took turns watching the five-year-old in his GI Joe frogman mask as he splashed the water.

Mickey turned to him. "Is Lisa coming? Is Lisa coming? Is Lisa coming? How many times are you going to ask me? I think what you are really asking me is – is Jean coming with Lisa? I think you're in love."

Mags jiggled a laugh, "Ooooo, Danny's in love!" His jovial body moved in unison from under his T-shirt. He usually wore his clean white T-shirt at the pool with his bathing suit. He believed it concealed a good portion of his body. His official story was, "My Mom wants me to wear it because I burn easily."

"So what if the man's in love? There's no law against that," said Sanners. "Hey, by the way, man, you should have said something when I danced with her. Heck, I didn't know you liked her."

"I never said I liked her or fell in love with her. I just think she's nice," said Danny in an unconvincing tone.

Mickey smiled. "Ya right, for the last two weeks. That's all we've heard, 'Jean, Jean, Jean!'"

"That's not true," said Danny, trying not to seem overanxious.

Mags and Sanners each followed with a, "Ya, right."

Danny stood up and decided to join Spikes. He held his arms over his head and took huge steps across the pool. Spikes saw him coming out of the corner of his eye and let out a bloodcurdling scream. It was time to play "creature of the black lagoon," Spikes's favorite pool game.

When Lisa and Jean arrived, Danny was not only chasing Spikes but also a dozen other kids who had joined in the fun. At the moment he realized the girls were watching, his face looked as though he were sunburned. *Oh God, how embarrassing! Is this the best I can do? The first time I see her, I make a fool out of myself, and now to back it up, she sees me as a clown.* Danny put his arms down and walked to the edge where Mickey sat. *Maybe she didn't see it. Yes, she did.*

In one smooth gesture, Danny sat down and tried to make his blush go away. He couldn't stop staring at her. She was even more beautiful than the last time he saw her. "Hey, Lisa, hey, Jean, how are you guys?" said Mickey.

Spikes waded over. "Come on, Danny, why did you stop?" Danny acted as though he didn't know what Spikes was talking about. Spikes pulled off his frogman mask. "Hi, Lisa!" He ran to her and gave her a hug. He looked up at the stranger who came with Lisa and asked, "Who are you?"

"This is Jean. She's my friend. Jean, this is my cousin Mark, but we call him Spikes."

Spikes stared up at her and smiled. "Hi! Know what? Danny loves you!" Danny's heart was now palpitating out of control. The beat red color came back to his face.

Mickey started to laugh. "Go play, you little squirt."

"Aren't you guys going to swim?" asked Lisa.

"You go ahead. I've got to watch Spikes."

"I'll relieve you in a while," said Danny.

Danny joined the girls in the four-foot-deep water. "How was the rest of the dance?" asked Danny. *She probably met some guy who she now dates.*

"It was okay. We didn't stay long after you left," said Jean.

"Sorry, I had to cruise early, I had a . . . a family thing." *Please don't ask.*

Danny was much smoother this time. His plan was to try to avoid the dumb questions. In anticipation of seeing her this week, he sat in front of the mirror every day rehearsing more intelligent conversation. The plan was to be slick, but how do you get her to talk about the important things in her life like, does she have a boyfriend?

The rehearsal plan went well as they talked for most of the morning. He found out that she loves tennis, Monkees songs, but she doesn't watch the show very often, and she's not a baseball fan. *Drats, that's okay, nobody's perfect.* She hadn't seen the *Apes* movie, but she wants to go see the new James Bond movie, and the best news of all – no boyfriend. *Is that possible? Someone as pretty as her?*

Later, when they were leaving, Danny took a series of deep breaths and made his best attempt to throw out the line he practiced at least ten thousand times the week before. "Umm . . . Jean?" *Say it, just say it now dammit.*

Jean's smile moved him. It made him feel like he was more than the insecure self-doubting person he had come to know. "Yes?"

His hands started shaking again. *No pockets. Hide the hands.* Danny put them behind his head. Immediately they came down. *There's not much hair under my arms yet. It makes me look like only a boy and not a man.* Finally, he put them behind his back. "Umm . . . Jean? Umm do you like . . . have a bike?" *She's got to know where I'm going with this question. She'll probably make something up like – .*

"Ya, my dad bought me a Schwinn ten-speed last year, why?"

Don't be afraid, boy, shoot the question, go now! The words stammered out, "Well, I just, um, I know that you are new to the area and umm . . . umm . . . would you like um . . . like um . . . to like ride around? Like sometime? You know, like I could show you some cool places around here." *There, crap, I said it. Now get ready for the big "forget it pal," "not really, I've got other things to . . . "*

Jean smiled, and her eyebrows went up. "Sure, I'd love to! Let me write down my number. That would be cool. Can you call me?"

Can I call you? Hell, I would jump face-first on a stack of burning coals for you. The jackhammer in Danny's chest was about to crush his ribcage. He kept the hands behind him – they were out of control. "Ya, um maybe we could um . . . like ride around like this weekend or something?"

"That would be cool," she said as she handed him a small piece of paper.

"Ya, that would be cool. See yuh." Danny watched her as she caught up with Lisa. His heart was still out of control as he watched her get in the car with Lisa and her dad. Danny watched the car drive away, then looked down at the paper she handed him.

"Oh shit!" He was sweating so badly that it caused the numbers to run. He gently held the corner of the paper and blew on it to dry it off. Danny took in two big sighs. *Oh geez, I can't believe it! Is there such a thing as levitation? There has to be because I'm floating.* He jumped in the air twice, then quickly looked around to see if anyone saw him. He spotted only a couple of kids next to the fence. He pumped his fists in the air and jumped again.

Louis Garrison's hangover pounded at his head, and he was pissed off. His first week back from the state pen wasn't the dream he expected. Things shouldn't change this much in five years. No former girlfriend waiting with open arms. The bitch stopped writing. She has another boyfriend; she'll pay.

9

Night Class

"IF YOU ARE not making your life what you want it to be, then what is your life becoming?" Megan scanned her class, looking back and forth. She was in the middle of trying to make a point for the students in her group counseling class. It was the only class she taught as an adjunct professor at Denver State University.

A silent figure entered the back of the classroom and sat down. She smiled. On occasion, Meg and Shaw would drop in on each other's classes when it wasn't too intrusive.

"Excuse me, Dr. Talden, could you repeat that?" As Shaw spoke, the students turned their heads; most of them didn't hear him sneak in. Some were immediately suspicious. Graduate students had a tendency to see teaching as a very formal process. *There must be a reason why he's here. She's probably being evaluated. They must be reviewing the curriculum for this class. Maybe they are considering her for a full-time position, and Dr. Durneck has to assess her effectiveness as a professor.*

"Certainly, Dr. Durneck. As I said, if you are not making your life what you want it to be, then what is your life becoming? Where I'm going with this is to ask ourselves the question, what are my goals? For instance, if I say, 'It's been a goal of mine for years to take up running and get in shape,' is this a goal, a decision, or an idea? What's the difference?"

She hated to answer her own questions. It either meant they weren't getting it, or she wasn't being clear enough. She figured she wasn't being clear. "A goal involves measurable behavior and progress. An idea is simply a thought. A decision is that bridge between the idea and the behavior. Have you ever heard someone say, 'I have a goal to renovate my kitchen or stop smoking or write a book,' but they never get around to doing it. They never have any progress. Our lives are filled with ideas that never come to fruition because we never *do* anything different. For that reason, when I screen for groups, I ask the members to set goals and constantly reevaluate them throughout the group. If they can't make progress, then they haven't made any decisions regarding their ideas. It's still abstract, and they need a new goal. Think about your own lives, we say, 'I want to make my life like this or that. I want to be more loving, patient, confident, or strong.' But the question is, what are you *doing* that reflects your wants? Again, if you are not making your life what you want it to be, then what is your life becoming? Our goals are the essence of our purpose in life, but our behavior is the evidence of our efforts toward them. Does that help?"

Most of the students didn't get it but scratched furiously in their notes to get it down on paper. *Maybe it will be on the midterm.*

Shaw nodded and smiled. As a professor, Meg often felt inadequate around Shaw. At times, she had seen him whip his classes into a near frenzy with the right discussion questions at the right time. She saw him as a master of class facilitation. *Very unorganized, often unkempt, but what a great professor.*

Megan glanced at her watch. "Oh, we've gone a little over our time. I'll see you next week." The class shuffled out.

"Hey, Dr. Talden," he said.

"Hey, Dr. Durneck." As an ongoing joke, Meg and Shaw called each other by their formal names when they were on campus. "What are you doing here tonight? Besides, of course, giving your friends a hard time in their classes." She walked to the back of the classroom where he was sitting and pulled a chair around to sit facing him.

"Oh, you know, the life of an important professor, meeting with the board of trustees. I was talking them out of naming the new building after me. I realize I'm famous and special, but hey, they could at least wait until I die."

Meg laughed, "Grading papers at the last minute?"

"Ya, I have this bad habit of waiting until the day before I give them back, so I figured I would barricade myself in my office and work on them until they are done."

Meg knew his habits and joked, "For me personally, it's tough to concentrate during ESPN *Sportscenter*." Meg rarely watched television, but knew Shaw's habits of grading papers while watching a ball game or *Sportscenter*.

"Ya, I know what you mean. Hey, I needed to ask you, are we ready to have my grad assist run the data our screenings?"

"Sure, I wrote up the results of my men's group," said Meg.

Megan and Shaw had been working for a year on a paper they were coauthoring on screening for groups. The paper emphasized how specific intake questions could identify multiply disordered clients who would not be well suited for the group process. They both believed the most productive outcome of group therapy was for its members to discover their personal "blind spots." Meg and Shaw used the term "blind spots" to describe the personality traits that keep one from being productive in relationships.

Shaw, like Megan, believed that most people are oblivious to the aspects of their personalities that keep them from moving toward healthier relationships. They had seen many clients who created shields in their relationships that kept them from becoming more intimate. In group, the feedback from others would help the members to drop their shields and take risks to move beyond their self-defeating styles of relating.

Megan used some of her assessment techniques when assessing Terrence, Daniel, and the other group members. Dr. Ferron's concern was that Terrence's depression may be too severe for the group, but Megan determined through screening that his problems may be related to some addictive tendencies and some unresolved relational issues. His interactions with others did not indicate that he was out of touch with others perceptions, and he could benefit from a group.

"Are we ready for our new group?" asked Shaw.

"I think so," Meg replied. "As usual, I have no idea where the group will go, but it seems strong."

"You say that with some doubt in your voice," said Shaw.

Megan looked away, avoiding eye contact as she thought about her words. She knew she had to have complete honesty with Shaw in order to be effective as a co-therapist, but she couldn't put her finger on why she was unsure of herself. "I'm still thinking about Ferron's reservations about our group."

"You mean the two guys?" asked Shaw.

"Yes, you know" – she paused, staring down for a moment before looking back up – "Terrence and Daniel, there's just something out there that's a mystery. In screening, Daniel said they were old childhood friends, and in a follow-up interview, I found out that they had been disconnected for years. Now, in hindsight, I'm wondering – doesn't it seem odd to have a support partner that you've been out of touch with?"

"I guess, now that you mention it, it does a little, but I wouldn't worry about it. I don't see anything there that should alarm us," said Shaw.

Meg was still second-guessing herself. She held a finger over her lips and stared into space. "Hmmm . . . I suppose you're right."

10

June 14, 1968
First Date

MICKEY'S EYES WERE locked in a tight focus on Mags. The connection between the two had become a choreographed dance. At times it was at near perfection. Mags crouched behind the plate. Over the years, he had studied the craft of catching from watching the Denver Grizzlies. From the bleachers, he used his binoculars to study the catchers and made hundreds of mental notes that came in handy when he played. Mags called for a fastball by holding a finger deep in his crotch. The concealed fingers did not allow the runner on first base to see it.

Mickey pulled off his hat and wiped his brow. The afternoon sun was still warm, but it wasn't the reason he wiped away the sweat. It was a signal to Joey Pelloman on first base that he was going to try to catch the base runner off guard and pick him off. He peered over his left shoulder and fired the ball. The runner got back on time. Joey threw it back, and Mickey set himself again on the mound. The runner on first took another lead. Bottom of the ninth, one out. St. Anthony's was two outs away from winning the opening day game. They hadn't played great, but they played well enough to have a 6-2 lead. Mickey reared back and threw the heater. The Notre Dame hitter sliced at the ball and sent a roaring shot down the third-base line. Sanners dove to his right and snagged it out of the air. He then rolled to his knees, rotated, and fired a bullet to Tom Dunlap at second base. Sanners threw harder from his knees than most guys could standing up. The ball stung Tom's hand as he caught it. He instinctively whirled and threw a rope to first base. Nailed him by a step. Game over. St. Anthony's 1968 season starts at 1-0.

The players jogged in and went through the postgame protocol of lining up to shake hands with the opposing team. Eggs then assembled the team and reviewed the game. "Great job, gentlemen. A good start for us. A couple of us were intimidated by the pitching. We've got to work on *not* stepping out of the box."

Eggs never humiliated anyone in front of the team. Even though it was always "we" and "us," the boys knew who he was talking about. Mags was the worst culprit. He had been stepping out of the box since he was nine years old, and the habit kept coming back.

"Some of us have also got to stop trying to kill the ball. We only need base hits." Mickey threw an elbow into Sanners's side. Sanners smiled; he swung for the fences on every pitch, knowing that his only goal was to send the ball into orbit. He went one-for-four on the day, but the one he connected with sent the Notre Dame centerfielder on his heels running after it. Sanners could have circled the bases twice in the time it took him to retrieve the ball. "Our fielding was shaky, we had five errors, but none of them managed to hurt us. Next week, we've got Saint Rose. They're a decent team and a lot better than Notre Dame. We've got the potential to go places this season, but we've got work to do. Mickey, nice job on the mound and nice wood." Mickey went three-for-four with three RBIs and stole two bases in a typical day for him. Whenever Coach Eggs wanted to talk about performances on the field, he heaped them on for the almighty stat for the RBI's. To Eggs the RBI was sacred ground. It was the least appreciated, and most important stat in baseball, next to fielding stats, of course. The RBI was the *run-batted-in* stat. At least once a year he gave a speech about how most people are consumed with hits and homeruns, but real players know that the RBI said a lot about a man. If a man could bring another man off the base with the right hit at the right time – he was everything, a good hitter, a man who could hit in the clutch, a man who was selfless, a team player. "Hits make a player feel good, home runs make the crowd feel good, but an RBI? That makes the team win."

Mags went zero-for-two but drew two walks. He received the "good eye" praise. Danny went one-for-four, but the one was a two RBI gapper to right field, better than a homer according to Eggs.

"All right, gentlemen, bring it in here. Let's hear 'Falcons' on three." The team gathered around Eggs, and each placed a hand stacked on the others. "One, two, three." The team shouted, "Falcons!" in unity.

The boys picked up the gear and placed it in the bag as Joe Hannigan pitched to Spikes on the empty field. Spikes donned an oversized batting helmet that was ten sizes too big. In his best stance, he scrunched his face into a big-league stare while he waited for the pitch. Mags ran behind the backstop and immediately started into his best radio announcer voice, "Myyyy goodness, will you look at the size of that rookie for the Falcons. Number 4 – Spikes Hannigan from Denver, Colorado. Yessiree, he is a monster. The Falcons just called him up from their farm team, and this kid can play! He takes a pitch!" Spikes swung the oversized bat with all of his might. "Oh! suh-wing and a miss. The count goes full. My goodness, if he would've connected with that one, it would've cleared center field here at One-Mile Park! This kid is a monster! He waits for the next pitch." Spikes took another whirlwind swing that resulted in ten-foot dribbler in front of the plate. "It's a line drive up the middle, wow! What a shot! He's safe at first, but wait! He's trying to stretch it for a double. He's headed for second, will he make it?!" Spikes's puppy dog legs churned wildly as he ran for second base. The distance between the bases was three times as far for him. Joe picked up the ball and started to chase him. Spikes glanced over his shoulder to see Joe running after him with the ball. His giddiness combined with laughter while he ran in a spastic gallop. He let out a yelp as he glanced to see Joe closing in him.

"Oh, would you look at the rookie's speed! He's gonna do it. HE'S SAFE AT SECOND BASE!" Spikes hurled himself headfirst as he threw his arms around the base. The helmet went flying another three feet past the base. Joe grabbed him by the britches and in one motion threw him up on his shoulders. Spikes was now overtaken by his own hysterical laugh.

Since it was a home game at Harvey Park, most of the team arrived and departed on their bikes. The home games provided the opportunity for the parents to arrive at game time and not have to deliver the boys for warm-ups. Mickey wanted to hang around with Danny after the game to get the details on his bike ride with Jean. Mickey told Mags and Sanners that they would catch up with them at the Hots and Suds eatery on the way home. Every good game deserves a postgame meal.

Mickey and Danny stuffed their gear into the canvas bags on their paper bikes. The great thing about paper bikes is that you can carry all the necessary tools of life in the large bags wrapped on either side of the wide handlebars. The items may vary between sodas, baseball gear, sweatshirts, hats, slingshots, or sneakers. The two camped under a full-leafed green tree close to the backstop. The grass served as their meeting area.

"So what happened, man? How did it go?" asked Mickey.

"Well, I called her and then picked her up. Her mom is nice. We rode our bikes to Ruby Hill and talked for a while. That was about the only place we went. It was pretty cool." Danny's face glowed as he forwarded the details. He met her parents, and Mr. and Mrs. Sommers seemed to be nice people. He didn't get a chance to meet her older brother, Lance. He was going to be a senior next year, and he owned a Yamaha motorcycle. Her dad was a plumber and looked like the plumber type, a guy who could swing a fifty-pound pipe wrench with little effort. Even though he was a little intimidating, he reached out and shook his hand man-to-man. He had a big round face that bore a welcoming smile, but he also looked like the kind of blue-collar man that you didn't want to mess with. After years of hard labor, he had a broad chest and huge arms that looked like they could lift the end of a truck with little effort.

Of course, her mom was like a typical mom; you had to sit down and have some cookies and Kool-Aid and tell her a little about your family. Danny was slightly embarrassed when she asked, "What does your father do?" He was accustomed to it as he went through the full explanation and then waited for her mom to say, "Oh, I'm sorry to hear that." Danny hoped it didn't leave a bad impression.

Mickey imagined the two of them riding their bikes to Ruby Hill, then sitting alone, and staring out over downtown Denver. He also imagined that there must have been more than just talking. "Ya, sure, just cool, huh? You're nuts over her." Mickey picked up his glove and threw it at him. Danny ducked and laughed. "So how did it go? What did you do? Hold her hand? Kiss her? Come on, man, what happened?"

If he was in any other company, he would have blushed, but with Mickey, their lives were an open book. "Naw, we just talked." Danny recounted their bike ride. She even looked graceful riding a bike. He was awestruck in her presence and stumbled for words most of the time. His huge grin revealed how exciting it really was for him, but his shyness was evident as he looked down; this was new territory for him. All the other guys seemed to have more charisma when it came to girls, and he sometimes felt like he was the only ninth grader on earth to have never kissed a girl. All the guys knew it, but they never ribbed him about it. Hell, even Mags has kissed Jennifer. Sanners and Mickey also had tales of romance but not Danny. He often wondered if he ever would. It took all the guts he had just to talk to this girl.

Mickey reached over and slapped Danny on the shoulder. "Keep up the good work, man. She's worth it."

Danny picked up his chin and chuckled. Danny felt lucky to have a best friend like Mickey. On a bad day, he could pick any guy up. His confidence was contagious, and he was a natural leader that had compassion even for the little guys. He could even take a kid like poor little Stevie Burman and make him feel like a king. Stevie was one of those little guys who was destined to be a perennial late-inning right fielder. Mickey would throw his arm around him after he struck out and tell him, "Stevie, I'm going to need your strong arm in right field to hit me on the cutoff. You could be one of the most important keys in our win, and I know you'll be ready." While most kids were consumed with their own performance, he never thought about himself and always had empathy for the kid who bobbled a ball or struck out. Mickey single-handedly brought the team to another level. The guys also knew to never criticize a teammate in his presence, or they might get the business. The weaker kids at school or on the team were safe in his presence. It created an atmosphere of a single unit. When a kid was around him, they didn't feel like just another eighth or ninth grader; they felt important.

Mickey didn't want to put him on the spot any more than what he was comfortable with. "I think I see the whole new Danny boy coming through." He grinned, then gave him a comforting slap on the back. "You're all right, dude. I'm proud of you. Come on, let's go catch up with those guys before Mags eats all the fries at Hots and Suds."

The two saddled up and began pumping their bikes across the park.

11

Session 1

MEGAN FOLLOWED A consistent format for each group she facilitated. Shaw was familiar with the routine and sat at his normal position slightly off center on the opposite side of the circle of group members. When Meg and Shaw facilitated the process of group therapy, it was more like a well-rehearsed performance on a ballroom dance floor. The dance could sustain any bobble or mishap and finish with ease and grace.

The group room had a dozen huge pillows with support backs to allow a person to lean back. Some therapists felt the pillows were a throw back to the sixties, where everyone sat on the floor and "experienced" each other. As a therapist, Megan had no ego so she did not lose any sleep over other people's perceptions of her group's furniture. She also preferred them because of their casual touch and insisted the center keep them.

Megan had very few critics, but her most vocal detractor was Darion. Darion's ego forced him to make a daily stop at his office door and admire the door tag. A quick nod to the "Dr. Darion Walsh MD" door tag confirmed that was certainly the most important clinician in the building. This ego, however, disallowed him from doing any group therapy. Dr. Darion Walsh MD was above sitting on the floor and privately referred to Megan as a "fake." He once told Shaw, "Since she can't analyze her clients like the rest of us in the field, she wants to do that circus crap that gets her in touch with her real self." He emphasized "touch" with heavy sarcasm in his voice. Darion shared those comments with Shaw over lunch a year ago, before he realized that Meg and Shaw were old friends. Shaw regretted sharing the exchange with Meg; it only made her angrier with Darion.

Each of the opening exercises were "sandwiched" between Megan and Shaw. One would begin an exercise, and the other would end it. In between, they would do a round with the group members.

From an ethical and legal standpoint, she started each group by clarifying the limits of confidentiality. Each member had to agree that anything they talked about in the group would not be discussed outside the group. As experienced therapists, they knew there would be some conversation outside the group, so they tried to discuss it before it happened. "You may be affected by what takes place in the group," said Megan as she turned from left to right and back again. "And you may want to talk about it. If you do, such as with your partner, I would like you to only talk about yourself and not other members of the group since they are not there to defend themselves. If you have issues with other group members or with Shaw and myself, please bring it up *in* group. Shaw and I will have discussions in private regarding the group because we want to try to work together to bring you the best experience possible."

Megan dispensed with other group information, legal disclosure documents, and the guidelines for the group. "Speak only for yourself, stay in the moment, try not to ask questions, and keep a confidential journal. Shaw and I will facilitate the group, but we will not be responsible for its content. This will be up to you." She scanned her head from side to side to make eye contact with everyone. "Does anyone have any questions?" Megan knew when to allow silence. She waited patiently and smiled as she scanned the group again and waited.

Lisa spoke first, "When you said 'a confidential journal,' will we bring it here?"

"Absolutely not," Megan first looked at Lisa, then her partner, then looked back and forth, talking to the entire group, hoping to model expected behaviors.

"I appreciate you asking that question. As a matter of fact, I personally believe you should show your journal to no other person on earth. And knowing that others are writing a journal, we should *never* ask to see them. The purpose of the journal is for reflection, perhaps to look back on your thoughts as we go through the group. I like to jot down a few of my thoughts every day, and I find it real helpful, especially when I am struggling with some issues. It's like a private conversation with myself. On record of course." Megan smiled widely and looked around again.

Megan's professional craft was an extension of her personality. She was genuine, and most of the time others picked up on it and immediately trusted her.

Shaw smiled and followed her lead by also scanning the group. His smile and slight nod of his head were his response to Megan's statement. Shaw was well aware that he was a good therapist, but behind his smile he was thinking, *I can't hold a candle to her.* In one brief moment, Megan had connected more with her group than most therapists do in weeks. Her professional demeanor, warmth, body language, and openness made quick connections. She was unaware that a short self-disclosing statement about her own journal had gained even further ground. In mentioning her own journal, it normalized the assignment. *Journals were not just for people who were struggling with issues in groups. Even therapists have journals.* What most of the group members heard loudly was *"when I am struggling."* Immediately, it disbanded hierarchies in the group and put everyone on the same level. *She struggles too.*

Many therapists take years to develop skills like hers, but Megan was unaware of her ability; she was just being herself.

After a few more questions about the length of group, commitment, and responsibility, Megan began some of her opening exercises. "Tonight I will be leading the group with a few exercises. Then next week the group will be responsible for what we talk about. I would just like to do a few rounds tonight to get to know each other. First of all, I would like us to introduce each other," Megan explained a process for a quick one-minute interview in which each person was paired off with another, *but not* their support partner; that would be too safe. "You can ask no serious data questions like, How old are you? Where are you from? Why are you in group? Or, what do you do for a job?' I want none of these questions. I want questions like, 'If you won the lottery, what would you do first? If you were stranded on a desert island, which book would you most like to read?' These questions can reflect anything *except* data. Of course, on occasion I've heard some great questions such as 'for $1,000 would you eat a bowl of live ants?'" The group laughed as Meg waited for them "So all questions are okay as long as they are not about data."

Megan and Shaw also paired off with different people in the group and went through the exercise. Afterward, in an orchestrated sequence, she went through a series of "rounds." Megan continually experimented with several different methods of starting a group. It was important to establish the norms of the group from the very beginning. In deliberate fashion, the first session was taken through a series of leads in ascending order from safe to risky disclosure.

When the time was up, she and Shaw carried out a closing round, again in a careful but-well coordinated manner.

After the group, Shaw and Meg closed the door to her office to review the session.

"UH ... OH ... !" Shaw slumped in Megan's desk chair then grinned. "Looks like you won't be needing me. Jan can help you with the group!"

Megan didn't appreciate the sarcasm; she rolled her eyes. "It's okay. She's just a typical junior Freud. But for the life of me, I don't know why some counseling students do that." She was referring to Jan Simper. Her husband had been struggling with recovery for years, and now they decided on group. Somehow, Megan had missed a couple of minor details in the screening. One minor detail was that Jan was pursuing her master's degree in counseling, and now after only four courses, decided she was ready to be a therapist. When the group introduced each other during one of the opening activities, Jan was the only one who stopped the group member who introduced her to add a few other details.

"I'd just like to attach a side note – that I'm excited to be here, and I wanted to let you know that I'm working on my master's degree in counseling, and Megan, Shaw" – Jan nodded in both of their directions – "I think I can be of help in counseling the group."

Meg didn't miss a beat. Not wanting to single her out, she scanned the group, "Thanks for your offer, Jan, for now though. I think that each member" – she looked from side to side making eye contact with the group – "should focus on what you came here for, which is to support each other." Megan smiled and motioned to Jan's left to continue the introductions. Jan's words stopped, but the nonverbals were screaming. Shaw and Meg continued with the group, but both noticed the pursed lips and folded arms; Jan was done speaking for the day. Even in the closing round, she refused to speak and decided to "pass" when it came to reflecting on the first group session.

Jan fumbled with her coat and waited until all of the other group members left before cornering Meg. She went directly to the source that threatened her power in the group. "I have to be honest." Jan stood, paused, and refolded her arms. "I felt embarrassed, and I *do* believe I could help run this group. In my group counseling class, I think I learned a lot about ways to help others – "

Meg made eye contact and gently cut in, "I apologize if my intentions were misinterpreted, but I think we have to stop here. One of our agreements was that we couldn't talk about group issues outside of group. Perhaps we could open the next session and you could – "

"No." Jan's anger was mounting. "This is not about the group members. It's about leading. My group counseling professor said I had some good leadership skills, and when I joined this group, I thought I could – "

"Jan, I'm sorry, but we have to stop here for a second. I really believe that Donald could benefit most from your presence as a group member, a source of support. Shaw and I will help each other to facilitate the group, and that will allow you to focus on your role." Megan offered an encouraging smile.

"Okay." Janice partially closed one eye, tilted her head, then offered a sarcastic smile. A smile that had "pissed off" written all over it. A smile that said, "How dare you demote me to the level of these people."

In a rapid tone, Jan offered her final jab, "Let's just hope I come back." She abruptly turned and walked out. Taking five steps, she stopped, waited, glanced back, then stomped out. She was now even more angered because one of her manipulation tools had failed. When she stomped out of a conversation, the other party usually tried to stop her. In this case, Megan simply nodded and said, "I hope you do come back. Let me know if you're not. See you next week."

"What are we going to do about her?" Shaw rubbed his index fingers to his temples in a sarcastic gesture. He and Meg knew each other too well. One of her gestures when she was stressing was to slowly massage her temples.

"Stop it!" The pantomime got a laugh from Meg. "We'll just continue as usual. This could be very good for her. Eventually, the group will confront her. Then we will see the real fireworks. Did you notice how quiet Donald was? I think he's used to her domination."

"Yes, I did. Since we started with these two, shall we keep going?"

They proceeded to discuss each of the members and take notes. Megan was compulsive about notes on her groups. When she taught group counseling as an adjunct professor at Denver State U, she always emphasized taking notes *immediately* after each session. She believed it was practically unprofessional to write up case notes at a later time. She also became angered any time she worked with a therapist who kept incomplete case notes or records. Note taking was one of her pet peeves.

Other observations were noted. Tony and Rose were the most uncomfortable. Meg agreed with Shaw that they would be important members of the group but also noted that Tony's male pride may be the product of his cultural norms. He was gentle and sensitive, but asking for help was out of the question for the oldest male in a Hispanic family. Pride and vulnerability were at stake.

Doris and Earl had been in family therapy in the past, and group seemed to fit. They wanted help, and both were willing to be open with the group.

The closest couple was Lisa and Gerri. Often, during the group exercises, they seemed to have tears in their eyes at the same time while the other was talking. "Tell me what you think about their fit." Shaw wanted Meg's input first.

Meg smiled. "I always go first, give me your thoughts first."

Shaw took a deep breath. "I have some concerns, not with Lisa and Gerri, but with the level of acceptance of the rest of the group. In some ways, I'll bet that right now Tony and Rose are the only ones who are really aware that they are a lesbian couple. Tony seemed to connect with them and glance back and forth while they spoke. It's just my hunch, but I'll bet that Tony and Rose probably have a gay or lesbian friend or relative and are sensitive and accepting to the relationships."

The reason Shaw brought up the "fit" up is because Jan spouted a little "holier than thou" speech during the intake. She seems a little suspect of everyone in the group and somewhat self-righteous.

Shaw continued, "Right now, we seem to have some nice balance because we have a male couple and a female couple. It's just that I don't know if I can handle another 'Campbell incident.'"

"If we handled the Campbells, we can handle anything, but I don't want to survive that scenario again." Meg leaned back in her chair and gave a slight shake of her head.

They were referring to Bill and Paula Campbell. Two years ago in a similar group, Meg and Shaw ran a group that included a gay couple. The Campbells had driven to Denver from Colorado Springs, an hour away. They wanted their therapy to take place in another community far from their own. In Colorado Springs, they were deeply involved in a large church that saw gays and lesbians as the work of the devil. In this case, they decided to use the group as a forum to talk about the issues of "the wrath of God, living in sin, and heathen lifestyles." With their prayer books in hand, they saw it as their mission to save the group. The results were catastrophic and made Shaw and Meg nervous about dealing with people who had difficulty accepting differences in others.

Shaw said, "Speaking of our male couple, did they look as uncomfortable to you as they did to me? And what about Terrence's answer to the nickname question?" Shaw waited through Meg's silence.

Meg leaned forward, stared at the floor, and sighed twice before responding. "I hope I didn't make a mistake with them. I think they both feel like they don't belong in the group, and I'm beginning to wonder myself." Meg knew she took a gamble with Terrence and Daniel. They were the only couple who were there for each other's support but were not an actual couple. "They were definitely the most quiet, and I did find it a bit odd how he stammered with the nickname round."

Early in the group, they went through a series of rounds that were intended to break the ice like *a favorite childhood memory, one important possession in your life,* and *a nickname from your youth.* The group divulged a few with *Lisa Pizza, Rosey, Danny, and Earl the Pearl.* When it came to Terrence, he stopped, and a serious look came over his face, unlike the mood of the rest of the group. He looked down and opened his mouth twice before he spoke. It was as though the words were trying to crawl out but were stopped by some barrier. He then stammered "I used to be . . . once was called . . . Mi . . . Mi . . . Mick . . ." Tears began to form in the corners of his eyes before he gulped, "I never had a nickname."

"I suppose we'll see next week," said Shaw.

Megan nodded as they finished their case notes.

"How are you doing, pal?" Daniel sat on a chair in the lounge but couldn't take his eyes off the bandages on Terrence's wrists. He felt a lump in his throat but couldn't figure out why.

"Actually, pretty good." Terrence smiled, wondering if Daniel believed him. Breaking the awkward silence, he asked, "What do you think of the Canterosa trade? Stupid or what?"

"It depends, he wasn't producing, so maybe they've got some hope in a couple of minor leaguers." They both sat straighter in their chairs. Switching the conversation was an awkward and predictable move, but at the same time, it was safe. Baseball talk was always secure ground. They could talk about trades, the game, and ballplayers, and feel comfort – at least for that moment. Maybe it wasn't just a move to safe conversation but a move to soothing conversation. For the love of spring, summer, and the baseball diamond. *As long as it stays safe, we won't have to talk about ourselves or feel the pain in our hearts.*

On her way to her office, something caught Meg's eye as she passed the lounge. Terrence was lit up in conversation; she had never seen this before. Sitting across from his support partner, Daniel, he was more animated than she had seen him in a month. Daniel was simulating a throwing motion with his arm. She watched from the doorway as the two laughed together. Feeling as though she was intruding, she turned and continued on her way to her office. *Maybe they are closer than I thought they were.*

Daniel sat in his car for ten minutes and stared at the Shiler Center. He felt sick to his stomach. *Maybe it's the flu. Maybe Terrence's mother dying. Maybe just seeing Terrence like that.* Daniel felt self-conscious as he sniffed. He picked up a tissue and blew his nose. He wasn't afraid of his emotions; he just didn't want to show them. Glancing back and forth over both shoulders, he wanted to be sure that no one in the parking lot was around to make a judgment about the man sitting in his car with tears in his eyes. Most of all, he didn't like emotions that he couldn't figure out. *Why the hell am I so sad right now?* He picked up his son's baseball glove off the seat and worked the pocket by popping his fist into the palm. The ball glove was new, and it needed breaking in. "Helluva a way to start the summer," Daniel said to himself as he slapped the palm of the glove. The feel of the leather and the smell of the glove oil seemed to have a calming effect. He ran his fingers over the leather laces. A wave of emotion hit him. His lips began to quiver, and suddenly his eyes blurred with tears. He held the glove to his cheek and whispered, "What the hell happened to Mick – " Tears ran out of both eyes. Daniel couldn't finish the name. He picked up another tissue and blew his nose. "Oh, Mickey, old buddy, I miss you so much." He wondered if he would ever call him by his nickname again. It was as though using the old name could bring him back.

Daniel popped the baseball glove with his fist once more for good measure. Tossing it on the passenger seat, he started the car and drove out of the lot.

12

June 21, 1968
Teen Swim

MICKEY AND DANNY arrived ten minutes before the opening of Teen Swim. Every Friday night from five to seven, the Y had a special swim time for teenagers. When they were younger, they were envious of those Y members who had the coveted TEEN stamped on the card. When time came to finally attend the Teen Swim, it was like having a tattoo across your chest that said, "Now I am one of the big guys."

Mags huffed as he pushed down the pedals on his bike. He pulled up next to Danny with his trademark smile. Every day was a great day when you were Mags. A few minutes later, they noticed Sanners approaching. When he was "up to no good," his lip curled at the top like a junior Elvis. Mickey spotted the grin and immediately knew what he was up to. He sported the devilish grin as he pedaled in two big circles around the boys. As he got closer, he yelled, "Hey, Mags! Would you like to trade some ball cards?" Sanners's grin turned to a laugh. Mickey and Danny also started laughing because they knew what he was up to. He had his sneaky methods of getting on Mags's nerves. When Mags heard the rat-a-tat of Sanners bicycle, he grew a startled look on his face. Sanners steered his bike just close enough so Mags could recognize the baseball cards that he had clipped to the front fork of his bike to make the rattling noise. "Hey, Mags, how would you like to trade some Pete Rose cards? Or how about some Carl Yaztremski cards?"

Mags dropped his bike and took off in a sprint. From behind, he looked like a bowl of Jell-O with legs. "You son of a biscuit!" Mags had been trying to trade him for those cards all week and now *that dumb idiot had them in his spokes!* To Mags, the desecration of a baseball card was a mortal sin. He gently handled every card in his collection and ordered them neatly in shoeboxes. To Sanners, they were cardboard meant for reading, flipping, and trading. Beyond that, they were just cardboard.

Sanners laughed with delight as he pedaled just fast enough to stay out of Mags's reach. "Hey, Mags, how about a Gibson or a McClain?"

Danny and Mickey shook their heads as they watched the cat-and-mouse game that Sanners had carefully orchestrated.

The trip to the pool culminated another perfect day of summer. School was out. The weather grew warmer with each passing day. Baseball was in their blood. The St. Anthony Falcons trounced the St. Rose Knights by a score of 10-1. Mickey pitched the first six innings and didn't allow a base runner to get as far as second base. Eggs brought in Danny for two innings of relief, and Joey Pelloman pitched the final inning. The one run was scored off Danny. He loved to pitch, but the pressure was always overbearing. Center field was his home. Eggs always had a couple of guys getting experience just in case he needed them at some other point in the season. Danny was their second best pitcher but sometimes had control problems. Mags had a great arm, but it was reserved for throwing out base runners who tried to steal. Sanners had a cannon for an arm but would lose his concentration as a pitcher. Last year, Eggs tried him for one inning, and he hit two batters. He hadn't pitched since.

In many ways, the boys sensed this was the last summer of true freedom. All four of them would turn sixteen in the coming year, and when you enter the "working age" you no longer own your days in the summer. *You are expected to find a summer job.* Minimum wage, of course, a whopping $1.35 an hour. They knew they would probably end up sacking groceries or bussing dishes somewhere. Maybe they also wouldn't do the thing that summer nights were made for – sleeping out.

Now that school was officially over, they had permission from their parents to drag their sleeping bag over to a friend's house and sleep out in the backyard. This also meant that they not only owned the city from five to six thirty every morning, they also owned the night. It was simple. Throw the sleeping bags out in the yard, talk about baseball and girls until the parents were asleep, stuff the bag so it looks like someone is still in it, then belly crawl to the alley or behind a garage and mount the mighty two-wheel steeds and go out for a midnight adventure.

Plans were already being made for their first outing. Mickey stood behind Danny as they waited for their turn on the diving board. "Did you ask your mom if you could sleep out?"

"Ya, but she said she still she wants to speak to Mrs. Magliano. She trusts me, but she always has to check it out." Danny stepped onto the board and attempted his best swan dive. Mickey followed, then swam over to meet him at the edge. "What about Sanners?"

Mickey glanced to the shallow end where Sanners was in the process of dunking Mags. "He never asks. He says his dad wouldn't remember him asking anyway, so he just grabs his bag and goes. So he's cool for the night."

"I kind of feel sorry for the guy sometimes," said Danny. "It's great that he can do anything he wants, but sometimes it's nice to know that your parents worry about you."

When Teen Swim ended, the boys made their trek to Mags's with their sleeping bags stuffed in their paper-bike bags. Mags dragged his things out into the yard along with two wind-up alarm clocks. The boys never had to worry about getting up on time to deliver, not with Mags around.

After the boys were settled in, they reclined on their backs and stared at the stars. The discussions involved the varied teenage intellectual issues that popped into their minds. *Wouldn't it be cool if you could own every baseball card ever made? We should go watch St. Augie's play a game some time, you know, scout them out. Sunday papers are a pain in the ass. The Gazette is a stupid paper. They deliver Monday through Saturday in the afternoons then deliver their Sunday paper in the morning. How stupid is that? Why do they deliver in the afternoons? Nobody wants an afternoon paper. Someday I'm gonna have a big house. Who invented sleeping bags? The guy's probably a millionaire. I wished I had arms like Charles Atlas. I think chicks dig that.*

The talk eventually progressed to the grilling of Danny regarding Jean. He saw her three times this week. No hand-holding yet. The guys backed off. The questions made him nervous.

The conversation shifted from subject to subject until Mags delivered the showstopper. "This guy I was talking to in the cafeteria a few weeks ago, he was um . . . like a new kid at school. I don't remember his name. Um . . . he um . . . he said that he wakes up some mornings with a stiffy. He also said that sometimes when he kisses his girlfriend, he gets a stiffy. You suppose there's like something like wrong with him? You know, like if you're not like thinking about a stiffy, can you still get one? Not like I would know or anything, it was just some kid at school."

Dead silence filled the air. No response. None of the boys even turned to look at each other. They were incapable of doing anything except staring straight ahead. They remained motionless staring into the Denver night sky, their minds in shock. It was as if the world stopped rotating on its axis. Nothing to say, only a lot of thinking; they had watched all of the sex education films in junior high, but no one ever asked this question. The films were usually fodder for laughing fits at a later time since they never really were helpful or informative. The last one they had seen was the most hilarious of all, *How To Know When You've Gone Too Far.* They had seen it in an all-boys gym class. The guy in the film would hold a girl's hand, and the announcer would say, "Gary has not gone too far." The next segment would show a guy moving his hand up above the knee on his date's leg and say, "Clarence has gone too far." Later that day, the boys laughed until they cried with Mags imitating and replaying all of the scenes.

This new subject, however, was foreign territory. They could easily talk about most subjects on earth, but no one brought this one up before. Macho guys bragged about getting to second or third base with girls, but no one ever mentioned hazardous or awkward situations. Mickey stared ahead. The guy had an intelligent answer for everything, not this one. An answer may incriminate you. Danny's thoughts drifted. *Oh my God, what's going to happen if I ever kiss Jean? Oh my God . . . No way, a guy can control that, can't he?*

In a bold move, Sanners broke the still air in the eye of the hurricane. "I don't think there's nothin' wrong with that kid." It was time to *immediately* change the subject. "Hey, guys, it looks like the coast is clear. Let's cruise to the Quick-Ten and grab some sodas." A sigh of relief fell over them.

Mickey followed. "It looks good, men, let's book."

It didn't matter if they were thirsty or not. The sheer thrill of these missions was enough to pump extra blood into their arteries. After stuffing the sleeping bags, they crawled in silence to their bikes behind Mags's garage and then sped down the alley. As they pedaled, Danny was still wondering, *A guy can control that, can't he?*

13

Too Good

MEGAN FLINCHED IN her office chair. A five-page paper fell from her hand to the office floor. It didn't make enough noise to wake her. She had closed her eyes for only a few moments, but it was enough to send her drifting into a nap at nine o'clock at night.

Megan's office was efficient but not compulsively ordered. It was impersonal but not by design. Many of the other therapists at Shiler had pictures of their families and loved ones on the walls, and most of them had already gone home to those loved ones by now.

Megan's office walls had her college degrees, a few pictures from her fishing outings in the Rockies, but other than that, the office was sterile and stacked with books and papers. Only one picture had a personal touch; it was of four smiling faces in caps and gowns from years ago. Meg, Shaw, Pentral, and Hensman.

Professor Hensman tried to scoot forward in his chair to gain a comfortable position in his graduation gown. The tassel flopped back and forth and brushed his cheek. Sitting in metal folding chairs and wearing academic regalia were incompatible duties. Dr. Hensman looked down at the blue velvet slashes on the sleeves of his gown and smiled. He calculated in his head that he had worn the cap and gown forty-two times, twice a year, through twenty-one years of graduation ceremonies. As department chair at Southern Colorado State University, he had participated in dozens of *hooding* ceremonies for doctoral students as they walked across the stage.

The event was held outdoors on the SCSU campus, and when the weather cooperated, it was even more special. The portion involving the doctoral hood was the most prestigious segment of the university graduation ceremony. One of Dr. Hensman's favorite students beamed as she walked across the stage. He did not have the honor of "hooding" her because he was not her research advisor. Nonetheless, he took great joy in the occasion. Dr. Hensman loved every graduation ceremony he attended. He just hated the boring speakers and the uncomfortable gowns.

"From the School of Arts and Sciences . . ." The muffled stage announcer spent extra time introducing the doctoral candidates "A doctor of philosophy in professional psychology, Megan Marie Talden, Dr. Talden's dissertation study . . ."

Dr. Hensman nudged his fidgeting friend, Dr. Pentral, and leaned over to whisper, "She's *too good*." Dr. Pentral adjusted his hood as it slightly choked him when he turned. "I agree," he whispered. "She may be the one of the best we've had in the program."

"Too good" was a term shared by the faculty in the professional psychology department at Southern State. It was used only on rare occasions to describe those students who were heavily invested in the field. "Too good" described those students whose lives were being transformed within the profession, and likewise, they would transform the lives of others. Some enter doctoral programs for career changes, financial rewards, power, position, prestige, challenge, or any combination of life's needs. And there are those few who enter the profession because it is was a true extension of who they are. They are so deeply invested in others that they often forget themselves. The term "too good" was coined to describe them. With this investment were also greater pains. Dr. Hensman had seen a few during his tenure at Southern but none like Meg. At times, he shared his fears with his friend Dr. Bill Pentral. He had seen others like Meg and knew that if she wasn't careful, she could feel too much of other's pains, too much of other's hardships, and identify too much with the struggles of her clients.

Megan had a tendency to piss off some of her fellow students in the program. It wasn't on purpose. It was due to the academic standard she set for herself. The compulsive ones were more concerned with getting the "right answer" than they were with the profession. Megan always seemed to be one step ahead, one reading assignment ahead, one research article ahead, and one insight ahead of others in the program. She had more than a personal opinion; she was able to be introspective beyond the level of the average student. She was driven to "get things right" for herself, not for her grade or for her professor. When she studied, it was for her clients, not for the program and the grades. The compulsive ones were often jealous. It seemed that even when she made mistakes or went out on a limb with a new idea, she was held in higher esteem than other students. She often viewed the issues in a creatively new framework and was simply on a different track rather than being completely wrong.

She was also a loner; her only real close friend in the program was Shawnon Durneck, who studied with her because he wasn't intimidated by her and had deep admiration for her original thinking. Many of her colleagues had money, and some were flat-out spoiled. Most of them also drowned themselves in beer on weekends if the stress in the program got too high, and Megan had given up that scene a long time ago.

Meg was also plain and simple. She rode her bike and racked up student loans to get through school.

"We have to know when to cut ourselves off . . ." Dr. Hensman used to lecture in his classes. "We need to continue to be empathic and care for our clients, but we can't take their problems home with us. We need to take care of ourselves first. If we take their problems home with us, we won't have a life of our own. We won't be able to nurture our relationships and our own lives. It doesn't mean that we don't continue caring for them. It simply means that we can't carry the burden of their pain with us twenty-four hours a day. As the old saying goes, 'Owning other people's problems only makes them twice as hard to solve.'" Dr. Hensman spent a lot of time in his courses preparing his students for *life* as a therapist, not just a career. He also knew that it was impossible for good therapists to leave all of their problems at the office, but what he feared most was for those therapists who were *too good* and took too much home with them.

"Please join me in as we congratulate and welcome to the community of scholars, Dr. Megan Marie Talden." Dr. Hensman applauded as he leaned over to Dr. Pentral and whispered, "We're going to miss her." To that, Dr. Pentral nodded and noticed Hensman's eyes welling up. He smiled and thought, *The old guy never fails to get choked up every year at these things.*

After the ceremony, Meg, Shaw and the two professors posed in their graduation gowns for a keepsake photo. Hensman thought, *One day, these two will be a couple of marvelous professionals, perhaps too good.*

A soft knock on the office door startled Megan. "Dr. Talden? I'm sorry. I didn't mean to scare you." Frank, the custodian, stood next to her office door. "Would you like me to vacuum your office tonight?"

Meg sat up straight in her chair and drew in a deep breath of air. It took her a moment to take in her surroundings. She shook her head and looked at her office clock. "I'm sorry, Frank, that's okay. I must have drifted off." She looked at the vacuum cleaner next to him. "Please, go ahead. I'm on my way out the door anyway, thanks."

Megan threw a handful of folders into her backpack and made her way down the hall. She shook her head and spoke to herself, "Oh shit." She looked at her watch, *I've got to get home and clean Carl's cat box and feed him.* Carl was known to be passive aggressive and tear things up if his needs weren't being met.

She stepped into the lot, unchained her bike, and pedaled home.

14

June 29, 1968
Hots and Suds

UNCLE BUD SLAPPED a glass of orange juice and a donut on the counter "Hey, Mickey, I heard you pitched a heckuva game against St. Rose."

"It was okay, you know Danny pitched too." Mickey reached to his left and smacked Danny's biceps. "The man's got a great arm, and speaking of arms, did you know that Mags caught two guys stealing, we couldn't live without the big guy behind the plate. He also caught all nine innings."

Mickey habitually deflected attention. He loved it like any other guy but was uncomfortable if it wasn't distributed among his teammates. The difference between Mickey and most others his age was that he enjoyed attention but he didn't need it.

Bud poured coffee on the other side of the shop but his booming voice carried like a built in microphone. "Tell you what, I'll try to make the Trinity game tomorrow."

The boys were not too anxious about Holy Trinity. Weak pitching, and they were 1-1.

Three of the four boys were already into their donuts. Sanners had another late delivery of his papers. Mags snorted through his hot chocolate as he read the Alley Oop cartoon aloud. Mickey planted a soft jab to Danny's shoulder. "So how did it go, man?"

Every time Danny was questioned about Jean, he blushed. This time he didn't. His grin grew wide. Taking a bite out of his donut, he looked over at Mickey and raised his eyebrows.

"Aha, my man Casanova has come through! Did you even watch the movie?"

"Maybe."

The day before, Danny went over to Mickey's prior to his bike ride to Brentwood theaters. It was a date to see a movie, but it really wasn't a date. Mickey gave him some advice on how to nonchalantly reach over and hold her hand. Danny's hands shook for the first hour of the movie before he finally reached over and gently touched her fingers. Jean slipped her fingers inside his, and Danny flew on a one-way ticket to heaven. He could hardly summon the courage to look at her. His mind was going crazy. He could no longer follow the plot to the James Bond movie *You Only Live Twice*. He could hear the characters speak on the screen, but the plot was lost. *Maybe she just grabbed my hand by accident. Look at her. No! don't look at her! Look at her! No don't! Oh God my hand's shaking again.* When Danny finally glanced at her she smiled. Danny smiled, then quickly turned back to the screen. *Oh God, is this a "just friends" holding of the hands? Or, does she really like me? I hope she likes me. This is the softest hand I've ever touched.*

Danny chewed his donut and continued to smile as he remembered the feel of her soft skin, her luminous smile. It was as though she was capable of glowing in the darkness of a movie theater.

"I see that smile, you hound dog, what happened?"

"We just you know, held hands and watched the movie."

"Oh my goodness, the world has come to an end, my man Danny made the move." Mickey stood up and placed an arm on Danny's shoulder. "Attention, everyone, I have an announcement to make!"

A look of panic came over Danny. *Oh no, please don't, come on, Mickey, I swear I'll never talk to you again, you son of a . . .*

"I would like to announce that Danny has claimed . . . that he . . ."

Please don't Mickey, please . . . Danny's chin fell to his chest.

"Has claimed he will hit a homer against Trinity tomorrow."

From across the coffee shop Buds hollered, "Good for you, boy!" Danny balled his fist up and planted a friendly sock of relief to Mickey's stomach.

It took time, but Pats eventually understood the sense of reverence that Danny experienced with his baseball games. Three years ago she stopped complaining about his need to wear brand-new blue jeans to his baseball game. At first, she thought of it as only a game. She later realized that young boys see baseball as something much bigger than their own lives. For that reason, she bought him a new pair of blue jeans every summer.

Danny walked from the shower to his bedroom with a towel around him. He looked at his clean-pressed blue jeans neatly lying across the foot of his bed. Next to the jeans were a pair of socks, his hat, and white shirt had big block red letters on the front proudly announcing FALCONS.

Baseball players are men of rituals. Before each game, they know that you have to do everything a certain way. Uniform, meals, warm-ups – everything has to be in order. It helps keep you focused on the importance of this duty you are about to undertake. When your foot steps out on that diamond, you represent all the honor and tradition of the St. Anthony's Falcon senior team – even if that tradition is only three years old.

In Danny's mind, he was stepping into the clubhouse of a great major league team. In front of him was his uniform in all its glory. In his mind he imagined the old and trusted clubhouse equipment manager carefully placing it there before he arrived. First the underwear, then the shirt, followed by a pair of blue jeans. Next went on the *good* pair of white high-top shoes.

When it came to buying clothes, Pats had to go with the budget. The only problem is that everyone knows that any serious game cannot be played in those dime-store reject shoes with the hard rubber soles. It's entirely possible to kill a young man in those darn things. It is of vital importance to have Converse Chuck Taylor high-top shoes, affectionately known to athletes as "Chucks." In order to own them, Danny had to contribute ten dollars of his own. A worthwhile investment when one's life is on the line.

After Danny precisely tied his shoes with double knots he attended to one last detail. The cards. Ever since he could remember playing with the guys, they had the time-honored tradition of placing a baseball card in each of their back pockets. This

was strictly for good luck – which meant you had to select your cards very carefully. One had to be your favorite hitter and the other had to be your favorite fielder.

The cards were symbolic and the behaviors surrounding them were ritual. If you were going out in the field for defense, you had to slap one of your back pockets with your glove for good luck. If you were going up to bat, you would slap the other pocket for good luck at hitting.

In his right went the Willie Mays for fielding; in his left went Ernie Banks for hitting. He stood in front of the mirror and adjusted his cap. Ready for action.

Mags looked at himself and adjusted his rolls. He loved catcher's gear because it covered up some of the bigger ones. He reached to the top of his dresser and picked up a brand-new 1968 baseball card of Harmon Killebrew, a great hitter. The other card was handled with special care. He beamed at the smiling image as he gently handled it. It was a 1954 card he picked up with a shoe box of other cards at a yard sale. The name was Roy Campanella.

Campanella hadn't played a major league game since an accident paralyzed him ten years ago. It didn't matter to Mags. He felt a connection to the three-time MVP catcher from the Brooklyn Dodgers. Two years ago he mentioned to Mr. Magliano that he thought his fat thighs didn't allow him to run fast. Mr. Magliano knew that his son was self-conscious about his weight. It would have been easy for him to tell his son that he should like himself, no matter what you look like, but for Mr. Mags life's lessons were better learned through stories. He told him a story about the greatest catcher of all time, Roy Campanella. Roy had legs that some said looked like a pair of watermelons under his uniform. Powerful legs that could squat down for hours. Powerful legs that allowed him to put zip behind his throws to nail base runners at second base. That's right, Roy Campanella thighs. Ever since that conversation, Mags was damn proud of those Campanella thighs. The day he found the card he pedaled his bike home until his legs were numb. He had to show his dad. Until that time it seemed like Campanella was a mythical character. Now he would serve as Mags's strength. Mags also dug up more information on Campanella in the public library. Campanella's mother was black, which kept him out of the majors for years. But, in an almost mystical sense, like Mags, Campanella had an Italian father. In his mind, this great Dodger was practically his blood brother in baseball.

Mags reached to his dresser and picked up the bottle of Hai Karate aftershave lotion. Big leaguers probably put on a little before every game. It was in his stocking last Christmas. At $1.33 a bottle, no kid can afford this stuff. *A little dab here, a little dab there, this stuff will last until next Christmas.*

Mickey pulled on his hat, then turned to his younger brother Spikes. Prior to each game, Spikes would watch Mickey prepare himself. It was like staring up at Mount Olympus as Hercules readied himself for a feat of strength.

"Hey, slugger, you choose." Mickey held out three cards in each hand. Spikes reached out and pointed. "This one and this one." He reached up and handed them to Mickey. One was Eddie Mathews, and the other was Bob Gibson. Two good cards, a slugger and a pitcher. Mickey wasn't as picky as the other guys, but he still believed in tradition; it was important to have those cards.

He stuffed them in his back pockets and whipped Spikes around. "All right, little partner, the others go in the back pockets of the best batboy in the history of the Falcons." He spun him back around and hoisted him up in the air for a hug. "I'll see you there."

"Thanks, Mickey, see yuh there." Spikes reached into his back pockets to feel the cards. These were special, they were Mickey's cards.

Sanners grabbed a stack of cards and shuffled through them. He made sure one was Brooks Robinson, his favorite third baseman. The other will be decided later. No one was home to see him off. No one that was interested anyway. His father was gone, and his mother slept on the couch. He quietly stepped past her to the backyard, where his bike leaned against the house. He pedaled off to the game.

Hots and Suds was one of the boys' favorite eateries for their pregame meal. When you think of baseball and food, you have to think of hot dogs. Hots and Suds had the best foot longs in the area. They also served great root beer. The place was not the Buckingham Palace, but it had character. It was run down and rarely had more than a few patrons. The scuffed tile floor and the faded counter were testimony to years of business. The faded ten-foot long hot dog on the front of the building seemed tacky and could only be appreciated by hungry teens.

The daily special was two Hots with fries and a Suds for forty-nine cents. Each of the boys dove into the plastic baskets when they arrived.

After his first dog, Sanners reached four fingers into his glass of water and turned toward Mags. "Ah ah ah choo!" He faked a sneeze as he flicked sprinkles of water on Mags's face.

"Knock it off, man, that's sick," said Mags as he grabbed a napkin and wiped his face. He shook his head with a *what an idiot!* gesture.

Sanners followed with a self-appreciating laugh. He got a kick out of having a leg up on his practical jokes directed at Mags.

Mags reached over the counter and slid the bowl of ketchup and mustard packets closer. Along with relish, he was ready to adorn his second dog when a serious look fell over his wide cheeks. He picked up a mustard packet and turned it over in his hand. He folded it and turned it from side to side. He then picked up a ketchup packet and did the same. The wheels were turning in his head.

Mags had an ongoing fascination with those little packets. Throughout his junior high school years, he was well-known for his discovery of at least a hundred creative ways to smash the little things. If you placed them on the table, you could smash them with your fist and make them spray in one direction or another. If you placed them on the floor, you could stomp on them and get the same results. Three out of four times it would end up on his shirt, pants, or shoes. But, nonetheless, his cafeteria reputation was legendary. His great claim to fame was the day he got a weeks suspension from the lunchroom. With one graceful smash, he shot a full mustard packet ten feet away, only to land on the side of the face of the school cafeteria monitor lady. It wasn't on purpose, but as legend has it, he took careful aim and nailed her as an act of revenge. The entire place erupted in howls at the sight of her trying to wipe the yellowish splotch off her face and hair. It was good-bye Mags, but he was a hero that day.

Mags woofed down his second dog while his hand nonchalantly slid two mustard and two ketchup packets into his pocket. The wheels were not only turning in his head; they were on a collision course with paybacks. Mags headed off to the bathroom.

A few minutes later, he returned and sat back down at the counter. He was quiet and more nervous than usual. With nothing better to do with his hands he arranged all of the shakers and napkins on the counter. Finally, after a wait that seemed to last forever, he watched Sanners get off his stool only to utter the sweet words he had been waiting for, "I'm going to take a dump."

All of the boys had their pregame rituals, and Sanners had one that was as predictable as a Rocky Mountain sunset.

As soon as the bathroom door shut, Mags listened for the bolt to lock the door. At the sound of the *click*, Mags sprung off his stool and bolted for the door with the determination of a small rhino who just discovered his hindquarters were on fire.

Mickey and Danny both had a puzzled look on their faces as they watched him jump on his bike and begin peddling as though his life depended on it.

Sanners stepped over to the only stool in the bathroom and dropped his drawers. Sanners never dropped his drawers much below his knees, a trivial fact only remembered by Mags. The other part of this perfect equation was the fact that Sanners hadn't noticed that the toilet seat was slightly elevated. Mags had meticulously placed two mustard packets and two ketchup packets under the knobs of the toilet seat where they made contact with porcelain bowl.

The instant Sanners sat down, there was a slight popping sound of the bursting packets. What followed was a bloodcurdling scream that pounded through the walls of the small bathroom and echoed through the normally quiet Hots and Suds establishment. "Maaaags! Maaaags! you sonnnn of a biiii . . ."

Mickey and Danny were still oblivious to what was happening. It then became apparent as they saw Sanners come bursting through the door. "Maaaags!" He looked at the two boys with the face of a crazed rabid animal. "Maaags! Where is that son of a . . ." He turned and ran out the door.

As Sanners left, Danny and Mickey could see two large splotches on the rear of Sanners pants. One was mustard yellow, and the other was catsup red.

"We better go save Mags," said Mickey. They hopped up from their stools and took off in pursuit.

By the time Mags saw Sanners closing in from behind, he was covered in ten pounds of sweat. Legs of fear are no match for pure angry locomotion. Mickey closed in on Sanners and knew he better catch him before he got to Mags. If Sanners got there first, it would be certain death. Mags turned behind the Brentwood shopping center. It was a wide-open chase through the middle of the parking lot.

When Mickey came within shouting distance, he began yelling at Sanners. Sanners was a wild African water buffalo leading his own personal stampede. Mags resembled one of the *Mutual of Omaha* documentaries where the helpless jungle animal is being chased by the vicious beast, soon to be his dinner. When Sanners finally got close enough, he reached out and grabbed Mags's belt. The rotund ball of sweat tumbled in a heap.

Mickey arrived just in time to throw himself between them. "Sanners! We need a catcher today! Sanners! stop!"

Sanners's eyes were bugging out as Mickey placed his hands on his muscular chest. "Listen, I'll let you kill him after the game, but for now cool down."

Sanners took a deep breath but his eyes were possessed. "I'm gonna kill you, Mags, look at my pants, what am I supposed to do now? I can't play like this!"

Mags sat on the asphalt as though he had been snared in a net. "We're even now, man."

"No, we're not. What am I gonna do?"

In a few minutes, Mickey calmed everyone down and convinced Sanners that he could hardly see the stains, and he needed to play. They finally mounted up with

Danny, and Mickey making sure they were between the guys for the rest of the trip.

The boys settled under their favorite tree and dropped their bikes. As usual, they were the first to arrive. Sanners had cooled down by the time they arrived. He was quick to anger but also quick to forgive, especially when it involved his best friend. "All right, I admit that was without a doubt the topper of them all. That was awesome paybacks."

"Man, you should have seen your face." Danny fell on his back and popped his hand in the palm of his glove. He was relieved to see Sanners composed.

Mickey started laughing, "You should have seen both of your faces! Mags knew he was going to die. He ran out of that place like crazy. And then when we saw you, we also knew he was going to die. Hey, Mags, when did you think that one up?"

"I don't know, I just made it up, it was the ultimate." It was the first time since the incident that he was truly able to appreciate the magnitude of such a scheme. Those splotches on the back of Sanners's pants were not mere stains; they were a work of art.

Sanners stood up and tried to look at the back of his pants. "You can still see this can't you?" He turned from side to side.

Mickey lied, "Naw, it's not that bad." Danny shook his head and put his glove over his face to cover his smirk.

The game went well against Holy Trinity. Everything started out well until Lisa showed up with Jean during the first inning. Mickey called Lisa and invited them. After they arrived, Danny struck out four times in a row and dropped two easy catches in the outfield. As he roamed center field, he wondered *Why the heck Mickey didn't tell me they were coming. Craps.* With every mistake he made, it got worse. The harder he tried, the more he failed. He wanted so badly to impress her, but he couldn't come through. There's something so humiliating about trying to be a manly man and ending up looking like a wussy.

The final score was 7-4 but didn't start so well. It was the first time they had to fight from behind. They trailed 4-0 after six innings but tied it up in the seventh and went ahead in the eighth for good. Most of it came down to the performance of a lifetime by a mammoth third baseman.

Sanners felt comfortable and believed no one could see the catsup and mustard stains on his jeans until just before game time when Eggs asked, "Hey, Sanners, what's that on your butt?" He then realized that his buddies were lying to him. From that point forward, he never got up from the bench whenever they were in the dugout. This way, no one could see the embarrassing stains. He sprinted out to his position at third base each time they took the field. He would then abruptly turn around so the crowd couldn't see his backside. When he stepped to the plate he swung with the deliberate precision of a seasoned woodcutter. Each time it was on the first pitch, and each time he connected. One of the pitches was way outside, and two were nearly over his head, but it didn't matter. He didn't wait for a pitch that he could kill; he had to get on base. Overall, he went four for four at the plate with three doubles and a single. He stretched out the doubles because he figured that if he was standing on second base, then no one could see the stains. He looked like a major leaguer with incredible hustle.

Coach Eggs complimented him on not trying to kill the ball. *This was necessity, man – this is pride, this is survival of the ballplayer's pride.*

The final result was a good game in front of a great crowd. When it was over the team and the parents milled around on the grass behind the backstop. When the team had a good game, it was like coming out of a big-league locker room afterward. The boys talked to the supporters and waited for compliments on their hitting or fielding. Sometimes it was the best part. Today it was glory for Sanners except he did not move from his position of sitting on the ground and leaning against the backstop until everyone had left. He didn't have his own parents to congratulate him; but he had the Maglianos, Hannigans, and Pats to comment on his hustle and hitting. Even Uncle Bud showed up and promised him an extra donut on Sunday.

The day belonged to Sanners but was out of reach for Danny. He talked to Pats and Joe Hannigan but his chin went to his chest when Lisa and Jean approached him. "That was a great game Danny," said Jean.

"No, thanks to me," he said. *Why couldn't she see me when I really kicked butt?* "Ya, boy, that Sanners did great, did you see him? Oh by the way, whatever you do, don't mention his pants. I'll have to tell you about it later."

The two talked for a while before she caught a ride home with Lisa and the Hannigans.

After everyone had left, Mags, Mickey, and Danny all wandered over by their favorite tree. Mickey yelled in the direction of the backstop, "Hey, Sanners, you can get up now!"

"I'll be over in a minute!" he replied.

After a few minutes of reveling in their triumph, they noticed Sanners still sitting over at the backstop with his head down. From a distance Mickey sensed something was wrong. "Come on, guys," he said to the others. Mickey guided his bike over and sat down in front of him. "Hey, Sanners, what's up?"

"Nothin." His usual robust voice seemed meeker than Mickey was accustomed to hearing. Even though the guys who meant the most to him in life surrounded him, he felt more alone than he had ever been. He wished he had a brother or a sister or a father to be there to see his best game in years, but he couldn't bring himself to tell his buddies. It seemed to hit him all at once. If the guys weren't there, he probably would have cried.

Mags felt the silence. He had no clue. "Hey, man, sorry about your pants."

Sanners forced a chuckle then looked up at him. He loved the jolly guy like he was his own brother. "That's okay, man, but I owe you for the next twenty years." He leaped forward and tackled his legs. If he couldn't have a mom or a little brother to hug, sometimes grappling with your buddies at least lets you grab someone.

They rolled around for a minute while Sanners pinned him down and jabbed his knuckles in his chest. "Say it, Mags, who's the coolest guy on earth?!"

Mags resisted for a while and repeated, "I am," until the pain finally gave in. "Okay! Sanners is the coolest guy on earth!" he laughed as Sanners released him from his powerful grip.

On the way home, they continued to heap compliments on Sanners. It was a lonely day for him, but in the scheme of things it was as good as it gets.

As they were parting ways, Mickey turned to Sanners, "Hey, man, I'll ride you home." They rode in silence until Mickey brought up his performance again. "I suppose in the long run you have Mags to thank. Without him you wouldn't have had to hustle today."

Sanners agreed, "That son of a gun, that really was the best paybacks he's ever had. Sometimes, I swear, the man's a genius."

Turning down the block toward Sanners's house, it was easy to pick his out from the rest on the block. There was a car on blocks in the driveway that had been there for as long as Mickey had known him. The shrubs in the front yard had grown so high they covered some of the kitchen window, and the grass had a number of dead spots. When Sanners stopped at the foot of his driveway, he looked up at the chipped paint on his house. Immediately, his chin went to his chest.

Mickey had intended to comment on Sanners's glum mood but now had mixed feelings. Some things in life were just the way they were, and the right kind of words don't always make them better. Finally, he had to tell his buddy what he was seeing, for better or worse maybe he could help, maybe not. "Hey, Sanners, after such a great game, you look like someone just punched you in the gut."

As the lid of the cap slowly came up, Mickey could see a tear rolling down the cheek of the toughest kid in the history of Kepner Junior High School. On the outside he often had the misleading appearance of an adult, but the guys knew that on the inside he was still a kid at heart.

Mickey's comment was right on target. Sanners felt a huge knot in his gut, and it grew larger all the way to his house. It was always easier to just pick up his junk and meet everyone else at Mags's house or at the park. To have a buddy come by and see his house or talk to his parents was too risky and too embarrassing. The scenario could change with every time they arrived. On one occasion, his mom might be asleep on the couch, other times she might be full of hugs, but the hugs often became a shameful scene when they were accompanied by slurred speech and the smell of bargain bin wine. On other occasions, the boy's had encountered Sanners's dad playing poker with his two brothers and other assorted friends whom they had never seen before. If it was early in the evening, they would be loud and happy. If it was late in the evening and someone was losing money, it was a scene to be avoided. Tempers could flair, and fists could fly. On those evenings it was not uncommon for Sanners to show up on Mags's doorstep. The Maglianos never asked, they knew the whole story, and were more than happy to have him over. The closest thing Sanners had to a family was the Maglianos. It was a great place to eat, laugh, and feel like you were part of the *Leave it to Beaver* lifestyle. Actually, it was better. The Cleavers never had that much fun. Sanners was always amazed that a family could have that much fun just playing a game of Monopoly or Yahtzee.

Sanners reached up and wiped away a tear. His lower lip slightly quivered, it took every ounce of his courage to even speak. Mickey was the last guy to ever pass judgment – he was okay. The words trembled out of his lips, "You guys always seem to have . . . like brothers or parents there, I guess I just wish sometimes that I had someone there too."

Mickey knew he couldn't mix words. There wasn't much to say about that. He couldn't say, "Hey invite them to a game sometime," or "Maybe they'll come." Everyone remembered the last time that Mr. Sanners attended a game two years ago. He was drunk and tried to pick a fight with an umpire. Sanners always secretly hoped no one would remember it; unfortunately it was a game that no one would forget. He had to be bodily removed during the fifth inning, and Sanners rode away on his bike in a different direction. Pats, along with the Maglianos, and Hannigans drove around southwest Denver until midnight when they finally found him parked under a tree near the ballpark. From that time on, they simply welcomed him into their homes without questions and often felt better that he was with them rather than at home.

Mickey knew it would be stupid to suggest that things may get better. He also began to wonder if it was such a good idea to ride home with Sanners; it may have only made the situation worse. He also was unsure of how to comment on his situation without insulting his parents. After a moment of silence, he spoke his carefully chosen words. "I wish you had them there too, Sanners, but maybe there's some things we can't always change. But don't forget who is there, man – Father Abbie, Eggs, Uncle Bud – and some other families – you know what they see? They see the same thing I'm seeing right now. A great guy who worked his ass off to do great things with himself. A great guy who an awful lot of people depend on. A lot of your buddies need you, and I'm one of them, I don't know what I'd do without you. You're a good man, Sanners."

After a moment of silence, Sanners picked up his head to reveal a smile. Mickey never said anything he didn't mean. Therefore, when he said something like that, it was as authentic as an old leather glove. It was as real as anything he ever knew. Mickey stuck out his hand. "I'm glad you're my friend."

Sanners reached forward and shook his hand. Man to man. It made him feel like he could take on the world. Mickey patted him on the shoulder, then began to ride away. When he got two car lengths away, Sanners sighed. He then found the energy to yell through the choked feeling in his chest. "Hey, Mickey! I'm glad you're my friend too! Thanks, buddy!"

Mickey smiled, waved back, and rode on.

That night Louis Garrison experienced his first good drunk since being out. His parole agreement was on the edge. A night out with the cousins. A couple of fights. Freedom is good.

15

Carl's Message

THE APARTMENT DOOR swung open as Megan walked lopsided through the door. Her face was red as she began to cool down from her daily 6:00 a.m. run. "You are so fat and lazy." She talked to Carl, a cat she had rescued from the pound last year. He stretched in the windowsill, barely noticing her as she came through the door. She held one running sneaker in her hand. She always tied her apartment key to the laces on her left shoe, so she had to take it off to open the door. Kicking off her other shoe, she took in a deep breath. *Don't smoke, don't drink, but I looooove my coffee.* The smell of French vanilla coffee permeated the three room flat. She would often say to others, it was her only vice. *Caffeine, gotta have it, love it.* She felt as if she needed to explain herself to others. *Yes, I do drugs, but nothing stronger than caffeine and aspirin.*

If you broke into Megan's apartment and studied it, the place would reveal very little of her personality. A stereo, an eclectic collection of music – mostly jazz, new age, and scatterings of folk. On the walls were a few photographs she had taken herself when visiting some of the Native American ruins throughout the southwest. Her grandmother was Navajo, and it was the only cultural aspect of herself that she nurtured. Whenever she was stressing, she tried to reconnect herself to the mountains and the earth. She only shared that side of herself with close friends. Spirituality to her was not some trendy fix or a conversational piece, but a part of her.

Another picture was of Megan in her fishing vest holding a fly rod with the Poudre River behind her. She looked natural with the Poudre Canyon, the green pines, and blue stream flowing around her. On many of her free weekends, she would journey into the mountains to fish. To Megan, fly-fishing was part art, part philosophy, part spiritual, and part healing. To cast a fishing rod with a hook was more than an exercise. Her place in nature was one of respect and reverence for the creatures who shared this space. To cast a rod with a small hook – one that had the perfect combination of thread, and other assorted items to make it represent an actual fly, was a sacred event. If a rainbow trout latched onto that hook, it then became a match of will between the human and the fish. When it is finally captured, it is to be appreciated and respected. Megan never brought home a fish that she did not eat. It would be disrespectful to be anything other than a meal. She only took from the mountains and streams those things that she needed.

Shaw would often jokingly refer to her as a fish murderer. Meg didn't like the gender biased term "fisherman," so she proudly called herself a "fishergal." In one corner of the living room sat a handmade oak box filled with fly tying equipment. During the cold winter months she would tie flies and listen to Native American music as her means for reducing her workday stress.

"Hooked on Fishing" was the title on another picture. It was an eight-by-ten enlargement of a picture of Shaw. He was standing next to a river with his arms folded and a very angry look on his face. Upon closer examination the picture revealed a fly with a hook in the cheek of Shaw. "Don't stand behind me . . ." were the last words he heard before her back cast whipped and caught him in the cheek. It remained in his cheek for several hours that day because the barb in the hook prevented him from pulling it back out. It could only be removed with wire cutters, which were left back at her truck.

Whenever Meg was having a bad day, all she had to do was look at the picture, and she would begin laughing out loud. The day it happened Meg laughed so hard she rolled on the ground with no muscle strength left in her body. She was laughing so hard she was afraid she would have a bladder accident. When she went into the woods to relieve herself, Shaw could still hear her laughter through the trees. He was screaming back to her, "It's not *that* funny!"

Shaw vowed to never try fishing again. It was his first and last outing. She told him he would get hooked on the sport and come back begging to her to teach him how to tie flies.

In the rest of the apartment, the furniture was practical and not fancy. When the student loans are paid off, she decided she would treat herself. She still had two years to go. On a small wall of shelves next to the windows were mostly books. Two shelves were reserved for pictures. Five of them had people in them, mostly friends. One picture showed Megan in her cap and gown graduating from Southern Colorado State over six years ago. Another picture of her graduation with Dr. Pentral, Dr. Hensman, Shaw, and herself once sat there but was eventually displaced to her office at Shiler.

Last spring she placed the picture in a drawer for a month. She found herself wanting to cry every time she looked at it. The picture showed four bright smiling faces, two of them old, two of them young. Each in graduation regalia, her arms draped around Shaw and Dr. Hensman, with Dr. Pentral holding two fingers up behind the head of his buddy Hensman.

Two months after Hensman retired last December, he had a stroke and died only a week later. The phone call from Bill Pentral struck her like lightning. She cried every day for two weeks; her mentor had died, and she never got to say good-bye. After a month she finally made peace and put the picture in her office at Shiler.

She sat down at her desk in front of the pictures and sipped her coffee. "It's probably for you," she said, referring to the blinking light on her phone machine. She punched the button and a voice came through. "Hey, Carl, give me a call when you learn to dial the phone with your paws." It was Shaw, as always, he left his messages for the cat and not her. It was his mindless way of jabbering to the phone machine. Megan wondered, *How in the hell could anyone have a sense of humor this early in the morning?* "And would you please tell Meg to give me a call, tell her that her boyfriend has been acting up again."

The machine shut itself off, and Megan groaned as she scratched Carl behind the ears. "What the hell is he up to now?" She was referring to Dr. Darion Walsh, the clinic's psychiatrist. Whenever Shaw talked about Darion, he would sarcastically refer to him as her "boyfriend." She sipped her coffee again and began to peel off her socks. She threw her running outfit in the corner and headed toward the shower. "Just what I need, another fun day with Darion."

16

July 7, 1968
The Plan

"LISTEN UP, GUYS, I've got the plan." Mickey hunched over the counter at Bud's before engulfing a bite of his donut. It was early morning, and the boys had just finished their routes. Danny was directly on his right, and Sanners to his left with Mags on the other side of Sanners. Mickey's eyes became focused and dead serious. When the boys mapped out a plot, a plan, or a scheme, they had to consider all the details. He had been working with Lisa for a week on a plan to get together, but not in broad daylight. The situation between Danny and Jean had gone on long enough. This hand-holding thing was going nowhere. Every time the boys knew that Danny had been out with Jean, they would ask, "Well? Did you kiss her?" Each time the answer was the same. Mags, Sanners, and Mickey all wondered if he would ever have the guts. Danny was beginning to wonder himself. Mickey had talked with Danny in extensive detail about how to set it up. *Make it romantic . . . Make it dark . . . Nighttime . . . After a date.*

So far every effort had failed, but now Mickey had concocted the perfect scenario. Jean's father owned a pop-up camper trailer that was kept in the rear of their backyard near the alley fence. Lisa and Jean had spent several nights at each other's houses during the summer for sleepovers. The last two times, Jean had convinced her dad to let them sleep in the camper. It was like their clubhouse, much better than a basement floor. Mickey developed a seamless plan, but it would need input from the others for the details. The guys would sleep out in the backyard and take a midnight cruise on their bikes for a special visit. The three other boys leave a little early, and bingo! Romance – a good night kiss under a tree behind the camper trailer to seal the evening. Lisa concurred; it was the perfect plan.

There are many pivotal points in life, and most of them lie right between childhood and adulthood. Somewhere during that time, a guy knows that he is an adult, but he still possesses the talents of a child. One of those great talents is the ability to know true thrills, true highs, and maybe the last great pure intoxications of one's life. The greatest rushes in life are those moments where you blatantly create your own rules and laugh like heck as you bolt the other way. The boys would never do enough to be thought of as real criminals, but there's nothing wrong with using one's strength and power to tease authority. The enjoyment is the rush of fresh air behind you as the consequences for mischievous behaviors nip at your heels while you run like hell in the other direction. These are the greatest of the last great highs in life. Only kids truly know how to get high.

The boys knew how to taunt that line. Going off in the middle of the night on their bikes had a thrill all its own. Of course the thrills can even get greater if you have minor brushes with jerks in authoritative positions.

One such occurrence took place a month ago as Mags and Sanners rode their bikes home from practice. They decided to pull into the Quick-to-Go filling station on Florida Avenue. While Sanners dropped his money into the soda machine and pulled out an Orange Nehi, Mags rode in circles and rang the bell by running over the air hoses in the driveway. The ringing generally signaled to the attendant that someone wanted a fill-up. Sometimes you had to pop a wheelie in order to pounce on the hose just right. Bicycles didn't have the same weight as cars. Mags was not trying to rile anyone; he just liked to hear the bell ring.

"Hey! What the hell do you think you kids are doing?!" A bulky pot-bellied mechanic in his early thirties came out stomping snakes in the filling station driveway as he walked. His hairy belly braggingly revealed itself at the bottom of a grease stained T-shirt that stretched at his well-fed waistline. He looked like he hadn't bathed or shaved in a week. He pointed a foot long crescent wrench at Mags. "You want this on the side of your head, boy? Here I am working under that car, and I damn near kill myself to get out here only to see some fat ass kid on my service bell."

Sanners was halfway through a sip on his Nehi when he swooped in between the two in one gentle motion. He held his palms out in a gesture of kindness, "Sir? Sir? Sir? Please, sir, allow me to apologize. I'm very sorry if you were disturbed. We didn't mean to do any thing, please accept our apology. I promise it won't happen again."

Mags was still shaking, but listened in awe. Sanners was not Sanners, this was definitely a polished speech, and it was impressive. Sometimes when Sanners did this he knew he was being manipulative. In these moments the boys called it his Eddie Haskell charm. Eddie Haskell was a character in one of their favorite TV shows called *Leave it to Beaver*. Eddie was a sharp up-to-no-good influence on other kids and he could turn on his charm with adults.

The mechanic didn't know how to respond to a polite teen so he figured he would assert his authority once more for good measure. "You bet your ass it won't happen again, or you'll have this upside your head." He pointed the wrench again. "I guaran-damn-tee it! You here me, boy?"

Mags apologized, "Yes, sir, I hear you, sir." He followed Sanners's polite lead. The two rode off down the street carefully checking over their shoulders to see if he followed. They knew he wouldn't follow, but it's instinctual to look back after a brush with trouble, just to check anyway.

It would have been easy to sass back at the jerk, but that was for amateurs. It takes real talent to even a score. Ten minutes later the two peered into the station from behind two shrubs on the other side of the street. "Are you sure he's under there?" asked Mags.

Sanners spotted the feet of the mechanic sticking out from under the car. "Ya, it looks perfect."

With stealth precision, the two boys road their bikes to a point where they were just out of eyesight from the mechanic's bay. All at once they pounded the bell hose with relentless strikes from the front tires of their bikes. The sound of the incessant ringing of the bell caused an electrified charge of adrenaline to surge through their bodies. That feeling, that high – it is pure and it is glorious. But mostly, it is one those great exercises in fairness. *When a person treats others in a mean spirited rude fashion, they deserve a little frustration in return.* Mags and Sanners were giddy in their execution because they knew that the potential scenarios in this purposeful and deliberate act could be dangerous.

After the initial stimulation comes the real high. Trouble is a lot of fun when it's deliberate. On the other hand, it's a real drag when it's a mistake. All kids make stupid mistakes like breaking mom's lamp when they know they shouldn't have been wrestling in the house. Or jamming a lawn mower's blades with the hedge clippers when they knew that they should have picked up the yard before cutting the grass. However, trouble for the sake of fun is a completely different and one of life's most invigorating experiences. It envelops that perfect balance between fear, thrill, and the athletic ability necessary for human survival.

The boys had experienced this before, and now they would face it again in the form of the beer bellied mechanic. Upon hearing the bell ringing, he waddled off his back from underneath the car. He still held his crescent wrench, except this time he was in a sweat-covered fit of rage. "Why you cocky sons-a-little-bitches! I'm gonna kick your puny little assess!" The pursuit was on. The fun was nearly at its apex. Unfortunately for the mechanic, his energy was wasted because he did not realize that in nature, waddling water buffaloes will never capture frightened cheetahs. Especially if they have to chase them through the cheetah's own jungle.

The average teenager can set a world record on a bicycle pedaling when his life is in danger. Mags and Sanners churned their legs with savage energy as they laughed and half-screamed at the same time. Mags was thrilled but afraid. Sanners was laughing hard and hollering, "I'll guaran-damn-tee it, boy! I'll guaran-damn-tee it!" Sanners was not as fearful as Mags. In the back of his mind, he knew that if the guy caught him, he could probably take him. After the first twenty yards the race was over. They glanced back to see the swearing barrel of lard bounce up and down. This made them laugh even more.

In situations like these, Mags would become a mishmash conglomeration of emotion. He loved the thrill but was afraid he might pee his pants in the process. His mind was also busy at work. He was wondering, *What if he recognizes my bike? or tracks me down and calls my parents? What will I do then? Oh, for sure he will track down the bike. Everyone knows there's only two or three Carrier's Specials in this city. Oh no, he probably already knows who I am. Maybe he saw my picture in the paper for carrier of the year. My parents will never forgive me!*

The only thing that went through Sanners's mind for the next few hours was the humorous image of a fat guy swearing as they rode away. The sight of him running after them was worth all the risk. By the time the story was shared with Danny and Mickey it got better and better. The guy got larger, louder, meaner, and closer with every recount. That's the beauty of a great exhilaration like that; it can be relived again and again. Certainly, they talked about movies, TV shows, and other exciting scenarios in life; but there's no high like being there. It was the stuff of legendary adolescent fables.

This morning they were planning another adventure that had implications for more excitement. The midnight ride had to be carefully plotted through alleys and drainage ditches. The key was to not get caught. The motive had to do with setting up a buddy to take the next big step with his girl.

Mickey revealed the intent of the evening's plan to Mags and Sanners but not to Danny; he will be left alone and he will have to figure out the rest on his own. The remainder of the plan was up for public discussion. "All right, guys, all we have to decide is this. Whose house do we sleep out at? Mags's, Sanners's, Danny's, or mine?" The boys thought for a moment. Obviously, huge life decisions are not to be made quickly or without extensive thought. The intelligible solution would come down to Mags's or Mickey's. They never stayed at Sanners's and Danny's didn't have an easy escape route.

Sanners forwarded his opinion, "I say Mags's house, with the alley, it's easy in and easy out." Of course Mags's house had its hazards too. Mrs. Mags was too protective. She would sometimes bring out extra blankets if she believed they may be too cold, mosquito spray if she thought the bugs were bad or cookies and milk if she sensed they were hungry. This could ruin a good conversation about girls, but the cookies were never refused.

The boys considered Sanners's idea, and they nodded. *This is pretty big stuff, everything has to be executed in perfect detail.*

Somehow, when these schemes evolved, it made sense to defer to Mickey for leadership. He never lacked confidence, and nothing can go wrong when he leads the way. "All right, men, here's the deal. Everyone knows where Lisa and Jean live. It's about a thirty-minute bike ride. We have two main streets to cross, Evans and Federal. Gentlemen, we need suggestions."

Mickey had a route in mind, but it always felt more powerful to have the team collaborate for the plan. Sanners suggested going under Federal Boulevard at the Gunnison gulch culvert. *Federal is often busy at night and cops could be among the cars. Excellent insight.*

Mags suggested cutting through the Federal Heights apartments. *This reduced one more public street. Safety factor. Good.*

Danny threw out another suggestion for a north-south passage that could involve alleys most of the way. Everyone was contributing. *The adventure will be carried out with perfection.*

Baseball, a hot summer's day, and sleeping out under the stars are the sum total of the ingredients that add up for perfect summer day. The Falcons were undefeated and were on their way to their best season ever. At 3-0 they were out to earn their fourth win of the year. Coach Eggs knew they had a walk-over game against the All Saints Cougars. The pathetic Cougars had the weakest team in the league, and sometimes they hardly had enough players to make the squad. This was one of those occasions where Eggs believed it was good to shake up the complacency and make the boys think about their game. He often did this to the initial dismay of some of the players and sometimes in disagreement with some of the parents.

"Gentlemen, sometimes when you play a position too often, you tend to daydream, you don't think about where the throw is going or where the cutoff man is going to be. As I've told you before, you should always be prepared to play any position on the field, and occasionally I like to see if you are up for the challenge." He didn't feel the need to explain himself any further. They would now have to think when they played today. This was also Egg's way to put most of the benchers at the top of the order and play critical positions in the infield. Some of the stars may start on the bench and fill in. Eggs would do this two or three times a season and did it regardless of whether they were having winning or losing seasons. Some teams had kids that never got to feel important. Eggs's team members always got their chance to be a hero.

"All right, at the top of the order is Stevie Burman at shortstop, followed by Bennie Garcia at second, followed by . . ." He went through the lineup, and the boys listened intently. The guys who were most often at the bottom of the lineup were now puffing their chests and feeling important. The better players had to temporarily step aside. Danny would start at catch, Mags in center field and Sanners and Mickey would start on the bench.

It was a chance for a lot of guys to be stars, and it was a thrill for them. As expected, the Falcons won easily. Mickey came in for the last four innings in left field. Danny caught two innings, and then later pitched two. Some of the guys who normally didn't see the top of the order got to score some runs. Three of the runs were scored on walks, stolen bases, and balls that got past the catcher. Eggs always had a back up plan, but never needed it as the Falcons cruised to a 12-7 win. It was also good for All Saints who scored more runs in this game than their previous three games combined.

After the game, Joey Pelloman's father pulled Eggs aside and asked him why all the "scrubs" were in the game. He also made certain that Eggs understood that he significantly reduced his chances for winning every time he messed with the lineup. The boys kept their distance whenever a parent was going off their nut. It was an embarrassment. Mr. Pelloman had a reputation as one of those parents who knew it all. This type of parent espouses the belief that they are in it for the kids, but the bottom line is that they want the win and see "my kid" win. He was a little incensed that one of the better players, Joey, had to sit the bench for the last four innings. Coach Eggs handled him well and told him everyone sits once in a while because "it's a team sport." Many parents didn't understand this basic concept, but Eggs did. One of the reasons why the Falcons had become so good over the last two years was because a parent *didn't* coach. There's no better way to pollute the objectivity of good coaching than to insert a dad. Most of the time the kids don't perform as well with a dad for a coach.

The Falcons also prospered because Eggs treated them like they were men. They could even swear! With "discretion" according to Eggs. This was the first time they ever had a coach or an adult who had even talked to them about cussing. No adult had ever done that. Most of them just said, "Watch your mouth!" Then ten minutes later they would hear them cussing the same words that prompted the scolding. Eggs gave several preseason speeches about behavior, team, how to conduct yourself if you were upset with an error or a strikeout, and setting an example. The boys could listen to him because he wasn't a parent. Most parents live in a make-believe world about the things they believe their kids did and didn't do. Eggs never forgot that he was a kid, and swearing was part of the territory called adolescence.

Eggs would start his speech with, "Gentlemen, have you ever heard me swear?" None of them raised their hands. "All right, how many of you believe that I've never cussed before in my life?" Mags was the only one to raise his hand and the team chuckled. "Sorry, Mags, but I've got to tell you guys that I've cussed up a blue streak on occasions. Once I hit my thumb with a hammer, and I didn't think I would stop cussing for weeks!" The guys started laughing, trying to imagine this trusted adult in a fit of swearing. "Why, gentlemen, I've cussed some words that are so bad I hope you never hear them in your lifetime." By now they were all laughing. "But you know what? You've never heard me. Your parents have never heard me. The people in the supermarket never heard me. And none of those people ever will. Do you know why? Because everything I do says something about me. Am I a gentleman? Or a slob? I have to think about how others see me. You hear a lot of language in your schools, in the halls, out in public. But you *should not* be one of them. A guy with class will never be heard swearing his brains out in public. Now, gentlemen, if you are out riding your bikes, or sitting in your basement farting and looking at girlie magazines with your buddies and you want to curse up a storm, that's all fine with me. Out here, you represent the Falcons. But it should go beyond that. In your schools, in life, you don't need to cuss and swear to be cool. Only those without class do that. It's not about *not* cussing. It's about discretion. Use discretion. I'm going to let a few words go here and there during practice, if there are no parents around, *but* never do I want to hear it in public situations."

By this time all of the guys were nodding and thinking, *This is like too cool. No one ever talked to us about cussing before. This makes sense. We can cuss, real men cuss, just not everywhere. What does the word discretion mean? I think it means sometimes.* The guys loved Eggs because he simply wanted them to do their best in life. He also had a knack for knowing when and how to praise a kid.

The star of today's game was Ben Garcia, who scored three runs. He walked once, was hit by a pitch, and got his first hit in over a year. After the game, Eggs was certain to heap praises on his performance and how courageous he was to keep playing even after a wild pitch glanced off his helmet. To Ben, this will be a game he will one day tell his kids about. If guys like Pelloman coached, they would deny Ben's future kids of a great story. Over the years it will probably grow.

The guys began dumping their bags in Mags's backyard. They had an hour of daylight before the plan kicked in gear, but for now they would just enjoy the beauty of another Colorado sunset. When people talk about the west or big sky country of the northwest, it's about the dry air. One can see forever in the dry air and growing up in Denver, it's easy to learn your directions. Find the mountains on the horizon and it's always west.

Mags's backyard had a short-sloped hill facing west, and it was perfect for watching the sunsets. The Maglianos liked to sit on their backyard deck and have barbecues in the summer evenings. The boys picked a spot for their bags that was strategically located just out of sight of Mags's parents' windows. This also allowed for an easy belly crawl to the shed near the alley where their bikes were parked.

Mickey and Danny had a few dozen baseball cards spread out on their bags. At this point in the summer they had each purchased at least ten packs. Most kids their age had given up on ball cards, but to these boys the cards increased in their value. Rookie cards are the least valuable; you may as well save them for flipping, pitching, or simply attach them to your spokes. Late-veteran cards are the best because they have the most statistics on them. A 1951 rookie Mickey Mantle card may as well be thrown away; but a new 1968 card has years of statistics on batting averages, hits, RBIs, and of course, the almighty homers. The cards also served as volumes of encyclopedic facts about a ball-player's hometown or their height or weight. How else would a guy know that Harmon Killebrew was born on June 29, 1936, stood five feet eleven inches, weighed 210 pounds, and hailed from Ontario, Oregon?

Sanners sat up staring at the sunset. Mags laughed out loud as he read a Richie Rich comic book.

Danny stared at his cards and made his best attempt at a poker face. "I'll trade you a Clemente and a Drysdale for your Banks."

Mickey saw through his gamble. "Wishful thinking my friend, wishful thinking, but I'll tell you what, you make it a Mays instead of the Clemente, and it's a deal."

Danny knew it was his only chance at the Ernie Banks card. Ernie Banks was the name on his own Louisville slugger bat; it was a "must have" card. He paused and acted as though he was bidding $10,000 at an auction. "It's a deal."

The two continued to trade as Sanners commented on his deep thoughts continuing a conversation that began at Uncle Bud's this morning. "I would own ten Harley Davidson motorcycles, that's what I would do."

The sports section reported that New York Jets quarterback Joe Namath had just signed a big contract for $400,000. *It's nearly a half-million dollars. That kind of money would keep you rich for the rest of your life.* The boys discussed at length how they could buy a huge house for $40,000, then live on the remainder for the rest of their life. *A guy could vacation at far away places like Disneyland, Mount Rushmore, or Yellowstone Park. Or you could spend $6,000 and own two huge luxury cars.* Sanners had even looked at the ads in this morning's *Times* to find a new 1968 Dodge Charger for $2871. *That's so much money!* The wish list went on and on. Everyone's wish list included the obvious life necessities of a big color TV, a console stereo, and a new Schwinn ten-speed.

"Young men?" A soft voice and the sound of a squeaky screen door broke into their conversation. Mrs. Magliano's voice never seemed to waiver from daisies and roses optimism. She could report that an atomic bomb had just gone off and a person would still think that they were just about to eat cake and ice cream.

"Young men? I have some good news and some bad-but-better-good news." She chuckled at her self-amusing comment. It was easy to see where Mags got his laughter. "Here's the good news, I've got fresh baked cookies." She held out a plate in front of her. The boys had already perked up before she spoke. The waft of air containing moist chocolate chip cookies soaked into every sense in their bodies. It was as though the smell took over their brains the instant it hit them. Being boys, they could do nothing else, think nothing else, and feel nothing else until the taste of the cookies hit their tongues. The paws of four teenage starving wolves leaped for the plate at the same time.

Some cookies have the capability of melting in a person's mouth. Mrs. Magliano's cookies permeated a kid's entire body. The boys chewed the cookies like mesmerized zombies when Mrs. Mags broke the air with her announcement, "My young men, the bad-but-better-news is that we are expecting rain. I've pushed the chairs aside in the den so you can sleep right in front of the TV set!"

All of a sudden the cookies tasted slightly bitter. They simultaneously stopped chewing as the three visiting boys all looked over at Mags. The only one who has a chance of overruling a parent is the child of that parent. It would be very uncool for Sanners, Danny, or Mickey to speak up. They continued to gape at him until he finally spoke.

"Ummm ... Mom, that's okay, we won't get that wet." The lightbulb went on in his head. "Hey we could use Uncle Ray's tent and set it up right back here." Mags beamed an *I'm a genius!* smile.

"I'm sorry, Thomas," said Mrs. Magliano, "but Uncle Ray came by last week to get his tent."

Mags's idea went sour, and he realized that he actually sealed his own fate. By suggesting the tent, he admitted that they may need a tent. "What do you think, guys?" The boys looked at the scattered clouds. They gestured with supporting shoulder shrugs and agreed, "It doesn't look that bad to me . . ."

"Now now now, what would your mothers say if you caught a cold while sleeping out in the yard? What kind of fun would that be? I'll tell you what, I'll pop some popcorn, and you boys can enjoy watching TV. *Bonanza* is on tonight, you know. Get your bags." She turned and walked inside.

Mickey threw his head back on his sleeping bag as his brain churned with ideas. *Should we switch houses? Should we beg to sleep out anyway? How about a makeshift lean-to made out of a canvas tarp?* Most of his ideas would come up short in the Magliano household. Once Mrs. Mags was set on her idea, it was over. They could already hear the popcorn beginning to pop in the kitchen.

"See you boys in the morning," shouted Mr. Magliano from the top of the stairs. "Don't forget the door cop!" The boys lay on their backs and stared at the ceiling. The *door cop* was Mr. Magliano's proud invention he had attached to the top of the front and back doors. It was his idea of a homemade security device, and he took personal delight in the name he gave it at its christening. Mr. Magliano was one of those middle-to-lower income dads who could fix most anything and on occasion would improvise his own solutions to meet the needs of the household. He had been looking at security systems for homes over the past three years and always decided against them because of the price. Then came the door cop. He created a device that would set off a ringing bell if someone opened the door in the middle of the night. It was simple. There was a spring loaded pin that was compacted against a plate that stuck out from the door jam. If the door came slightly ajar, the pin would shoot out to set off an ear-piercing bell. It ran on four-D batteries and looked like metal coffee cup saucer attached to batteries and wires.

Before the boys went to bed, he instructed them on how to deactivate it in the morning. "Before you go out for your routes, remember, you turn this switch to pull back the plate, then you turn this switch to turn off the battery juice, then you turn this switch so you can open the door." He pulled and twisted on one side then the other. The boys didn't pay any attention because Mags would always take care of it; he had done it hundreds of times. Every time Mr. Magliano showed off his *door cop,* he followed it with, "You know, someday I should get a patent on this thing and sell it. A guy could make a lot of money on a thing like this."

Sanners sat up. *That's it! The door cop!* He looked as though he just discovered the cure for arthritis. "Hey, guys, what do you say we just sneak out the back door! We can still make it!"

Mags's head was shaking involuntarily before he even got a word out. "Oh, no no no, no way, man." His speech sped up and was nearly out of control, "Oh, man no way! That would be like illegal!"

Sanners, Danny, and Mickey all snorted with laughter at the same time. "Illegal?" asked Sanners.

Danny was holding his stomach. "We might get arrested by the door cop!" All three were now rolling on their bags.

"You know what I mean!" Mags became defensive. "You can sneak out of a backyard, but not out of a house. That's like running away or breaking the law or something like that!"

"No, it's not," said Mickey. "It might not be a bad idea. We sneak out, and then we sneak back in. Nobody will know the difference."

"Well, I'm not going then." Mags folded his arms across his chest. "Forget it. Do you know how much trouble I would be in? I would be grounded for ten years!"

The boys mulled it over. Three of them were in, and one was out. It was tricky, but it will work.

Two hours later in the pitch-black darkness of the basement, Sanners nudged Danny, and Danny nudged Mickey. It was time to go. They begged Mags, but he would have no part of it. They had waited long enough, and now it was time to carry out the mission. The three bold teens started out by creeping up the stairs on all fours. Their greatest enemy was noise, so each placement of a hand or foot had to have the deliberate softness of an Indian scout. When they reached the back door, Sanners reached for the door cop. "No no no!" whispered Mickey. He reached up to the bell and tapped a switch. "This one first!" he said in a hushed voice. Sanners carefully looked at it in the dark shadows of the kitchen. He felt like he was on the Denver Police Force bomb squad. The success of the mission depended on his perfectly calculated movements.

Sanners took a deep breath and twisted the knob. Without warning, the explosive noise in the kitchen sounded as though someone had slapped a grenade onto the back door. The bomb went off. A nightmarish scream of the *rat-a-tat* bell was enough to put a civil defense drill to shame. In his haste, Sanners jerked hard at the door. Danny, in his panic, retreated down the stairs to find Mags to shut it off. The ringing only seemed to get louder. Dogs in the neighborhood began to bark. Mickey and Sanners fumbled madly at the switches – trying them all. At this point, their ears were destined to a state of eternal deafness. The boys were now yelling at each other, "Shut the damn thing off!"

"I'm trying! I'm trying!"

"Let me do it!"

"Go get, Mags!"

The kitchen lights went on. Standing in the doorway was a figure that resembled a sumo wrestler in paisley boxer shorts. He wielded a baseball bat in his hands and he was ready to strike at the intruders. The sound was so loud that neither boy could hear each other, but they could hear one voice above the ringing, and it was loud. It was a dad voice. Mr. Magliano brought his bat down to his side and screamed, "What the hell are you boys doing?!"

Dads never seem to be embarrassed when they parade around in their boxers; it's what dads do sometimes. When a guy is growing up, he never seems to see a mom in their underwear or bra walking around the house, but he always seems to see dads in their boxers. In a man's castle and he shall do as he pleases in that castle.

Mr. Magliano made his way across the kitchen and reached for the switches. The incessant ringing resembled a belligerent brat that taunted authority. It was stuck, and it wasn't about to stop yet. Sanners had turned a switch so hard that it jammed. Mr. Magliano pulled over a chair and stood on it. He wrestled with the device, but the ear-piercing pounding of the bell only seemed to get louder. His next move was what any self-respecting dad would do if gentleness didn't work on a machine. He pounded it with his fists.

If they weren't in so much trouble the boys would have laughed at the sight of the backside of the extrawide paisley boxers and its occupant swinging wildly at a bell with wires.

Being woken out of a dead sleep is enough to cause the sanest of people to act irrationally. In the case of Mr. Magliano, his door cop was a rabid animal that had gone out of control. Like any bad animal, it would have to be put down. The deafening sound needed to be silenced.

He placed both hands on the door cop and pulled as hard as he could. The separation of the door cop with the wood made a loud crunching sound followed by Mr. Magliano falling backward over the chair with the device still in his hands. Shards of wood from the door were still attached to it, and it continued to ring. As Mr. Magliano fell backward he tumbled head over heels across the kitchen floor. He looked like a prized State Fair heifer that had just fallen off of a cattle truck while going down the highway. It was a lot of beef, and it was still moving. As he stumbled to stand up, he clutched the door cop, and it continued to ring.

Holding the door cop over his head he slammed it to the kitchen floor. A couple of pieces went flying across the kitchen and the ringing only got louder. Desperate situations call for desperate measures. He reached for the baseball bat and swung it in a massive Paul Bunyan – like arc. Each smash of the bat sounded like a collision on a demolition derby raceway. On his third strike the ringing finally stopped.

The stillness of the kitchen became a quiet and eerie scene. Nobody moved. By now there was a crowd. Mrs. Magliano stood clutching her robe, the four boys were in shock, and the only sounds in the stillness of the kitchen were the echoed ringing in their ears and a few neighborhood dogs barking from somewhere far away. If the boys' hearts could be heard; they would sound a lot like construction site jackhammers.

The boys alternated their stares between the red-faced huffing Mr. Magliano and the dead door cop. Mr. Magliano still clutched his bat, and the machine was dented beyond recognition. It was mercilessly murdered before their eyes in Mags's kitchen.

Mr. Magliano pulled in a deep breath before speaking in a frighteningly controlled voice. "Is . . . there . . . some reason . . . why you boys . . . would be opening this door at midnight?"

The boys stared at him, knowing that they knew they had to lie, but it better be good. *He doesn't look like he's ready to put down that bat just yet.* Mags spouted out the savviest lie he could create in this moment of truth. "Mickey had a headache, and he needed to get to his bike to get some aspirin, and Sanners needed to check the air on his bike tires. They've been leaking lately."

"Thomas Magliano," his father responded through gritted teeth, "I'm not *even* going to ask you if you expect me to believe that. All I'm going to say is that you boys have exactly ten seconds TO GET YOUR ASSES DOWN IN THAT BASEMENT AND GET TO SLEEP!"

Mags turned to run and fell flat on his face at the top of the stairs. The other three tripped as they fell on top of him in what looked like a choreographed scene from a *Three Stooges* episode. After the grunting, bumping, and clawing to get through the doorway, the door was pulled shut behind them as Mr. And Mrs. Magliano listened to eight panicked teenage feet stomping their way down the stairs.

The boys sat in silence, their hearts still beating out of their chests. Each had different thoughts. Mickey was wondering what Lisa must be wondering. Danny was sad because he really wanted to see Jean. Sanners was wondering if they would have to pay for the dead door cop. Mags was trying to reach back into his memory for recent "groundings," and figured *this one will be worth a good three to four years.* None of the visiting boys were worried about the incident getting back to their parents because they knew that Mr. Mags was good about addressing their troubles in house.

In the silence the boys could hear a mixture of muffled giggles from the upstairs bedroom of Mr. and Mrs. Magliano. *What could they be laughing about?*

Mr. Magliano was not ashamed of parading around in his skivvies, or the destruction of the door cop. The only thing that bothered him was cursing in front of the boys. He believed he needed to set an example. He quickly got past it and laughed at the thought of how it affected the boys.

The main reason why Mags was so close to his dad was because Mr. Magliano may have been quick to anger about kid things; but he was also quick to forgive, quick to cool down, and quick to find humor in most situations. Most of all, he trusted Thomas.

Mrs. Magliano lay next to Mr. Magliano on their bed. She was laughing so hard she had to stick a corner of the pillow in her mouth. She pulled it back out and wiped a tear away. "You should have seen the look on those boys' faces when you were beating the beast to death!" she squealed as she said it.

"Tell me truthfully, dear. Was I pretty sexy in my boxer shorts?" He rolled over with another laugh and kissed her on the cheek. "Bet it kind of turned you on, huh?"

"Oh yes, my dear, it was straight from a chapter in the 'everything you ever wanted to know about sex but were afraid to ask' book. Women are definitely turned on by sexy, manly men who can save their families from the ringing monsters of terror!" The two laughed together at the thought of the boys seeing the fierce display.

Jean sat up in the silence of her father's pop-up trailer. "Did you hear something?"

Lisa had answered this question twenty times over the last two hours. It was now midnight. "No, it was just another dog barking down the street."

Jean lay back on her pillow. Her eyes welled up. She wanted desperately to ask Lisa all the questions that were running through her head. *Am I pretty enough for high school next year? Maybe I'm too much of a tomboy. Does Danny really like me? He must think I'm ugly. Why doesn't he want to kiss me? We've been holding hands for a month, maybe we're in a friendship relationship, but not a love relationship, but I didn't know it. Is something wrong with me? Is he getting ready to break up with me before we ever really got together? Maybe he went to see some other girl tonight.* She fought to hold back the tears. She wondered what it would be like to really kiss someone.

Earlier in the spring, Jean attended a backyard birthday party for a friend. Toward the end of the evening she danced with an older boy, a senior in high school. At the end of a slow dance he leaned over and kissed her on the lips. It was kind of sick. He tried to french-kiss her, and she pulled away. He thought he was Mr. Cool, Mr. Suave. He was really Mr. Sweaty and Mr. Ass. His whole body smelled like a big underarm. She pulled away and went to the bathroom. Oh, how she wished she had her toothbrush! She spit in the sink and wiped her lips. *Yuck!* Jean locked the door and fumbled through the drawer next to the bathroom sink. She found an old toothbrush and washed it off. Anything had to be better than the taste of Mr. Underarm. After brushing, she spit continuously for the next minute. *Yuck! I am not counting* that *as my first kiss.*

Jean still wondered what her first kiss would be like. She wondered if there was a possibility that she would ever kiss anyone.

17

Session 2
Norms

Personal Journal 1

Dear Dr. Megan, sorry if I'm late on my assignment, but I'm not sure I really want to do this anyway. Here it is anyway. I know that you said that these journals would be confidential, but I know they are not, so I'll be to the point. I realize that we will all say that "these are our private thoughts," but I think I know how these groups go. Sometime later in our sessions we will all be told we can share them if we want. So, I'm a step ahead, I'll just go ahead and write it to you since you'll be reading them anyway. Okay, first session – fine, my friend was suicidal, depressed, and a former alcoholic. The group – fine, some a little nuts, but I'll deal if it helps Terrence. What else? I think we all should have talked about our real feelings and beat on pillows for a while then talked about our innermost feelings a little more. We're all healed. Love, Daniel.

Personal Journal 2

Okay now for Session 2
Dear Dr. Megan again, or are we close now, and I can call you Dr. Meg? Sometimes I think I'm waiting for Jan to call you Nurse Ratchet and we turn this into the

Cuckoo's nest. She's pissed and an odd bird, but I suppose we all are odd birds; otherwise we wouldn't be here. But I guess I'm a little pissed too, who's turning my friend into a zombie? Do you really think that's going to make him better?

"I'VE HAD ENOUGH for one day," said Megan as she slumped in her office chair. She found it difficult to stay focused; her thoughts juggled back and forth between her concerns for Darion, Terrence, and the group. "Thank God for you, Shaw, you carried me in group today."

Shaw sat up straighter. "Hey what are friends for?" Shaw poked his head into the hallway then looked back at Megan. "So, did your boyfriend leave for the day?" Shaw said with grin. As soon as he spoke the words, he regretted them. He loved to joke with Meg, but it was obvious that she was on overload. She sat in silence.

"I'm sorry. Is there anything I can do?" he asked.

"No, I've got to take care of it. Tomorrow. Thanks, Shaw." She threw he head back in her chair and inhaled before slowly blowing the air back out. "Were you ready for today?"

"Hey, I'm ready for anything these days." He sat down in a chair across from her.

"Shall we do our case notes?" she asked.

The mood in the room lightened. They had work to do. It was 6:00 p.m. and group had just finished. It was time for Meg and Shaw to staff the group and draw up their case notes. When Meg referred to being "ready" she was referring to the second session. Earlier in the day, she received Shaw's phone message referring to her "boyfriend" acting up. The night before, Shaw was leaving the clinic and stopped by the lounge to see one of his inpatient clients. During his short stop, he had a brief conversation with Terrence who was in a near comatose state on his feet.

Shaw often followed his hunches regarding his clients. He also was privy to nearly any information he wanted at the center. Even though he was only part-time, he was treated much like the resident teddy bear. Everyone loved him and a few innocent questions here and there about medications and other information seemed to easily find there way to him whenever he asked for it. Last night his hunch was on target and he determined that Terrence had been overmedicated. His attending psychiatrist was Dr. Darion Walsh. Ever since Shaw shared the information with Meg, she seemed to be preoccupied with it all day.

The stress carried over into group, and Meg's mind seemed to drift to other places. "Expect the unexpected" is a motto that Meg and Shaw both seemed to agree with when it came to group therapy. Most group work runs like clockwork, even bad therapists can run a group and move through the stages, but the "unexpected" was in regard to *how* the group formed its identity.

This group, like all others, started with its members testing the water with unconscious struggles about *how safe is it in here?* and *how social I should be with these people?*

Meg sat back. "You go first," she said. Shaw could read the exhausted look on her face.

"It was kind of fun," he said with a smile. Shaw experienced most groups as exciting and sometimes entertaining. "But the session was a drag in some other ways. Jan was definitely rehearsing her best therapist role all week. I think in some ways it helped move the group along. In other ways, I was wondering about the members of the group that pulled back. In particular, our two guys. They really pulled back. What did you think?"

Meg had been stressing all day over whether Terrence would arrive in an overmedicated state, and she was unprepared for the anger expressed by others. It didn't bother her; it just got things going early.

After each session she tried to play back the group in her mind.

"Sometimes we will start with an exercise, but for the most part, the group is responsible for the content. Each week I will open up with 'new business' and 'old business' where anyone can comment, if they wish, on last weeks session or move to anything new you would like to bring to the group." After Meg opened the group, she glanced at Jan, who left angry the week before. Jan responded with a sweet smile.

The group started smooth and was fairly predictable for an early session, in what Meg often called the *pseudosharing time*. The members tend to share a lot of data about themselves but not much about how they are affected by it. Her experience with group was that they don't often share feelings, but mostly stories "my mother was a drunk . . . I was abused . . . I started drinking . . ." Meg's patience allowed her group members to transition into a more difficult stage in which they would talk about themselves and not just the data regarding their personal histories.

In time, the members talk about themselves after they go through a stage in which they are conflicted with their own feelings. The inner conflicts revolve around how to bring those emotions to the group. Meg and Shaw had experienced all different types of groups, and for the most part, they seem to follow the same patterns.

"I have something I would like to start with." Rose's voice trembled. She swallowed; most group members sensed it was taking all of her courage to be the first one to speak. "We've both, Tony and I, have been sober for a few months now, and it's maybe the greatest feeling I've had in our relationship. But I'm afraid. I'm afraid I'm going to lose it, and I've been wondering if anyone else has felt that."

Immediately Jan leaned forward and steepled her hands in front of her. She tilted her head and said in a soft voice, "How does that make you feel?"

Shaw had to restrain himself. "Jan, I'm wondering if you can say what you want to say without asking a question."

Jan clenched her jaw. "I just wanted to know how she felt." She immediately glanced back toward Rose as though her move was rehearsed. *Another defensive style.*

Meg immediately thought, *Oh no, hear we go with the Junior Freud. Anybody who has taken a psychology course believes that the six golden words "how does that make you feel?" automatically qualifies them as a master therapist.* Jan's agenda was clear: she wanted to be a counselor and not a group member. Meg knew that it would be easy to jump in at this point. However, she had learned a long time ago that it was important to let each co-therapist handle their own conflict so as not to make a group member feel like the facilitators are ganging up on them.

Shaw handled her masterfully. In most groups he asked the participants to avoid questions. Jan was not in the present, nor was she really saying how she felt, "I guess I'm sensing that Rose's statement affected you and that's why you asked." He waited through a moment of silence. Jan folded her arms.

"Is there like a rule now? That I can't ask questions? That *we* can't ask questions?" She was trying to pull the others in with her, perhaps to align against *them*. Shaw remained patient, her behaviors were consistent with a fragile ego, and he had been down this road dozens of times before. Jan was feeling persecuted, in danger of losing control over others, so she was blaming others rather than look at her own behavior. As if she was saying *please join me in my paranoia*.

Shaw stayed with her. "No, as we mentioned at the outset, no rules per se, but staying with the moment and speaking for yourself can be more honest."

"Are you saying I'm dishonest?" She was quick to defend.

"What I'm saying" – Shaw looked from side to side – "is that at times, we can all be a little dishonest, not in a malicious way, but we avoid our feelings by asking questions. For instance, if I ask, 'How does that make you feel?' It's probably because I felt or perceived something. Perhaps, being more genuine I might say, 'It makes me sad to hear you say that' or, I might speak for my own senses by saying, 'I sensed that made you sad.' In either case, if we come here every week and do nothing more than interrogate each other, we are not speaking for ourselves."

In Jan's case, her personality was incapable of understanding her emotions when *others* felt something. Shaw often referred to this as the "duck and cover!" civil defense drill. She didn't know how she felt when others had emotions.

In the few silent seconds that followed, Jan held a cold stare in his direction. As he glanced around he waited for someone to speak. No one stepped forward, so he continued to lead. "It seemed like we left Rose hanging, any reflections on what she said?"

Meg wanted to speak, but she and Shaw had a teamwork style that avoided facilitator following facilitator talk as often as possible.

Gerri was the first to talk, "I think my greatest fear is losing Lisa. Not just physically, but emotionally." She couldn't make eye contact with Lisa when she said it. She glanced down and continued to talk. Eventually she glanced back at Rose. "Sometimes I think it's just my crap coming up. I'm too possessive or something, or too insecure, I don't know"

Bingo, We're back on track, thought Megan. Maintaining her silence, she watched the group establish their own norms. Instead of responding to Jan, they got on to business. It seemed a little too early to begin to subgroup, but Jan was doing her best. Megan had experienced insecure group members try to form alliances with others against the leaders. They need others to be *on their side* because they see the group leaders as a threat. This is why Jan asked, "We can't ask questions?"

Despite Jan's discomfort, the mood of the second session was lively. Doris and Earl both talked about their fears. After a few other exchanges, Lisa finally responded to Gerri and with a nervous voice. She acknowledged her fear of being alone and talked briefly about her need to "numb" herself with her drinks. "Because at first, it seems safer than the real world, but the more I drink, the more unsafe it becomes." Others contributed as they talked about relationships and fears.

Nearly all of the members added something to the group, but Terrence spoke only briefly. When the group was well along, Tony held a gaze in the direction of his wife Rose and thanked her for bringing him to the group. It was his way of saying *I love you, I'm afraid, and I don't want to lose you,* all at the same time. His pride kept him from being able to say all of those things out loud.

If the group ever left some members out of the conversation, Megan had a gut feeling for when to stop and use a round. "Let's stop for a second because it seems like we haven't heard from everyone for a while." She noticed that she hadn't heard from Terrence and Daniel, and of course Jan, with arms and legs crossed, went into shutdown mode.

"Let's do a quick round, one sentence or less." She always threw that one in order to avoid anyone dominating the round with long talk. "Finish one of these leads 'some of the conversation has made me feel . . . ' or 'today's session makes me think about . . . ' and of course with any round, you have the option of passing."

As they went around the group, it went as expected for most of the members. When it got to Daniel he stayed unemotional and felt the need to justify his silence "Some of the conversation has made me feel like this group is helpful. I'm feeling kind of quiet, just kind of thinking that there's a lot of pain around these issues."

Meg took note that Daniel's brief statement revealed his distance. He mentioned "feel" twice but never mentioned any real feelings. Shaw and Meg didn't call him on it, it was too early, but they both noticed that "this group is helpful" and "quiet" weren't real descriptions of his feelings. Daniel's silence tended to mirror his friend's silence.

When it came to Terrence, even though he was in a fog, he surprised Meg with his empathy. With a slight slur he said, "I'm feeling a bit sad, hurt, and even lonely. I think it takes guts to bring these things in here. I wish I could help."

All of the members responded with some emotion except Jan; she would glance at each of the leaders and mutter, "Pass."

Later in the closing, Meg repeated and acknowledged, "How tough it is to say what we want to say in group."

The two hours flew. Meg and Shaw self-disclosed on occasions, Shaw more than Meg. He never hesitated to recount images of a drunken father on Christmas and how he was reluctant to trust as a result of some of his memories.

As Daniel listened, he continued to wonder why he was there and maintained his silence in order to align himself with Terrence.

In closing, Meg always chose a member to give a summary. The reason she did this at the end was to revive her own memory. In a quick recount at the end, she could have all of the conversation ready to be translated to her notes a few minutes after the session. Sometimes, (she often admitted this was the case) she forgot things and she needed to sum it up at the end. In her final round, she started to her left and went around the group. "One quick final comment about your feelings as you leave today."

Gerri sighed, "I guess I feel relieved."

Tony fidgeted. "Um, I think I'm uh going to pass, sorry."

"I feel good to be here," said Doris

Jan folded her arms. "Pass."

Terrence smiled. "I guess I'm like Gerri, I feel relieved. This is better for me than I thought."

Don looked up and hesitantly said, "I feel somewhat anxious." Immediately he looked at Jan and knew he would get an ass-chewing in the car for not simply following her lead with a "pass."

Shaw was in the mood to crack a joke, his usual departing conversation, but he held his humor in tact for the serious needs of the group. "I feel good for myself and good for so many people who took some risks tonight and weren't afraid." He glanced to his left, indicating he was done. He knew that the final closing job was Meg's.

"I'm glad to be here," Lisa said with a warm smile.

"I feel like I'm ready to get to work," said Earl. No one else knew what he meant except Doris. Earl was ready to truly commit himself to his sobriety this time.

"I feel good but in other ways I wonder if I belong," said Rose. After she said it she knew she would dwell on it during the week ahead. What she meant was not that she was above the group, but in some ways she felt below it. Because of their finances, she had earlier told Meg in the screening that she couldn't afford it, and Tony did not have insurance. For that reason, they, like some others were not asked for any reimbursement. Rose was still concerned how others would take her statement.

"I just want to repeat what Terrence said. It does take a lot of guts to bring these things in here, and I'm feeling happy for the group, and" – she paused – "I just want to say thanks, see you again next week?" She looked around the group and smiled.

After Shaw had made his initial observations of the group, he asked Meg what she thought.

Meg smiled. "Jan's armor sprang up quicker than the defensive shields on the Starship Enterprise." They both chuckled.

Shaw added, "Then she set her stare beams on stun. I think the only one she hit was poor old Don himself."

For the next few minutes, Shaw was on a roll with his *Star Trek* analogies. "Then, Megan the Klingon leader sought to take over her empire, but the good admiral Jan ran out of dilithium crystals and was unable to achieve warp speed out of the group." By now Meg was laughing hysterically. "Captain, I caaaan't give you any more power," he said in his best Scotty voice.

The two were not laughing at anyone's expense. But Shaw knew his friend needed to relax. She wasn't her normal self today. She was concerned about Terrence and needed to let some of her stress run off.

Eventually they got around to the issue of Terrence. "I see what you mean about Terrence." Meg referred to Shaw's observations regarding Terrence. "He was completely out of the group." Shaw suspected that his medication had been changed, courtesy of Dr. Darion Walsh, the friendly neighborhood shrink. Not only could Meg feel her blood beginning to boil, but she knew it was time to confront him.

18

July 14, 1968
The Kiss

MAGS MAINTAINED AN intense and frustrated look on his face. Whenever he started holding his head, it was his sign that he was becoming temperamental. He sat on his sleeping bag behind Mickey's house. The other three bags were also laid out, and Mags sat cross-legged across from Sanners. He looked like a fire and brimstone preacher holding up a copy of *Science Digest* like it was his Bible. "Okay, listen again." His eyes focused on Sanners, "What the theory says is that the universe is three-dimensional. It's like, all the matter is in one place. The universe doesn't actually go on forever."

Mags was certain that Sanners was just confused. Sanners was certain that it was just another idiotic idea from Mags because he reads these *Science Digest* books, and he doesn't know the difference between science facts and science fiction. "So you're saying that the universe ends. How stupid is that? So you go way out in space and all of a sudden there's like what? A brick wall? Ya right it ends. Well, what's beyond that?"

"Don't be such an idiot. It ends because the theory says there is no more matter, that all the matter is contained in one place." Mags held out his hands, moving them around an imaginary ball.

Mickey and Danny were lying next to each other and trying to get better reception on the transistor radio. The Grizzlies were playing. The argument didn't help them as they tried to listen to the game. "I don't know, it doesn't *matter* to meeee . . ." said Danny with a laugh.

"What matters is the matter in which it matters to you," said Mickey with a laugh.

Now Mags was even more frustrated. "Okay listen, the article said that a long time ago the universe was like all in one place, and it blew up in what was called the big bang."

"It was probably the fourth of July," said Danny with a sarcasm-laced voice. He and Mickey were getting their kicks out of egging them on.

"Shut up you guys, I'm serious, you guys are just too stupid to get it." Mags rolled on his back and folded his arms.

"Oh, I get it, like there is a huge stop sign out there," said Sanners. He then turned back to Mags. "It's just plain stupid. You're saying that the universe ends. Well, what's on the other side of that? It goes on forever. It's infinity."

"No, there's nothing there."

"How can that be? There's the universe, and it goes on forever. There's something, it's called space."

"It's nothing, and nothing is nothing."

Sanners looked at him shaking his head. "Nothing is something, and it's called the universe."

"Gawd, you're an idiot. Nothing is nothing."

"You guys need to shut up, you are giving me a headache, and the Grizzlies are down 9-2. I can hardly hear them on the radio," said Mickey.

"They are always down 9-2," said Danny.

It was now 10:00, and Danny's nervousness was escalating. They would leave in two hours for their second attempt at operation "pop-up-trailer visit."

After their last bumbled attempt, they finally met up with Lisa and Jean at Teen Swim and explained the mess. To entertain the entire group, Sanners graciously acted out the role of Mr. Mags beating the door cop into submission.

Jean had a sigh of relief. She and Danny were becoming mirror images of each other in their sense of personal self-doubt, but at least this eased the awkwardness for a while.

Their new location for the sleep-out was Mickey's backyard. Even though the cookies and popcorn were always a hit, they were no replacement for the opportunity to go out for midnight rides on the bicycles.

The summer was moving at its usual summer pace. As they grew older together each summer season felt like a page in forever. There's something magically slow about a summer in which there is no schedule to be somewhere or plan something. They could never understand why the adults would continually ask, *where the hell did my summer go? Where the hell did my vacation go?* The boys' summers felt like a perpetual experience without beginning or end. Every true summer has no boundaries or definitions, a lot like infinity.

While Mickey tuned into the Grizzlies game and Sanners continued to argue with Mags, Danny's mind flowed into his self-doubting thoughts, *I'll never kiss her, I'm such an idiot, she has to think I'm a fool.*

Despite his lack of confidence, he had worked up enough guts to ask Mickey about the art and craft of kissing, but it seemed to leave him with a lot of questions. *Are you supposed to move your head fiercely from side to side like those lovers in movies? If the heads come together to kiss, which way do you turn your head? Because obviously the noses get in the way. A straight on kiss will definitely result in a nasal collision. How do you initiate a french kiss? What the hell is wrong with me? Some guys my age are doing a lot more than I am. At least they say they are.*

Danny was overwhelmed, nervous, unsure, and excited all at the same time. He had been fortunate to grow up in a house with a caring mother who sat them down to talk to them about respecting girls a long time ago. Danny knew that the speech was intended mostly for Aaron, but it felt good to know he had a mother that actually understood the real world or at least acted like she did. "There's a lot of boys your age who are already fathers. It's because they let their penis do their thinking for them instead of their brain. Now neither one of you have any business thinking about having sex at your ages, but when you eventually fall in love, you sure as hell better be ready for the consequences."

Pats had told them about pregnant young girls, unwed mothers, and boys having to support kids before they got out of high school and the like. *A great way to screw up your early adult life.*

Pats also had a hands-on plan for educating her boys. Last summer, when her sister Laurelyn and her newborn visited from out of town, Pats had Aaron and Danny do all of the diaper changing for three days straight. She also had them launder the diapers, which was even worse than the changing. The boys were thrilled when Laurelyn finally left. Pats then sat them down and looked at both of them straight in the eye and said, "You know, boys, you are capable of having babies just like the one you took care of for three days. And when you think about having sex someday, think about what comes with it."

Pats was also smart enough to take Polaroid pictures of Aaron and Danny holding and changing the baby, then place the pictures on the boy's dressers. *A gentle reminder.*

Danny had listened for years about the fantasy exploits of a lot of junior high school kids who claimed they got to second base or third base or scored a home run with some girl. Danny knew most of it was ego-driven, guy-talk lies, but he was still frustrated to feel like the only ninth grader on earth to never even get a hit. Hell, he not only never got up to bat, he never even got out of the dugout.

Finally, it was 11:30. Time to go. The plan had been created with perfection and precision. Nobody awake at the Hannigan household. The boys stuffed their bags and crawled to their bikes. The moon was full, and the night was young.

When they arrived at Jean's block, they found the unoccupied house a few doors down and parked their bikes behind it. Jean informed them that the neighbor was on vacation. Their approach route to the house was carefully planned as well. *Which houses had lights on? Which backyards could you crawl through? Which ones had dogs?* All the details had been worked out, mostly because Mickey thought of everything.

Mickey was the first to reach the pop-up trailer. He gently knocked three times with his middle knuckle. The door slowly opened on only the bottom half. The top half stayed zipped. *Bingo! We're halfway through the mission!* The four boys crawled inside then sat around the fold up table inside the pop-up trailer. On each side were two beds with thin mattresses where Jean and Lisa had rolled out their bags.

Danny was the last to enter and at once made eye contact with the most beautiful sight on the planet. Mickey had already moved aside so the only place Danny could sit was right next to Jean.

"Hey, Lisa!" whispered Mickey. "How are you guys doing?"

"We're doing great!" whispered Lisa in return. "How long will you be staying?"

"Only a while, we have to get back to get some sleep. We have routes to deliver in the morning you know." This was Mickey's manly way of saying, *Hey, you know how it is when you are a working man.* In reality, teen bodies don't work that way. You could stay up for three days in a row if you had to and then sleep for three days in a row. It all evens out in the end when you have the physical resiliency of a cheetah in its prime.

The boys had little to talk about except baseball and girls, but in the presence of girls, you don't talk about girls. That cuts down on about half of the things that you can talk about in life. Sanners leaned across the table. "I have a question: does infinity go on forever?"

Lisa looked at him like he just fell out of the sky. "What are you talking about?"

Mags held up both hands and said, "Oh, for crying out loud, that's not what I said, I said the universe doesn't go on forever, not infinity!"

Now everyone was confused, except for Mags, who just sat there shaking his head.

Mickey interrupted, "You guys shut up, I'm sick of this stupid conversation. Lisa, Jean, never mind the two stooges here."

The conversation went on tangents about important subjects like Schwinn ten-speed bicycles, Teen Swim, an upcoming dance, and which songs were the coolest on the radio these days. Eventually, all of them had noticed, in the dimly flashlight lit confines of the pop-up trailer, that Jean had reached over and was now holding Danny's hand. *It was time to go.*

"Hey, guys," said Mickey, the platoon leader. "It's time to cruise." The others nodded.

"I need to ask you about something," said Lisa as she waved a *follow-me* motion with her hand to Mickey and crawled out the door.

Mickey elbowed Sanners, who elbowed Mags. Then Mickey said, "Hey, Danny, we're going to get going, catch up with us at Schmitt Elementary."

Danny wondered why he was being abandoned, but he didn't seem to mind. After a minute of small talk and fidgeting he stood up. "I better go now."

Jean stood up next to him, then reached out to hold both of his shaking hands. The two were nearly the same height, and he now stared straight into her eyes.

"Ya, I better go. Good night. Will you be at Teen Swim this week?" *Dumb, Dumb, Dumb, you idiot, she just said ten minutes ago she would be there. Why ask again?*

"Ya, I'll be there."

"Well, good night."

"Ya, good night," she said, as she waited for what seemed like an eternity.

Danny was ready to turn to crawl out the door when she said it again "good night," but this time he could feel the softness of her hand as it gently rested on the side of his neck.

His mouth began to resemble the Sahara desert. *Is it possible for an entire body to be a shaking hand? Oh gawd, what do I do now? She's moving closer. Oh gees, should I tilt my head to the side? Will our noses collide? If we kiss should I move my lips? Should I hold my breath? I hope my breath doesn't stink. I'll hold my breath. Should I close my eyes? Oh gawd, she's closing her eyes!*

Danny could feel her hand gently pull on the back of his neck. He closed his eyes as he could feel the warmth of her breath on his lips as she moved closer. He then felt the most incredible feeling of his life as his lips gently touched hers. His arms came up around her waist, and he held her in a timeless place where he had never ventured before.

Her lips were softer than anything ever known or described in human nature. They were warm, gentle, perfect. They were rose petals, spring rain, and a summer's evening all in one. They were more than anything he ever imagined. They were perfect, and this was simply the most perfect moment in his life.

All of his fears instantly dissolved. Not only did it go okay, in that moment he was whole. He never knew he had the talent to actually kiss someone. He just knew that if someone could screw up a kiss, it would be him. But he didn't screw it up. He had just felt the lining of heaven. He wished he could hold this moment forever.

When she finally pulled away, she whispered "good night" again.

Danny whispered, "Good night," but noticed that the shaking in his hands and voice had stopped. His life was complete.

Danny crawled out through the door and saw Lisa standing next to a tree. "Those guys said they would meet you at Schmitt."

"Okay," he said through a stunned grin. He mounted his bike and rode away.

As Danny rode away, all he could do was smile. He could only think about how soft her lips were. Her lips were so different than any others he had ever kissed. Moms, aunts, and grandmas give you those slobbery kisses on the cheek while you writhe to get away; but this was the most incredible thing he had ever felt. He could still smell her. Danny closed his eyes as he rode through the silence of the night. When he was safely a block away, he popped a wheelie on his bike and screamed at the top of his lungs. At this point in life, he could do anything.

When Lisa crawled back into the camper, she climbed on to her sleeping bag and put her head on her pillow. She looked at her friend and whispered, "Well?"

Jean smiled and whispered, "We kissed." She grabbed the pillow and put it over her face and screamed into it. Lisa grabbed her pillow and did the same. For the next few minutes, the two kicked their legs and screamed into their pillows.

As Danny approached Schmitt Elementary, he knew where he would be able to find them. There was a pitch-black area where no lights were mounted in the middle of the courtyard next to the building. It was a safe place to wait. They had been there before

Danny couldn't help but wonder why adults become so nonchalant when they kiss each other. It's like a kiss good-bye, or a kiss hello. *How could they kiss someone and just walk away like it was nothing? How could they not scream every time? How could they not just fall on their backs and smile every time they kiss? Don't they feel anything anymore? Don't they know what a great thing this is? I'll always feel this way after every kiss, I just know it. I hope I can kiss her every day, unbelievable!*

Danny rode his bike toward three shadows in the courtyard of the schoolyard. He felt at least six feet five inches tall, his chest was at least twenty inches larger than before, and a smile had never spanned this far across his face before.

As his bike slowly rolled toward the figures he could hear argumentative voices coming from the shadows. "If the universe ends, then what's beyond that? It just keeps going because it's nothing space, but that's something!"

He could see a shadow of an animated Mags waving his hands. "Nothing is there, so that's just it! Nothing is nothing! There is no longer a universe!"

Sanners fired back, "It's just space, and it goes on forever and – "

"Will you guys stop it?" said Mickey. "I wish I had a rocket, I would send you both into space. Quiet! Here comes Danny."

The four looked at each other in a moment of silence. Mags, Sanners, and Mickey all noticed his sheepish grin. His teeth seemed to glow in the dark. Mickey nodded upward with his chin. "Well? All we've been doing is arguing about nothing. For reals. What about you, pal? Anything new to report to the team?"

Danny blushed for a moment then confirmed, "I kissed her good night."

The three moved their bikes toward Danny and began congratulating him. "All right, man! Good job, man! Good work, my man!" Danny felt like he was being congratulated for hitting the winning home run in the World Series. But this was better, much better. He would take this over a home run any day.

Mickey was the first to extend his hand to shake Danny's. "Cool stuff, man. I'm proud of you, my boy." Mickey had a way of shaking another guy's hand that made him feel like he was a man. It was firm, with eye contact and a pat on the wrist. Danny had just made it to the big leagues.

Sanners reached out and shook his hand. "Good work." He gave him a pat on the shoulder.

Mags could think of nothing better to say than, "Hey, man, did you french-kiss her? As my cousin would say, 'Did you stick your tongue down her throat?'"

Sanners wheeled around and slapped Mags's hat off. It went flying to the ground. "Shut up, man, I can't believe you. This is his woman you are talking about. You're an idiot."

Mags got off his bike and retrieved his hat. "Sorry, man."

"We better get going," said Mickey.

The three boys were already pedaling before Mags could mount his bike. He pulled on his hat and pedaled to catch up.

Danny was too pumped up to sit on the seat of his bike. His energy poured out in all directions, and his legs pushed hard on the pedals. Somehow the night air smelled better than it ever had before. Somehow his body had more energy tonight. Somehow, he believed, this grin would never go away.

Sanners and Mickey flanked him on either side as Mags fell three lengths behind. Sanners tried to permeate Danny's world with an important question, "Hey, man, are you going to ask her to go steady with you?"

Danny's smile grew wider. He had never even thought about that. *Wow, this is really big stuff.*

From twenty feet behind the others, a burst of energy hit Mags's legs. It wasn't just a light that went on in his head. It was more like a floodlight, a spotlight, or a lighthouse beacon. His eyes got bigger and he looked as though he had just discovered the lost tomb of the pharaoh. He pumped his legs furiously to catch up with Danny. He thought about the ring that Jennifer's mom made her give back to him.

"You're going to ask her to go steady? Hey, you're going to need a ring! I've got a ring! Do you want to buy a ring?" *Let's see, my cousin bought it for $10, I bought it for $8.50 from him, and five bucks would seem reasonable. I could put the money toward a new pair of Converse shoes or go to a couple of movies, or . . .*

The next day, the Falcons defeated St. Catherine's by a score of 8-2. Willie Mays played in center field for Saint Anthony's. Danny's performance was nothing short of remarkable. He looked like a minor leaguer who was about to make the leap to the majors. Everything he did was perfect. He went four for four at the plate, stole two bases, threw out a base runner on a throw to home plate from center field, and jacked a three-run homer in the fourth inning. Hell, when you are a man, you can do anything.

19

The Cave

"**I** LOVE THE cave," said Megan. She threw her bike helmet on the floor and sat on couch.

Shaw sat on the other end of the couch and grimaced. "I hate the cave."

The "cave" was the nickname the professors at Denver State University gave to Shaw's office. His fourth floor office was one of several rooms in a building that were converted from a former dormitory. The second and the third floors were devoted to counseling services and a lab for training masters degree counseling students. The offices were oversized and allowed Shaw to keep a couch he bought at a yard sale. Over the years, Shaw bought most of the furniture himself. Asking a state university for office furniture was about as promising as asking pigs to fly.

Megan was still breathing fast from her bicycle ride to his office. The ride was only twenty minutes from her office, but a casual ride was not in her character: she liked to move.

The Shiler Center was located in a well-populated area on North Federal Boulevard but nowhere near the congestion of the area around Denver State University. In order to get to DSU, she had to cross the Platte River and go into downtown Denver. She tried to visit Shaw a couple times a month to go out for lunch.

Meg stood up. "You know they should just turn this place into a shrine. You could charge admission." She threw her arms in the air. "You could have a family rate. Here, kids! Look at the cave! You could once see walls and a floor in this office, but now it's covered with stacks of paper. Here, kids, take the beef jerky and feed the professor, now don't get too close! We don't know if he bites."

Megan was in a mildly euphoric mood. She was getting a charge out of herself at Shaw's expense. He enjoyed her banter.

Meg's visits often coincided with times when her stress was running high at Shiler. Getting away to Shaw's office was always a treat. Shaw's office was a minor miracle. He probably had not thrown out a scrap of paper in six years. It was a metaphor for his life. Always wanting more order – but never getting it.

"Shall we go to lunch?" asked Meg.

Shaw hesitated. His hand went down to his belly and with a slight rub he pinched the fat. His body was also a metaphor for his life. Shaw was never excessively overweight, but he was always in need of losing *those last twenty pounds*. During his doctoral program, it was *those last forty pounds*. His five-foot-eight-inch frame had not been well conditioned since his undergrad college days. By the time his senior year rolled around, he began to brandish the body he now occupied.

The pinch on his belly was a compulsive habit that went back to the days of the Special K cereal commercials, *if you can pinch more than an inch* . . . Shaw always thought *it depends on where I pinch, over here is fine*. He contemplated lunch long enough to assess the damage. "Ya, I could use a salad." He knew it would end up being a cheeseburger and fries.

Thirty minutes later, they were eating lunch. "I wish we could run clinics the way they run the major leagues," said Meg as she glanced at Coors Field. Their favorite deli had outdoor tables and was located just down the street from the Colorado Rockies Major League Baseball Field. It was only a ten-minute walk from his office and one of Shaw's favorites because he was close to the field. When it came to baseball, Shaw never aged a day past twelve. He was like a little kid who soaked up the atmosphere like a sponge. His favorite times were during afternoon games when he could hear the roar of the crowd. Shaw had always dreamed of attending a World Series game and when the Rockies did the impossible and finally made it, like thousands of other Coloradans, he was unable to get tickets. The next best thing was not a television broadcast but sitting outside the stadium with a radio. He felt like he was one of the crowd.

Shaw took a bite out of his cheeseburger, and the slice of avocado began to slip out. "What do you mean by that?"

Meg took the opportunity to entertain herself. "We could send Darion back to the minors. We could make him bring his average back up."

"Or" – Shaw swallowed then reached for his fries – "we could trade him."

"For what?" asked Meg. "A dog?"

"Ya, you're right, there wouldn't be much we could trade him for. Besides, what the hell would you do with the dog? The best you could get would be a yapping poodle that wants to hump everything in the neighborhood. The only joy we would get would be when we had to have the poor old Mutt put out of his misery. Sorry, boy, no one wants to adopt you."

Meg snorted. She tried to laugh but had a mouthful of food. Her milkshake nearly made its way up through her nose. Shaw loved to make her laugh, but he knew she was at wits end with Darion. "Did you finally get to see him?"

"After two days of avoiding me, I finally cornered him. He knew that I was coming to see him, and he finally cut down on our client's medications. He claimed that because our client was suicidal, the medications were a means to protect him from harming himself. But nothing happened until I went to Ferron. I think we'll see a different group this week, at least on our client's part." Meg glanced over both of her shoulders. There was no one within twenty feet of their table. She rarely talked about her clients outside of the office in order to preserve the confidentiality of the client-therapist relationship. Without mentioning his name, they both knew she was talking about Terrence. She felt a little uncomfortable discussing their group over lunch. She had professional issues with Darion, and it was his practices that prompted her stress.

20

July 21, 1968
The Ring

THE BOYS HUDDLED under a tree. The game was an hour away. The four boy's heads nearly touched as they hovered over the small item in Danny's hand.

"Let me see it," said Mickey as he held out his hand. "It is a beauty, I have to admit." Mickey examined the ring again. Mags polished it for the possibility of a sale. It was a standard gold-tone band that could be purchased at most department stores. It looked fairly new, and on the inside it was stamped 14K.

Mags argued that "14K" mean that it was solid fourteen-karat gold. The ring was cheap but had the appearance of a nice piece of jewelry.

"But it's the wrong size," said a disappointed Danny.

Sanners interjected, "I'm telling you, man, that it doesn't matter. I've seen chicks put just about any size ring on their fingers. I'm telling you, man, if it's a little tight, it's okay. She won't lose it."

"It's too small." Danny said with a half frown. The boys had just spent the last twenty minutes discussing the fact that Danny would save so much money if he went with Mags's ring. Mags had gone all the way down to five dollars, final offer. Danny was anxious and disappointed. *So much to think about, so little time. She would be coming to the game. It would be a perfect time to give her a ring – right before the game.*

In order to obtain the precise ring size, Danny carried out carefully planned strategies. The boys had created a perfect plan for obtaining Jean's ring size. When he went for his most recent bike ride with Jean he wore three different rings that the guys had dug up that week. One was a gaudy turquoise ring that Mags had been given as a child. Another was a Boy Scout ring that Sanners retrieved from his brother's collection, and the third was a small Saint Christopher ring that Mickey had from his first communion ceremony at the church when he was in third grade. The key to the plan was to have three different ring sizes. The guys carefully designed each step, and each step would need to be perfectly executed. When she notices the rings in conversation, you slyly take them off, goof around and have her try them on. The result? *Bingo! you've got the girl's ring size, and she never knew the difference. These guys are geniuses.*

Unfortunately, Mags's leftover ring from his short-lived "Jennifer-nearly-going-steady" escapade was too small for Jean's ring finger on her right hand. Her size matched up with the Saint Christopher ring, and the Jennifer ring was too small. The ring had to be for the "going steady ring finger," and that's all there was to it.

Danny's chest drew in a deep breath before he let out a slow exhale. Maybe Sanners was right, maybe girls could squish rings on their fingers, and all would be okay. With a ball game ahead of them, a crystal blue sky, and all the stars properly aligned, it just had to be the day. He took another look at it. "Okay, I'll take the ring." He reached in his pocket and pulled out three dollars. "I'll get you the other two after I collect for papers this month."

He looked at the ring and smiled. *Look out, big leagues, here I come!* He was ready, and the time was right. His chest inflated another two inches. *Having a real girlfriend, a real "steady" girlfriend. It doesn't get any better than this.*

Danny began to warm up with the others when he noticed Lisa and Jean riding up on their bikes. The important thing was to not act like you saw them, then perform some superhuman athletic feat, and then nonchalantly walk over to them.

Danny was hitting fly balls to the guys with the bat when he decided to begin hitting them all over their heads. That would definitely be impressive. He tossed the ball in the air and swung as hard as he could. The only sound was the whiff of the bat. Danny nearly stumbled as the bat wrapped around him. The instant redness filled his face. He picked up the ball and swung even harder. This time he tripped forward after he missed the ball. "Shit," he whispered under his breath.

By now the guys were laughing. On the third swing, he finally connected, and the ball went flying over their heads just as he had planned. It was time to quit. He then acted like he just noticed the girls and wandered over to talk to them.

"Hey, Jean, Lisa." He nodded to both of them and reached down to feel the ring in his pocket. His heart began to pound out of his chest. It was game time.

The girls said hi, and Lisa went over to grab the bat. She yelled at the other three to stay put. She picked up a ball and slashed a line drive to the three waiting ballplayers. Everyone knew of Lisa's athletic prowess. Growing up with Mickey, she was his equal until only two years ago when his body started changing. She was probably a better player than half of the Falcons, but they had no girl's league in the DCYBA. Equality for the girls wasn't even a concept in their minds yet. Occasionally, they patronized the girls in the parish by having a "powder-puff" football game or a couple of softball games for the girls. In each of them, Lisa ran roughshod over most of the other girls.

Danny watched with slight embarrassment as she pasted ball after ball to center field. He nervously sat down next to Jean and started the conversation with safe topics like, "Did you watch *Twilight Zone* last night?" To no avail, his conversation was dead. He had spent the entire morning with no loss for words as the boys discussed Drysdale pitching six straight shutouts or going to see a new movie called *The Devil's Brigade* or the temperature or even revisiting the subject of infinity. But now he was out of words, time stood still, and he wanted to ask her to go steady but didn't know how.

Mickey had once revealed the slick art of asking girls questions with the "you probably wouldn't want to . . ." preface attached to them. His theory was that it was hard for girls to say no if you popped questions like, "You probably wouldn't want to go to a dance with a guy like me . . ." These types of questions, Mickey determined, made it more difficult for girls to say, "Ya, you're right, I wouldn't."

The beauty of the "you probably wouldn't . . ." questions was that it was harder to shut you down. If you asked outright, "Would you like to go to a dance this Friday?" the girl could always say they were busy or going somewhere, but if they turned you down on a "you probably wouldn't" question, it almost made them seem cruel.

Danny nervously attempted to craft the conversation toward a "you probably wouldn't" type of a question. "I had fun riding to Ruby Hill with you yesterday. You probably wouldn't want to do that again sometime would you?"

Jean tilted her head and thought for a moment. It was an odd question. Of course she wouldn't mind, she had been doing it all summer. "No, I wouldn't mind doing it again. That would be groovy."

Yes! It worked! You probably wouldn't, you probably wouldn't, okay how do I ask this . . .

"Cool, let's do it again sometime." He ran his fingers over his pants pocket. He could feel the outline of the ring in his pocket. It was time to ask her to go steady.

"Hey, I remember Lisa saying that she went steady with some guy last year. That's really something isn't it?"

"Ya, that is . . ." Jean wondered where the conversation was going. Somehow it was strange that all of a sudden Danny was nervous, and the conversation had gone from the *Twilight Zone* to bike rides to Lisa's past all in one minute.

"Have you ever gone steady with someone?" *Please say no, please say no, I can't bear the thought of you saying, "Yes, forty times . . ."*

"No, I never have . . ."

Hallelujah! Hallelujah! Hallelujah! Now say it, say it now! Ask! Now!

"You probably wouldn't want to ever go steady with a guy like me, would you?"

"I would love to go steady with you, Danny."

Danny wasn't ready for such a quick and direct response. He fumbled in his pocket for the ring. With his best attempt to coyly conceal the ring in the palm of his hand, he hesitated. *Wait a minute, did she say yes? Wait, did I really ask her to go steady? Does a "you probably wouldn't" question really count? Oh my God, what if she really didn't mean to say . . .*

Jean leaned over and kissed him on the lips.

Danny's heart came up into his throat; it was the first time he had actually kissed her out in broad daylight. Doing that in front of the guys took another kind of boldness.

"Mine!" Mags called the pop fly in center field.

"I'll be damned. Did you see that, my boys?" asked Mickey.

"That son of a biscuit is making out with her right here at the ball park," said Sanners in disbelief. It was such a new sight to see Danny do anything that required confidence.

"Crap! I missed it," said Mags as he stared in past the dugout to see them. "Ya, Danny! Thataway my boy!"

Sanners reached over and knocked his hat off. "Shut up, man! Don't embarrass him. He embarrasses easily enough."

Danny still had his eyes closed. He could kiss her all day. This feeling was the greatest he had ever experienced. To be kissed by someone who really cared about you was something beyond his life expectations. This is something that only happens to other guys.

He unfurled his hand to reveal the shiny ring. "I have something I want to give you. Um . . . if you want it."

"It's beautiful. Here, put it on me." Jean held her hand out in front of his lap.

Danny shook so bad he had to clutch the ring with both hands. He wasn't sure if he could accurately put it on the ring finger of her right hand. That was the place that all "going steady" rings were to go.

As he slid the ring on her finger, it stopped at the middle knuckle. *Damn! It's too small, I knew it! I knew I shouldn't have listened to those idiots!*

Jean reached down and pushed the ring. It wouldn't budge. She twisted and pushed again, only this time much harder. It finally made it over the knuckle. Her heart pounded as they sat in silence. "Thank you, it's beautiful."

Danny beamed and leaned over to kiss her again. It was the first time he had initiated a kiss with her. The only things left in his life were a driver's license, a draft card, and the legal voting age; and he was a total man. At this point everything was crystal clear and in order. He took a deep breath. He was a man with a steady girl.

Danny looked over Jean's shoulder and saw Coach Eggs approaching with the bag of baseball equipment. It was time to start thinking about other manly things like their game with St. Luke's. A formidable opponent, but it would be men against the boys today. Willie Mays would be playing in center field again.

Danny said his good-byes and went over to help Eggs with the equipment. In the meantime, Mr. Hannigan arrived and helped Eggs by warming up the outfielders.

Danny breathed in the day with his newest sense of confidence. He had seen other guys his age react to their age and development with cockiness, rebelliousness, or defiance. In his case, Danny had a newfound sense of pride.

His heart beat with a fresh confidence that was more like his idol, Mickey. He was the perfect friend, and whenever Danny was around him, he felt stronger. Unlike other teens who vied for position by proving their power over other guys, Mickey never needed that, he already had a firm sense of who he was, and he didn't need status by belittling or creating rumors about potentially threatening people.

In Danny's eyes, Mickey's quiet but confident swagger summed up the ideal way to enjoy life. No issues were too big to keep you up at night, and no trial was too small to not be acknowledged or appreciated. He wasn't the strongest, fastest, or most brilliant kid to make it to junior high; but he was the most complete package. Even the most cocksure, brilliant, and bold seemed to envy him. He was the guy they all wanted to be.

Danny watched Joe Hannigan belt the balls with a smile and an effortless swing. If there was an adult image of Mickey, it was Joe, and if there was a kid image of Mickey – it was Spikes, running after each ball in a carefree connection to the energy of a ball field. Mickey was the middle of this sandwich between the hearts of the two special people in his life.

Danny began to feel some of the confidence that he had desired for so many years. The self-reliant poise was always the end product in a recipe for which he could never find the ingredients. Until now. Somehow, by trial and error, a few risks taken with a girl; he was feeling life the way it was meant to be felt. It was a manner of approaching life where the end product is not always perfect, but it always turns out right.

The game went pretty much the way everyone thought it would. Mickey pitched all but the last inning where Joey Pelloman came in to pitch with the lead at 10-2. Everyone got a lot of playing time. The guys could start to feel the makings of their best season ever. They were melding into a single unit of coordination and grace.

Danny's game went well. His first two at-bats produced a ripped line drive down the left field side for a stand-up double, and a two-RBI single over the pitcher's head into shallow center field. Just before his third trip to the plate he stood in the on-deck circle taking swings when he noticed Jean running over to her bike and peddling away from the game. Danny struck out in his next two attempts because of his worry.

He stood in center field and pounded his glove as his mind was racing. *Was she not interested in the game? Maybe she was having second thoughts about the game. Are we not a steady couple anymore? Maybe she was wondering if it was really 14-K gold? Maybe it was the stupid "you probably wouldn't" questions. Does a "you probably wouldn't" question count when you are asking a girl to go steady? I should have never asked. I'll bet she hates the ring. I'll bet she figured out that it was Jennifer's. No, she doesn't know Jennifer. Maybe Mags told Lisa and . . .*

A crack of the bat interrupted his thinking. A thundering shot from one of their best players, Davie Clickner. Danny knew from Eggs's signals to play him slightly toward left field because Clickner was a lefty and swinging a little late on each pitch. The perfect position paid off for an easy pop fly to center field.

Stevie Burman called out, "Can of corn, coming at you, Danny." The *can of corn* expression was new to the boys until this year. Eggs had referred to an easy catch as a can of corn. It's history, he explained. It went back to grocers in old food markets who would have things stacked high on their top shelves. They would take a stick or broom to knock off a can or box on top which resulted in an easy catch. Hence, the "can of corn" meant an easy catch. Somehow the term stuck with ballplayers for at least a century.

Danny centered himself under the ball but couldn't stop thinking about Jean. *Maybe she doesn't think we're actually steady . . .* The ball glanced off the heel of his glove and hit the ground. It was two outs, and the two base runners for St. Luke's were off and running. He fumbled for the ball and accidentally kicked it. The lead base runner scored. He tried to pick it up and dropped it again. Another man scored. He finally picked up the ball but threw it so hard it went over the cutoff man's head. Danny's chin fell to his chest. He was back to his old doubting self.

The only two runs scored by St. Luke's were due to Danny's triple-error play. It didn't affect the outcome, but he felt bad because he cost his buddy the chance to pitch a shutout.

After the game, he confided in Mickey about his new worry.

"Are you kidding me?" said Mickey. "Is that what was worrying you? Girls get up to leave all the time. Haven't you ever noticed? They leave classes, they leave games, they leave movies, and they leave all the time. Don't you get it, man? It's *womanly* things. You know, womanly things." He emphasized "womanly" again as he said it.

A light went on in Danny's head. *Oh ya, that's it, womanly things, that's why she took off. It had to be.*

Mickey patted him on the shoulder. "Don't sweat it, man, it had to be womanly things. Womanly problems sometimes result in womanly emergencies, and they take off at the craziest of times."

Danny nodded and added a big sigh of relief. *Ya, that had to be it.*

"No, Daddy, please don't, no, Daddy, please don't." Jean's face was covered with tears. She was standing next to a workbench in her father's garage as the air filled with a thick fog of emotion. Mrs. Sommers held Jean's right hand in a gesture of comfort, but she felt helpless in finding a solution. For the past two hours, they had tried soap, motor oil, ice, and Vaseline. The ring would not budge. Her finger had now turned deep purple.

"I'm going to have to cut it off," said Mr. Sommers. He held a huge pair of sheet metal sheers in his right hand.

Jean was shaking, crying, and hysterical.

"I'm sorry, honey, it's either cut it off or we go to the hospital."

Mr. Sommers's huge callused hands were the evidence of his life as a plumber. His grip could break a pair of pliers if he commanded them to do so. Today, however, they were gentle as he held his daughter's swollen hand. He watched her cry and felt helpless. His large puppy dog eyes slightly welled. He knew this was the only possession in her life that was meaningful at this time.

"No, Daddy please, let's try one more time, please, Daddy."

"Your father's right, Jean, he's got to cut it off."

Mr. Sommers looked through his tool box for a smaller pair of wire cutters or another set of sheet metal sheers. A plumber by trade, his tools were his life and were top of the line.

A fourth voice rose from the corner of the garage. "Don't worry, Jean, maybe your rich boyfriend will buy you another one!" Jean's brother, Lance, was six months away from turning eighteen. He leaned back on his Yamaha 175 motorcycle and cackled after his comment. Most of the time he tried to keep a composed James Dean swagger, but his spare tire belly detracted from his persona. Ever since Mr. and Mrs. Sommers agreed to the motorcycle, they had regrets. For the last two months, his cockiness kept brewing as he approached his senior year in high school.

The garage grew stuffier, and the air was getting thicker by the minute. The four personalities were all focused on the phenomenon of the purple finger, but the emotions were incompatible. A frantic crying teen, a hysterical laughing egotist, a consoling mother, and a confused father. It was like walking into a chemistry lab and arbitrarily throwing chemicals into a beaker. Pretty soon something had to happen.

"Tell the cheap jerk to buy you a ring that fits next time! Ha! I can't believe it. Check the label on it, maybe there's an emergency number we can call at the crackerjack ring company!" Lance leaned back on his cycle clutching his helmet over his round belly as he laughed.

The words did not even register with Mr. Sommers. He was like a surgeon collecting his composure and searching for the right scalpel. Jean did not hear him either. She could not believe she was about to destroy the first ring ever given to her.

The chemistry in the garage continued to swirl, but sometimes the smallest of sparks can set off the explosion. Lance's words eventually mixed with the wrong chemical. "What's your boyfriend's name? Danny Einstein?" He laughed again.

Mrs. Sommers suddenly dropped Jean's hand as she abruptly turned around. Her face had the look of imminent detonation, and in moments a flash from a mushroom cloud would destroy everything in its path. This bomb had a target, and someone tauntingly entered the drop zone. This bomb was igniting out of maternal protection. Mrs. Sommers's eyes bulged, the finger pointed, and the legs were in gear. With furled eyebrows and gritting teeth, only one word was necessary. "OUT!" she screamed. Inaudible mumblings were escaping from her clenched jaw as she began to make her

way across the garage. "I'm going to tear . . . rip . . . take you apart . . . shut your . . .
so help me . . ." Lance dropped his helmet and started looking for a bomb shelter. He
glanced around for a corner, door, or window. He was panicking. Escape was essential
for survival, and the once cocky animal sensed his life was in danger. He ran for the
door. The bomb had detonated and the shock waves were coming. Mrs. Sommers
was right behind. She lunged with her hand and narrowly missed his back as he flew
through the screen door. He was lucky to escape the flying shrapnel. She grabbed the
back door and heaved it to a slamming finale. The garage was once again quiet.

Mrs. Sommers turned around and wiped her brow as she made her way back to
the workbench. The stress in the garage had just been reduced by a hundred notches
on the tension meter. The volatile element had been removed.

Jean continued to plead. Mr. Sommers was trying to determine how much damage
would be done to the finger as he would try to snip it in one clean cut.

"It's the only way, sweetie. I've got to do it."

"But what about the ring, Daddy? It will be ruined! Daddy, please don't, don't
ruin the ring. Please don't." Jean was now sobbing, losing her energy and her ability
to hang on. Her body slumped next to the workbench as she sat on a stool. Her hand
was still on the bench as she looked at the deep blue color. She was beginning to
realize that she may lose her prized possession.

"I won't ruin the ring, I promise. We'll get it fixed, or I'll get you a new one."

"No, Daddy! I don't want another one! I want this one!"

Exasperated, Mr. Sommers ran his fingers over his brow. "We've got to do this, and we've
got to do it now. It's either the ring or your finger. Which one do you want to lose?"

Jean stood up and placed her face on his huge barrel chest. He gently held her in
his arms and felt his own eyes beginning to well. "Just do it," she said.

Mr. Sommers waited until she was ready and pulled away. She sat back on the
stool, but her hand was shaking. "If you squirm around, I might cut your finger, so
you've got to hold still."

The brawny plumber had enough confidence to create precision pipe fittings that
would withstand thousands of pounds of pressure for decades to come. This small
piece of cheap metal however, created apprehension, and a soft purple finger caused
self-doubt. His heart pounded as the sweat covered his forehead. He wasn't sure of
his confidence this time.

Mr. Sommers opened her hand, put on his reading glasses, and carefully held the
cutters as close as possible. The swelling made it even more difficult to get close.

Mrs. Sommers held Jean's left hand with her own while holding her other hand
over her mouth. There was no good outcome for the ring episode.

The snip was quick and accurate followed by a quick bend in the ring so the finger
could slide out. He cut some of the skin on the inside of her hand. Blood immediately
oozed from the wound. Jean jumped up and ran from the garage with Mrs. Sommers
close behind. She ran to her room, and Mr. Sommers knew she would probably stay
there for the night.

He sat down on the stool and looked at the mangled piece of tinted metal in his hand. He turned it from side to side as he examined the damage and tried to push the lump back down in his throat. In his business of working with metal all day, he estimated its value at about thirty-five cents. He also knew that the girl sobbing on the other side of the wall valued it at over a million dollars.

A few minutes later, Mr. Sommers knocked on Jean's bedroom door. Mrs. Sommers opened it. She had been consoling her daughter. "Come on, she wants to sleep." She placed a hand on his big shoulder and turned him toward the living room. The two made their way into the kitchen and sat down.

"How's the hand?"

"She won't need stitches, but I did put a butterfly on it and wrapped it up good. I don't think she'll get an infection." She paused, then reached out to put her hand on his. "Can it be fixed?"

He held out the twisted ring and shook his head from side to side. "Are you kidding? Take a look at this thing." It was badly mangled. He pursed his lips and sighed. "It was a stupid thing for him to put that damn thing on her finger." He shook his head again, picked up the ring, and stood up. Turning toward the garage, he said, "I'm going to have to do something about this."

Five thirty in the morning.

Danny folded his papers and smiled. An anxious Scooter waited for his chance to go out on the route. His tail wagged as he waited. It was the high point of his day. Danny could not remember being any happier either. A punch from Cassius Clay couldn't wipe this smile off of his face.

Most mornings when no one was around, Danny spoke to Scooter as though he were human. Scooter's loyalty was undeviated and eternal. He wagged his tail as Danny spoke through a big smile on his face. "I'll bet she sat up all night and looked at her ring. She probably called Lisa and the two of them sat around and looked at it. I'm glad I got the ring from Mags. It was perfect."

Mr. Sommers hunched over his morning cup of coffee at the kitchen counter. He poured the remainder of the coffee from the electric percolator into his thermos. He looked out the kitchen window and straightened up with attention when a one-ton pickup truck stopped in front of his house. The truck had panel compartments on each side over the truck bed and had the appearance of a well-used work truck.

Mr. Sommers walked out to the garage and picked up a six-pack of beer that had been sitting on the bench. He dropped by his local liquor store last night to buy a special six-pack of Irish ale. An old friend named Harvey Treston managed Tom Dooley's Liquor Mart. Harvey highly recommended the ale for special occasions.

With the six-pack in hand, he opened the garage door and walked toward the truck. He made his way to the driver's side, where the window was already rolling down.

The driver grinned and nodded. "I think you were wrong, Pete," he said. "The ring wasn't quite worth thirty-five cents. I believe I would place a value of about fifty cents on it." Both men chuckled.

"How did it go, Cliff?" asked Mr. Sommers.

"OK, but it was about as tough as trying to weld two tin cans together." He held out the ring. At the place where the ring had been cut, there was a short section of a shiny silver band that contrasted the gold-colored plating on the rest of the ring.

Mr. Sommers looked at it and turned it over. "How much bigger?"

"About two sizes. The color is not the same. It took me awhile just to get the metal to bond. I won't even begin to wonder what kind of cheap metal that thing is made out of. But I can tell you one thing, you won't be cutting through the part I welded, so don't try!" The two men laughed again.

Mr. Sommers carefully looked at it again. "It looks better now than it did before."

"Ya, I hope you don't mind, I took the liberty to polish it up for her. So now what? You want me to go rough this kid up for you?" he asked jokingly.

"Naw, Danny's a good kid. But tell me, how long did it take you?"

"Well, at welder's wages I would say that the ring is now worth about a hundred bucks. I won't say how long it took, but I'd do it for free for my little Jeannie. But then again, I guess my little Jeannie isn't so little anymore if she's getting rings."

"Naw, she's not so little anymore. How about buddies wages? Will that take care of it?" He held out the six-pack.

"Buddies wages are free, but I'll tell you what, the six-pack will cover the tip."

Mr. Sommers handed him the six-pack through the window. "Thanks a bunch." His big hand reached through the window and patted the top of his shoulder. "I owe you."

"You don't owe me a thing. It was my pleasure. Give little Jeannie a hug from me." Cliff nodded and drove away.

Mr. Sommers walked back into the house and glanced at the kitchen clock. It was nearly 6:00 a.m. He had a few minutes before he had to leave for work.

He walked to Jean's bedroom door and noticed it was slightly ajar. As he pushed it open, he saw his youngest child lying in her sleep with the bandaged finger next to the pillow. Pete Sommers had lived through a lot in his life, but he wasn't ready for his little girl to grow up. He sat down on the chair next to her bed and stared at her. Above her bed on the wall was a Bobby Sherman poster. A year ago it was a poster of Minnie and Mickey waving from the seat of a cartoon car. He always liked that poster, but now it was probably rolled up in the closet or in the trash. He looked over to her dresser and saw a stack of *Teen Beat* magazines, where comics used to lie.

The huge callused hands reached out as he gently slid the ring on the middle finger next to the bandaged finger. He smiled as he admired the craftsmanship of Cliff. He looked at her sleeping and glanced back at the poster. His face rounded into a sheepish smile as he felt a tear roll over his large round cheek. Another tear formed in the corner of his other eye. It's hard to grow up. It's hard for dads too.

Pete stood up and left the room, gently pulling the door shut behind him. He pulled out his handkerchief and blew his nose.

He walked out to the kitchen where Mrs. Sommers was sipping her morning coffee. When Pete kissed her good-bye, he held her for an extra long time this morning.

An hour later, Jean woke up and felt something new on her finger. She screamed into her pillow, called Lisa, then ran into the kitchen to show her new ring to her mother.

Louis Garrison awoke with another hangover. Last night he sat in a borrowed car in front of his former girlfriend's apartment. Waiting, watching, more drinking. She will pay. There are a couple of scores that will have to be settled in this world. She is one of them. Another is with Harvey Treston at Tom Dooley's Liquor Mart. There won't be a botched holdup this time.

21

Session 3

MANY OF THE doors in the residential wing of the Shiler Center were open. During visiting hours, people walked and chatted in the halls and rooms.

The door was slightly ajar as Daniel checked the number. He had been here before, but it was always good to make sure. Number 204. He knocked.

"Come on in."

He heard Terrence's voice and peered around the door as he stepped in. On the bed sat a tired disheveled friend who looked as though life had dragged him around in the past few days.

Terrence appeared ragged and defeated.

"Hey, pal, how you doing?" asked Daniel. His friend looked pale, and Daniel imagined that he hadn't had any decent sleep in days.

"Not bad," he said in an unconvincingly tone.

"You look tired, are they working you hard here?"

Terrence had been working at the center for a month. After hitting rock bottom, losing a job, and a marriage, he was pleased when Ferron offered him a month-to-month position at the center.

Over the years, with managed care out of control, it was difficult to get clients the services they needed. Ferron and Meg created a program where clients could work at the clinic if they had no insurance or if their coverage ran out. The clinic needed cooks, janitors, and groundskeepers. Since many of the beds were not filled, they would provide therapy and a place to stay for a limited time. Daniel's room was on the second floor and overlooked the Denver skyline.

Meg always felt that it was her most important duty to provide long term care for her clients, but in doing so, she often felt like she was reduced to begging. She often referred to herself as a "prostitute of the system." Managed care systems would often only allowed seven-, fourteen-, or twenty-one day inpatient care. The rest they had to beg for. Meg, as well as other therapists would find themselves negotiating with providers for twenty-one-day services for the price of fourteen or fourteen for the price of seven.

Some clients needed extended long-term therapy, and her program created ways to keep the clients in therapy. These were things they didn't teach you in graduate school. No graduate program has a class that teaches you to beg.

"There's plenty of work here," said Terrence. The color came back to his face. "It's kind of strange in here sometimes but hey, I can't complain, I'm dry." He was happy to be sober, and his message was genuine. "You remember those dreams I told you I kept having in high school and in college? They're back. I don't know what to make of them."

"Do they bug you?"

"A little," said Terrence as his chin went to his chest.

"I've been thinking about you a lot. After group this week it seemed like you were back to feeling like the old friend I used to know, but I'm still worried." Daniel was having a hard time saying what he wanted to say.

Terrence answered his question for him. "I'm not going to try to kill myself if that's what you are wondering."

"Actually, that's what I was wondering. I don't want to see you go through that again. Tell me what's up with the dreams." Daniel surprised himself; he didn't think he was bold enough to ask about them.

"I die, plain and simple. It's a little different with little twists in each dream that were different than the one before." He added a nervous chuckle, "I guess it's just my death wish again. Same theme though, I'm taking a bullet."

"Have you talked to your counselor about it?"

"Actually I have two counselors. I see a shrink every couple of weeks. He thinks his shit don't stink, mostly he just prescribes meds. I always feel like he is psychoanalyzing me. Last week he said, 'I think you may have been sexually abused as a child and either you've blocked it into the unconscious, or you are in a state of denial.' Then he asks about how I'm feeling, asks me if I would like to try something new in a medication, then he leaves. My other counselor is a young guy who's interning from CSU. He's actually the best counselor I've ever had. He really seems to listen. He's asked me the question that I've asked myself a million times – 'what kind of meaning do *you* attach to the dream?' He told me he's not really into dream analysis, but the dreams could be important if they are affecting my everyday activities."

"What do you say?"

"Nothing really, I haven't told him everything. I don't tell anybody everything, probably never will."

"What can I do?" Daniel wanted more than anything to help Terrence but he had wished that for years. Nothing had changed.

"Coming along with me to group, believe it or not has been great. Thanks, buddy."

"To tell you the truth, that's part of the reason I'm here. I feel guilty as hell. I don't say shit in that group and I sometimes I feel like I'm letting you down."

"Naw, don't worry about it, you're with me and that means a lot to me."

"Did you ever think about being a counselor?"

Terrence leaned back on his bed and laughed, "What the hell's that supposed to mean?"

"No, really, you seem to help those people. They listen when you speak, and they look to you when things get tense. You've got a heart, man. It's like you can feel what they are saying and help them out with it. Except for Jan, and that poor sonofabitch married to her. Can you say henpecked?"

"Thanks, but I don't think I'll be studying to be a counselor in the near future. I just want to get a job, keep it, and try to get back on track and help my family."

Daniel had no reason to doubt him. He had many faults, but a lack of loyalty wasn't one of them.

The conversation eventually changed course. It was as though both of them knew they wanted to stay with the serious stuff for only a while. Terrence asked about Daniel's family last week, and this time Daniel brought pictures. Daniel gave him all of the details on Monica, the girls, and his son.

Later, the conversation took its usual course to the stuff that spring and summers are made of – baseball. The brightest part of their visits always seemed to be baseball. The standings, averages, homers, upcoming games, bullpens, and predictions of things to come. Baseball is what kid's hearts are made of, no matter how old they get.

Personal Journal 3

Dear Dr. Meg, I saw my buddy this week. There's a lot of stuff you don't know about and you probably never will. But I feel bad, I feel like he's been reduced to the status of a skid row bum. You don't know his heart and you never will. As far as the group went – things are cool. It's great to get Terrence back. I was reminded that he is one of the best guys I've ever known. Last week he had as much personality as a washrag, but this week I couldn't get over how much he seemed to help the group. It's like when everyone else was missing the point, he had tears in his eyes, and would say something to the person telling their story and you could tell he really cared. He seems to know both sides of a relationship; he kind of makes everybody feel that they are okay. Especially the Hernandez couple, they started talking more because he could relate to their struggles. He's really okay, Dr. Meg, you may never understand that. PS, Sorry I don't speak much, but what the hell, I don't really know what to say. Love, Daniel.

"Do you think it's possible to have an intimacy paradox?" Meg pulled back the fly rod and gently whipped it back and forth. Shaw sat to her left on the grass and watched her graceful art. She was practicing her casts on the grass behind her apartment. He knew better than to stand in front or behind her. He didn't want another hook in his cheek.

Shaw vowed to never fish with Meg again, but he enjoyed her immersion into her hobby. He once told her that she was a "symphony of fly-casting." He had never seen anyone look so graceful in the sport of fishing. To him, she looked like an art form in motion. With each practice cast the long pole and line made a swishing sound that seemed so controlled and purposeful. Her casts were effortless. She didn't seem to concentrate; the motion was a natural extension of her. Her little finger on her casting hand stuck out at an angle curved away from her hand. She had shared a story with Shaw when she was in high school and broke two fingers while trying to catch a pass in a basketball game. The third finger curved in permanently bent at the top and her little finger bent in two directions. It seemed to give her grip a style all its own.

When she chose her apartment, she purposely favored her current residence because it backed up to an elementary school. The large grass play area provided an unhindered wide-open space where she could practice her fly-casting in the evenings. She would often place large sheets of white butcher paper on the grass. She would put small rocks on the corners to keep them from blowing away then practice gently laying the fly down on the sheet of paper from distances that varied from ten to twenty-five yards. It would also give her the opportunity to see how the fly looked when it gently landed. Today she was testing the weight of some her new flies.

Meg's fascination with fly-fishing was a combination of sport, hobby, intellect, obsession and art. The art was in creating something that resembled the appearance of a real life fly. During the cold winter months in Denver she tied her summer collection. When her stress was high she would even go as far as researching her art. She read up on fish, flies, temperature, seasons, water, habitat, fishing lines, hooks, casts, rods, reels, position of the sun, and the direction of the wind. She attempted to master any variable that might affect the catch.

"What do you mean by an intimacy paradox?" asked Shaw. He could tell that Meg was having one of her days where she was off into philosophical land. She probably read theory or philosophy this morning.

"An intimacy paradox is when we need love so much that we don't pursue it for fear that we won't obtain it." She began to change her casting style to make smooth elongated figure eights over her head. Shaw stared at the smooth strokes in awe. She would create different casts that allowed her to fish under trees, over bushes, in the wind, or in other unexpected circumstances.

"So tell me, what does this have to do with catching fish?" he joked.

She smiled and decided to jab back. "Glad you asked, you see, I have this hypothesis. There are two kinds of people in this world, those who can fish and those who can't. Fishergals are innately self-actualized healthy personalities, nonfisher types often become out of control psychotics."

"Ah-ha," screamed Shaw "That's it! That must be why I have this driving need to go see Darion for medication!"

Meg's casts flew over her head. "Do you want to try a few casts?" she asked.

"Only if you promise to stand behind me," said Shaw.

Megan chuckled "One of these days you're going to come around begging me to teach you how to cast and tie flies." She stopped and sat down next to Shaw. "Seriously, think about it Shaw. Think about so many of these people we see in therapy – especially in the alcohol and substance abuse cases. They are either trying to numb themselves or become delusional in their drunken state to tell themselves 'my life must be okay. My love must be okay.' Do you know what I mean?"

Shaw nodded.

Meg continued, "Then they wake up, and there they are, lost again and lonely again. There's something to be said about running our couples groups because of our focus on people, not just the substance. I've thought a lot about our couples' group this week, everything is right on track, but there's a mystery hanging out there."

22

July 28, 1968
Late Swim

A DAY AFTER the ring fitting Jean told the story of the enlarged ring to Danny. He confessed to her that he was so embarrassed that he avoided her house for the next three days.

Danny eventually worked up enough nerve to visit her house. He was hoping he would see no one but was warmly greeted by Lance perched on his motorcycle in her driveway. "Hey, loverboy, how's the jewelry business?" He threw his head back and roared with a self-appreciating laugh. He had been looking forward to his lines for days. "Let me give you a piece of advice loverboy, don't buy her a necklace, you might choke her to death!" He bobbed his head again and screamed with another round of laughter. He then put on his helmet, threw a smirk in Danny's direction, then flew down the street on his Yamaha.

Danny stood in her driveway and put his hand over his eyes as though he was temporarily shutting the world out. He also dreaded the inevitable; sooner or later he would have to face the family.

The first was Mrs. Sommers, and she was exactly as he expected. Her manner was warm; never mentioning the ring. Next came the large paternal protector – Mr. Sommers.

The two were sitting on her porch as Danny inspected the bandage on her finger. A noise came from the side of the house as he heard the sound of a garage door as it opened. The slow ominous sight of the door moving made his heart pound as he realized what he was about to face. *He's coming out of the garage, and he's coming this way!* Danny's heart resembled a percussion band. He always remembered Mr. Sommers as big, but today he even looked bigger, stronger, and more intimidating than ever. *Maybe he's been lifting weights and waiting for his chance at me.* Danny's heart jumped to his throat and began to choke him as he noticed the pipe wrench in Mr. Sommers hand. At once, he saw his life flash before his eyes.

Mr. Sommers was so huge it only took three steps to make his way to the porch. He stopped in front of Danny and switched the pipe wrench to his left hand. *Oh God, this is it. My life is over. Damn that Mags. I can blame him for the ring. Quick! think of an excuse. The ring must have shrunk! Her finger must have grown! Think of something!*

"Hello, Danny," he said as he wiped the grease off his right hand and held it out to shake his hand. "Pardon the grease."

Danny reached up with a trembling hand and quickly shook his hand. *Maybe it's a trick so that he can grab my hand and then quickly smash my skull!* "Hello, Mr. Sommers." His voice shook and his mouth turned dry.

"What are you kids up to tonight?"

"We might go to Teen Swim," chirped Jean.

Mr. Sommers smiled and walked into the front of the house. "You kids have a good time."

The danger was over. Danny had seen all three of the occupants in the Sommers household, and he survived. The only negativity was from Lance, and he was a jackass anyway. Danny had a newfound respect for Mr. Sommers and a fleeting moment of envy. *It must be great to have a cool dad.*

The best thing about Teen Swim was that it was only for teens. The YMCA closed off the pool to everyone else on Friday nights from seven to nine. It was *your* place to go if you were a teen. It was *the* place to be if you were a teen. The lights were turned down a little lower; there was dancing on the pool deck, cool music, and girls. Danny had an interest in only one girl, and he spent this evening with her.

This was the first time he had gone to Teen Swim with Jean since they officially became a couple. They joined the other kids at Teen Swim staying in the shallow end for a game of water volleyball or horsing around.

None of the teens in attendance were aware of how their behaviors were a metaphor for the struggles they were experiencing in life. The shy ones sat near the edge, hopeful for one chance that maybe, and just maybe, someone of the opposite sex would notice them tonight. The bold ones were just as inadequate in their attempts to communicate. The girl's methods included a few verbal jabs, and the boys tried to say *I like you* through the only method of communication available to them: wrestling or dunking them in the water.

Each boy and girl had a desperate voice inside them praying, *Please, God, don't let me be the only one to never fall in love. Please God don't let me leave this world alone.*

The shy ones, the not-so-perfect ones, and the not-so-popular teens often sat on the perimeter of the action watching the popular carry out their archaic ritualistic attempts to impress others. At this juncture in life the less-than-popular ones often envied the popular ones, thinking that life would be better if they could be that way.

The popular ones were often envious of the not-so-popular ones believing that life would be better if I didn't have all this pressure to always be the achiever.

Unbeknownst to both groups was the fact that they all feared the same things. They feared they wouldn't fit in. They feared they would die alone. They feared that their acne would flare up. The girls feared that their periods would start at unexpected times. The boys feared that they would be the only guy on earth to turn eighteen and not sprout a pubic hair yet. Most of all, the greatest fear in life is not death, injury, failure, or loss of property. The greatest fear that exists is embarrassment. One can survive nearly anything but public humiliation. The teens did everything in their power to avoid this god awful worse-than-death feeling.

It's a tough world when you are a teen. No adult will ever understand that. When adults grew up it was probably so much easier than it is today. Adults are well-meaning, but they are also the most oblivious creatures on earth.

Danny followed suit with the other boys with the belief that it's okay to touch the opposite sex in public if it's done through wrestling. It's simply too tough to touch them in another way such as a gentle pat to the shoulder or a gesture that reflected softness.

As the evening went by there was a mixture of dancing, more horsing around, and some talking. For the most part, as far as Danny was concerned, it was about the closest thing to heaven that he had ever experienced. It was now 8:30, and there was only a half hour to go. After a few more barbaric dunks in the water Jean took Danny's hand and pulled him away from the rest of the crowd to a corner of the pool where they both waded and held hands.

Danny was now growing accustomed to kissing her. In his mind, he was damned near an expert at this. Jean pulled him closer for a kiss. "Let's just stay over here," she said.

With the lights turned low, it was not uncommon to see couples making out in different areas of the pool grounds, and Jean was content to be one of those couples.

To Danny, this kiss was different from the others; this is like really making out – this was an extended kiss. He kept his eyes closed and felt his entire body move into a state somewhere between ecstasy, meditation, and pure joy. He felt the softness of her lips and the warmth of her tongue. At that moment, he knew that nothing would ever go wrong in his life again.

A screaming whistle invaded their perfect moment as a lifeguard stood perched on his stand. "It is now nine o'clock, and Teen Swim is officially over. You have five minutes to clear the pool."

Danny slowly pulled away from his embrace with Jean. His heart was pounding. This was unbelievable. He sluggishly opened his eyes and then realized that something else was also unbelievable. His face revealed a look of panic. Jean could sense that something was wrong. "I . . . I . . . I . . . can't get out of the pool yet."

The lights were dim, and the water partially covered Danny's worst nightmare – a public stiffy. His head viciously turned from side to side as he looked for anything – a friend, Mickey? A towel? Mags? Sanners? He spotted his towel on the pool deck about twenty feet from the water. *Think! Think! Think! There has to be a solution!* Danny put his head under the water and swam for the deep end of the pool. It was the only thing he could think of.

Jean watched as his legs thrashed in a ruffle of waves as he swam away. She could also hear a slight muffled sound from the bubbles of water that surfaced near Danny's head.

Danny kept his head underwater as he felt overwhelmed with panic and desperation. He lifted his head to the side to gather a breath of air and then stuck it back under the water. Instead of merely blowing out the air bubbles, he screamed under the water. "Shiiiit! Shiiiit!" He reached down with his hand and attempted to adjust nature's nightmare. It was not going away. He swam into the deeper water. *Yes! Sometimes the deeper water is colder! It will have to go away!* He reached down to adjust himself again. Plan B wasn't working.

Danny surfaced in the middle of the deep end to notice that he was only one of three teens left in the pool, and he was the only one in the deep end. A sharp blast of a whistle ripped through the air. An angry lifeguard stood on his tower with his hands on his hips. "Hey, kid! Teen Swim is over, out of the pool!"

The second whistle seemed to summon the attention of most of the free world. Now all of the teens slowed down in the middle of their walk to the locker rooms. The same instincts that say *STOP! Is that a fire? A car wreck? A fight?* were now the same ones that now held the morbid curiosity of at least one million teens on the pool deck. *Is there trouble? Stop and look. What is it? Could it be? A kid defying authority?*

Danny's head bobbed in the middle of the water. He looked for anybody, a friend, anything. Mags and Sanners were close to the locker room entrance when he spotted them. "Mags!" He swam to the edge as quickly as he could. "Mags! Give me your towel!"

Mags furled his brow and cocked his head in his confusion at the request. Danny's hand grabbed the edge of the pool; the other reached out like a beggar needing just one thin dime. "Mags, give me your towel, now!"

"Hey, kid, out of the water!" The riot police were now bearing down.

"Mags! Please!" He gritted his teeth. "Mags!" Mags couldn't understand the request or the anger. Danny reached up with an arm and screamed through his teeth again. "Mags, give me your damn towel!"

"What for, man?"

"Just give me your damned towel!"

The whistles now resembled a civil defense drill. They came from all sides. He blew again and the lifeguard bellowed another threat. "Hey, kid! Get out of the water! Get out of the water! Teen Swim is over! Move it, kid!"

By now it occurred to Danny that he had single-handedly created a scene. His nightmare was now escalating to the status of a lifemare. This is the worst thing that could ever happen to a kid in the history of his life. He realized that the attention of at least one million teens was turned to the kid in the pool and the rebellious kid is defying requests to remove himself from the pool.

He reached down into his swimming suit with the hope that things had settled down. No chance.

Mags stood confused at the edge but still did not hand him a towel. Danny pushed off and swam for the deep water again. His head went back underwater. His life had just turned from heaven to hell in the span of a few short minutes. The bubbles came up from around his head as he screamed into the chlorinated water. "Shiiit! Why meeee! Shiiiit!"

When his head surfaced under the diving boards he could hear the orchestra of what sounded like a hundred whistles. The collective voices of other lifeguards screamed the same commands to the brazen disobedient. He now also noticed that at least one million teens had stopped and were pointing and laughing.

The cat-and-mouse game went on for at least five more minutes. The lifeguards were moving around the pool and trying to get close to him to pull him out of the water. "Hey, kid, I'm warning you! If you don't get out now, I'll have your Y-teen pass suspended."

Suspended, sushmended, WHO GIVES A DAMN! I'm dying here!

Two of the lifeguards pulled out the ten-foot-long hooks that are generally used to reach small thrashing kids who accidentally swam in water over their heads. They poked them in the water in a futile attempt to snag the brash rule breaker. As the laughter escalated, Mickey had joined Mags and Sanners on the edge as they were also caught up in the comedy show. It was particularly humorous for them because Danny was the type of kid who never challenged rules or authority. In their eyes, the scene was beautiful, foolhardy, bold, and reckless all at the same time. No kid in his right mind would pull off a stunt like this, but soon it will be a legendary tale. The only thing they could not figure out was *why?*

One of the lifeguards was growing tired of these antics. He dove in after him. Danny swam in another direction. Another lifeguard dove in. He swam in another direction. A third dove in and now had him trapped like an escaped convict. There was nowhere to go. He finally gave in. He held his hands up as though he was surrendering. *I'll go quietly. Take me away. I'm guilty.*

Two of the lifeguards grabbed him under his arms to enforce their military escort to the side of the pool. When they reached the edge, the largest one barked, "You're in a heap of trouble, kid, you're going to need to report to Mr. Richards, the pool manager. Who do you think you are? Some kind of clown?"

Danny had no response. He grabbed the edge of the pool with both hands. Another lifeguard pushed him as though it would help him out.

"Just a minute!" He turned his head to shout at the pushing guard. With one hand he reached down into his suit. *Hallelujah! Hallelujah!* Life was all right again, except for the fact that he would have to report to Mr. Richards, a fate much easier than death via public embarrassment. As he pulled himself out of the water, the teens surrounding the pool applauded. Most acts of teenage authority defiance are worthy of adulation. In ten minutes his entire life's existence had gone from heaven, to horrific, to heroic status.

23

Jan's Visit
Session 4

"HI, JAN, WHAT can I do for you?" Janice decided to visit the threat to her power before group this week.

Meg left her office door open during most of the day. She didn't expect to see anyone this morning but always encouraged group members to drop by if they needed to talk about nongroup issues.

"I've got a problem with the group."

"Before we get going, I have to remind you that we have to talk about group issues *in* group, in order to protect the confidentiality that we all agreed upon. But we can certainly talk about anything else."

"Okay, that's fine." She placed her bags on the floor, folded her arms and paused.

Meg informed all of the members early in the sessions that she and Shaw would discuss the dynamics of the group before and after the sessions. This was to plan for each session, but they needed to respect the goals of the group by bringing any issues *about* group only in the group sessions.

"Okay, let's do it this way. This is a question about counseling theory." She settled back in her chair and folded her hands. A couple of counseling classes made her an expert in the field.

"If a group facilitator decides to make a rule that we can't ask questions in a group, wouldn't that seem to disagree with many counseling theories? Such as the theories that suggest *questioning* is a method of interaction in therapy that is beneficial in assessment and goal setting. As you may know, a form of Socratic dialogue."

Meg could immediately sense where Jan was going with this. Janice took issue with the fact that Meg and Shaw had stopped each group member to rephrase their questions. They asked them to form statements to reflect what they were personally feeling at the time rather than voicing their curiosities about others. It was a method of creating group norms. If group members do nothing more than ask questions, it becomes a barrage of interrogation rather than meaningful communication. Members who struggled with this often had authority issues, asking themselves, *Should I try to control the flow of the group? Or if I involve myself, am I letting the group control me?* In Jan's case, she needed to control the outer world because her inner world felt out of control.

"Sounds like you are fond of counseling theory."

"As a matter of fact, I am, and as you probably know, in cognitive therapy, the method of Socratic dialogue involves a lot of questions." Jan felt confident in her ability to show this therapist that she knew her stuff. She could run a group and could get things moving as a leader.

Meg decided to avoid Jan's interpretation of the group. Jan was upset because she couldn't control the group. Meg also knew that paranoia also needed to be treated with kindness not defensiveness. She leaned forward and said in a soft voice, "I love to talk about theory. Perhaps you can tell me about a cognitive theory that uses individual therapy techniques in a group format." Meg had taught counseling theories for years and understood the relationship of cognitive techniques in therapy but also knew that no theory of group counseling involving a focus on interrogations.

The confidence Jan possessed two minutes ago was fading like a bad sunset. She was careful in her homework and had her lines ready to fly but stopped short when she was unsure of if she would lose control in her discussion with Meg. The Junior Freud stance was growing thin. Psychologizing family and friends occasionally dazzled her working class relatives, but today she was caught in her own arrogance, and escape was becoming difficult.

"I just think that these type of rules . . ." Jan smacked her lips. Her nervousness was now visible as her mouth became dry. "These types of rules are inappropriate," she stammered again looking for the right combative line.

Meg leaned forward; she did not want to make Jan feel uncomfortable. "Let's just say, as a therapist, I've found that there are a lot of things in group that make us feel uncomfortable. For me personally . . ." Meg self-disclosed rather than to assign blame, "I find that, as a member, the first task for me is to try to ask myself 'why am I here?' Then I can look at how I can benefit everyone in the group. By doing that, I think I have more to offer. I know for me, I often feel uncomfortable because each group is unique, and our roles will change with every group. For instance, I was once in an Adult Children of Alcoholics group. What helped me the most was to continually, week by week, look at what I wanted from the group, and most importantly – ask myself, 'what am I doing to work on these goals every week?'"

Jan sat quietly in confusion. "I'm not sure you're getting what I'm trying to say, never mind." She reached down and pulled her bag up to her lap. "It's not a big deal. I'll see you in group."

Personal Journal 4

Dear Dr. Meg, what is it the fourth time we've met? I'm sorry but I didn't write last week. I feel helpless. When Terrence said, "I'm alone," it scared me. I'm tired as hell tonight, and I want to help him. I'm thinking of coming to talk to you, but I won't. We can't talk about group out of group. So who the hell am I supposed to turn to? When my wife said, "Don't worry, this won't mess up your summer," she was wrong. I didn't want to bring up this shit again in my life. I worked for years to not bring it up. Help. He's a good man. He's in pain, and I'm starting to get some of his pain. Love, Daniel.

"I'm pleased with the last couple of sessions," said Meg as she started to write her case notes.

Shaw noticed that she seemed more upbeat after the fourth session than she had after any of the previous ones. It wasn't an issue of whether or not the sessions were going well. It had more to do with her stress over Darion and Terrence.

The third and fourth sessions melted together with some expected resistance, but it was clear that as each member explored their issues in more depth, they were moving toward more of a working stage.

"I'm fairly pleased too." Shaw reviewed the last session in his mind. He and Meg purposely introduced a couple of activities that were intended to move them toward more receptiveness.

Meg started the third session with her usual lead of "any old business?" If the group members had any issues with the previous session, they could bring them up. Jan had old business for each session but never took the lead. Meg then followed with, "Any new business?" About half of the time in the early sessions, someone would start with either of the leads. If neither lead was taken, she would ask the group where they would like to begin. She would also have a number of group activities prepared but only use them when the group needed to process their current status.

The third session started with Rose taking the lead for "old business." She shared with the group that she wondered if she fit in. From there the group took off. Terrence seemed to connect with Rose at first, then her husband Tony. He reflected on discomfort in situations. As the two hours went by, the time seemed to fly. The group was now getting used to speaking for themselves and commenting on their reactions and emotions to the issues. They were also getting used to speaking to each other and not just the leaders. Jan continued to believe she was a quasi-expert on human struggles, and each time she did, her husband, Donald, would shut down.

Rose's issue of "belonging" snowballed into issues that many members of the group shared. It was not hard to find people with substance issues who also didn't have family issues. Terrence seemed to sense other people's feelings, and soon they were looking to him as well as other members.

Meg and Shaw had experienced this mutual dependency on many occasions and saw it as a good sign that the group was moving. In the early stages, the members always seem to want to direct all of their comments toward the leaders, and Meg was accustomed to this. In time she knew that they would feel comfortable with trust and not be afraid to confront others.

"I was especially pleased that the group felt confident enough to take a few risks," said Shaw. He was referring to Jan during the fourth session.

The session began with no one responding to the "old business" or "new business" leads. Shaw led the opening activity. "This is the fourth time we've met, and tonight I would like to start with a something we can reflect on. When you are taking care of yourself, you naturally take better care of others, and you are working toward those things in life that you want for yourself. Write down two things you've tried or two things you've done that would illustrate how you've tried to take care of yourself in the group. Part of this has to do with your personal goals you set before the group began." I won't ask you to share these. I just want you to write them down." Shaw and Meg had used this opener before. Often they would use it when a group was stuck and needed to be reminded that they made a commitment to work on their goals in the group.

After the group finished writing, Shaw asked for a quick round of one sentence that described what they were thinking about as they were writing. Some commented on commitment, others on opening up, and some were reflective. After the round, Meg asked, "Any reactions to the group?"

Terrence looked to Doris. "I don't know how to say this without asking a question, but, Doris, I heard you say that you were so upset with yourself, and you didn't want to carry on the family tradition. I guess I just wanted to let you know that I felt sad for you. You had tears in your eyes when you said it." The room got quiet, and Doris's eyes welled up. She had involved herself in all of the group discussions so far but never really opened up.

"You should see her, my mom," Doris's voice began to tremble. She looked down, and a tear streamed down her cheek. "I don't want to become like her. She is full of years of excuses, looking twenty years older than her time. She's in the hospital right now waiting for a liver transplant. All those years of drinking, forgetting school plays, embarrassing us with whiskey on her breath at back-to-school nights. I looked in her eyes about a month ago, and I saw myself." She looked at her husband. "I'm so sorry." Doris knew it was her last shot to really commit herself to her goal of sobriety. "My kids are now in grade school. I want to give them something different. This is like the tenth time I've tried to stop drinking." She wanted desperately to hug her husband at that moment. She stared down at her feet and wiped both eyes. The group remained quiet.

Jan spoke up, "I know she loved you. All mothers love their children. I know she must have loved you."

Shaw wondered, *Where the hell did that come from?* She was violating the group norm of speaking for others, but it didn't surprise Shaw. Jan had trouble speaking for herself, telling others how they felt allowed her to remain in control. The group waited to see if Earl would comment. He was stuck, feeling emotions for his wife. Shaw desperately wanted the group to respond.

The group was surprised to hear an opinion from a deep voice that rarely spoke. Tony's thoughts had been relatively quiet through the first few sessions, "You can't know that." He said with firmness in his voice.

"Yes, I can, I've been there! I know what you are feeling," said Jan.

"I think you can only know how you feel," said Terrence "That's all any of us really know."

The group immediately erupted. They confronted each other for the first time. The talk went back and forth, recognizing that they hadn't lived Doris's life and couldn't possibly know how she felt. Doris felt herself getting smaller feeling backed into a corner.

Terrence spoke up again, "I feel bad because I feel like . . . like we overlooked Doris in all this." He looked at Doris. "I can't imagine how hard that must have been to see yourself, especially in the state your mother is in. I'm sorry, Doris, I wish I could help."

The group stopped in their tracks. Collectively, they realized that they ran away from Doris's feelings. She was in pain. Jan grew angrier as her face turned red. She didn't know how to handle a challenge from the group.

Earl finally spoke up and talked about how tough it was to see Doris's mother too. Doris smiled and mouthed, "Thank you."

From that point on, the group moved to personal feelings. Lisa talked about being a child of hippie parents in Boulder and how she watched the euphoria of substances, alcohol, and free love slowly drain the life out of her parents as the drugs turned to numbness. Daniel pitched in a few words for the first time and recognized that he could relate to a relative who is still struggling with alcoholism.

The group wound down into a subdued mood. Meg gave the group a short lead for their final round, "Finish this statement for yourself, tonight I learned . . ."

The closing was marked with Terrence commenting, "Tonight I learned that I need to push for quality connections in my life." He sighed and continued to look around as he tried to keep the tears in his eyes. His lip quivered for a moment before his next words could come out, "I guess for the first time in my life I realized that it's not a bad thing to scream, 'I'm alone, please help me.'"

Daniel felt like the whole room was staring at him. They weren't. He looked down and realized his fists were clenched. He felt guilty for not saying more in the group. He thought, *I feel like I'm the only one here who can't help his partner.*

As Meg and Shaw processed the group, they went over its progress. They both agreed that the group was bonding and feeding itself.

Meg said, "I don't know though, have you noticed that even though Terrence seems to take the group to another level, he doesn't really talk about himself. It's like he's here struggling with all of these issues but without a personal history. I don't think the group will ever ask him about it because to them it probably seems like he is sharing his feelings."

Shaw replied, "I know, he has such great empathy for others, but no sense of emotion for his own issues. Hell, we don't even know what his issues are. He's had a long struggle with dependency, suicide attempts, and depression, but doesn't talk about it at all."

"I think I hear what you mean. We may have to eventually say something," said Meg. Inside she was hoping she wouldn't have to be the one to say anything. She was really beginning to grow fond of Terrence and knew that it would be painful and could potentially shatter the fragile door on his closet of secrets. Shaw looked at Meg and noticed she was staring blankly ahead, trying desperately to figure it out.

"I think it's his support partner I'm starting to feel sorry for," said Shaw. "I sense he feels more out of place than anyone."

Meg was silent as she nodded. She finally spoke, "Let's just play it by ear."

24

July 31, 1968
The Big Plunge

MICKEY ENTERED BUD'S coffee shop and filled his lungs with the aroma of donuts and coffee. He waved at Bud for "the usual" and smiled as he approached the other three boys. *It was confession time for Danny. He had to come clean.* Mags and Sanners had already begun the grilling as Mickey overheard the interrogation.

"Why did you do it, man?" asked Mags.

"What did Mr. Richards say?" followed Sanners.

Mickey joined in before Danny even had the chance to speak, "Ya, man, what did you tell him? What did you tell him?"

Danny turned beet red. He had only one mode of communication when it came to his own life. It was one of brutal honesty. He could lie for his friends, he could lie to cover up for others, but somehow he couldn't lie to cover his own tracks.

"I told him the truth."

Danny stared down at his donut; he couldn't look his friends in their eyes. Yesterday, on Monday he faced Mr. Richards. He was a young college graduate with a recreation degree, and this was his second year of managing the YMCA pool. Danny told him the whole story. He figured this young guy would understand that if a young guy was kissing his girl that sometimes things might get out of control. He did understand, and even though Mr. Richards laughed until his eyes watered, he handed Danny a token five-day suspension.

Somehow it was easier to tell Mr. Richards the story than it would be to tell his friends. The guys kept grilling as Danny stared at his donut. *What were you trying to prove? What was going on? Did you just want to put on a show? Were you showing off for Jean?* Finally, Danny raised both of his hands to each side of his head and whispered, "It's a private matter."

Mags, Sanners, and Mickey all stopped and leaned in. They were ready for Danny to reveal some bold plot he had to show off at the pool, to show off for the world, to show off for Jean, to boldly challenge the lifeguards. Three chins dropped in silence as they heard Danny whisper "I had a . . . I had a . . ." He gulped, picked up his head, and spoke straight ahead, looking at no one. He finally pushed the words out, "I had a public stiffy, and I couldn't get out of the water."

Mags's eyes bulged. "You what?"

Sanners slapped his hands to the sides of his temples. He tried to imagine what it would be like to have that happen to him.

Mickey waited, then smiled wide. He slapped Danny on his back and grinned. Mickey stood behind Danny with both hands placed firmly on his shoulders and raised his voice. "Attention to all of my good friends at Bud's coffee shop . . ." Danny was now blushing out of control, his first instinct was to plant a quick jab into the ribs of Mickey, but he let him go. "I would like to announce that my good friend Danny has proclaimed that he is so much in love that he . . ."

Danny's hands trembled, *Please, Mickey, please, Mickey, don't . . .*

"He is so much in love that he has promised to hit a home run for his girlfriend in the game against Holy Names this weekend."

Danny grinned as Mags and Sanners laughed, clapped, and whistled. A handful of patrons joined in with few scattered claps. Poking fun at each other and suffering the abuse of a few minor discomfitures were components of the language between the boys. These were not gestures intended to humiliate; they were ways of expressing loyalty. Danny was grateful to have Mickey in his life. He was the one guy who could unearth all the best qualities in others. He elevated everyone's game. The small display of public humiliation deflected his embarrassment from having to come clean with his friends. You laugh about it and move on.

Sanners continued to sit in the stillness of his own thoughts with his hands on the side of his face wondering how a human being could actually survive such an incident.

Mags offered meaningless solutions with questions like, "Why didn't you just borrow my towel? Why didn't you just try to get out of the pool right away? Why did you start kissing her in the pool at a time so close to closing time?" Mags tried to save an incident that already passed.

Mickey simply smiled and slapped his friend on the shoulder with warmth that indicated his loyalty and understanding. It could happen to anyone, and the slap reinforced a sense of safety. You didn't like to share these kinds of details with everyone in your life; they had a tendency to ruin a guy's image for the remainder of his time on earth. It was like the incident with Buddy Callahan three years ago. He got an erection during a wrestling match in gym class and had been nicknamed Boner ever since. Adolescents have a way of never letting you forget an embarrassing moment. Clinging to another's faults helps them to maintain their sense of superiority. The biggest goal at this time in life is avoid embarrassment and to fit in. To hell with being successful, just don't be embarrassed, and you'll do okay.

The rest of the week went like clockwork. St. Anthony's drilled Holy Names by a score of 9-2. Mickey had another terrific pitching performance, and the Falcons jumped to a 7-0 record. The boys were warming up their season for the grand finale, a confrontation with their biggest and most hated rival – Saint Augie's. The schedule had one game against a very challenging foe, the St. Stephen's Bears first, and then they would take on an easy Saint Paul's Buffaloes team who had only won one game all year. St. Augie's would be undefeated at 9-0 going into the final game, and if all went according to plan, the St. Anthony's team would also be undefeated and challenging them for their first league title. Something inside the boys told them that this was the year. This was their 1955 for the Brooklyn Dodgers; this was their "next year."

Mickey, Mags, and Sanners remained loyal to their fallen comrade and did not go swimming at the Y without Danny. Danny never explained to Jean exactly what happened; it would have been too embarrassing. Since the pool was out of question, the boys needed some other form of excitement for the week. Mags was generally the most tentative when it came to planning for excitement, but this week he had a good one. They hadn't pulled off this kind of a trip in over a year. The mission? Skinny-dipping, it's time to crash a swimming pool in the middle of the night.

One of the great built-in components of being a teen is the knowledge that kicks are simple. You evaluate your life by your "kicks." It's a personal question and a group question. What are we doing to get our thrills – our kicks out of life? You're too young to get overly involved with alcohol to alter your consciousness, so you rely on creating situations where you utilize as much of your natural resources as possible. It's called adrenaline, and it's the perfect high. When you have plans to go skinny-dipping, you really don't need drugs. Incidents like these assist in the ultimate thrill of walking the tightwire between mischief and safety. There's no feeling in the world like the adrenaline rush from being devious or running from some yahoo who is mad at you.

The boys returned from their routes and finished a donut at Buds, and now they sat at Danny's table making last-minute arrangements for their evening out. Pats had gone to work, and Aaron was still asleep in his bedroom. Small details were being laid out for the evening's escapade. Danny's backyard would serve as headquarters, and they would sneak out the alley and swim at the Y sometime after one in the morning.

As the boys finished their plans, Aaron strolled into the kitchen. A mouthful of his bad breath permeated the room. His wayward bed hair matched his odor. He spent another late-night out in his make-believe world, where he was grown up. Overhearing the plans he poured a glass of orange juice and sat down at the table. "Kid stuff," he said without looking up.

Mags stared at Aaron's lopsided hair. One eye that was partially closed with sleep goo, and it made him look like he was drugged. "What do you mean kid stuff?"

"Just what I said, kid stuff. Going skinny-dipping isn't a big deal. Everyone does that. You ought to go to the Big Plunge, but you guys probably aren't man enough to pull it off." He threw out an insult and a challenge all in one sentence.

Sanners scrunched his face in confusion. "The Big Plunge is an indoor pool. What do you do? Break in?"

Aaron shook his head with a condescending *how can you be so young and stupid* look. "Of course you break in, but not through the doors, you fools. Everyone knows that all you have to is get on the roof of the building and open a ceiling hatch door and drop down to the middle of the pool and let the rest of the guys in. It's easy."

In their excitement, all four boys hunched forward. This was excitement and in comparison to a simple skinny-dip and jumping over a barbed wire fence at the Y, this was on another level of grandly proportioned devious schemes. The Big Plunge was a longer road trip, and actually the pool wasn't that nice. It had been the only indoor pool in southwest Denver for years and had been run down for as long as the boys could remember. But the idea of this adventure had all of a sudden taken on a certain intrigue. This was much bigger than your routine skinny-dip.

The boys were now interrogating Aaron for details. *When was the last time he went? How do you get on the roof? Where is the opening on the roof? How far is the drop? Can you see the water from the opening in the roof?* With each answer from Aaron, the excitement grew. It was like being in the middle of a scene in a scary movie just before the monster is coming around the corner. You don't know when it's going to happen, but the excitement keeps building. Each of the four boys could feel the hair on the back their necks standing up. This was going to be a real kick.

The rest of the afternoon was spent planning. Everything had to go like clockwork. The Big Plunge would clearly be one of the major adventures of the summer; it was more than just a mischievous escapade, *and* it was flirting with the law. Should this be classified as a skinny-dip? Or is it breaking and entering? After some discussion, it was decided that it was a skinny-dip. They weren't breaking anything, and they weren't stealing anything; they only wanted to swim. Besides, "skinny-dipping" was easier on the conscience.

As usual, Mrs. Magliano had to speak with Pats first in order to make sure that sleeping out in the backyard would inconvenience no one. Mickey got the approval from his mom, and Sanners simply told his mother where he would be. It wasn't as much of an approval process as it was an informing one. They probably wouldn't know the difference if he was gone. In some way, it was an issue of pride, to be like the other guys, Sanners felt he should get permission too.

Mags glanced at his watch and hummed to the music that played over the radio. His one earphone plug hooked into the side of his transistor radio. Sanners and Mickey had temporarily drifted off into sleep. They could always count on Mags's compulsiveness and Danny's restlessness to wake them in the middle of the night for their missions.

Danny hummed the last song he heard when he danced with Jean at Teen Swim. It was a song by the group named Flannery Row. "I pray every day that I'm not asleep. This is not a dream that will go away when I wake . . ." Danny decided at that moment that "I Pray Every Day That I'm Not Asleep" would be "their song." Every couple needs an "our song," he decided.

Mags whispered a different song, "Life's so short! Life's too short! I'm not gonna live a short, short life!" The tune, along with his nervousness, made his heart race. Mags's adrenaline escalated with each passing moment. He needed to get psyched up for events that may compromise his guilt. *What would my parents think if they knew I was about to break into the Big Plunge? But then again, I'm not really breaking in. I'm just skinny-dipping, but then again, what would my parents think of me skinny-dipping? Is it really illegal? Or maybe just bad? My parents probably never did anything bad like this.*

Mags glanced at his watch again. Twelve forty-five. Time to wake the troops and get started.

By the time the boys rode their bikes up the alley behind the Big Plunge, it seemed to loom much larger than it ever had in real life. It was the only indoor pool in southwest Denver, and it wasn't much to look at. Now, however, it seemed to stand before them like an intimidating Mount Everest. The roof was a little more than three stories high. The green outer paint had peeled and cracked in places to match the reputation of its run-down and out-of-date condition. The BIG PLUNGE was painted in big black letters along the side of the building with peeled chunks missing, and the *N* in "Plunge" almost faded into the green color beneath. Alongside the name was the silhouette of someone in midflight doing a swan dive. It was easy to imagine how fifteen years ago the building was an attractive sight with waves beneath the letters going from one end of the building to the other. The boys followed Aaron's directions to place their bikes behind a garbage Dumpster in the back.

"I don't know if we should do this," whispered Mags. His doubts grew, and it started to feel a lot more illegal.

Sanners grew more excited. He peered at the rod iron rail ladder that scaled the side of the building. It was brown and rusted in places but seemed very inviting. Mickey smiled as well. Without discussion, it seemed fit to send the two boldest to go up and look for the roof entrance. Mags and Danny would wait below and come in through the back door.

Sanners didn't hesitate. "I'm going up." Mickey followed as they quickly scaled the metal ladder attached to the side of the building.

Mags and Danny watched them move over the top edge, then backed themselves to the rear door to wait.

Sanners crawled on his belly to the spots he remembered where Aaron told them to go. Aaron had warned them that there were three roof panels that could be opened, and two of them were not directly over the pool, so they had to be careful. After crawling around for a few minutes, Sanners located the panel they would try. Mickey tried to visualize the interior of the building and determined that they were close to the center of the pool. They each grabbed a corner of the panel and folded it back. They could hear their voices echo in the building but could see nothing but pitch-blackness.

"How do we know if we are over the pool?" asked Sanners.

"I'm already one step ahead of you my friend," replied Mickey as he drew a handful of stones from his pocket. He anticipated this dilemma and came prepared. Staring into the blackness he whispered, "Listen," then carefully dropped a stone. The two held their ears next to the opening and listened intently. A small splash was echoed from below as they both smiled. Mickey was excited, but it seemed like they had to wait too long for the sound of the splash. It was a frighteningly long wait even though logic told them that the drop was only about thirty feet.

"I'll go," said Mickey, "you bring my clothes around." He peeled off his shirt and shorts. He edged himself over, then hung for a moment. His heartbeat was like a hummingbird's. He felt panicked and exhilarated at the same time. After dangling for what seemed like an eternity, he released his grip and fell into the abyss. Mickey's hands went straight out to his sides as he waited for his feet to make contact with the water.

From above, Sanners could hear the splash below as he waited breathlessly to hear his voice.

As Mickey fell, he trusted that he would hit the water, but a fleeting doubt in his mind had him wondering about worst-case scenarios. His toes touched, and he could feel the water engulf him as he slid into the deep water. As his head went under the water, he felt a sharp pain in his right wrist. When he came up, he realized why it hurt so much. He had missed the edge of the pool by only a foot, but it was close enough to clip his hand. As Mickey reached for the edge, he could hear a voice above him.

"Are you all right, man?"

Mickey reached for the edge. Something was wrong. Only his left hand could grip the edge; the right hand was numb. He gently pulled himself up to the edge, then yelled, "I'm okay, meet me at the door!"

By this time, Mags and Sanners had grown restless. Each car that passed was imagined to be a cop car or worse – it might be a parent who knew them. Finally, they heard a thump on the ground next to them. It was a pile of Mickey's clothes hitting the ground. Sanners made his way back down the ladder. "He's in and coming to the door, get ready!"

Before Sanners made it to the ground, the heavy metal back door creaked open. "Come on, guys, quick!" Mickey peered through the door.

For the next half hour, Mags, Sanners, and Danny were jubilant. The nearly pitch-black pool provided the most exciting adventure of their young lives. Mickey swam for the first fifteen minutes, then sat at the edge rubbing his wrist. The numbness was beginning to be replaced by swelling. At first, he was convinced it was just a bruise, but as the swelling continued, he knew something was wrong. His grip became weaker, and the pain was increasing at a steady pace.

Mags, Sanners, and Danny dove off the edges, chased each other, and reveled in their victory. They conquered the Big Plunge. Mickey sat on the edge and rubbed his wrist in hopes that the pain would go away. He was too hopeful and too proud to mention his injury, so he simply watched and laughed at their antics. It was a moment to be rejoiced.

When it was time to leave, the boys borrowed towels from the supply room, dried off, dressed, and snuck out the back door. As they flew down the block, the wind in their faces was fresh and spoke volumes about how great life really is. A new mission of excitement had been accomplished. Mags and Sanners took a side-by-side lead down the alley as they recounted the excitement of their adventure. Danny was two lengths back. As he glanced behind him, he noticed that Mickey was swerving trying to catch up. When he turned again to look back, Mickey was falling down on the gravel in the alley. The crash woke up a few dogs that started barking.

Mags and Sanners looked back in shock as they saw Danny racing toward their fallen companion. Something was wrong. Very wrong.

By the time Danny reached Mickey, he was sitting upright holding his wrist. His good wrist. His throwing wrist. The wrist that attached to the arm that held all of their baseball season dreams and hopes. Reality was beginning to set in for Mickey.

"What's wrong, buddy?" asked Danny.

"I think I messed up my wrist. When I jumped in the pool, I think I hit it on the edge." He looked up grimacing.

"Let me see." Danny looked at his worst nightmare. The wrist was blue and swollen. He held it gently as Mickey winced in pain. If this wrist was messed up, the entire St. Anthony's season was down the tubes. There was no replacement for a team's superstar. The seriousness of the situation sunk in when Mickey said, "I can't even grab my handlebars."

By this time the other two had pedaled up and stopped. Mickey explained the dilemma as all three stood in shock. This was the toughest human on earth. None of them had ever seen him injured before. This was new territory, a shocking development in what was supposed to be their greatest season ever.

As they rode back to Danny's house, the silence engulfed them. Each of the four boys were deep in thought and regretting the mission. A night of victory was spoiled.

By the time they reached Danny's house, they had decided that an explanation would be in order for Mr. and Mrs. Hannigan. Somehow, they had to explain the injury. After a short contemplation of the truth, other possible explanations arose: hit by a pitch in a practice game? *No, why would we be playing in the middle of the night.* Injured wrestling Sanners? *No, we hate to pin the blame on anyone.* Finally, Mags came up with the best explanation – *a dog ran in the way of his bike while delivering the route. He swerved to miss the dog, and he took a bad spill.* It seemed to be the best explanation. If you made up a story about screwing around or wrestling, it would seem irresponsible. A crash in the line of duty was certainly more respectable. But it would have to look good. After the morning deliveries, the front wheel would have to be jarred at an angle. With the loosening of a couple of bolts, it could look real. Reloosening and moving the wheel back in line could also repair the bike at a later time. The boys rehearsed the story – *a big brown dog? No, an evasive small black dog that could have been killed if he didn't swerve!* This made the scenario seem nobler, more in the line of duty.

The biggest worry was the swollen wrist. As soon as it was reported, Mrs. Hannigan would surely cart him off to the doctor's office.

25

Graduate Counseling Class

"THE GREATEST RISK we can take in life is to enter into a relationship with another human." Meg tried to make eye contact with her class of twenty graduate students. "This seemingly innocuous gesture can be as momentary as a dialogue with a store clerk or as momentous as a marriage. We hope, sometimes in vain, that we will not be rejected, and we create an expectation that this connection will be a worthy risk and will make us stronger and healthier."

Meg glanced around her classroom. The class was getting late. She had about fifteen minutes left in the class she taught for DSU. The benefit of being an adjunct professor was that it also allowed a practicing therapist to put things in perspective. For Megan, she could reflect on her practice and think out loud. She loved teaching group therapy, but sometimes grad students can be too cerebral. She also hated it when her grad students had their noses on their notepads for the entire class. Too much note taking and not enough listening. Sometimes to really hear something, you need to stop wondering whether this will be on the midterm and listen.

Meg repeated herself. "Now I want you to think about this for a minute. The very things we lose in life are the things we want people to gain in a good group experience. Listen to what I just said: the greatest risk we can take in life is to enter into a relationship with another human being." She paused, hoping they would all look up at her. When all the eyes were fixed on her, she continued, "This is *not* fulfilled with an obsession with another or by simply being obsessed with love, but by nurturing the formation a healthy dependency." She paused to let it sink in. "When we connect, we open our hearts and become more sensitive, more vulnerable. This can be frightening. As a result, if we can't get our needs met in a relationship, we defend the ego by compensating with excessive work, obsessions, drugs, or we may simply push them away.

"The other major problem is the trend in our culture to beat up the idea of dependency. All of these books out there talk about unhealthy dependency. We have codependency, dependent personality disorders, and overdependency, but what we are failing to recognize is that dependency is the very essence of the human experience. We, as humans work in packs, educate in packs, cooperate in packs, and organize ourselves in packs. In spite of our 'pack mentality' our culture screams out messages that insist you must not need others! Don't depend on others! And heaven forbid you should allow yourself to become weak by having significant others in your life. This is hogwash." At this point in her lecture she stopped and allowed the students to work in smaller groups to describe an example of dependency where the result was positive.

After regrouping the class she asked each student to briefly comment on what they had learned. After summarizing the student's comments she continued. The students became accustomed to Meg's fervor and sensed it in her body language. Whenever Meg became passionate in her lectures, her arms would move in front of her. The tone of her voice softened, and she put her hands over her heart. "We need others not just for our needs, but because we are human. A denial of our need for others results in psychopathology. The great author Leo Buscaglia often asked, 'How is it that we are surrounded by millions, yet we are all dying of loneliness?' The goal should not be to move away from dependency, but toward it. The goal should be to move from infantile helpless dependency to a mature helpful dependency." Meg wasn't much of a lecturer, but she often went on a tangent when it came to issues of the heart. She tried to pull the class into her thoughts. "Can somebody give me an example of how we lose this basic instinct of a healthy dependency?" She scanned the room. Those who didn't have an opinion kept their eyes fixed on their notepads.

A bright-eyed woman in her midtwenties spoke up, "Dr. Talden, I'm not sure, but could it be because our boundaries have been violated?"

"Excellent, give me an example."

"Like if a child is abused, then they may not learn how to trust others?" The uncertainty of the student was reflected in her answer phrased as a question.

"Good, any other examples?"

A man in his midforties raised his hand. "How about trauma?"

"Right, can you think of an example?"

The man thought for a minute. "My sister was in a car wreck once. She wasn't hurt, but it scared her to death. She became a nervous wreck, and it seemed like all she could do was push people away. She shut herself off from all of those who wanted to help her. She didn't know how to ask others for help."

Megan pulled a chair up in front of the room and sat down. Whenever a student offered something personal, Meg appreciated the risk. "I'm sure it must have been tough for her. Something like that can happen to any of us. We like to think of ourselves as strong, but we are fragile creatures. Sometimes when our personal reality is damaged, on some level, our brain is saying, 'This is not the way life is supposed to be,' and then we don't know how to ask others for what we need. Why do we do this?"

The man continued, "Could it be, Dr. Talden, that maybe we think we are smart enough to be able to figure it out on our own?"

"Excellent observation, I think you're right." She smiled at him. "Any other reasons?" The class seemed stumped; some were paging through their books and notes – *this wasn't in the textbook*. She waited through the silence. No one was ready to speak. "Sometimes" – Meg paused – "we just don't know. We just don't know. The mind so desperately wants to survive anything that is thrown its way." Meg's gestures reflected her empathy; she squinted, gazed upward, and gently held her two fists in front her. She inhaled deeply and continued, "But we just don't know why the pain is there. It's a mystery to us, and getting back to group, in group counseling our goal is to learn to trust again, throw down our guards, discover those mysteries, and go back to a safe and healthy dependency. Most importantly, if you run your groups right, you will create such an environment. And, my oh my, what a wonderful thing it is when it happens! Group can be the most gratifying experience you may ever have as a counselor. You get to witness true recovery in action, not just in thoughts or ideas." Her smile radiated warmth across the room.

Students never wondered if Dr. Talden was passionate about therapy. It was evident that she had felt those emotions.

"All right, we're about out of time. Don't forget that your papers on a group proposal are due next week. See you then."

As the class shuffled out, Megan's mind was on her groups. Like most other times, the flow of her groups were right on target. But her couples group had something going on that she couldn't understand. *I can't seem to put my finger on what's happening. The two guys have more to them than I'm seeing – but what?*

Her bike trip home would be spent in heavy thought.

26

August 4, 1968
St. Stephen's

MOST OF THE members of the St. Anthony's senior team sat in disbelief when Eggs informed them that Mickey would be out for next week and a half. Their chins went to their chests as they contemplated their destiny.

It wasn't a matter of a lack of confidence in the rest of the team, but it's hard to pump blood through the veins when the heart has been removed. Fortunately no bones were broken in the fall, but the wrist was badly bruised and had been strained. He might be able to throw for the final chapter of the season – the St. Augie's game.

The team had to create a new game plan for the St. Stephen's matchup. St. Stephen's was a scrappy team from the west side of Denver. They hadn't won the league in many years but regularly served the league as the spoiler. They could knock off the best of teams on a given day, and now Eggs informed Danny that he was the starting pitcher. For him, it was the biggest game of his life. He would have to keep the undefeated season intact. Mickey would sit and watch from the bench.

The tension built with each passing day. All of a sudden, the perfect summer of romance and victories had gone sour by dropping through the roof of the Big Plunge. Danny tried to focus each day to bring his wild pitching under control.

By the time the game rolled around, the easy-going week-to-week cockiness of the Falcons had drifted away. In order to have a shot at the title, the entire team would have to come together.

Nothing about the day seemed to go right. The clouds had been gathering since early morning. Danny, Mags, and Sanners thought of little else as they delivered their papers in the morning drizzle. Joe Hannigan helped Mickey load the car. For the next few days, he would deliver the papers from a vehicle instead of his bike. By midweek, he would probably be able to grip the handlebars.

The slight sprinkle of misty rain wouldn't be enough to cancel the game, but it was fully capable of casting a blanket of gloom on the Falcons. In the first inning, Danny's hyped mood resulted in a number of wild pitches. He loaded the bases early and walked in a run. The next batter popped up on a foul ball to Mags. Sanners then caught a line drive and doubled up the runner on first to end the inning.

Danny breathed a sigh of relief, and Eggs reassured him that all would be settled in the innings to come.

The crowd was exactly what the boys expected. They had had grown up knowing the St. Stephen's reputation – they had seen this group before. Win or lose, the St. Stephen's families from west Denver seemed to make a habit of a festival at the games. The beer at the picnics had a tendency to bring out hostility in some of the parents and relatives of the young players. These were working-class people. Some lived in housing projects, but most lived in modest low-income one-level housing. The rest of Denver may have had enough money to pay to see minor league ball games or go to a college sporting event, but not on the west side of Denver. This is community pride with community volume in their cheering for the boys.

Eggs warned his players to never respond to the other team when these things occur. He tried to educate them in how to keep their cool in all situations. He would tell them, "In tough situations, your energy gets drained by poor judgment."

Sanners had a three-year battle going with the biggest kid on their team, Wally Fontman. Wally pitched a tough inside game and had hit Sanners in each of the past two years. Since Sanners played third, it was difficult but not impossible to get his revenge. Last year, when Wally was trying to leg out a triple, Sanners tagged him with his entire upper body to flatten him. By the time Wally got up, the benches had cleared, but fortunately no one got into fisticuffs.

Danny led off the game as the first batter and quickly grounded out a ball to the pitcher's mound for the first out. Pelloman grounded out to the first baseman, and Sanners was up with two outs. Wally glared into his catcher with a smile, then proceeded to nail Sanners square in the back. It seemed like Eggs had jumped up and yelled to Sanners to get down to first base before the ball even hit him. It was as though Eggs knew it would happen. In his usual calm voice, he continued to manage without bringing attention to it.

The next two innings went scoreless, and St. Stephen's held on to their 1-0 lead. In the third inning, all hell broke loose. Danny walked the first batter, then tried to throw an inside pitch to Fontman. It drifted a little too far inside and careened off his elbow. Fontman was certain it was an intentional payback and took off for the mound. Fontman stood six inches taller and weighed thirty pounds more than Danny. He threw down his bat, then turned to stampede in a blaze of fury toward the pitcher's mound. The charging bull caused Danny to freeze – a state of uncertainty of how to handle this impending doom. As Fontman charged the mound, Danny stood paralyzed in his steps. He braced himself for the inevitable contact with the enraged rabid animal. He stiffened his fists as it seemed like the pursuit was in slow motion. Contact couldn't come quick enough. Danny muttered, "Shit," under his breath as he prepared to close his eyes for the beating. At the instant before contact, he saw Fontman rear back with a fist destined for the side of his head. Suddenly, a white flash blew in front of his eyes, and Fontman was gone. It was as though the hand of God had reached down and brushed a train off the tracks to make the danger go away.

Fontman's misfortune was his failure to realize he was steaming down the train tracks at the wrong time. Danny realized it wasn't God at all. It was Sanners. Sanners had charged from the third base side and delivered a linebacker's blow to the side of Fontman. His body lay limp, and his batting helmet rolled another ten feet beyond his crumpled body. It was as though someone had knocked Wally's head cleanly off his shoulders. Sanners stood over him with a finger pointing straight down in a warning for him to not move. His job was to protect his pitcher, and no one would do that job better than he.

Sanners stood for a moment in disbelief and wondered if he killed him. Wally wasn't moving. Danny turned away because he knew Eggs would be on Sanners in a New York minute. Things had to settle down quickly before they could become worse.

In what seemed like an eternity, Eggs finally got to Sanners. He turned him away and began to push him back to his position. Unfortunately, he didn't see Wally's uncle who had consumed five beers prior to the first inning and now saw it as his duty to coldcock Eggs. Eggs went down in a heap, and Wally's uncle and father proceeded to jump on Sanners. Within seconds, there was a mixture of ten grown men and fifteen players in a crowd at the mound. The umpire screamed at the top of his lungs and finally got everyone split up. The park police showed up and escorted three of Wally's relatives from the field.

Eggs was delirious as he wiped the blood from the corner of his lip. He regretted that he didn't see it coming. All of his years of experience as a player had taught him to have peripheral vision whenever a fight breaks out on the field. He was more concerned about Sanners and let his guard down for a second too long. Sanners was ejected from the game, and since he didn't have a parent to take him home, Eggs took a few minutes to sit with him on the bench and convince him to get on his bike and ride home. It would keep him safe from being an after-game target for the St. Stephen's crowd. The boys watched in silence as the large figure pedaled away on his bike through center field.

Danny was so overwhelmed with confusion that he couldn't regain his composure. He gave up four more runs while being jeered by the St. Stephen's crowd and bench. He didn't even make it through the inning.

The team watched in disbelief as their first perfect season drifted away in a 9-3 loss to an inferior team. Eggs's postgame speech commended the boys for keeping their cool despite being harassed by the crowd for the remainder of the game. He named the practice times for the week, then sent them on their way.

Even though the game was played five miles away, the boys decided to ride their bikes home instead of opting to have them thrown in the back of Joe Hannigan's truck. They had a duty to their teammate, and they knew where to find him.

Mickey steered his bike slowly with one hand as he rode behind Mags and Danny. All three were grieving inside, but none worse than Danny and Mickey, who personally blamed themselves for the loss. This was the first time all season that a postvictory meal or root beer was not in order.

As the boys approached Harvey Park, they could see on the other side of the pond where Sanners's bike leaned against a tree. The rain now poured harder, and it seemed to fit the mood of the day. They were about to meet up with the one person who took the loss harder than they did.

Sanners didn't look up when the bikes rolled up. He stared ahead and asked, "What was the final?"

Mags gulped then said, "We lost 9-3." They were the only words he muttered, not offering any details.

Mags, Mickey, and Danny were all thinking of the same thing. A deep fear loomed for Sanners's condition. Not a fear of him – but a fear for him. Did he really have a boiling point? Could he really go over the edge?

None of the boys mentioned what they saw, but it struck fear in their hearts. At eye level, the bark on the tree had been torn away in a patch the size of a Frisbee. It was covered with blood where the bark had been ripped from the trunk. Sanners's knuckles on both hands were missing several layers of skin and were both covered in blood. For the last hour and a half, he had punched the tree, and now he sat collapsed beneath it.

His hands shook, and the sight caused tears to run down the cheeks of Mags. He knew that his best buddy was hurting like he had never hurt before. As he left the ball field, he determined that he had left his team, coach, and friends down. He lost his cool trying to protect Danny. To the adults, it was just another example of the short-fused kid from the short-fused family.

The boys sat in silence for the next twenty minutes under the rainy drizzle. Mags preferred it that way; no one could see his tears. Mags was less affected by the loss of the game than the other three who were all personally holding themselves responsible. Mags hated to see Sanners in so much pain.

After the silence passed Mickey stood up quietly and spoke to no one in particular saying, "Let's go home." The other three followed.

On the way home from the game, Spikes was writhing in the front seat of Mr. Hannigan's truck. He had what Mr. Hannigan called the disease of the young – IBB or itty bitty bladder. Joe didn't mind; he would swing by Tom Dooley's Liquor Mart and let Spikes run in to use the bathroom. He knew the owner, Harvey Treston. Most people in the neighborhood knew him well. On this particular night, Harvey wasn't working, but the hired help knew Joe and let Spikes run into the bathroom before he exploded.

Louis Garrison wavered in the aisle. His head swam from another day of drinking. He looked around at the liquor bottles. A child and his father came in. The boy darted to the bathroom. This was the scene of his failed robbery years ago. The bastard Treston sent him up to the Canon City state pen years ago. He's not working tonight, but he will pay. One day he will pay. Garrison bought a pack of cigarettes and drove away.

The next morning turned from panic to glee for Mags. He finished his route close to the 6:30 deadline. For him, this was unusual. It also was the first time he had been beaten to the punch by the *Gazette* carrier who delivered the same route – Johnny Gonzales. On Sundays, the *Gazette* and the *Times* were both delivered in the morning. It infuriated Mags to see so many papers neatly delivered to each doorstep. Mags slept a little later than usual, and the thought made him feel irresponsible. There was another reason Mags was behind schedule on this Sunday morning. He concocted what he considered a brilliant idea. It came to him in the middle of his delivery. With every house that also had a *Gazette* delivered, he carefully placed the enemy's paper on a bush next to the door. *When my customers see my paper on the porch and his in the bush, it will make him look like an idiot!*

After a dozen misplaced papers, Mags was beginning to laugh out loud and recall the half-dozen times that Gonzales had beaten him up in junior high. Pretty soon he was giddy with excitement and gleefully pranced between doors trying to imagine Gonzales's face if he received a complaint for his errant deliveries. Gonzales had haunted Mags for years and made his life miserable. Mags was the lame duck – the easy kid to pick on in gym class. He never fought back. He was the perfect bully's target. Mags never resented anyone for it, but today was his day. Each carefully placed paper removed the pain of a punch to the face or a notebook thrown down a hallway or a push down the stairs. Each paper was a small victory.

Mags raced off to Buds to catch a morning donut and was excited to see the other three. Danny told Mickey the night before that he would get up early to help with his route. Mr. Hannigan offered to drive the two boys in the pickup truck because the Sunday papers were so heavy, and Mickey was operating with only one hand. They finished both routes in record time and had already polished off their donuts and juice.

Delivering from the back of a truck was cake and lifted their spirits in this time of need. Joe Hannigan seemed to sense they were feeling down from the night before.

The boys stared at Sanners hands. It was not a "mom" first-aid wrap. It was easy to see that Sanners had done it himself. Pads of tissue were covered with masking tape across the palm of the hands and his knuckles. Around the edges, the crusted blood peeked out. Sanners seemed to be in good spirits despite the loss. Somehow he found a way to get back on track and finish before his usual Sunday-morning time of seven.

Conversation picked up where it left off earlier in the week except that the game was not included. Box scores, movies, bikes, and girls were the topics of the morning.

Danny and Mickey left Bud's first, and Sanners turned to Mags shortly thereafter. "Sorry I let the team down yesterday." His eyes went down to the counter. He was certain he single-handedly cost them the season.

Mags consoled him, "Eggs said that if we win the last two, we will win the league. We would end up in a tie with St. Augie's. St. Stephen's has already lost a couple, and if we won the head-to-head contest with St. Augie's, we would win the league on a tiebreaker."

Sanners perked up, "Really?" His eyes leaped with hope.

"Ya, really, Eggs said we are not out of it yet, but he also said we have to win them one game at a time."

For the next few minutes, the two dreamed out loud about how it would feel to hold the league trophy. Mags nervously thought about how he would face Gonzales and what would happen if Gonzales found out about his paper switching. *Naw, not a prayer, nobody saw me.*

Mags stared blankly ahead when Sanners tapped him on the shoulder. "Hey, I want to give you something." He motioned with a wave for Mags to follow him outside.

When they reached his bike, Sanners unfolded his canvas bag wrapped around the handlebars. He pulled out a cigar box and handed it to Mags. "I know I upset you yesterday when I beat up the tree. Somehow though, when I saw you ride up, I didn't feel so all alone anymore. I wasn't sure if I would see you after the game, but seeing you made everything okay. I've just been meaning to give you these for a while for thanking you for being my buddy."

Mags opened the box to see about a hundred baseball cards. Many of them were cards that Mags had been trying to trade from Sanners for years. Sanners never treasured his cards the way Mags did. Mags's collection could practically beat out the Topps Baseball Card Company all by itself. Sanners held on to certain cards over the years just to keep a bargaining grip on Mags. It was as though the gesture was letting go of petty kid competitiveness and saying in one display of gratitude that *we are beyond all that now.*

Mags's jaw dropped; he couldn't believe his eyes. These were the best cards in Sanners's collection. He was speechless for the first time in his life. "Wow, Sanners how come . . ." his voice drifted away. He wasn't sure of what to make of it.

"I don't know, I guess I just got tired of them, you know . . . I guess you'll just owe me."

Mags rode his bike away and felt closer to Sanners than ever before. As he negotiated the last few blocks of his trip home, Mags couldn't wipe the smile off of his face. He was giddy to get home and catalog the cards in order with all of his others.

Suddenly the smile and all of the feelings in his heart were gone. Mags hit his breaks halfway down the block and instantly turned around and started pedaling the other way. Two other bike riders had been sitting in the middle of the street waiting between him and his home. It was Gonzales and another *Gazette* carrier whom Mags recognized.

The pursuit was on, and Mags realized he would not make it home before he was caught by his two hunters. Mags felt the sweat soaking his body as his legs furiously pounded the pedals. Alongside him on both sides swarmed the two bicyclists on their paper bikes.

"Hey, Mags!" screamed an angry Gonzales. His gritted teeth reminded Mags of an angry dog as he glanced to his left.

"Hey, Mags!" shouted the other carrier. "In a hurry?"

Mags glanced up and recognized the face of Rich Baker – another *Gazette* carrier and also another bully that hassled Mags in junior high. He seemed to attract most of them throughout his life until he and Sanners became close friends. After that, most of the bullies left him alone.

Gonzales cut him off, "I heard you were moving some papers this morning, Mags!" He veered his bike into him. Mags pumped his legs harder in vain to try to outrun the bigger and stronger enemy.

Every time Mags glanced up, Gonzales seemed taller, stronger, and more muscular than he remembered him at the close of the school year. It had been a confrontation that he hoped would go away when they reached high school, but he didn't expect to meet up with him this summer.

Mags tried to evade. He slammed on his breaks and turned sharply. The box of ball cards went flying out of the canvas bag and landed on the street. Mags immediately turned his bike around to retrieve them. As he jumped off his bike and bent over, a set of laces from a pair of gym shoes connected with his nose causing Mags to fly on to his back. Gonzales connected with a cheap shot kick as his bike flew by. Gonzales then spotted what Mags was trying to reach and rode toward the cards spread on the asphalt. With perfect timing, he hit the brakes on his bicycle as the rear wheel rode over the cards. Mags nervously shook as he saw the cards being ground into the street. "Aww, look at that, did I mess up some of Maggie Faggie's pretty baseball cards?"

Gonzales's partner did the same and joined in the taunting as they rode circles around a frightened Mags in the middle of the street. He was praying that Sanners would come around the corner and send these guys into orbit. *No such luck.* He watched as his eyes welled with every card that was being destroyed. These were special gifts being ground helplessly into the asphalt.

Finally, Gonzales headed for the cigar box itself and slammed on his break as it glided over the box. The result was a loss of control that sent the back of his bike careening toward the street. Gonzales slid two body lengths on his side before he was able to stop. He got up and looked at the side of his jeans. Fire seemed to come out both sides of his eyes. He stomped toward Mags. "Look at what your cards did to my jeans! You fat little son of a bitch, you're going to pay now."

Mags tried to move from his butt to his knees. As he stood up, Gonzales's fist sent him reeling back to the ground. He followed it with another kick to the head. As he continued to flail on Mags, he spoke between his relentless punches and kicks. "If I – ever – hear – of – you – touching – my – papers – again – so help me – fat boy – I'll kill you." He took one last swing, then pulled at his own pant leg to check for bleeding. "By the way, fat boy, I heard you lost to St. Stephen's. It's just as well. St. Anthony's will never take St. Augie's. You're just a bunch of sorry-ass losers, and we are looking forward to kicking your asses."

Gonzales got back on his bike and laughed. Mags could hear the two of them laugh as he tried desperately to pick his cards up off the street. With tears streaming down his face, he carefully picked up the ruined cards and gently placed them in the broken cigar box. About a third of them were torn and ground. These were cards that he had his eyes on for years, and now they were embarrassing garbage. All he could think of was how he could hide them from Sanners. Sanners must never know. He would commit murder.

27

Session 5

FOLLOWING THE GROUP session, Terrence went back to his room. He still had to mop the cafeteria that night. It would only take about an hour, but at this time he felt a desperate need for reflection and time alone. He threw himself facedown on the bed. After each group session, he needed to wind down. Each session seemed to take more energy out of him. He wasn't sure whether he wanted to invite the group to go to the places where his demons lived. Terrence knew that everyone had demons, but *once you rile them up, can they ever be put to rest? Was this the place where I want to bring them to life? What would the payoff be? More pain? Less pain? Are my problems any worse than anyone else's, or am I just too weak to confront them?* He wanted to take a fifteen-minute nap to reenergize. It wasn't going to happen. He headed for the cafeteria.

Daniel came through the door. "What are you girls still doing up?"

"Wrestle with us, Daddy!" screamed Sarah. She and Christina each attacked one of his legs.

"Oh no!" he yelled. "I'm helpless, the evil swamp monsters have my legs! For the love of Captain Crunch, will somebody please help me! Oh no, I'm melting into the quick sand!" He fell over in the living room. "Oh no, they're dragging me down!" He fell limp to the carpet, and the girls jumped on his back. His muffled voice moaned, "But wait, when the giant man was sucked into the swamp" – Daniel jumped to his feet and began screaming in an animated voice – "he then became the biggest and meanest monster in the swamp. He could only survive by eating the little swamp monsters!" He stood up, raised his hands over his head, and roared, "Awwww!" The girls screamed and ran toward their bedrooms.

"No more eating swamp monsters until they brush their teeth," said Monica as she came around the corner. Behind her followed Grammy Pats, the grandmother who set the standard for all other grandmothers. She had just returned with girls from a trip to Circus Playland, the mall, and a burger-and-fries dinner.

"Hi, Mom," said Daniel, "did you spoil my girls again?" He laughed, hugged her, and planted a kiss on her cheek.

"It's a grandmother's job to spoil her grandkids!"

"Of course, then just walk away and leave us in the aftermath!" Daniel had always appreciated Pats but even more now that he had his own children. In his mind, Pats was perhaps the most selfless mother who ever walked the face of the earth. She now had the chance to do it again, but with the grandkids she had a lot more time for herself. Two years after Daniel and Aaron left home, Pats fell in love with a man who shared her sense of humor, and a year later they married. Daniel cried at her wedding when he realized how selfless she had been for all the years she had raised the two boys. Now, after thirty years together, Pats and Paul were two peas in a pod.

"How is Paul?"

"He's great, and he's looking forward to taking Marcus and the girls camping this weekend. But hey, I better be on my way, he's cooking me dinner tonight. My favorite – burritos."

Daniel helped her with her coat, then hugged her, and kissed her good-bye. "Love you, Grammy Pats." Daniel turned to yell down the hallway. "Girls? Come here and thank Grammy Pats for taking you out today!"

The girls sprinted down the hallway and flew into her arms. They squeezed her and hugged both of her cheeks. "Thanks, Grammy Pats!"

As Pats stepped out the door, Daniel turned around and threw his arms straight in the air. "Ahhh!" He began to stomp down the hall in a Frankenstein-like trance. "There is only one safe place on earth! This is in the tower of the bunk beds! If the little swamp monsters are not in the tower in five minutes, they will be eaten alive!" The girls screamed and slammed the bathroom door shut behind them.

"How was group tonight?" Monica walked to Daniel and kissed him.

"About like before, Terrence keeps telling me that it's doing him some good, but it surely isn't because of me. I still feel like I'm not offering him a lot of support, but then again, he doesn't seem to have many others in his life right now."

"Do you know why he chose you?" Monica was asking a moot question. She knew the answer

"Ya, I do," he said matter-of-factly. Daniel sat down in his recliner. He was out of words. He and Monica had talked about each of the sessions. He was faithful to the confidentiality of the group. He told her there were five couples but was careful not to describe them or mention names. Mostly he talked about himself and Terrence. On occasions, Monica noticed that Danny would be talking about Terrence and accidentally call him by his boyhood nickname, Mickey. He hadn't used his nickname for years. Monica was curious about the details but never pushed him. She wondered with him about the final outcome of the group counseling. The whole story of Terrence made both of them sad.

"I talked to Maggie this week. She wants to go to lunch next week." Since the group began, Terrence's wife started calling Monica about once a week. Years earlier, the couples would see each other at least twice a year for a barbecue or a night out but the get-togethers slowly evaporated over the past decade as Terrence made excuses and isolated himself from others. Monica missed them.

Daniel looked up. "How is Maggie? I know Terrence has been talking to her since they separated. He mentioned her last week but didn't say they had any plans. I know that she and Jessica visited him a few times. He really lights up when he talks about her."

"Maggie seems okay considering all things. I hope they can get back together. Has he said anything?"

"Only once, I think he believes he doesn't have his act together well enough to be a good father or husband again. I hope it works out okay."

They sat for a moment of silence as the girls came out of the bathroom. Daniel let out a roar, and they ran off to their bedroom shrieking along the way. Monica stood up. "I'll tuck them in, but of course they'll want a visit from the big swamp monster." She smiled and walked down the hall.

Daniel sat quietly and thought about the past year. When Maggie and Terrence separated, they both agreed it was for the best. Terrence's life was falling apart, and the drinking was reaching a level of uncertainty and distress for all those around him.

Daniel stood up and glanced out the window. Marcus was engaged in a game of wiffle ball with the neighbor's kids. The sun was nearly down, and it was becoming difficult to see. They played in the shadows of the halogen lights hanging above their garage. He turned around and walked to the girls' bedroom. The girls giggled with affection as he gave them a snarl and a kiss good night.

Daniel went back to his recliner and picked up a spiral notebook and a pen. He sighed and fingered his pen. The tone of his journal writing mirrored his suspiciousness of the group and its leader. He continued to believe that sooner or later, it would no longer be confidential, so he continued to address each journal entry with those sentiments.

Personal Journal 5

Dear Dr. Meg, I'm running out of things to say. Where are we going with all of this stuff? What conclusions are we reaching? I know we've all got goals that we are supposed to be working toward, but what's the bottom line when this is all over? Are we all just going to bring up miserable issues that will remind us of the troubles we have? What then? Well, I did finally share tonight. I guess I'm proud of that. It was weird to talk about my brother, the alcoholic – those are some odd thoughts I have. I also remember my mother consoling him when he went through therapy. None of that had done him any good. I think he was born to be an alcoholic. Some who have these problems were not born that way. I think of Terrence. No one in our group will ever know how much he was filled with life at one time. This guy was and still is special, but maybe all that "special" has been silenced. I know why, it's just that I don't know how to help. Anyway, I hope you were proud of me today. D.

28

August 11, 1968
Rebound

THE TEAM WAS scheduled to practice on Monday, but Mags didn't show. He also wasn't at Bud's on Monday morning. After practice Mickey, Danny, and Sanners went to his house.

Mags confessed the entire story to his parents but was afraid to tell his friends. It was sad, embarrassing, hurtful, and he felt like a loser. Worst of all, he looked like one. His upper and lower lips had been split. His left eye was blackened, and his right cheek was purple and still swollen.

Mags told his father only on the condition that he would agree to not call the police. Mr. Magliano reluctantly agreed to the terms, and Thomas told him of the last two years of harassment at school. Mr. Magliano was shocked but kept his promise. He then made Thomas agree that the next assault would result in the intervention of authority. Mags pleaded with his father to understand that this was a problem that he had to deal with, and no one else could solve it for him.

When the boys arrived at his house after practice, they stood in disbelief as they looked at his face.

The rage began to boil in Sanners. He knew someone was guilty, and someone would have to pay. Mags made them promise the same thing his father did, that they would not intervene. When he finished his story, Sanners tore out the door. "I don't give a shit what I promised. I'm taking Gonzales's head off."

Mickey and Danny chased him out to the yard and tackled him. Sanners had the strength of three men and wriggled free, throwing them in opposite directions. Mickey tackled him again, and Danny followed. It wasn't until Mags jumped on his legs that they finally subdued him.

"You promised!" screamed Mags in a half-panicked voice. He knew that Sanners would not stop until he found Gonzales and personally murdered him. The boys held him down for another ten minutes with all of their strength.

"Cool it, everyone!" screamed Mickey. "We have to be smarter than those guys. If we go pick a fight, our season is over. If we go mess with him, we end our chances for a league title. We've got to do this right!"

Sanners finally stopped struggling. He wanted a league title as bad as anyone. He, like the other three, had never won a championship in anything. This year could still be special. "Okay!" he screamed. "I'll kill his ass after the game! That son of a bitch is dead."

"No, you promised, and you can't," said Danny.

"Then I'll steal every one of his goddamn papers next Sunday and throw them in the Platte River myself. I'll fix him good."

Danny and Mickey laughed at the thought. When they finally realized that Sanners was no longer a threat to humanity, they sat in Mags's front yard. The boys had a restless feeling in their hearts, and each had different emotional reactions to the crisis. Mags felt defeated. Mickey was deep in thought with possible solutions. Beating them for the league title was enough for him but maybe not enough for the crew. Danny had dreams of a 20-0 shutout. Sanners stewed in thoughts of revenge, it was impossible for him to be rational, and he could only react.

For the rest of the week, the boys immersed themselves in the heart of the summer. Lisa and Jean were never told about what caused Mags's injuries. He begged the boys to keep it private. He wanted to take care of it in his own way. The boys followed Eggs's advice and focused exclusively on the upcoming St. Paul's game. It inherited the title of the "rebound game." Eggs reminded them that tough circumstances not only builds character, it reveals it as well. He told the team that this game, more than any other game this year, would reveal the character of their team.

After the Tuesday-morning routes were completed, Mickey walked into Bud's after the other three and sat down. The boys were sensitive to each other's emotions, and as the summer grew, they became closer and more aware of each daily mood.

Mickey seemed businesslike and quiet. He smiled at Bud and ordered the usual; but the mood was direct, fixed, and obviously preoccupied. Mags and Sanners discussed the August standings in the majors. McClain and Gibson were each pitching storms in their leagues, and the arguments revolved around whether it was more important to have a pitcher with more wins or a lower earned-run average. Mags and Sanners also began to argue over a new song on the radio titled "Classical Gas." They had also heard it on the *Smothers Brothers Show*. Sanners contended that it wasn't really a song because it had no words. Mags argued that you didn't need words in a song for a song to be a song. Sanners believed you could call it a musical piece but not a song because it was only musical.

The conversation eventually went to Danny who was interrogated by the group to fill them in on his love life with Jean. He continued to float through heaven. The summer had its bumps, bruises, and disappointments; but overall it could be the greatest ever for him because of love, true love.

Mickey sat silently and listened but contributed very little. He scratched notes on a napkin. "Boys, what's happening this morning? Can we meet? This is important."

The guys stopped and stared. When Mickey said it was important – it was very important. Something's up. Something big, and it needed attention. Private attention. The boys all agreed to meet in the privacy of Mags's basement in one hour. It gave them enough time to take care of morning chores.

Mickey was the last one down the stairs. He had a rolled-up piece of paper in his hand. "I've got a plan, but I need some brilliant minds to help me pull it off." The other three immediately sat up. Hearts started pounding. Danny nervously was thinking, *Another Big Plunge?* Questions started rolling around in Mags's head, *Skinny-dipping? Girls? A ball game?* Sanners smiled. *Beat the hell out of Gonzales? I'd be happy to.*

Mickey had the look of an officer in the barracks in the movie *The Great Escape*. He had "serious scheme" written all over his face, but the other three had no idea what he was up to. His demeanor, intensity, and wisdom commanded their attention. If he were in uniform, he would've looked like a four-star general setting up a D-day invasion.

"We're going to pull off the greatest heist in the history of the *Times*. We're going to screw the *Gazette* carriers like they've never been screwed before. We're going to throw the whole system into disarray, and no one is going to know better." He stole the "disarray" line from the movie *The Great Escape*. "For one Sunday, everyone in southwest Denver who subscribes to the *Gazette* will be angry and upset, and it will all be because of us. We, my friends, are going to steal all of their papers."

None of the boys knew where this plot came from. Mickey lay in his bed for the past two nights pondering whether some things were better left alone or whether some form of retribution, justice, or fairness needed to be exacted. Gonzales had tortured Mags for years, but that was only part of it. They had a deep-rooted hatred for the *Gazette*. There were also three carriers who played on the St. Augie's team. In every way, these guys needed to be dealt with. In other ways, it was a matter of Gonzales having to take the brunt of the revenge in the name of the *Gazette*.

For a moment, the boys sat in stunned silence, and each of them went to their instinctual reaction. Danny felt safe under Mickey's direction; he was naturally a follower. Mags wondered, *What will my parents think? What if we get caught?* Sanners grinned. His only desire in life at this time was to make Gonzales suffer – his time had come. He wanted all of the *Gazette* carriers to suffer.

Mickey unrolled three carefully prepared sheets of paper. One was a map, another a list, and the third was a list of times and dates. "Gentlemen, as you know, the *Gazette* carriers all meet here at the 1210 Raritan house for their drop-offs each day." They all nodded. It was common knowledge that the *Times* and the *Gazette* operations for paper distribution were different. *Times* paper bundles were dropped off at each carrier's home. *Gazette* carriers had to report to a drop-off garage of a district manager where the boys would meet, fold their papers, and go on their routes.

"On weekdays, the papers are dropped off at about three in the afternoon. Every Sunday, the papers are dropped off here" – he pointed to the sheet – "between 3:00 and 4:00 a.m. The *Gazette* carriers never show up before 5:00 when they start folding. Our papers don't come around until 5:00. This gives them the jump on us every Sunday. This is why they can get up early and porch most of theirs long before we get there." All three nodded; it was disheartening to deliver your papers on Sunday mornings only to see the enemy had arrived before you had. Resentment for this inferior paper was overwhelming.

"We can locate ourselves in the alley here." He pointed to the map. "Then heist the papers shortly after they are delivered. Each of us will have a mission to dispose of at least four bundles of newspapers. We will have to split up. If we are ever caught, we must remain silent."

The guys were beginning to feel like the destiny of the free world rested on their shoulders. This was by far the most important mission of their lives.

Mickey went through each of the details. They were familiar with the *Gazette* operation. They had slept out in their sleeping bags last year and rode their bikes in the wee hours of the morning to spy on the delivery of the early-morning *Gazette* paper bundles being dropped off. They had seen the delivery truck come though in the early hours of the morning. Last year, Sanners wanted to insert firecrackers in the bundles to blow them up or start them on fire. They never followed his suggestions.

Mickey seemed to have most of the details worked out. They would need to sleep out this Saturday night after the St. Paul's game and time the delivery of the truck; they would need to take a dry run. Questions had to be answered: *Could they get away? Would they have enough time? How many bundles could be stolen?*

As the boys discussed the plan, it seemed to be more of a perfect idea each time they heard it. The conditions included swearing to secrecy. For the rest of their lives, they could never tell anyone, not even their parents or Lisa and Jean.

As the week passed, the secrets of the universe were falling back into place. A summer that started so perfect had gone foul in the blink of an eye. Somehow, magically, it was being pieced back together. Danny was still in love, and friends were still loyal. The last real summer of freedom, baseball, and duty were coming together for a chance at a league championship. With each practice, Eggs had them believing they were thoroughbreds with the Kentucky Derby ahead of them. No mercy on

St. Paul's this week. Everyone would play their best; this would be their momentum going into St. Augie's.

It was also common knowledge that there was a social history between St. Augie's and St. Anthony's. Father Abercrombie was the long-standing and respected priest from St. Anthony's. It was no secret he loved baseball. He would attend games that went from ages six through the older boys. He would buy kids root beers after the games; he would make bets with priests from other parishes. The most familiar rivalry had been an ongoing bet with the parish priest from St. Augustine – Father DiPaulo. Father DiPaulo was a student at the Saint Christopher Seminary several years ago when Father Abercrombie taught courses there. The mentor relationship developed into a long-standing but light-hearted competition. It was much less serious than the attitude the two teams of boys had cultivated. Father Abercrombie was in his late sixties and contemplating retirement while Father DiPaulo was in the prime of his midthirties.

Father Abercrombie always told his parish that the good Lord was saving up one big task for the wager with Father DiPaulo. Unfortunately, Father Abercrombie had to fulfill his end of the bargain for the past four years. The senior boys' teams were the focus of the bets, and St. Anthony's didn't have it in them to beat the tradition of the St. Augie's team. Last year, he painted the picket fence in front of St. Augie's as the Falcons lost 5-4. The year before, it had to stain the doors of the church, and the year before that, he had to fix the broken kneelers on the old pews in the choir loft.

The good-hearted bets between the two always seemed to make their way into each priests' sermons the week of the game as the senior boys' teams got ready for the showdown. The two priests also arranged this game on a Sunday afternoon; and parents would use the event to line up fundraisers, pie sales, and a grand-scale picnic.

Father Abercrombie had the same wish list for the last three years. He wanted the bell tower in front of St. Anthony's to be painted, and he wanted to see the young Father DiPaulo on a scaffold up there painting it. He insisted that the good Lord wouldn't let an old priest climb that high, and as soon as the tower was ready for a painting, a young priest would be up there doing it. Some of the parishioners offered to help. The paint had been peeling for three years, but Father Abercrombie was patient. "It's in the Lord's hands," he would chuckle.

These little additions were meant for lighthearted fun, but to the boys, it only added to the pressure. The showdown was becoming bigger than life this year.

Throughout the week, Danny's focus went between the three most important things in his life: Jean, pitching, and the plot. The order of importance seemed to go back and forth. By Saturday, they were ready for two of their tasks, the St. Paul's game and the heist. What they weren't ready for was harassment at the game.

The St. Augie's team won their second-to-the last game of the season by dusting off St. Stephen's 6-0. This gave them momentum. They were undefeated. Since St. Anthony lost to the same team a week ago, it only seemed logical that they would do the same to them. As Mags, Sanners, Mickey, and Danny warmed up for the game, they noticed four bicycles making their way to an area behind the backstop to blend in with other spectators. Immediately, Mags felt shivers move up his spine as he noticed that one of them was Gonzales. His nervousness resulted in errant throws and misplaced swings of the bat during warm-ups. The mere presence of this entity created fear in his heart. By the second inning, the jeers were coming in waves.

"Hey, Fagliano! Why are your lips so big? Been kissing your ball cards?" Mags tried not to glance in his direction. He didn't want to look at them. In between each of the comments, the other boys would laugh. Mags's swings at the bat resembled his mood. He swung in haste at three straight pitches, then had to listen to their comments as he ran back to the dugout.

By now, Mags, Mickey, Danny, and Sanners exchanged whispers regarding the hecklers. They fingered three of the four boys. Along with Gonzales was Rich Baker, his accomplice in Mags's beating. A third person was St. Augie's premier and most feared player, Chet Anderson. Anderson was nearly the size of Sanners but had the coordination of a guy like Mickey. Anderson was the heart of the St. Augie's team; he pitched to perfection and slammed homers on a regular basis. Unlike the other boys, he seemed quiet and did not join in the razzing of Mags and the St. Anthony's team.

After the third inning, the coaches from the two teams met with the umpire behind home plate. A few minutes later, the umpire approached the four boys. "Gentleman, I know your coach from St. Augie's, Tom Parker. He's a good man, and he wouldn't approve of your behavior today. I'm going to tell you right now that you are going to either leave the field or keep your mouths shut for the rest of the game and watch it like everybody else." He drew his hands up and placed them on his hips. He stared down at the four boys, waiting for a reply. They sat in silence. Despite their oppositional dispositions, they held a certain amount of reverence in the presence of an umpire.

"Hey, it's a free country, we can say what we want," said Gonzales with a smile.

The umpire removed his mask and bent down closer to Gonzales's face. The other three boys' eyes grew large as they felt compelled to avoid eye contact and take a sudden interest in their shoelaces. Their cockiness was now dissolving. They noticed the face of the umpire turn to a glare with a clenched jaw. "This is a free country. But you're not free on this field. Not on my field, boy. You're gone." The umpire pointed to the other side of the park without looking in that direction. "You get your cocky smart mouth off my field now, or I'll personally remove your ass right now."

"Ya, right," Gonzales said. He stood up slowly and threw a leg over his bike. When he got a safe distance away, he glanced over his shoulder as he pedaled. "Yes, sir! Mr. Umpire, sir! I will remove my ass from your field right now, sir!"

The umpire turned to the other three. "Open your mouths boys, and you can join him." The other three stared down, feeling embarrassed to be a part of the charade.

The umpire walked back to the game and resumed play. An inning later, the other three boys quietly rode away but not before Mags had struck out again out of sheer nervousness. Sanners lost his focus too. He was seething and muttering beneath his breath. His nervous legs paced the dugout like a caged tiger. He continued to walk back and forth while glancing at his potential prey. Mickey kept close proximity in case he needed to pounce on Sanners if he took off. Mickey knew full well that he stood a better chance of stopping a cannon ball with his body than he did of stopping Sanners if the powder keg went off.

When the three rode away, the entire team cooled down. Sanners continued to boil over. Images of Gonzales hitting Mags kept running through his mind. When he stepped to the plate in the fourth inning, the Falcons were leading 4-1. With two out and men on second and third, Sanners swung as hard as he could on the first three pitches thrown to him. It was as though he wanted to hit the ball in the way he would like to hit Gonzales. The first two swings were in vain; the third sent the ball into the deepest part of center field.

In DCYBA competition, a player never gets the chance to admire their home runs like the major leaguers. Since there are no outfield fences, a guy has to run as hard as he can no matter how far he hits it. By the time the center fielder reached the ball, Sanners was already on third. At that point, he glanced over his shoulder to see the hapless fielder was still running in vain in the opposite direction. The hasty fielder's job would be to chase it down and throw it in as fast as he could. Perhaps in an effort to save some pride, perhaps just to get rid of it and take the attention away from him. A dreaded task for any losing team.

Sanners still had Gonzales on his mind until he looked up to see the crowd of his teammates waiting just past home plate. At that point, he realized that his feat had permanently altered the game. He coasted in and sat on the bench. Taking in all of the pats on the head, back and shoulders, he finally smiled and enjoyed the moment.

The Falcons cruised to a 9-1 win behind Danny's pitching. He gave up five walks and five hits but always seemed to get out of trouble behind good fielding. He was anxious to get Mickey back on the mound so he could return to center field for the last game of the season. Danny became more relaxed as the team scored more runs as the game wore on. His greatest fear was a close game, where attention goes to the pitcher. Fortunately, he never had to face this fear.

"Did you see the look on that centerfielder's head when that ball sailed over his head?" Mags's body jiggled as he opened his eyes wide in a mock impression of the St. Paul's centerfielder. The boys sat at the counter of Hots and Suds, reveling in their victory.

Mickey leaned in, then raised his root beer in a toastlike gesture. "That, my friends, was a true spanking, and that ball was the whack of the paddle that hurt the most." The boys laughed at his analogy.

"I think it would have left Yankee Stadium!" added Danny. He sat at the counter shaking his head. They all shared the wonder to behold, the miracle, and the unsurpassed beauty of watching the simple contact of a ball on a bat. They had all played other sports, but they knew that no other sport or event instantly captures a moment like baseball. In football or basketball, the excitement is great, but you always have to wait for the referee's call or a penalty flag to see if the event would stand. This always leaves a slight tarnish to even the greatest of feats. In baseball, the thundering crack of a bat causes an instantaneous emotion. Recalling the event causes one to sit and shake their head. This was the reason the game is perfect in the boys' minds.

The boys often discussed the rarity of home runs, the frequency of failure, and the challenges to one's pride in this sport. For these reasons, they often proclaimed it to be unarguably – the greatest sport on the face of the earth. The best hitters aren't even close to a 50 percent success rate, which means one has to focus more on team than individual successes. But when those individual successes do occur, they are bigger than life itself.

After the game, Eggs sat them down and scanned the excited faces of the boys. Some were still shaking hands.

"Gentleman, a good victory." He paused to make eye contact with every member of the team. He then nodded and continued, "And as you know, our season is almost over. We have one game, and we all know what we are in for." He placed his hands on his hips and smiled. He knew what the boys had been talking about all week, and he decided to address those issues.

"I want to mention a couple of things, and after today I won't mention them again, and in a minute I will tell you why. First, we know that if we win, it's for the league championship, and St. Anthony has never won a league title." The boys suddenly fell silent. Most of them stopped, and a few had shivers run up their spines. A couple of others drew in a deep breath and stopped fidgeting.

"Second, it will be the biggest crowd of the year, thanks to Father Abercrombie and Father DiPaulo, who seem to let everyone know about their running bet. And third, St. Augie's is by far the best team we will play all year. We are in for a game with a lot at stake and a lot of distractions. But let me ask you guys a few questions. When Roger Maris stepped to the plate in the last game of the 1961 season, what was he thinking about?" Eggs smiled. The boys didn't have an answer, as though maybe it was a trick question.

"Sanners, what do you think?"

"Out of the park, out of the park, he was thinking – smash it!"

"Joey, what do you think?"

Joe Pelloman scrunched his eyes for a moment, then answered, "I think he was thinking about Babe Ruth and the record of sixty home runs."

Eggs looked at the team. Not unlike a classroom, those who weren't sure if they had the right answer avoided making eye contact. Mags was one of them. "Mags?"

"Umm . . . I don't know, like maybe he was thinking, I hope I don't screw up?"

"Actually, gentlemen, I don't believe he thought any of those things. As a matter of fact, I believe if he was thinking about any of those things, he would have failed.

What's the most important thing he needed to think about when he was standing at the plate?"

Mickey began to see where Eggs was going with this. He nodded and calmly spoke. "The next pitch."

Eggs pointed to Mickey. "Right! Now somebody tell me why."

Some of the boys remembered a speech Eggs gave earlier in the season. Tom spoke up, "Because if you think about all those other things, you can't concentrate on your job."

Eggs affirmed him loudly, "Right, Tommy! So tell me, guys, what was his job at that moment?"

Four or five voices seemed to find a chorus at the same time as though it became an "*ah-ha!*" experience for the group. "His job was to hit the ball!"

"Right, guys, the answer is the same for all of those questions about great moments in baseball. What was Sandy Koufax thinking about when he threw the last pitch of his fourth no-hitter? What was Bill Mazeroski thinking when he hit a homer to win the World Series in '60? What was Don Larsen thinking on the last pitch of his perfect game in '56? What was Ted Williams thinking when he hit a homer in his last at-bat of his career? The answer is the same. They were all thinking about their job – the task at hand. They were thinking about pitches, strike zones, connecting with the bat, throwing the ball. The reason why they can concentrate is because they are focused on their job, not the reward, not what happened before or after. They were only thinking about what they needed to do at that moment. As long as you think about your job, you will have a great chance of succeeding. It's the mark of great ballplayers. Great ballplayers are never bothered by two annoying little nuisances: the fear of failure and the fear embarrassment."

The boys all nodded, understanding why this was so clear to Eggs. Some could see Eggs standing at the plate when he played in the minors with a huge crowd at One-Mile Park. As the boys nodded, they were affirming the wisdom of the sage. The man had been there.

"Now, boys, I told you that I would only mention the situation once." He overly emphasized "situation" as he spoke. "The situation may have many distractions, but you are good players, and good players play the same in all situations. We will *only* focus on the job this week. Each of you has a part of a team job. It might be throwing, swinging a bat, catching, running, or even cheering on your teammates. These are the things we will focus on. All right, let's bring it here!" he said with a snap. The boys all stood up and put their hands on a pile in the middle. "Falcons! On three . . . one, two, three!"

The boys all shouted in unison. "Falcons!" Eggs's smile grew wide. He knew they would all be nervous as hell, fearful as hell, and intimidated by the big game. This was the most enjoyable part of it all, and he knew it.

"I think we are going to whip St. Augie's this week, and I'm going to enjoy every damn minute of it," said Danny. He was starting to get cocky now that he knew that Mickey would be back on the mound. The pressure was thrown back on his shoulders, and 100 percent of the members of the team would rather have it on his shoulders than anyone else's.

Mags slurped his straw as he tried to inhale remnants from what was left of his shake. "Gads, I can't wait to hold that trophy, I'm gonna – "

Mickey cut him off, "Remember what Coach Eggs said, don't think about the prize, only your job."

Mags nodded and reached for another fry.

Mickey looked from side to side then grinned. "Speaking of jobs, my friends, we still have one job to do. Is everyone ready?" All three responded with a nod.

29

Nightmares

TERRENCE STOOD HIS ground. "Make it be me, NOW! Make it be me! *I'm* the one who deserves this. NOW!" The bullet exploded into his chest. His body crumpled to the floor. It burned, but it didn't really hurt. Lying on his side, he yelled, "Run! Get out of here, you'll be safe."

The small child looked over at him and said, "But Mickey – "

"Go now!"

The little boy ran out the door.

Terrence awoke from his dream and rolled over in his bed. He looked at the clock to see the red glow of 3:30 a.m. He reached up and turned on the lamp next to his bed. He sighed, picked up his paperback novel from the nightstand, and began to read. It was a lesson in futility to try to sleep again tonight. Whenever he awoke from his dreams, it took him a good hour to get back to sleep. *This is becoming a habit. There's no symbolism left to explain in these dreams, only pain.*

"I saw some good counseling today." Shaw glanced at the six students he supervised in his practicum in counseling class. "But again, our instinct is to jump from *A* to *Z*. You've learned all this great stuff in your program, and I can't blame you for wanting to jump to conclusions and answers for your clients, but take your time. They don't need a room filled with theoretical concepts. They need a person, focus on being there for your clients." His students looked drained. By the end of the week, they had seen a number of clients in sessions, and he knew that could take a toll, especially for rookie counselors.

Practicum had a tendency to be one of the most stressful courses for graduate counseling students. At DSU, they had to take the course toward the end of their program. They would see clients in sessions behind two-way mirrors. By this time, they had heard all of the horror stories about past students having to take practicum over. Counseling someone is stressful enough as part of a graduate program, but to be watched through a two-way mirror and have your sessions videotaped was another story.

"There are some parallels between your lives and your client's lives right now. When we are educating ourselves, we are in critical times of growth. If we come across as too aloof, then we never relate. If we intimidate our clients, we may crush their spirits. Just be yourself – a good person first. Everything else will fall into place." Shaw's biggest concerns were the compulsive students who were too concerned with the A grade and less concerned with the well-being of their clients.

"Make it your goal to touch your clients each week. Not physically, but emotionally. Empathize with them. This is a scary place to be. These aren't objects for manipulation. These are people with deep lives – filled with fears, emotions, uncertainties, compassion, and love. Right now we live in a frightening world that lacks trust. The Internet is a great example. It's a great place to exchange information. Some people feel better by knowing that someone else experiences life the same way they do, but it can't replace touch.

"Let me give you something to think about. Then let's call it a week. Any of you ever had pets? How would they respond if all we could give them was a voice over a speaker? They may wag their tail when they hear you or even bark, but now think of the difference when you are *really* there. When you pet them, roll up next to them, or hold them. They come to life! They know you are really there for them. When I get close to my friends, I happen to purr." Some of the students laughed. "What I'm saying is don't be afraid to be there for them." Shaw glanced at his watch. "Write your case notes now if you haven't already. Otherwise, onward, young counselors, until we meet again!"

Shaw tried to live his life as a professor in the same way he wanted his students to counsel. *Be gentle. These are real people.* Shaw had struggled early in his career as a counselor. He had dealt with pompous professors, clinicians, and supervisors. His main goal was to have his students become caring people – the theory will have its place. He felt as tired as his students, but he had to do another group at Shiler tonight.

Shaw's practicum class was his favorite course. It took a lot of time, but he felt like it was the only course he taught that was the real world. A lot of disciplines at universities never get close to the real world. In practicum, students had to deal with real-life struggles, and they had to start to deal with the effect these relationships had on their own lives. Shaw was content to counsel on a part-time basis at Shiler. Some, like Meg, had the tools to do it full-time. Shaw also knew the risks associated with becoming too consumed with a client's struggles. He knew better, but he still took many of his client's problems home with him. He often lectured to his own students about one of the most difficult issues in a counselor's development – facing yourself when you see your personal struggle in your client.

Last semester, Shaw had to ask one of his counselors-in-training to stop therapy with her client. The forty-year-old graduate counselor was a single parent. In the process of therapy, the counselor told her client to stop her divorce proceedings and try harder to save the marriage. The client was agonizing over divorcing her abusive husband.

The twenty-year-old woman was a client who came to counseling to try deal with the pains of physical and mental abuse. She told her counselor that she was leaving her husband. The counselor immediately became obsessed with saving the marriage. When Shaw confronted the counselor, she became defensive.

"You have no idea what it's like to go through a divorce. I don't want to see her suffer through this."

Shaw tried to be gentle to no avail. "So what you are telling me is that you need to decide the fate of your client. You want to see her handle the pain of more bruises even if it is something she doesn't want."

"I know what it's like to go through a painful divorce, and I just don't want to see her go through that."

Shaw knew that his first duty was for the safety of the client, and the counselor jeopardized her safety. He pulled the counselor off of the case and strongly recommended she pursue counseling for herself. She needed to resolve her inability to stop projecting her own issues into therapy. "It's one thing to empathize with our clients, but when we lose our objectivity, it's time for the therapist to get help."

Lately, he had given a lot of thought to these issues. In group, he knew it was tougher because the therapist straddles the role of being a member and a facilitator. Shaw was concerned for Megan. He had worked with her in groups for four years and had never seen her become more emotional about a group. Most of her reactions were not overt, but Shaw was picking up on little subtleties. She was becoming more moody, silent, and unsure of herself. As her close friend, he picked up on her changes but was unsure as to how or if he should bring it to her attention. Something in her couples group was bothering her.

Personal Journal 6

Dear Dr. Meg, I was a little scared of today's activity, but it seemed to work well. I suppose we all have sides to us that are hidden. But don't you suppose there's a good reason for that? I think it's best to keep some things buried and throw away the shovel. Terrence is looking better in some ways each day. He has control over his life, but I also feel he's on the verge of going over the edge. When I see him in private, he's getting more nervous each week. He said he's not on any more meds, so what's up? Whenever I ask, he shuts down. He's a good man. Is any of this doing him any good?

With each session, the group moved toward greater trust. Each week Meg introduced activities that involved greater risk. As a veteran therapist, she could sense the progress of the group. Not all of the members move toward trust at the same speed but collectively each group has its own level of emotional closeness.

Meg would discuss possible leads, rounds, or activities with Shaw before each group. Sometimes she would use planned activities, and sometimes she would not. If the group took off in one direction, it was best to let them go, especially if it meant more progress. Most activities were meant to facilitate progress, and if the group was moving on their own, she let them go. After a brief discussion with Shaw in her office, Meg decided she may use the "if you knew this about me" activity. Shaw agreed that it may be a good time.

After no one responded to old or new business, Meg prefaced her activity with a short introduction. "Tonight I would like us to start with an activity. All of us can relate to certain situations or feelings that are common. Many feelings are universal. We've all felt elation, joy, sadness, loneliness, and even anger. In that sense, it allows us to relate better to each other. These are often easy to share. For instance, if someone in the group describes a family crisis or a relationship problem, many of us can relate to the feelings. But also there are parts of our lives that sometimes we are afraid no one can totally relate to. We keep these memories or issues close to our hearts, and we don't expose them to anyone. This is okay to do. There are parts of me that I would never share with anyone. There are parts of you that you may not share with anyone. It doesn't mean that you are avoiding them. It's just that you prefer them to stay in that safe place." Meg scanned the group and smiled. "Don't worry, I promise I won't make you share any of your secrets, but I want you to think about that side of you. Let's take a moment and think about one thing you would *never* share with anyone in this group." Megan sat back and stared upward. She was thinking of something too.

"Now what I want you to do is to look around the group and imagine what it would be like if others in here knew this about you. Think about that for a minute. What would their reaction be?" She paused for a minute. "What we are going to do is do two rounds. We will go around the group twice, and both times I want you to select someone other than your support partner and say how you think they would feel if they knew this about you. Let's try to call on all members of the group. But under no circumstances are you to share your secret nor will I or anyone else ask you to share it. For instance, I'll go first. Earl, if you knew this about me I think you would be confused but sad for me." She paused. "As usual, you can pass if you like." She looked to her left at Geri. "Let's start in this direction." Meg held up a hand and signaled to her left.

As each member looked around, they could sense each other's discomfort. Meg knew that the most important part of any activity is not the activity but the processing afterward. Meg often knew inexperienced group leaders who didn't focus on the processing of activities afterward. This, in her eyes, is a huge mistake. Group members need to step away from issues afterward and reflect on how they are affected by them.

Most of the members seemed to trust enough to go through it. They took the leads and went one by one. They spoke directly to the person they chose. It was a high-risk activity because of its personal nature, never to be used in early group sessions.

"Rose, if you knew this about me, it would probably make you sad. Daniel, if you knew this about me, you may be slightly amused. Gerri, if you knew this about me, you would probably understand." Each group member took their turn.

When the activity ended, Meg took the lead. "Now what I would like to do is to get your reaction, what kinds of things were you thinking about as we did it?

Earl was the first to speak; he had big grin. "No offense, Meg, because I trust what you say, but as I thought of something I wouldn't share, I actually thought of two things, like what if she now asks, 'Would you like to share your secret?' I thought of something safe in case, you know, we were going to."

Several members of the group laughed. Lisa spoke up, "I had the same fear, what could I share? I thought of something I wouldn't share and something I would."

A couple of other members laughed and said they were feeling the same. Some of the laughter was a release from the tension of the activity. Meg smiled and raised her hands in a fun gesture. "Don't worry, I won't ask. It's your business."

Jan chimed in, "I think we should share them, just to show how much we trust the group." She was squirming ever since Lisa said, "Jan, if you knew this about me, you probably wouldn't understand." Jan needed to know. She *had* to know. She was offended.

"No, we won't. Under no circumstances will you share it, and I will ask all of the members not to ask others to share no matter how uncomfortable it made you feel."

"I didn't feel uncomfortable. It's just that we need to show our trust. Let's vote on it. How many think we should share?" Jan was still struggling with control issues in the group.

Shaw stopped her, "I'm sorry, there's no voting, and I'm sorry if it made you feel uncomfortable, but we did the activity knowing we wouldn't share, so we need to respect that in others and not put them on the spot. But let's move back to your reaction to the activity."

"I said, I wasn't uncomfortable!" Jan folded her arms and sat back. *Closing time – shut down the factory for the day.*

The group moved on. Terrence got things back on track. "I think in the back of my mind I was wondering what others were thinking about, but I would imagine in some ways we are similar in that if our lives were all open books, it would be painful, maybe too painful."

From there the group took off, minus Jan. Even her husband joined in. The activity allowed them to feel more intimate with each other because they were able to predict how others perceived them but not feel overly exposed by their personal issue. They talked about guarding themselves, fear of their secrets, openness with others, and feeling vulnerable when someone really knows us. By far, it was the most productive group so far.

In closing, Meg facilitated a round and had them lead with "Something I learned today was . . ." She was careful to not say "learned about me or others." Each member's response would indicate their orientation toward an internal locus or an external locus of control. If a member said "what I learned about me," it indicated that they felt they were responsible for their own struggles.

When the round came to Terrence, the group stopped. "Something I learned today was that you don't get strong 'once and for all.' That, at least for me, strength is something that is step by step and not an event – not a magical incident."

"Well, what did you think?" Megan's voice was businesslike after the session.

"The best session we've had yet," said Shaw. "But you know I have a love-hate feeling about that exercise, sometimes I wonder like all the others, what is their secret? And why would I react that way?"

Megan massaged her temples; the exercise never affected her before, but today was different. She recalled when Terrence looked at her he had tears in his eyes; he said "Meg if you knew this about me, you would cry." It was a showstopper. Donald sat next to him and didn't know whether to move on or say something. It was the first time the group had seen an affectionate gesture on Donald's part. He gently patted him on the shoulder, then looked back to the group. "Rose, if you knew this about me . . ." It was his manly way of moving on and saying, "I'm with you."

Ever since Terrence said it, Meg wondered, *I would cry about what?* She stared into empty space as though Shaw wasn't there.

"Earth to Megan." Shaw waved a hand in front of her face. "Earth to Megan come in, what's up, buddy, something going on?"

"No, not really," she said in an unconvincing lie. It gnawed at her. "I guess I was still kind of wondering about Terrence's closing remark of 'you don't get strong once and for all.' What did he mean by that?"

"I don't know. He seems to say a lot of rather profound things as if he understands and feels a lot, but I still feel like I know nothing about him." She stared into space again.

"Well, let's write up notes and compare." His attempt to break through her trance was in vain. *It won't happen today,* he thought.

30

August 12, 1968
The Heist

MAGS LOOKED UP to see the other three in front of him as they walked their bikes through the silent shadows of the alley. Each step had to be slow, deliberate, and quiet in order to prevent any neighborhood dogs from barking. Whenever he felt nervous, his body told him he had to pee. Right now, he felt like he had a gallon in his bladder. The whole trip he was nervously singing a new song by the group named Bessie and Sadie. Trying to keep his voice down, he whispered the tune, "I know I'm just a dog . . .chewin' on a bone . . .but I ain't gonna share today . . ."

Sanners turned around. "Mags," he whispered, "you need to stop singing or you will wake the dogs around here." Mags stopped.

Danny was second in the line behind Mickey. He shared the nervousness.

Sanners's excitement grew with each passing moment. While the others all had fleeting thoughts about getting caught, recognized, or in trouble, the possibilities affected Sanners the least. *So what if I get caught?*

The four gently laid their bikes in the darkness next to a fenced alley. They crawled on their bellies toward the mouth of the alley, being careful to not be in direct line of the streetlights.

Mickey glanced at his watch. "T minus sixty minutes and counting."

The others lay on the ground next to him but didn't respond. Mags glanced over his shoulder looking for place where he could relieve himself. He held a glimmer of hope that Mickey would call it all off. Danny was caught in the middle; he would simply follow the crowd.

Mags pulled out a pair of cheap folding James Bond spy goggles out of his back pocket and held them to his eyes. He could see just as well without them, but they made him feel more like he was on a mission. All four stared at the spot where the bundles of papers would be dropped off soon. Not soon enough.

It was a perfect place to pull off a heist, and they had the perfect plan. The bundles would be dropped in a pile in front of a one-car garage facing the street. From where the bundles were dropped, you would not be able to see them from the windows in the house.

After lying in the shadows for what seemed like a lifetime, Sanners grabbed Mags's wrist to look at his official Boy Scout watch. It was 2:20; the bundles would be here in forty minutes. Mags rubbed his wrist, looked at his watch, and wondered *Should a Boy Scout be stealing papers?*

Danny felt thankful for his place in the lineup. He was second behind Mickey. The plan had been devised to consider every detail, and the boys reviewed it numerous times until it was memorized. They would wait ten minutes in the darkness of the alley after the papers were dropped off. Mickey would then go first with Danny. Only two would go at a time. They decided that if they were to get caught, it was better that only two get caught. They would load Mickey's bags; then he would help Danny load his. The huge canvas saddle bags that straddled their front tires would easily hold two bundles apiece.

After Danny, it would be Sanners's turn. Mickey would help him and then load Mags after that. When all were finished, Mickey would take off as well.

During the planning phase, each of the boys decided on where they would dispose of their papers in four different locations. Mags's was the closest; he would dump his in the culvert under Federal Boulevard, where the Gunnison gulch ran under the road. Since it was the closest location, he would go last. It was a decision he now regretted. He became more tense with each passing minute realizing he would be the last to leave, and he had to pee.

Mickey sensed the tension in the other three, and he began to feel the nerves as well. He also knew that it was important for the other three to not know this. There were even fleeting moments when he questioned the whole thing. *Stealing is wrong. But this isn't stealing. It's more like war. These guys deserve it.*

Danny never questioned it. *The plan is okay. Mickey made the plan. It's the right thing to do.*

Sanners grew more excited. *I wish I could be there to see Gonzales's face when he doesn't get his papers.*

"I've got to pee," whispered Mags.

Sanners turned to him like a child on vacation in the backseat of a car. "You picked a fine time! Why didn't you go at home?" He managed to whisper and yell at the same time.

"Shush!" Mickey turned to them both. "Shut up, both of you. Mags, crawl back down the alley and go!"

The other three shook their heads as he crawled away.

"Please please please don't wake up anything," Mags whispered to himself as he tiptoed down the alley. He found a place in the darkness where he began to urinate next to a garbage can. Over the sound of the small splashes in the gravel, he could hear the sound of a truck coming from a distance; it was moving down the street. From where he was standing, he recognized the side of the truck as it passed by the opening of the alley. A shudder went through his body the moment he recognized the *Gazette* logo as it passed the alley opening. "Oh shit!" he whispered, "It's a half hour early!"

Mags was halfway through his relief when the panic attacked. *What if they start without me? What if they leave me? Maybe I should stop peeing. But . . . nobody can stop peeing once you start.* Mags scrunched his face as though he was in pain. *Stop. Stop.* "Oh, that burns!" he whispered. He finally stopped, but his bladder still felt full. It didn't matter; the operation was in gear. Instead of lightly walking, he ran toward the others. Two houses down the alley, he heard a high-pitched bark breaking through the still air. Another dog joined in causing Mags to run faster.

"Mags! What the hell are you doing?" whispered Mickey. Mickey rolled on his side and motioned with his hand. "Get down!"

Mags shook with fear. He dove on the ground next to the others. The other three could see the silver-dollar-size wet spot on his pants, but none of them mentioned it. They watched the bundles of papers being thrown out of the back of the panel truck. The pile of bundles grew and seemed like a Mount Everest of newsprint. The magnitude of the mission was now a reality as they watched the truck speed away. The silence that filled the air just moments ago was now filled with assorted dog barks each triggered by the one before it.

The boys waited a few minutes, but the canine riot continued. Mags had riled all the beasts in the neighborhood, and now it was like a chain reaction out of control.

"Shit!" said Danny. "What are we going to do now?"

Mickey stood up. "We're going to start now. Come on, Danny." He picked up his bike and ran across the street. Danny ran close behind.

Mags and Sanners stayed on the ground half stunned. There was no discussion and no more "what do you guys think?" questions. Mickey took the bull by the horns. His confidence was reassuring, but it didn't seem to erase the night's terror-filled mission. Danny was mesmerized as he could do nothing more than be a good follower at this time. Sanners became alert and hypervigilant. He desperately wanted to get his hands on the goods. Mags's hands shook as he realized he was breaking the law.

Mickey and Danny picked up two bundles and loaded one on each side of the canvas bags, straddling the front wheel of his bike. They picked up two more and loaded them. Suddenly it occurred to Mickey that something had gone awry. There were twice as many bundles in the driveway than he thought there would be. *How can that be? There were eight routes. Two bundles per route. There are at least thirty here. Each boy is supposed to take four. We will never be able to take all of these!*

"Shit!" A light went on in Mickey's head. He slapped his hands on the sides of his temples. "I forgot the funnies!"

Every carrier knows that Sunday papers are double-sized because of the comics and ads that have to be inserted in each paper. Danny gasped. *How could we forget that detail?*

Danny glanced across the street at Mags and Sanners still lying in the shadows on the ground. Sanners remained crouched like a combat veteran ready to spring across the street when given the signal. Mags glared through his spy glasses whispering to himself, "Come on guys hurry!" His only wish in life was to get this damn thing over and go deliver his own route.

Mickey realized they would not be able to steal all of the papers. He turned to Danny. "Danny, I forgot about the funnies. We can't take all the papers, what should we do?"

Danny suddenly felt uneasy. *You're asking me?* He was too afraid to have to think and pull off this stunt at the same time.

"I don't know . . ." He looked around at all the bundles. "Take half?"

"Good idea, which half?"

There were two distinct types of bundles. Danny looked at the larger ones that were newsprint black-and-white. The rest were smaller and had color. These were the items that needed to be inserted, the ads and comics. "Leave the funnies, let them deliver the ads and funnies only and get no paper." He surprised himself with the sound of conviction in his own voice.

Mickey smiled. "Ya, that's perfect, newspaper bundles only!"

They looked at Mickey's bike. On one side were two larger black bundles, and on the other side was a large bundle and one smaller bundle of comics. They quickly pulled it out of the bag. Danny held the bike steady as Mickey whipped it to the ground and replaced it with a larger bundle.

Danny leaned the bike on the fence, then picked up his own. They quickly loaded it, and Danny became the first of the four to be on his way. He pedaled furiously toward his destination. Drop-off number one would be in the Dumpsters behind Skaggs drugstore on Federal Boulevard. *Easy access by alley and easy departure.*

Mickey watched as Danny's figure rolled into the darkness. He knelt down and signaled for Sanners.

Mags watched from behind as Sanners ran beside his bicycle across the street. Mags never felt more alone in his life. He silently watched what would be the quickest load of the four. While Mickey steadied the bike he whispered, "Big bundles only!" Sanners unquestioningly grabbed a bundle in each hand by slipping his hand under the wire binding. Most mortals would feel the pain of the tight binding dig into their palms; of course this was not the case for Sanners. He swung one bundle on to one side and then the other. He turned around and did the same with two more. Mickey shook his head and smiled in admiration of his strength.

Sanners mounted his mechanical steed and flew in a different direction down another street. He already had an imprint of his route to his destination in his mind. He would stash them in the trash Dumpster behind the Big-T Bar and Grill on Jewell Avenue. He already knew his covert route through alleys and back roads.

Mags waited for his signal, then ran to Mickey. His eyes bulged with fear as he received the "big bundles only!" command from Mickey. They loaded the bike with half the efficiency of the Sanners exchange. Mags had to grab each bundle with two hands instead of one. He hurried to load the first three, then glanced around for his fourth bundle. There were no more! He then spotted one last newsprint bundle underneath two other bundles of comics. With an urgent waddle, he scurried over to pick it up. As he grabbed the bundle to pick it up, he felt a bolt of shivers run from his toes to the base of his neck. He trembled as he read the single sheet of paper on the top of the bundle: *ROUTE # 409 – 84 PAPERS – JOHN GONZALES.*

Mags felt momentarily stunned by the memories of the last time he touched this person's property. *What will he do this time if he catches me?* With a gaping mouth, he spun and glanced over at Mickey.

"What's wrong, man? Come on!"

"The . . . the . . . this is Gonzales's papers," he mumbled. He said it as though he was hoping someone else would take them.

"Great!" said Mickey. "Hurry up!"

Mags loaded the last bundle, then moved around the bike. His eyes still bulged, and Mickey could sense his discomfort. "Let me get you started on Gonzales's papers." He parted the stack a few papers down and spat on the front page.

Mags chuckled with delight before turning to ride down the alley. Mickey smiled as he watched him speed down the street.

Mickey's destination would be the Dumpsters at the Sunnyside Retirement Home. If all went well, they would meet back at his place in a half hour.

In each of the four boys, uneasiness set in. Being in a group of four provided strength, but now that confidence was challenged as they rode by themselves through the dark lonely night.

The four boys' minds raced in different directions. Danny pedaled hard, but his silent thoughts now resembled Mags's sentiments, *Should we have done this? What would Mom think if I got caught? She would think that I was as bad as Aaron. Please, Lord, don't let me get caught.*

Sanners basked in the thrill. His butt never touched the seat of his bike. He flew toward the Big T with nothing but gratification written all over his face. His muscled legs were tireless pistons running on high octane. *Maybe I should keep a couple of papers and show them to Gonzales, then tell him to shove them up his ass.* He grinned at the thought and then imagined punching him out after he told him. This event was already a victory. *We won.*

Mickey was the mission leader on the final leg of the plot. He pedaled in silence and smiled. *All is well in the world. We will pull it off.*

Mags felt content to be in a quiet alley. He turned down one street before turning into the alley where he wanted to go. *One block left, I can make it.*

At the far end of the dark alley, he saw a car pass. It was no cause for alarm until he saw the car stop and back up. Mags immediately recognized the silhouette of the vehicle. *There's a bubble on top, it's a cop car!* His body reacted with panic as he slammed on his breaks. The quick stop caused the bundles to fly out of the front of the bags. "Aww, crap!" he whispered. He knelt down in a crouch, then crawled toward the bundles. The cop car was at least a half block away, and Mags was certain he would not be seen. Mags gasped. The car turned on its spotlight and slowly rotated its beam toward the mouth of the alley.

Danny arrived at his destination. The alley was deserted as he approached his drop-off site. The two huge industrial-sized iron Dumpsters behind the building were perfect. The papers would get mixed in with tons of other garbage, and no one would know the difference. The only difficult task was pushing them over the top. He pulled up and leaned his bike against the building.

Sanners rolled into the small employee parking lot behind the Big T. They had planned on the Big T Bar and Grill being closed by 4:00 a.m. The papers would go unnoticed in a Dumpster that was shared by several businesses. It was half the size of the big ones behind the Skaggs drugstore, so throwing them over the top would be easy. The boys picked this site because it was emptied regularly. Some of the bums in southwest Denver were known to go through Dumpsters behind large bars hoping for a small sip at the bottom of an empty whiskey bottle. Sanners leaned his bike on the side of the Dumpster, walked to the front of the bike, and pulled out a bundle. He lofted the first one over the edge.

Mickey arrived at Sunnyside. He liked the selection of this site because it was remote and quiet. He pulled alongside the small Dumpster and lifted the lid. *This is too easy.*

Mags trembled as the beam of the spotlight moved toward him. He hunched behind the bundles and peered over the top of them. The spotlight found the bundles and Mags on the ground shivering like a puppy.

Danny had to get up on his toes to push the last bundle over the top edge of the trash Dumpster. *Mission complete.* He was on his way back to Mickey's.

Sanners threw the bundles with ease over the top edge of the open Dumpster. *Piece of cake,* he thought. He pulled the fourth bundle out of his bag and lofted it to the far corner of the Dumpster. "Ahhh!" A muffled scream came from inside the Dumpster. Sanners's feet left the ground as his body involuntarily jumped away from the Dumpster in shock. His body turned into a piece of rigid steel readied for defense as his heart pounded. *What the hell was that? Was that an animal? Was it in the Dumpster? Was it a human voice?* It sounded like it was in pain – perhaps hurt, perhaps rabid. The sound was the last thing Sanners expected in the quiet, still air of the morning.

"Ahhh!" The sound came from the Dumpster.

Sanners jumped again as his body tensed into a fighter's stance. He rolled his fists in front of his face as he readied himself for defense.

"Ahhh!" It was definitely human. It was coming from the far end of the Dumpster, and it was right where he threw the last bundle of papers.

Mickey finished his job by placing the last bundle of papers in the Sunnyside Dumpster. He wiped his hands in the air in a gesture that signaled his pleasure for a job well done. He tipped his nose back and inhaled the peaceful night air for the first time that evening. He thought about the displacement of the four groupings of papers and imagined that the other three were already done.

Their plan was based on a mutual belief that if the papers were dispersed to the four corners of the world, then the job would be more complete. The truth was that they could have dragged them fifty yards down the alley and pulled off the same result. Nonetheless, the whole scheme made them feel like spies, secret agents, Old West men of justice, and geniuses all at the same time. The Hardy boys could not have pulled off a more perfect caper.

Mags watched in horror as the headlights methodically crept toward him. The cop car crept up the alley as the spotlight scanned the alley from side to side. His body shook uncontrollably. *Think! Run! Make up a story! Run! Ride away! Think! Omigod, I'm caught! I won't talk! Oh God! Oh shit, I think I'm peeing my pants!*

Mags reached over and tried to pick up a bundle. He tried to put it in one of the canvas bags only to cause the bike to fall over in the other direction. The cop car slowly rolled closer and now he was speaking out loud to himself. "I'll go to jail! Oh shit! My mom will be crying from the other side of the bars! I'll never graduate from high school! I'll never be named paper carrier of the year again!"

The cop car finally reached him as Mags continued to struggle with the bundles. The door opened on the driver's side, and the outline of a huge figure stepped out and walked toward him. "What are you doing out this time of night, son?"

Mags fell to his knees still clutching the bundle. "I'm . . . I'm . . . I'm . . . a paper carrier . . ." His head fell on top of the bundle.

The deep voice spoke from behind a flashlight. "I can see that, son, but what are you doing *here?*"

Mags picked up his head and glared into the beam of light coming from the cop's flashlight. He felt like an escaped convict that had just crawled over the prison wall. The blinding light made his eyes pour the tears he had been holding back.

"I'm . . . I'm . . ." *Think! Lie! Make up a story! Oh God, I'm too young for prison!* "I'm . . .
I was just trying to take my papers to my friend's hose, I mean house, and we were
going to fold our papers together . . ." Mags smacked his dry mouth; he knew this
happened when he lied. "And I was going to deliver them . . . and then I was riding . . .
and this dog chased me . . . and I was scared . . . and I tried to get away down this
alley . . . and then he bit me . . . I think . . . and I rode fast . . . then I crashed and now
I'm dead . . ." His head fell on the bundle.

"Well, son, I don't think you're dead, but you sure as heck are going to be if
you're out riding around all by your lonesome every night like this with four bundles
of papers. Do your parents know where you are?"

Is he? He's buying my story . . . He's believing . . . Mags picked up his head and
inhaled as he dug for his next words. "Yes, my parents, no, my parents . . . well, they
know . . . they don't . . ."

"Listen, son, here's what I'm going to do, let's get you loaded up, and I'm gonna
tell you what, this is the last time you need to be riding around like this. I don't
want to see you out again this time of night. I know you guys usually deliver around
5:30, and you better have learned your lesson. You get run down by some dog or
some car at four in the morning, and you're in a heap of trouble. Now here . . . you
hold the bike . . ." The cop kept talking as he helped load the bundles back in the
canvas bags. "You got no business trying to get up earlier than you need to. Now
I hope you learned your lesson next time that dog's gonna catch you, good boy,
and I ain't goin' to be out here to help you, you hear me, boy?" He loaded the last
bundle in the bag.

"Oh yes, sir. Oh yes, sir. Oh yes, sir. I will never. Oh, I swear, I swear, I will
never – "

"Just get on your way, boy."

"Oh yes, sir. Oh yes, sir . . ." Mags climbed on his bike and pounded the pedals
as hard as he could. "Oh yes, sir, thank you sir, thank you sir . . ."

The cop laughed and shook his head as Mags rode away.

Mags looked down at his pants. The wet spot covered his crotch.

Sanners waited as he heard the sound in the Dumpster again. "Ahhh!" The
grunt seemed to grow louder, and it sounded like whatever was in there was in pain.
"Ahhh!"

Sanners's body told him to run, but his mind said, *Stay – . what the hell is in there?*
He needed to know. He moved to the other end of the Dumpster and slowly climbed
up the edge. He raised his eyes just enough to look over the top. In the corner of the
Dumpster was a gray-bearded man pinned down by a bundle of papers. Part of his
body was covered by garbage. His head and arms seemed to flail in slow motion from
beneath a bundle of papers that rested on his chest. His eyes remained shut. "Ahhhh!"
he screamed.

"Oh shit," said Sanners as he shook his head. *Maybe I crushed the old man. Maybe he's dying. Aw, for goodness' sake, what the heck was he doing in there anyway?*

"Ahhh!" the old man screamed again. Sanners's fear left him as he rolled his eyes and jumped into the Dumpster. He knew he would have to pull the bundle off of his chest. He took three steps over the garbage, then stood over the old man. He could now make out a face behind a beard with eyes were nothing more than slits. Sanners caught the scent of what smelled old urine and whiskey mixed together.

"Ahhh!" he screamed.

"I learned mouth-to-mouth resuscitation in health class, and you know what? If you need it, I think you are going to die because you ain't getting it from me." Sanners reached out with one hand and pulled the bundle of papers off his chest. The old man inhaled without opening his eyes, then rolled over while mumbling incoherently.

Danny was the first to arrive in Mickey's backyard. He parked his bike at a distance and crawled to his sleeping bag. He now felt nervous, and the myriad of potential scenarios ran through his mind. *Did they get caught? I'll bet Mags got caught. I'll bet Sanners beat up some delivery guy. I'll bet Mickey had to – .*

He heard a rustle and noticed Mickey laying his bike down at a distance and making his way toward the bags. A few moments later, Sanners arrived and told them of his encounter with the drunk in the Dumpster. After fifteen minutes, they were all worrying. Mags was not back yet.

Mags glanced at his Boy Scout watch; he was way behind schedule. He pedaled harder, and eventually he reached the culvert that ran under Federal Boulevard. The air was still and had an eerie feel to it. The concrete walls were lined with old graffiti, and a stream of trickling water was the only sound. Above him he could feel the rumble of an occasional car passing on the street. Making his way to a spot near the center, he leaned his bike against the side and kicked his canvas bags until the bundles fell out the front.

Mags felt tired and defeated. This exciting plot didn't turn out the way he had intended, and the wet spot on his jeans was another sign that he wasn't cut out for this line of work. He gazed down, and a smile slowly appeared on his face. His bladder seemed to be very full again. A bundle of papers laid before him with the label *ROUTE #409 – 84 PAPERS – JOHN GONZALES.* The bundle beckoned to him.

A stray cat peered from one end of the tunnel at a darkened silhouette of a bicycle, paper bundles, and a human. The sounds of splashing water were immediately followed by what seemed like a maniacal laugh. The laughter echoed in the tunnel and was loud enough to send the cat running for cover. After the splashing ceased, the figure zipped up his pants, got on his bike, and rode away. The laughter continued to echo under Federal Boulevard.

31

Emotions
Session 7

Personal Journal 7

Dear Dr. Meg, you're an ass. I stand by what I said. You're an ass.

"WHAT THE HELL was that all about?" asked Shaw as he sat down in Meg's office. The group session had just finished. Meg sat down in her chair and closed her eyes. She leaned back and ran her fingers through her hair. Her face looked flushed.

Shaw waited through the silence; then Megan finally spoke "I have no idea, I have absolutely no idea. I'm lost. I have no idea what's happening."

After another long pause, she opened her eyes and leaned forward. "I know that partners often protect each other in group, but that was out of the blue." Her voice cracked; she sat in a state of shell shock. "I've never seen anger in the later stages. It always seems to be in the earlier sessions. Now *that* I was not prepared for."

Shaw and Meg retraced their steps in the group. They opened with the usual rounds, and the group seemed to be on track for another average session where the members had reached a healthy working stage. They trusted each other and were unafraid to explore their feelings. With about a half hour left, Shaw introduced an activity where members could identify two people in their group – other than their partner to whom they felt connected. Nobody mentioned Jan. She was incensed. She called the activity "nothing but a damned popularity contest."

Other members disagreed and said it had to do with how they related and who they felt connected with because of what they shared. The group seemed like most other sessions; then in a seemingly harmless moment Lisa said, "Terrence, I know I feel close to you in some ways because you seem to connect with me, but I feel distant from you in other ways because I know nothing about what brings you to the group." The group sat in silence as they watched his eyes welling up with tears.

Megan hoped the group would eventually say something as she followed, "I agree with Lisa. It's like there's a safe covering." Terrence wiped a tear from his face and looked down, unable to respond.

Daniel jumped in to rescue him, "I think you ought to leave him alone." His voice was crisp, and his glare threw daggers through Megan. His face, tone of voice, and words reflected anger.

Tears streamed down Terrence's face. "I know," he stammered for words. "I know I haven't . . ." His words trailed off as he wiped his face again and put his chin on his chest. His fists doubled as he held them to his chest. "I . . . I haven't said anything about my life." His voice cracked, and he began to rock forward and backward as though a tidal wave of nerves were about to burst through the dam. "There's . . . there's . . . there's a good reason." The tears were now flowing through the cracks in the dam; the walls were about to shatter.

The whole room sat stunned and silent. Meg tried to make eye contact. "Terrence, I – "

"I think you ought to leave him alone." Daniel's voice grew louder.

"I'm not trying to – "

Daniel pointed a finger; his voice became stern, "I think you ought to leave him alone!"

Terrence continued to rock in silence. Clenching his fists to his chest, his jaw tightened and he began to moan. His mind was racing between agony and fear. He did not want to live another moment in his past. He mumbled, "Please. Please."

"Terrence, I just want to – "

Daniel stood up and pointed at Meg. "This is fucking bullshit! What the fuck do you want from the man? What kind of fucking joy do you get from carving him to pieces? I think you ought to leave him the fuck alone! Did you hear me?!" His voice sent a shock wave through the room. Terrence's tears ignited a rage in Daniel that no one in the room had ever seen. It was as though a paternal instinct took over and he was fighting for Terrence's life. Meg sat with her mouth gaping as she searched for the right set of words to say. The rest of the room sat shell-shocked.

Daniel was now screaming as he whipped his finger through the air while pointing at Megan. "Leave it alone! Just leave it alone now!"

"Stop now! Stop!" Shaw's commanding voice broke in. He broke an informal rule between himself and Meg – they would never come to each other's rescue if a member of the group verbally attacked them.

"Please stop, everyone, please stop, let's all take a deep breath." His voice softened, "Please, Daniel, sit down, please." Shaw felt nervous but sensed Meg's fear and took over. He had been doing groups for years and had never encountered a moment like this.

The room was in chaos. A crazed fighter, a woman knocked off the road by a truck, a beaten and defeated man, silent bystanders, and one peacemaker who now spoke, "It's probably a good time to wind down, there is a lot of emotion in this room right now, and we all need to cool down." The group stared at him, waiting for his next words. "I really don't know what is going on in here, but let's keep our cool. We're going to close for today to give us all a chance to reflect and come back. One final round, please. Let's just continue next week." Shaw needed to put closure on the session but had no answers. He was stunned, and the group knew it. All of them were thankful that he broke in with, "Final comments please." Shaw's voice was controlled and comforting. He looked to his left and gestured to Lisa to start the round.

"I'm sorry, Terrence, I wish I could help," said Lisa. She was stumped but felt compelled to say something. Earlier, she mentioned that she felt closest to Terrence.

"Pass," said Earl.

Rose paused and shook her head; she was frightened. "Pass."

"I think you're an ass." Daniel looked straight at Meg.

Gerri's gaping mouth and empty stare summed her feelings, but she decided to take her turn anyway. "I'm ready to pass, but I've got to say, Meg, before we need to jump on Terrence because we don't know anything about him, I think I don't know anything about you either. You seem more guarded than Terrence." She looked down, unable to make eye contact with Meg.

Tony waited then said, "I think all of us need to go home and cool off."

"I'm sorry," said Doris, "I'm mixed up and confused and sad for Terrence, but I've got to agree with Gerri, I don't know you either, Meg."

It was now Meg's turn. At a loss for words, she stared into space and quietly said, "Pass." She had never ended a group in her life without saying something. *I'm a group leader for God's sake, and I'm failing.* She looked down to see her hands shaking.

Jan had a shocked look on her face; even Junior Freud couldn't save this group, "Uh, uh, pass."

"Pass," said Terrence through his tears.

"Pass," said Donald.

It was back to Shaw; he knew he needed careful words for closing. The group cooled down but still appeared to be staggered by the events. He drew a deep breath of air and exhaled slowly as though he was trying to breathe for the group. He then scanned the group members, trying to make eye contact with each of them.

"Sometimes, like today, we have a lot of emotion in group, we don't always know what that emotion is about, but for this group, we've come a long way. We've shared a lot, we've trusted each other, we've depended on each other, and we've leaned on each other. We've talked about life, love, struggles, and our fears. I think I'm afraid right now too." He paused and looked back at Meg staring into space.

"We are too strong of a group now to not move forward." He waited, sighed, and looked around again – feeling more like a coach than a therapist. He also knew he was violating a group norm by telling the group how they felt. Despite the violation, the members nodded with each of his words. "I know we are strong enough to get through this, but let's stick together, let's think about today, let's regroup our emotions and get a fresh start next week, okay?" He took a final scan of the group, trying to make eye contact with each of them. Daniel, Meg, and Terrence all stared down. The rest nodded in silence then quietly left the room.

Megan was still taken aback as she sat in her office. "It was like nothing I have ever encountered." She desperately wanted Shaw to rescue her, but he had no answers himself. "We're going to have to think long and hard about how we will open group next week." Shaw nodded.

32

August 18, 1968
Pregame

MICKEY, DANNY, MAGS, and Sanners sat in the second to the last pew in the back of the church. The very last pew was always reserved for those families with small children. Sanners fidgeted with the hymnal trying to act like he was really interested in what was on the pages. Mags sat up straight. He, like Sanners, rarely attended St. Anthony's. Mickey was accustomed to the long services, as was Danny. They were fairly regular. Most of the time, they would attend one of the early masses, either 6:00 or 7:00.

Today, all four were in attendance at the 7:00 mass. It was the day of the big game, and they knew that Father Abercrombie would mention the big game. It was like hearing your name on the announcements at school. Just hearing them made you attain a state of instant status. There was no way you could pass that up even if the service was long and could put you to sleep.

Sanners held a theory about Catholic masses. He believed that all of the responses, songs, changing of positions from standing to sitting to kneeling were purposeful gestures. They were not for religious purposes, but rather, they were designed to keep you from falling asleep during the long boring service. His family never went to church, so the few times he went during the summer was only with the guys. He found the whole thing to be rather mysterious, especially that white thing they give you for communion. *What the heck is that thing made out of? It's not even close to bread, so why do they then call it the breaking of the bread?* Mags and Sanners once had an argument over its content and ingredients. Mags said it had to be a form of bread; otherwise, the church was lying, and churches don't lie. Sanners maintained that it was made of paper that was designed to melt in your mouth. It looked like cardboard, it certainly tasted like cardboard, and it felt like cardboard, and therefore it must be. Sanners came to this conclusion last year when he went to communion and received the host on his tongue. He then hurried off to the men's bathroom and took it out of his mouth to examine it for the next five minutes. He eventually swallowed it.

Mickey paid attention as he waited for the announcements that would come at the end of the service. Finally, they started. "And Mrs. Gallup fell down her stairs and broke her hip last week. She is in Denver Memorial Hospital. If you would like to see her she said she looks forward to the company. We will also have a grand prize of a custom bowling ball at this week's bingo, complements of Arthur Lanes. Also, I would personally like to invite all of the parishioners to the senior boys baseball game this afternoon." All four boys immediately perked up and sat straighter.

"This year, the boys have a chance to win the league championship if they beat the St. Augustine's team. It's a big game, but as you know, it's become even more important to me." Father Abercrombie took off his glasses and looked out over the church members. Whenever he put on his serious face, the church members knew he would have something humorous to say. A few chuckles went up in various places throughout the church as all eyes were attentively on him. "As you know, I've had a running bet with Father DiPaulo for several years now." Assorted giggles echoed through the congregation. "All of you know Father DiPaulo – from St. Augustine's – you know, that other church." He rolled his eyes as he said "that other church." The congregation now roared with laughter. He then paused as he looked like he was delivering a campaign speech. His voice became raspy and took on the tone of compassion and conviction. "My, good friends, my parishioners" – he stopped again and took in a deep cleansing breath – "as you and I would both agree, it would be wrong to ask of the good Lord to have any influence in a sporting event, but as you also may know, our bell tower is in desperate need of a painting but" – he threw both hands in the air and looked up – "I'm sure that the good Lord would not turn his back on a simple prayer that we should never have to send your dear . . . old . . ." – he brought his hands down and purposely caused them to tremble over the pulpit – "fragile, did I mention 'fragile' . . . and 'old'?" By now the entire congregation joined the laughter.

"Anyway, I'm sure the good Lord would listen to a prayer requesting that we never have to send an old priest on any old rickety scaffold to paint the bell tower. So, as we bow our heads in prayer today, let us ask the Lord that one day we may see a young energetic priest, perhaps like Father DiPaulo" – he winked at the parishioners – "yes, like Father DiPaulo one day painting our bell tower. Let us bow our heads in prayer." The congregation laughed again as they bowed their heads in prayer. It was not uncommon for him to throw in humor; the parishioners all knew these were things they would never pray for. They also knew that his humor is what kept many of them connected to the parish. *Another Father Abercrombie sermon.*

While the parishioners giggled, Mickey bowed his head and sighed. It was beginning to sink in. *This is the game. This is the World Series. It's a championship game where all the eyes of the important people will be on you.*

Danny bowed his head. *No worries, the man will be on the mound. Center field? A piece of cake.*

"I still don't think we needed to leave this early," said Danny. He stood up on his pedals as the two bikes moved in unison up the hill.

Mickey glanced over his shoulder at Mags and Sanners ten yards behind them. "It's okay, it's what Mags wants."

Danny nodded. "Ya I guess it's okay."

After their last practice, Mags proposed the idea that they arrive at the ballpark much earlier than usual. The game was to be played at the Sixth Avenue fields on Federal Boulevard, just ten blocks south of One-Mile Park. The trek would take about a half hour, and Mags's logic even seemed to make sense. He had five reasons: first, if they got there early, they would not be tired from the ride; second, Mickey could check out the height of the mound; third, they could roll baseballs down the base paths to see if the ball broke toward the field or out of play. Sanners liked that idea in case someone bunted down the third base line. Fourth, they could check out their positions to see where the sun might be in the case of pop flies, and fifth, and perhaps most important in Mags's mind, it would give them time to trade cards.

The only problem with the plan was the one they hadn't considered – too much time. Within a little more than a half hour, they had completely checked out the field and had even made several trades. The only thing to do now was to get nervous, which seemed to be happening without any thought.

"What time is it, Mags?" asked Danny.

Mags looked at his wrist. "Eleven thirty."

Sanners threw his handful of cards into a gentle pile to his side. He then fell to his back. "Fer cryin' out loud, why did we decide to get here so early. The rest of the team won't even be here for an hour and a half. We're just going to sit out here and bake."

The other three sat in silence. *Too much time to think. No water. The temperature is going up.* "We shouldn't have come so early," said Danny.

Mags began to feel like they were ganging up on him. Although it was his idea, he never realized that they would just get more nervous as time went by. "Let's trade some more cards!" he said more gleefully. The other three groaned.

"I'm going for a walk," said Mickey as he stood up.

"Me too," said Danny.

The two wandered away as Mickey began to grill Danny on the latest status between him and Jean. It was hard not to be a little jealous. So few guys actually have girlfriends, but in his mind, it couldn't happen to a better guy.

"So what about when school starts?" asked Mickey.

"I don't know, I suppose things will just keep on going on. Maybe I could take her to homecoming."

"That would definitely be cool." Mickey wanted to talk about anything at this time to keep his mind off of the game. Danny felt the same way but dared not to say. They just wanted to play and play hard. Suddenly the quiet air was broken by a voice coming from forty yards away where Mags and Sanners were trading cards. The voice was faint, but the words and actions were clear.

"You son of biscuit!" screamed Mags as his arms flailed at Sanners. The two of them were rolling across the grass as Mags alternated between a death grip on Sanners's throat and erratic punches at his chest.

Mickey and Danny stood still, too shocked to react to what they were seeing. Mickey's mouth gaped open.

"Those guys are fighting!" screamed Danny.

The two of them took off in a sprint. Mickey quickly had a six-step lead on Danny. As Mags and Sanners rolled in a death lock, Mickey leaped on them at full speed. His initial impact separated them with a thud. He ended up sitting on top of Sanners's chest. As Danny approached Mags, he thought about grabbing him when he noticed that Mickey had cocked a fist behind his head and was screaming at Sanners. None of the three others had ever seen him this enraged. "What the hell do you think you're doing, Sanners!? Who the hell do you think you are! What the hell is your problem?"

Sanners lay on his back motionless, and for the first time in their years together it actually looked like Sanners was afraid.

Danny reacted out of fear, anxiety, and instinct. He leaped on Mickey and threw a bear hug on him as tight as he could. He fell to the ground with Mickey squeezing his eyes as tight as he could in a painful grimace. "Don't, Mickey! Don't, Mickey! Please don't hit him, Mickey!"

Danny stood up as a look of intensity spread over his face. The only thing the boys had ever seen spread over his face in the past was redness from embarrassment or paleness from fear. They had never seen this. He turned with his arms out and looked at the three.

"Stop it! Everyone! Everybody stop it right now. What the hell are we all doing!? We're supposed to fight the enemy not each other! We're supposed to put our energy into the game not into beating each other up!"

He spun his body around and pointed at Mickey. "What the hell are you doing trying to beat up, Sanner?!" Mickey stared up from the ground in disbelief at what he was seeing. Clearly, they were all out of character and half out of their minds, but this time Danny really lost it.

"I was trying to keep him from beating up Mags," he said in a half-frightened voice.

Danny turned and pointed at Sanners. If there was ever a moment in human history where smoke could actually come out of a guy's eyes and ears, it looked to all of them like this might be that moment. "What the hell are you doing trying to beat up Mags?!"

Sanners rocked up on his elbows and couldn't believe he was hearing this rage from Danny. *He's gone nuts,* he thought.

"Me? Beating up Mags? It's the other way around! I was trying only to keep him from beating up on me."

He finally pointed his finger at Mags. It was as though it had the potency of the lightning rod of Zeus himself. The finger was poised, and the look was frightening. "What the hell is your problem, Mags?!"

Mags sat up, and his voice turned mousy "He . . . he . . . tore my ballcard in half . . ." his voice drifted away.

"Are you kidding me? You want to fight Sanners over a ball card?!"

"Well ya . . . see, he said he didn't want to trade any more, and I said I did, and then like he got mad, and then he said well here have two cards instead of one, and he tore my Nolan Ryan – Jerry Koosman brand-new rookie card in half and said, 'Now you can trade two,' and then I got pissed, and then I tried to get him and – "

Danny threw his hands to his face. "Are you kidding me, man? You're seriously kidding me, man, you can't be real, a rookie card?"

Danny fell on to his back with his hands still over his face. "He rips up the most useless card on the planet, and you get mad? I mean who the hell is Ryan anyway? And Koosman's having a good year, but you've got to be kidding me. No one collects rookie cards! They're useless! They have no stats on them! They have no history on them! I mean seriously, would you rather have this year's Mantle card or his rookie!? The rookie cards are stupid! Stupid! Stupid! No statistics! You guys are crazy! Danny's hands fell down to his side as he lay on his back. He pounded his fists and heels of his shoes into the ground while he screamed again, "You guys are crazy!"

Danny rolled over on his belly and laid facedown on the grass. He screamed again, "You guys are crazy!"

The four lay still for thirty seconds; then without moving, Mickey began to laugh. Mags joined him a moment later, followed by Sanners as the chorus of hysterics became contagious. Within moments, all four boys were beside themselves.

For the next hour, the time went quicker. A game of five hundred, a game of pepper, and some catch made the time go by. As the team arrived, the tension began to melt off. Until of course, St. Augustine's showed up – in the church bus. They looked bigger than the boys remembered and resembled a big major-league team arriving at the ballpark. *We never go anywhere by bus. They look tough. They look cocky.* It was all the Falcons could do to stay focused.

The Sixth Avenue fields began to take on the atmosphere of a festival. While the boys were focused on baseball, the smell of fresh-cut grass blended with occasional aroma of picnic food. The sun partnered with the event – no clouds and a deep blue sky. The sounds of the voices of little children playing were mixed in with parents in conversation, and behind it all were the sounds of baseballs smacking into well-worn leather gloves. The sharp cracks of wooden bats connected with the horsehide balls to add to the sweet harmony.

The parents, families, and parishioners began to set up their camps on picnic blankets. Father Abercrombie arrived with Father DiPaulo as they threw out their own blanket. The final ingredient arrived in the form of an umpire. The game would start soon.

After batting practice, and taking some infield, Eggs signaled for the team to come in. "Take a knee, gentlemen, and listen up." The team knew it was now only a matter of time; Mags glanced at his Boy Scout watch, ten minutes until game time.

Eggs never wandered from his disposition. He never focused on the prize, only the task. Both teams knew what was at stake. You didn't need that carrot in front of these mules to get them excited. "Gentlemen, our job today is to play hard and think ahead. Don't let your minds wander on the field. With each count think about where the ball should be thrown. If it's a pop fly, think about where the ball will go if it's a grounder. Pay attention to Mags as he signals the number of outs after each batter. If we play every ball with our heads up, we will increase our chances of walking away with this thing. When you're at the plate, keep focusing on the next pitch, not the last one. We are the visiting team today, so we are up to bat first. Let's get a couple of pokes and show these guys how to play this game. What do you say we bring it in here. I want to hear Falcons on three."

The team rose to their feet, a few boys sported bulging eyes, and the rest could feel their hearts beating out of their chests. Mags hoped he wouldn't embarrass himself. Danny was just happy to be out in center field, in a place where he had the whole field in front of him. Mickey breathed deeply, he hadn't been on the mound in a while, but he knew he could get the job done. His team knew it too, and it was the main reason they felt confident today. Sanners ran images through his mind of belting the ball as far as he could. They all placed their hands on the pile and screamed, "Falcons!"

The first inning was a flop for the Falcons. Danny drew a walk followed by Joey Pelloman who tried to bunt. The ball popped up to the pitcher, and Danny was already halfway down to second. They easily picked him off for the double play back at first. Mickey ended the top half of the first with a long fly directly to the left fielder for the third out.

Mickey started out wild on the mound by walking the first two guys. He gave up two more hits and was lucky to get out of the inning giving up only one run. He left two more men on base. Gonzales was the only one to cross the plate in the inning. On his way past Mags, he said something to him that sent him into a frenzy. In the dugout, Mags threw his gear down in the corner.

"Mags!" Mickey hollered as he walked toward him. "What's the problem?"

"Nothing, except that sonofabitch Gonzales said, 'Get out of my way, fat boy!'" Mags threw down a shin guard.

"Remember what Eggs said. Your job is to focus on the next pitch. You're on deck, come on, man, we need you." Sanners was the fourth man in the lineup, followed by Mags.

Sanners stepped up to the plate and gleamed down the third baseline at Gonzales; he fixated on dreams of hitting him with a line drive. He swung hard at the first pitch and missed badly, causing him to spin around and nearly fall down.

"Come on, Sanners! You look like that tubby Mags!" Gonzales yelled.

Sanners gritted his teeth and connected with the next pitch to center field for a stand-up double.

Mags fell behind in the pitch count with two strikes and a ball before hitting a line drive directly at the first baseman for the first out. Gill Bankard followed with a strike out, and Tom Dunlop popped up to the infield to end the top of the second.

The next two innings went scoreless as St. Augie's held a 1-0 lead going into the bottom of the fourth. It appeared to be a defensive battle as Mickey was beginning to warm up. He felt his pitches getting stronger. He recognized all four of the boys who visited them during the St Paul's game. Gonzales was the one he pitched the hardest against, but he knew that the real threat was Chet Anderson, the hulking pitcher. He was also the best hitter in the league. Mickey knew it was a matter of time before Anderson would belt one deep; he was just hoping it would go Danny's way. Ray Bryant, one of the other four harassers, hit a cheap blooper over Sanners's head to start the inning. Mickey couldn't get his control back quick enough, and he walked the next batter to put runners on first and second with no outs.

Anderson stepped to the plate. Mickey knew him well. Anderson hit two homers off of Danny in the same game last year. Danny had started the game last year, then turned it over to Mickey, but it was too late. Last year's score was a disappointing 14-3. Anderson had the body of a Sanners but the cool controlled appearance of a guy about to be drafted to the minor leagues.

Even though Mickey had him scouted, there was no good way to pitch him. He had no holes in his swing. Mickey's first pitch went wild over Mags's head and the runners advanced. His next two were low, and he was now in the hole with an 0-3 count. He looked to the dugout to see Eggs giving the "pass" signal. Mickey was frustrated; he didn't want to walk him, so he threw one hard and away.

If you were an objective observer, you had to admire Anderson's swing. Some guys can put their hips into a pitch; for others it's all arms. For guys like Chet, the whole body turned into the pitch. A crack of the bat always sends a lump into a pitcher's throat, followed by a sick feeling in the stomach, and for Mickey it was no different. The ball went into deep right. By the time the players on both teams watched the ball descend, they could only see Stevie Burman's chubby backside run away in futility. St. Augie's now led 4-0, and Mickey could feel it slipping away. He allowed one more batter to get on but retired the next two with strikeouts to end the inning. When he came back to the dugout, he avoided eye contact with Eggs and moved to the end of the bench. It started to feel like they would never get to Anderson, and this could be as close as they ever got to the league championship.

Mickey's sulking was new to his teammates. They hadn't seen this before, and it immediately cast the team into a somber state. The mood stuck with them for the next two and one half innings. After six and a half innings the score stood at 4-0. There were only two at-bats to make something happen.

Joe Hannigan made a deal with Mickey a long time ago that he would never give him advice during a game. He told Mickey that a ballplayer should only listen to his coach during a game, and frankly no one else had any business giving advice. But there were rare times when they both knew that he could use input from those closest to him if it were done with the right tact and intent. As Mickey was ready to take the field for the bottom of the seventh, his chin was on his chest, and Joe Hannigan called out to him. "Mickey!"

Mickey stopped a few feet in front of the dugout and whirled around. Joe gave Mickey a big smile, then placed the back of his hand under his own chin, and tapped it three times. He then held his finger out in front of him and twirled around twice. He held a big smile the entire time. Mickey responded with a sheepish grin and a nod before jogging to the mound.

When Mickey reached the mound, he turned around and looked in at Mags who waited for the warm-up pitches. He then threw him a smile and a wink as though he was in perfect control. Mags smiled back. Mickey turned around after his last warm-up pitch, then hollered to the team. "On your toes, gentlemen, and we are going to be back in business before you know it!"

Mickey smiled at his teammates and remembered his father's signal. The tap under his chin meant just that, to keep his chin up. The circling of the finger was a sign to Mickey that he had to think about those around him, not just himself. Mickey knew they looked up to him and depended on his confidence. He also knew he had slipped in the last couple of innings. He was not at his best. It was time to throw hard. He shook off most of Mags's signs for the bottom of the seventh and threw heat. It was the middle of the order, and he was past the big guns. In thirteen pitches, he sat down the next three batters in a row with strikeouts.

As the team came in from the field, Mickey was already thinking ahead. Tom Dunlap and Stevie Burman were the first two batters up, and Mickey told them both to not swing until they had two strikes on them. Anderson had a tough time all day pitching to the shorter batters, and Tom and Stevie were their two shortest. Coach Eggs knew you could play a lot of Little League games and win them by preying on a pitchers control, but he always coached his players to play for the hit and swing at the ball. Unfortunately, Tom and Stevie swung at everything, and they usually struck out at the plate. This time, they heeded Mickey's advice, and both earned walks on the next nine pitches. It wasn't time to play the game in the most "right" way, but it was the time to play it for the win. It was now time for the top of the lineup and time to get things going.

Danny's head was everywhere but on his shoulders. He crouched and scooped up a handful of dirt. He tapped the instep of his shoes as though there was dirt clinging to them.

Most ballplayers are men of excessive rituals, and Danny proudly had his own. Most often the rituals are meaningless; they simply allowed the player the exact amount of time to get his act together and be perfectly poised at the plate. Danny felt the stare of Jean. He thought about the score. He saw Pats, and he heard the chatter of his best friends as the world felt like it was in slow motion.

As Eggs often told them, tough times not only build character; they reveal it as well. For Danny, he wondered if he had the character for the big one. Anderson did. He threw two hanging curves, and Danny swung over them both. On the third pitch, he altered his swing and swung under it.

The pitcher is the second person on the field to know where the ball is going; they can tell an instant after the ball makes contact. The first person who knows where the ball is going is the batter. At the moment of contact, the bat will ricochet in a direction that immediately registers in the brain. Often the player doesn't even need to see it or to watch it. Most of the time on the bad hits, the head doesn't even have to come up.

Anderson took five steps back and waved off the infield. He caught the pop fly in one effortless motion, then instinctively wheeled around to check the runners. His brain didn't even have to tell his body to do it. He was already there.

Joey stepped to the plate and grounded to Gonzales on third. An easy step on the bag kept the runners on first and second, and in the period of one minute, a rally turned into another lesson in futility.

As the boys grew up through the ranks of Little League, they began to develop the natural evolution of emotions that all ballplayers possess. The game becomes one of hidden emotion. When you are young, you can be fooled into false hope, but only the insane remain that unrealistic. Yet despite those untrusted emotions, all ballplayers and fans still lose a heartbeat each time a thunderous crack of the bat collides with the ball. Hope can come to life in a single split second. Nothing is contrived, the body reacts, the heart leaps, and the soul waits.

"It ain't over till the fat catcher sings! Come on, Mickey!" screamed Mags. A couple of the boys laughed at Mags's attempt to break up the intensity. All of the Falcons were now on their feet with their hands peeking through the chain-link fence on the dugout. Even Coach Eggs chuckled – he figured Mags must have been saving that one.

Mickey stepped to the plate and glared at Anderson. He was the best that the city of Denver had to offer, but Mickey knew that even the best make mistakes.

The chess match grew with intensity. Mickey fell behind 2-1 in the count, then fouled off two more as he did his best to protect the plate. The next ball was in the dirt, but the catcher knocked it down. Mickey stepped back and took a handful of dirt. He tapped his back pocket. Beneath the blue jean pocket was the card of Mickey

Mantle. He only used him in battle on special occasions, but this one had to be the one. It was a brand-new 1968 card.

Mickey kicked the dirt and dug in deeper. The 2-2 pitch was one that Anderson hoped he would overlook. Mickey anticipated the fastball, and his sinewy body ripped toward the incoming sphere. The collision was perfect, and Mickey knew it immediately. It was only a matter of whether someone could get to it in time in deep center. When Mickey rounded first, he saw the centerfielder turn around and begin running. At that point, he knew that it was a one-run ball game at 4-3. The Falcons had already evacuated the dugout and thrown themselves up in the air again and again as they ran for home to greet him.

Momentum can swing its ugly head, and after years of play, the boys knew that the delicate nature of emotions can make or break a team in a single play. Saint Augie's needed to stop the momentum. Anderson wanted to shut down the Falcon's screaming bench, and his best attempt would be an offering of his hardest pitch to the center of the plate. He forgot that Sanners had only one gear and ripped the ball cleanly to center field for a single.

Scores are meaningless in a ballgame when you are on your heels. Anderson felt the pressure and the possibility that the game could slip away even though they held the lead. He finally had a sigh of relief when he got Mags to pop up on a 2-2 pitch. As the two teams traded places, the emotion of confidence was replaced with doubt in only a matter of minutes, and the stalking Falcons were slowly moving toward their prey with each play that went by. Mickey ran images of the great Dodger pitcher, Sandy Koufax, through his mind and struck out the side to enter the last inning. But even Koufax's arm can grow weary. He struck out his last batter on a 3-2 pitch. The three balls he threw to the batter went all the way to the backstop. He wasn't losing his confidence, but he was losing his control.

"This is it, gentlemen!" Mickey greeted all of the players as they entered the dugout. No one sat down for the inning.

Sanners beat relentlessly on the fence with his palms. "Come on, guys! This one's ours!"

Mags and Danny both saw the same images in their minds. They were running scenarios through their heads and counting up the lineup. Both wondered and dreaded the idea that they may come to the plate with the game on the line.

Anderson knew the game was his, and he immediately went to work. *Three outs, and we have a championship.* Gil earned a strikeout by looking at the third pitch. It was a perfect curve over the center of the plate. Tom followed by fouling off the first two pitches, then swinging wildly at the third.

Anderson's engine now ran on high octane. *One out away from a league championship.* His team screamed, "Two down!" as he waited for the ball to make its way around the horn.

Anderson exhaled and tried to calm himself before throwing his hardest pitch. Ironically, it was perfectly suited for a guy who couldn't get out of the way of a slow-moving freight train. The tight fastball on the inside edge of the plate caught Kevin on the forearm. When he jumped up, it wasn't just a sigh of relief; it was a victory. Being hit by that pitch was as good as a hit. The Falcons jumped up and down like rabid animals as they placed the tying run on first. Saint Augie's was going just as crazy. The crowd reacted to every pitch.

Mickey stopped Stevie before he went to the field. "Don't swing until you have two strikes on you."

Stevie reverted to his low stance, and he took another walk. Now the go-ahead run was on first, and Danny's nightmare was coming true.

"Oh Jesus, oh Jesus, oh Jesus," he mumbled as he fumbled for his bat. "Come on, Ernie!" He looked at the Ernie Banks signature-model bat and reached down for a handful of dirt. He desperately wanted to be the hero but was petrified to actually take on the role. "Think about the next pitch, think about the next pitch . . ."

Danny looked like a mumbling psychotic that just stumbled out of a mental ward. He saw and heard everything but the pitcher and the pitch. He hoped for the same business that Stevie and Kevin got. He leaned over the plate hoping to get hit. It was all in vain, and he fell behind 0-2.

He stepped back out and heard only the voice of Mickey, "Hit the damn ball, man!"

Sanners gripped the fence with both hands. "Come on, Danny! Give it a ride, man!"

Danny stalled with another handful of dirt, a deep sigh, and a couple of taps to the insteps of his shoes. *Ready or not . . .*

He leaped on the next pitch to drill a liner toward Anderson. Stevie and Kevin were already running. The ball missed Anderson's glove by less than an inch and went straight to center field. By the time Danny rounded first, he didn't even see Eggs coaching third. He was on a dead sprint. He glanced up to see Stevie being waved home. At that point, he knew that Kevin was already scoring. Danny then took off for third as fast as he could. By the time he looked up, he realized he was being held up at second, but by now it was too late. He was caught in a pickle. Danny tried to backtrack, but Gonzales chased him down. Anderson stepped in behind him and took the throw. The tag wasn't gentle. It leveled Danny for the third out.

Nobody seemed to care. The two runs scored, and the Falcons were ahead. The Falcons were jumping up and down and screaming. Their emotions were on the outside, and all Eggs could do was smile. No matter what he said, he wouldn't be able to bring them down. They were just beginning to realize that they were the ones who were only three outs away from a league championship.

Mickey's arm was pumped with adrenaline, but the wrist was numb. He threw only two warm-up pitches, then signaled to Mags that he was ready. Mags had already envisioned holding the league championship trophy until he heard the voice of Eggs in his head. *The next pitch, gentlemen, focus on the next pitch.*

St. Augie's brought up the bottom-three men on the order, which suited the Falcons. All nine men on the field knew the game was in Mickey's hands. The first batter fouled off two pitches and took him to a full count. The next pitch got away, and St. Augie's put the tying run on first with a walk. The St. Augie's team was as loud as ever.

"Let's turn two men!" shouted Mags. In his heart, he knew Mickey would put an end to this, and they would all go home. The next pitch sailed over the batter's head, and the runner on first base advanced to second. The St. Augie's bench went into a frenzy. The whole team was on its feet jumping up and down and pounding on the chain-link fence

The next three pitches were just as bad, and the fourth ball nearly got past a diving Mags. The go-ahead run was now on first with no outs, and momentum had swung its ugly head again.

Mickey showed no emotion but knew his arm was spent. *One out . . . just one out at a time . . .*

He focused on two deep breaths before throwing as hard as he could right down the pipe. The ball missed its target and hit the batter. The bases were now filled, and each member of the Falcon team had tears on the edge of their hearts as they felt the game falling away. The St. Augie's bench now looked like the Falcon's bench just moments earlier. The parents of the St. Augie's team were now also feeling the victory only two bases away. The whole park buzzed, and every eye was on the pitcher and the batter.

Mags called timeout and ran out to the mound. Mickey couldn't make eye contact. "My wrist snapped. It's like my fingers are numb." He reached over and rubbed his hand.

"Come on, man, only three outs, and it's ours."

"You didn't hear me, man, my arm snapped. I can't throw shit."

"What the hell we gonna do, man? Just try . . ." Mags shook his head and realized the next three were the top of the order with Baker, Gonzales, and Anderson. Mags's eyes welled up in sadness. "Come on . . ."

By now Eggs had walked to the mound. "What's up, Mickey?"

Mickey looked down and rubbed his elbow. "I'm Casper Milquetoast, I'm spent, shit . . . I'm trying so hard, Coach, but I can't hit the plate."

Eggs never hesitated; he knew that if a guy's arm is gone, that's one thing, but if his confidence goes with it, they become a liability. He waved to his centerfielder, his best backup; it was time for Danny to steer the ship.

"Oh shit, oh shit, oh shit . . ." Danny saw Eggs wave him in, and he froze. He looked back to the ground and slapped his hand in his glove. "Oh shit oh shit oh shit oh shit . . ."

Danny slapped his glove again and stayed in center field. He looked over to Stevie in right field. "Come on, Stevie, stay on your toes out there, no outs!"

He looked back down at his glove and mumbled again, hoping the whole world would go away. He was in a daze like a man who just witnessed a bad accident, *This is not happening, please tell me this is not happening, oh shit oh shit oh shit . . .*

"Hey, Danny, coach is calling you in!" yelled Stevie. Both teams were now staring out to center field.

Mags looked at Eggs. "What's up with, Danny? What's he, deaf or something?" Eggs tried to catch Danny's attention as he waved once more.

"Ooooooh shit oh shit oh shit . . ." Danny was ready to die of a panic attack. He slapped his glove, put his hands on his knees, and looked up. *Eggs is waving me in.*

This time he couldn't fake it. He saw him, and he had to respond. He began to trot in. *Mickey's not coming out, no way, not Mickey. Eggs just wants my advice on how to throw to Baker, Gonzales, and Anderson . . . oh shit oh shit oh shit oh . . .*

"Danny, get warmed up, I'm putting Mickey in center field."

33

Session 8

Personal Journal 8

This is really strange, dear me, I finally realized that this journal really is just a letter to myself. When I look at my previous entries, I feel like a fool. I realize that I addressed them to Megan because I never trusted therapy, the process, or counselors. I thank God for them now. I guess for the first time I really trust what happens in group counseling. I always knew why Terrence chose me as his support partner for this group, but I never admitted it to myself. I guess I also realize the true destiny of pain.

MEG AND SHAW had no idea where this week's group would go. They arranged several leads to get the group going just in case they were to get stuck.

The group filed in to the room in silence. Megan opened with. "Any old business?"

Daniel was the first to speak. He looked directly at Meg. "I'm sorry, Meg. I was out of line last week. I really am sorry. You've been very patient. I have some things with Mick . . . uh . . . Terrence that we haven't talked about much, but I just want to say I'm sorry."

"I'm sorry too," said Terrence. "I hope no one is mad at Daniel, he's my pal, and I guess something went off inside both of us. Daniel and I talked a lot last week, and there's something I really need to bring to group, but I've never had enough guts to do it. I know why I've been too closed off, and I have had a life of all kinds of problems. Somehow, I lost my life a long time ago. It started on a day that was the greatest day of my life . . ."

34

Bottom of the Ninth

DANNY STOOD SPEECHLESS. His hands were numb and trembling.

"I can't . . . I . . . I . . ."

Eggs handed him the ball. "Warm up, we'll be fine. Mickey, take center."

Mickey turned to Danny. "I'm sorry, man, but anybody's better than me right now. Hell, Spikes could throw harder than me right now. Come on, Danny. Just hit Mags's target, and the game is ours. You can do it, man." He patted him on the back and turned to run out to center. Mags turned to walk to his place behind the plate, and Eggs left after one warm-up pitch. Danny felt the most profound sense of loneliness that he had ever experienced. The eyes of the entire world were upon him. Of the thousands of make-believe games he played as a child, he always imagined a day when he would be at the plate or on the mound in the World Series. The *cool as a cucumber* fantasy was easier than ever really facing such a situation. He now doubted his ability, strength, and leadership.

The first three warm-up pitches were wild. Two of them flew over Mags's head, going all the way to the backstop. He wasn't ready, but it didn't matter. Danny felt like he was standing in the middle of an eight-lane highway, and he wouldn't survive very long before a Mack truck would blindside him. He didn't feel fear in his heart – he was flat-out terrified.

He fell behind Baker 3-1 and sensed that any loss of control at this point would tie it or lose it. On the next pitch, he grunted as his best fastball left his hand. Baker surprised him by swinging and sending it back toward him. The ball caught a bad bounce, and the best he could do was throw his body in front of it. It ricocheted off his chest and fell in front of him. The runners were off, and one was headed for Mags behind home plate. Danny dove for the ball, wheeled to his knees, and threw a bullet to Mags. Mags touched the plate for the first out and held the ball.

The bases were still loaded. Mags looked up to see the next batter moving toward him. This batter was his nemesis. This batter held a constant sneer on his face – it was Gonzales. The umpire had gone to the dugout to get a fresh ball, and Mags stood face-to-face with the person he feared and hated most in this world.

"You're going to lose, fat boy."

Mags's voice was shaking. "Don't y-y-you deliver route n-n-number 409? That's right, John Gonzales." Mags stared upward. He swallowed and smiled. He was in control today. Mags always took a sense of ownership when he was behind the plate. This is not the street, this is his backyard, and he was wearing the armor.

"Hmmm, *Gazette* route number 409. Isn't that right? Weren't you missing some papers lately? Why I do believe I saw those papers. Why I do believe they were missing, and they ended up under the Federal Boulevard culvert." Mags's shaky voice now turned into one of spite and confidence rolled together.

"How the hell did you know we had papers missing?"

"Hmmm, good question. Oh, that's right, now I remember." Mags squinted with a sarcastic toothy grin. "Oh, I remember! I remember seeing a fat boy stealing them and then throwing them in the creek. Oh ya, and one more thing, I remember the fat boy pissing on those particular bundles." Mags moved within inches of Gonzales's face and forced the largest smile that his face was capable of displaying. "That's right! A fat boy was pissing right on a label that read Route 409 – 84 papers – John Gonzales. But you can still get them, Johnny boy. All you need to do is clean the fat boy's piss off of your name." Mags moved closer. "Psssssss . . ."

Gonzales took a step backward and shoved Mags at the same time. "I ought to kick your ass."

"Hey! what are you guys doing?" The umpire came back with the new ball.

"Nothing, sir," replied Mags. "Why, we were just discussing what a great game this has turned out to be. Isn't that right, Johnny? It'sssssssss great isssssssssssn't it?" Mags smiled at him again.

Gonzales now had fire in his eyes. It was as if he wished the bat in his hands could be used as a weapon. Mags raised his eyebrows and pulled his mask over his face – all the time smiling into Gonzales's face. He pulled his iron helmet over his head. This knight was now ready for a series of jousts. *May the best combatant win.*

Gonzales was seething. He was a loose cannon looking for a place to go off. Mags sent the signal down to Danny to throw outside. As he went into his wind-up, Mags put his teeth together to hiss "sssssss . . ."

Gonzales's body was a victim of his emotions. The only outlet was the swinging of the bat. He swung with everything he had and missed by a foot. He then picked up the bat and slammed it down on the plate.

Mags signaled for another outside pitch, then waited for the wind up. "Route 409, psssssssss," he whispered. Gonzales swung wildly again. This time after missing, he slammed the bat down on the plate with such force that it split. He then stomped over to the dugout and grabbed another bat. When he returned, he took a practice swing all the while that Mags was hissing from beneath his mask. "Pssssssss . . ."

His third swing was worse than the other two. It spun him around, and he landed on the ground all the while screaming as he swung. The anger filled his body. The frustration engulfed every ounce of common sense he had left. Every movement thereafter was mere instinctual reaction. He flew up from the ground, then leaped on Mags. Mags saw a fist moving toward his face at a speed that was propelled by the vengeance of a maniac. The knuckles collided with the catcher's mask with a snap that was evidence of a broken finger.

For the first time in his life, Mags laughed in the face of danger. This made Gonzales angrier; the next two punches were a blur. Neither had an effect on the catcher's mask. Gonzales's eyes bulged. By now there were at least three adults on their way to break up the melee.

The umpire didn't even have enough time to call him out when he found himself between them trying to break it up. The coaches pulled them apart and held Gonzales back. He screamed and writhed like a psychotic ready for the straight jacket.

After the scene cleared, the umpire called over both coaches to instruct them to tell their teams to keep their cool. Mags had blood streaming from his lip where Gonzales managed slip one last blow under the corner of the catcher's mask. It didn't matter; in fact, the blood tasted sweet. Mags glowed with delight. It was his greatest victory. He won the most important battle of his life with Gonzales. After all the years of bullying, he had beaten this man down and beaten him into submission, and he never swung a fist, making the victory even sweeter.

When the dust cleared, the players took their positions back on the field. The fight was enough to divert attention from Danny to something other than his performance. "One more out . . . one more out . . . I only need one out . . ." He was now mumbling incoherently. Somehow they managed to get the first two outs, but the bases were still loaded, and the greatest threat in the universe was stepping to the plate in the form of Chet Anderson.

Mags and Danny worked together for the first out. Mags was solely responsible for the second. The Falcons escaped with the second out without Danny throwing a single strike, but now he was on his own. The chess match between the pitcher and the batter was never better.

The parents, fans, and parishioners were now buzzing. This was Danny's high noon – his ultimate showdown. His mind could not center on anything. Anderson was taking practice swings with a determined look on his face. Danny was having nightmare visions running through his head. He was feeling like Ralph Branca staring down at his own Bobby Thompson when the New York Giants won the pennant on the last swing of the season in '51. He was the Yankees staring at Bill

Mazeroski who won the World Series on the last swing of the bat in 1960. *These things happen, and it's going to happen to me . . . I see Jean . . . Pats is watching . . . Father Abercrombie is screaming . . .*

Danny shook off six signals in a row, and finally Mags made his way to the mound. His chubby smile and jiggled run offered some comfort, but in this world of loneliness, it wasn't enough. Danny's hands were still shaking.

For the first time in the game, he was actually trying to think of strategies for getting a third out. He stared at the ground in front of Mags. "I've got to brush him back."

Mags shook his head in disbelief. "What the hell are you talking about? If you hit him, it will send us into extra innings. Are you out of your mind? Just throw the heat!"

"No, he's hanging out over the plate. I've got to brush him back so I can catch him on his heels and nail the outside corner of the plate. It's my only chance. He's a helluvan athlete, he'll get out of the way. Just let me do it, man!"

Mags shook his head and looked at Danny's trembling hands. "All right, one pitch, then follow my signals for the rest." He looked to Danny for a nod.

Mags then went down to a knee as if he were tying his shoe. As he grabbed the ball, he whipped the ball in one quick motion over the buckle on his catcher's shin pad. It tore the laces on the ball. His body jiggled as he ran back to the plate. "Umm . . . sir, I'm afraid we need another ball." Mags held the ball up to the umpire's face, where he inspected it and then turned and walked to the dugout to get another.

Mags stood alone with Anderson, and he knew he had only seconds. He spoke frantically and as quick as humanly possible. "Hey, Anderson, I swear, man, Danny's gone crazy! He says he doesn't give a shit about the game any more, he said, 'I'm just gonna hit that bastard Anderson in the freakin' head because that bastard Anderson hit a homer off me last year and I don't give a damn if we lose the game,' and I swear he's gonna throw at your head until he hits you. He says, 'I'll kill that bastard,' and you know what? I'm only saying this because I'm a nice guy, and I don't want him to smash your brains in, man, so please get the hell out of the way. He's crazy I swear." Mags finished his speech with panicked breathing as he watched for Anderson's response.

The umpire returned with a new ball. Anderson smiled at Mags and stepped back. "Ya right!" The hulking figure shook his head and stepped to the plate.

The first pitch was like a guided missile on a collision course with Anderson's chin. Danny was right: he was a tremendous athlete, and he hit the ground with a thud.

Mags snapped the ball out of the air, then quietly mumbled but loud enough for Anderson to hear, "I told you . . . told you . . . told you so . . . he's comin' again, he's gonna try again, I swear he's crazy. He said he's gonna kill you . . ."

Anderson's playful look was now replaced with gritted teeth. He kicked the dirt and dug in.

Mags mumbled in a whisper, "He's gonna do it again, I swear I swear I swear, watch out . . ."

Mags quietly set up on the inside of the plate and signaled for an inside pitch. Danny threw his best pitch for the low inside corner. The release of the ball made it seem like it was coming for him. Anderson stepped back and took a called strike on the inside corner. The count stood at 1-1 as Danny breathed a sigh of relief.

Mags called for another inside pitch and again accompanied the flight of the ball with his whispered warnings to Anderson. The ball broke too far inside, just missing the plate and sent the count to two balls and one strike. Mags kept up with his mumbling, "I'm telling you, man, he's a maniac. He's going to keep throwing at your head. Did you see that, man? He touched his head. That's his signal that he's comin' high inside, watch out, man."

Anderson stepped back in the box. Mags quietly shifted to the outside of the plate. The ball sailed waist high over the outside edge for a called strike to bring the count to 2-2. Anderson was fooled and was caught looking.

Danny filled his lungs with as much air as he could take in; then he slowly blew out all the air. He knew he was lucky to cheat the devil one more time. He knew in his heart that there was one last pitch in him. *The time has come . . . One pitch can end the game . . . One pitch . . . One throw . . . Think about what Eggs said about great ballplayers – they are only thinking about the next pitch . . .*

He shook off Mags three times. He wanted the fastball on the outside corner. Mags finally agreed. Danny conjured up images of the greatest pitchers he had ever witnessed and tried as hard as he could to put all of their talents into one pitch. The Detroit Tiger's had Denny McClain's high-leg kick. The Los Angeles Dodgers were blessed with Sandy Koufax's determination, and of course, the New York Yankees had Whitey Ford's composure. Now all those talents would come together for one pitch all at the same time. *Finish the game, right here, right now.*

In any athlete's life, they know those moments when a move, a shot, a swing, or a throw is perfect. Danny felt it racing through every part of his body. The leg kicked high, the step was perfect, the grip was hard, the release was flawless – it had everything he ever had to give. His body let out a scream as it left his hand.

In every pitcher's life, they know that feeling of the perfect pitch – the unhittable pitch, the immaculate pitch – the instant it leaves their hand. This was that moment for Danny. It was more accurate, faster, and more purposeful than any pitch he had ever thrown. The ball would paint the outside corner of the plate, and it would be impossible for Anderson to catch up with it. All he had to do was wait for the snap of the ball in the leather of Mags's glove. That sweet sound would begin the celebration of the Falcon's first league championship. He fell forward after the release and watched it sail. It felt gratifying to watch his work of art.

In every pitcher's life, there is also that moment when events don't go as perfectly as anticipated. Danny watched as Anderson strode into his swing. His entire body uncorked toward the incoming pitch. *It's on the outside part of the plate, he'll never . . .*

Emotions in sports are the best and the ugliest ingredients that life has to offer. When they are good, we want them to last forever. When they are bad, we want them to go away quickly. On a baseball field, if you are a fan, a player, a coach, or a parent, your emotions can swing as quickly as a bolo out of control.

Anderson stood in perfect balance when he swung his bat. Some kids swing with their wrists, others with their arms, and very few others can actually turn their hips into their swing. Anderson stepped into his swing. Power came from his wrists, arms, shoulders, hips, and legs as the bat collided with the ball. The perfectly placed pitch was met with a perfect swing. The thunderous crack of the bat was louder than a twenty-one gun salute. The sound was deafening.

The worst moment in a pitcher's life is the punch in the stomach when a ball leaves the infield. This one left faster than any that Danny had ever seen. Its destination was beyond right field – over Stevie's head. By the time Danny spun around to watch the ball, he could see a stunned Stevie looking up. Stevie knew where it would land – about thirty yards over his head. But . . . he would have to run after it anyway.

Danny fell to his knees and watched the ball sail. His perfect pitch was hit by the perfect swing from the perfect batter. The feel of the sun, the sounds of the park, and the smells of an afternoon barbecue were all melting together into a whirlpool of despair. Life could never get worse. The game would end on one swing.

The hearts of all the players, parents, and fans skipped a beat the instant the ball was his hit. The collision of horsehide on white ash wood provided a thunderous clap that could only deserve admiration. The glorious battle between two adversaries was nearing the end.

It seemed like Stevie could only run too slow toward an imaginary place where he might eventually catch up with the instrument of destruction. It all seemed in vain.

As Danny watched Stevie run in slow motion, another figure began to challenge the scene from far away. From center field, Mickey was already on a dead run to the deepest part of right field. He never thought about anything he did on the field. His body simply reacted. Good ballplayers start to feint toward one side of the field before the ball even arrives at the plate. Something in their brains calculate the speed of the swing, and their bodies start to move toward that side of the field. It's an inexplicable phenomenon that you see in old films of DiMaggio or Mays. They are moving toward the place where a ball will go long before others have thought about it.

Mickey's heels were flailing wildly as the back of his shoes carried some of the fresh-cut grass into the air. He hadn't looked toward the infield since the initial crack of the bat. His body continued to carry him faster than it ever had before. As Mickey's sprint turned to a blur, Stevie came to a stop. He realized his efforts were in futility.

Danny came back to his feet. Anderson was nearly to first base. Danny hopped up and down – as if his body language could help Mickey along. Mickey looked up for one last time, then leaped fully extended. His body shot out to a stiff flying prone position as he sailed the last ten feet of his journey parallel to the ground. Stevie watched in amazement as the flash of a figure moved like a cheetah into the deep abyss of right field. He saw Mickey leap and heard him grunt at the same time.

Mickey's glove stretched farther than it ever had as his body succumbed to gravity and contacted the ground. The white sphere came in like a guided missile to the very top laces of his glove where Mickey squeezed as hard as he could.

The entire park stood frozen and watched the gangly figure in deep right field stand up and hold the ball over his head. The infield umpire held a fist in the air, and the greatest athletic event in human history had finally ended. The Falcons were league champions.

You can throw away the Stanley Cup, the World Series trophy, and any old Super Bowl ring. Being on a championship team at the moment of victory causes the body to completely lose control. It causes mature humans to jump, flail, writhe, and scream simultaneously. There is no pride, there is no concern for appearance, and there is nothing else of any concern in the universe at that point.

After Mickey held up the ball, he watched the umpire pump a fist in the air to signal the final out. In his natural humility, he flipped it in the air and caught it in his other hand. He then bowed his head and jogged in. Modesty wasn't a quality he needed to work on: it was his essence.

Eggs always told his teams to never gloat or overcelebrate any occasion because you always have to remember how the other team feels. His words were not forgotten; it was simply a matter of being overcome by forces beyond the boys' control. The body and the mind simply celebrate. Sanners ran in from third and bear-hugged Danny. Danny threw his glove over his head. Stevie jumped on Mickey. Mags threw his mask in the air and spun around in time to see Gonzales pounding his fists on the chain-link fence.

Anderson pulled up his sprint halfway to second base and turned to walk to the dugout. Eggs closed his eyes and shook his head. In all of his years of professional baseball, he had never seen a catch like that one. He knew the game was over at the sound of Anderson's crack of the bat. He never dreamed it would end with a catch.

Father Abbie stopped clapping, then reached from under his blanket, and pulled out a paintbrush. "Father DiPaulo" – he gently tapped him on the wrist – "is this yours? Oh yes, look right there on the handle. It says in neat letters Father DiPaulo." He laid the paint brush on Father DiPaulo's lap and continued clapping. He had been saving the brush for years. Father DiPaulo chuckled, then planted a friendly slap on the back of Father Abercrombie.

Spikes climbed halfway up the backstop fence and shook it like a monkey trying to escape from his cage. The field was a boiling pot of emotions. The Falcons were league champions.

The celebration that followed was beyond anything the boys had ever experienced. The teams lined up to shake hands. Gonzales never even left the dugout.

The last two players to shake hands were Anderson and Mickey. Anderson smiled and held on for a moment. He looked him in the eye. "Nice catch, man."

Mickey smiled back. "Thanks, nice hit, I was lucky."

Archbishop Rogers was the DCYBA league director. Knowing that the league championship was on the line, he showed up halfway through the game and brought with him the trophy. The Falcons couldn't stop beaming. After the presentation, they screamed and all hugged each other.

The parents heaped on the adulation, and the boys couldn't get enough of it. Joe Hannigan hugged Mickey and held him tight. Pats hugged each of the boys. Spikes held on to Mickey's back pocket for the next half hour. He couldn't let go of the greatest ballplayer in the world.

Louis Garrison grew tired of waiting. Life on the outside wasn't going like he planned. Old tempers were brewing, and old habits came back. Going to bars, fighting, and drinking gave him back his same hangovers, his same mental fog, and the same temper. He called his cousin in California and decided to start a new life out there. He would leave tonight after he settled two items of business.

He sat in a car he hot-wired two hours earlier. No one would notice it was gone for a week. The family he stole it from was on vacation.

After two joints and a twelve-pack, it was time for business. He walked to his former girlfriend's apartment and pounded on the door. She made the last mistake of her life by opening the door. The flurry of fists lasted for two minutes.

He had only one last score to settle. He began to have flashbacks of his failed robbery of Tom Dooley's Liquor Mart. The manager, Harvey Treston, had wrestled him to the ground and hit him with his own gun. Louis knew the day would come when he would have to pay. All of his years in prison, he dreamed of paying him back. Treston joked with the cops when they cuffed him and led him away. *He won't wrestle it from me this time.*

The celebration went on for another half hour. The boys didn't want it to end. Eventually the parents drifted away until only a handful remained. Spikes let go of Mickey's pocket only long enough to imitate the diving catch and drink root beer.

The Maglianos had brought enough food to feed an army, and the boys ate and drank their sodas in their imaginary clubhouse. At least thirty people came up and shook Mickey's hand. Danny was fine with that. Mickey saved his life. The only thing people would have remembered if they had lost was "who threw the last pitch?" Now it didn't matter. They won – they were champions. The closing pitcher finished the job, kissed his girlfriend, and soaked up the best that life had to offer.

The four boys fingered the trophy every chance they got. But sooner or later, they knew they had to go home. There were now only a few people hanging around. After hugs, even Lisa and Jean went on their way.

"Hey, guys, what do you say we throw your bikes in the truck, and I'll drive you home?" Joe Hannigan offered.

Mickey picked up his bike and lofted it in the back of the truck. He picked up Spikes and put him in the front seat.

"I think we should ride the bikes," said Sanners.

"Ya, lets ride," said Mags.

Mickey turned to his best friend. "Hey, you, the winning pitcher!"

Danny smiled back at him. "What?"

"What do you think?" said Mickey. "Should we ride with these guys or take the truck?"

Danny tilted his head back and screamed, "Lets ride, this is too much fun!"

"All right!" He grabbed Spikes. "Hey, slugger, I'll meet you at home."

Spikes grabbed his T-shirt. "No, Mickey, go with us."

"Naw, you go with Dad. Here, buddy." He handed him his ball glove. "You can have it."

Spikes put on the oversized glove as his eyes lit up. "Thanks, Mickey!" he screamed.

Mickey went to the back of the truck and took his bike out. "I'll meet you at home, Dad."

Joe Hannigan walked to the back of the truck. "All right, buddy, come here." He signaled a wave to his oldest son.

Mickey walked to him, and Joe devoured him in a strong hug. Whispering in his ear he said, "I love you, Mickey, whether you guys would have won or lost – it doesn't matter. The image I'll always hold in my heart is of you with your friends, coming together in courage." Joe's voice cracked as they pulled away. Mickey noticed tears in the corners of his father's eyes.

Joe turned to the four boys. "See you back at the house, guys, and hey, Vic, nice game. Danny, nice pitching, and of course" – he paused and pointed to Mags – "you could've never done it without the big guy behind the plate." The four soaked up the compliments and gleamed back at him.

The boys waved and watched Joe, and Spikes close the doors and drive away.

Louis Garrison pulled up in front of Tom Dooley's Liquors. He could see the head bob back and forth behind the counter. Treston is working today. He reached into the glove box and pulled out a .38 caliber revolver.

He spun the clip, shoved it into his pants, and walked toward the front door.

"Did you see that catch?!" screamed Sanners. "That was the most unbelievable thing I've ever seen!" The four bikes cruised side by side down the street.

Mags threw his head back. "We did it! We did it!"

The boys rode together and reveled in the greatest day of baseball in the history of humankind. Tonight, the celebration would continue as they planned to sleep out in their bags in Mickey's backyard.

Louis Garrison paced back and forth by the cooler in the back of the store and occasionally glanced over his shoulder at the front counter. He waited until there were no customers in the store.

A voice came from behind the counter, "Hey, pal, anything I can help you with?"

Louis Garrison even hated his voice. "Yes, you can." He strode to the counter. "Remember me?"

A look of shock came over Harvey's face. He looked at the face, then remembered the tattoo on his neck. "Ya, I remember you. You're a son of a bitch, and you can get the hell out of here right now!" He turned to grab the phone. The police had informed him of Garrison's parole conditions and knew he wasn't to step foot in the store.

Garrison reached over the counter and tore the phone from his hands. In one swift move, he brought the gun face-to-face with Harvey. Harvey slowly brought his hands up and felt a chill spill down his spine.

"First, you can empty the cash register now!" He held the gun steadfast. Harvey followed his orders.

"Dad, I have to pee," said Spikes as he held his crotch with one hand and squeezed the baseball glove with the other.

Joe glanced over at him and continued to drive. He chuckled, "I knew it. I knew after your third root beer. Sooner or later, the old plumbing pipes would have to burst. Can you wait till we get home?"

"Noooo, I gotta go."

Joe smiled and began to look for a service station. He went another half block and spotted the store on his right. "Tell you what, buddy, you can run into Tom Dooley's and use the bathroom. I think Harvey's working tonight. He won't mind."

Joe pulled the truck near the front door and left the engine running. Spikes held on to the glove and opened the truck door. He had peed here before. He jumped out of the truck and ran for the door. Joe laughed as he watched him. He reached down to turn on the radio and then glanced into the store. He could see a man with a gun pointing it at Harvey Treston's head. A bolt of fear jumped into his body.

"Spikes, wait! SPIKES!" Joe flew out of the side of the truck. He watched Spikes open the door and run in. Joe was running on instinct.

A small blur flew in front of Louis Garrison. Maybe something was running – maybe toward him. He instinctively backed up and pointed the gun in that direction. "Hold it! Don't move!" screamed Garrison. Spikes stopped in his tracks. The gun didn't register in Spikes's mind. He looked up and had tears in the corners of his eyes. He was going to burst. He had to go.

Joe Hannigan ran in through the door and yelled, "SPIKES!" Garrison was already squeezing the trigger. The bullet hit the ball glove in Spikes' hand – then ripped into his shoulder and spun him around. The glove went flying.

Joe was still screaming as he ran toward his youngest child. "SPI – "

The second bullet went directly through Joe Hannigan's rib cage and entered his heart. His heart stopped beating before he hit the ground.

The sound of a cannon filled the liquor store. When Garrison turned away, Harvey grabbed a shotgun from under the counter and blew Garrison's face away. His body flew into a display of wine bottles and went careening across the store. Harvey emptied the other barrel into his chest.

Joe's heart immediately stopped beating as he went down. Spikes reached out and screamed, "DAD!" as he crawled to the lifeless body. Joe had only seconds of life left in him. He pulled him close and squeezed him. By now Spikes's bladder had emptied. He was in a state of shock seeing his father covered in red.

Harvey was already loading another shotgun shell as he stepped from behind the counter. "You son of a bitch!" He pointed the gun at Garrison and knew he was already dead. He took no chances and emptied one more shell into his chest. He turned toward the screaming child. It wasn't until that moment he recognized the two people on the floor. Joe Hannigan, a longtime customer and friend lay lifeless, and Spikes continued to scream uncontrollably as blood poured from his shoulder.

The boys arrived at Mickey's house and sat down in his room. They were still giddy from the afternoon. They would have to get their sleeping bags later. By now, Mags had told the story three times about how he got Gonzales riled up. The phone rang.

Seconds later, they all stopped as they heard a scream. Mickey jumped up. It was the voice of his mother. Moments later, the door flew open and Marilyn Hannigan screamed, "Mickey!"

The boys froze in their tracks. She was white as a ghost and shaking. "Mickey! We've got to go! There's been an accident! Where's my keys?! WHERE'S MY KEYS?!" Her hands went to her head. "My God! Where's my keys Mickey?!" Mickey jumped up and followed her in a state of shock. His mother was delirious and shaking.

The boys walked slowly from his bedroom not knowing what to do. "Come on, we've got to get to Denver Memorial Hospital!" She ran out the door as Mickey chased her. The other three stood in the kitchen and watched the car fly down the street.

Danny immediately called Pats and told her what few details he had. She was on her way. Mags called his mom and told her where they were going. Sanners had no calls to make.

Marilyn Hannigan and Mickey sat on the bench in the waiting room. A doctor in his midfifties with a gray moustache walked in. "Mrs. Hannigan?" She leaped to her feet. "Please come with me." Mickey jumped to his feet.

"This is my son . . ." her voice drifted off.

"I would like to just talk to you alone for minute. Please wait here." He signaled to Mickey to sit on the couch. He nervously obeyed the orders.

A few moments later, he heard a bloodcurdling scream from down the hall. It was his mother's voice. He rose to his feet. His mind was in a fog. His body shook as he moved down the hall looking for his mother. "Mom! Mom!" His voice echoed down the corridor. "Mom!"

A nurse emerged from an office and moved toward him. He continued to yell. He was lost and confused.

Mickey turned as he heard the patter of feet running down the hallway behind him. Pats ran at full speed with Danny, Sanners, and Mags behind her.

The nurse approached them in front of Mickey. Pats caught her breath as she joined them.

The nurse looked to the parental figure among them and asked, "Are you with the Hannigans?" Pats acknowledged. The nurse asked the four boys to wait in the waiting room while she spoke to Pats.

The boys sat down next to Mickey. Danny asked, "What happened?"

Mickey looked blankly at them. "I don't know. Mom said that Dad was in an accident." There was no Mickey grin, no emotions, only disbelief. All four were wondering, *What kind of accident? A car? What happened?*

The four boys waited by themselves. They were still wearing their Falcon T-shirts and ball caps, but the joy of what they represented was far removed. Instead, a mysterious mood of shock held them spellbound.

After minutes of silence, Pats appeared at the door of the waiting room. Her eyes were reddened, and her hands kept going to her face to wipe her eyes. The doctors informed her that Marilyn was nearly incoherent and in a state of shock. It was now the duty of Pats to have to tell Mickey what happened.

"Mickey," her voiced trembled. "I need to talk to you. You boys wait here for a minute."

She led him down the hallway and sat next to him on bench thirty feet away from the waiting room. Danny, Mags, and Sanners watched through the glass as she led him down the hall and sat down next to him. They watched as she talked while holding his hand.

When the doctors told Marilyn that Joe Hannigan had been shot, she completely lost control. The bullet entered his chest, and he died within seconds. Spikes would be able to pull through, but he lost a lot of blood before the ambulances arrived. Harvey Treston held him tight while they waited. Another customer came in and helped to hold bandages on his shoulder. The entire time he screamed for his father. Spikes was asleep now, and the doctors determined that he would make it.

The boys watched from behind the glass as they saw Mickey jump to his feet. They couldn't hear the conversation, but they could hear Mickey scream, "No!" They watched him hold his hands to his face as his upper body moved up and down. "No!" They could hear him scream again. His forearms went to the sides of his head as if he was trying to close off the rest of the world. Every time Pats tried to touch him or follow him, he pulled away. His hands went down to his side still balled in fists. He turned back toward Pats and threw his fists down stomping both feet at the same time. Then he ran down the hallway. Pats pursued him. *This isn't supposed to happen, not to my family, not to me, not in our neighborhood, and not in my life.*

The boys watched Pats race after him and finally catch him. He screamed, "No! No! No!" at the top of his lungs. He then fell against the wall. His face slid down the wall as he crumpled to the ground. Mickey's knees hit the floor as he brought his head down toward them. Holding his forearms to the side of his head, the boys watched him wail.

A couple of nurses helped him to his feet as the boys stared in disbelief at the scene. Somehow their perfect lives had turned to a nightmare, and somehow the strongest boy in the world was helpless.

Pats eventually came back to the waiting room and told the others. For the next hour, they cried and held each other.

Marilyn and Mickey held each other in Spikes's hospital room as they watched him sleep. Hours later, exhausted, she fell asleep in the chair next to the bed. On the other side of the bed, Mickey held Spikes's hand. For hours, he whispered, "I should have been there . . . I should have been there . . . It's my fault . . . I should have stayed in the truck . . . I should have been there."

Mickey finally drifted off to sleep somewhere around one in the morning.

Around four in the morning, Spikes's tiny heart stopped beating, and he joined his father, Joe Hannigan. The person who Mickey idolized in life and the person who idolized Mickey were gone forever.

The Mickey the world had come to know also died that night.

35

Session 8
The Story

TERRENCE FINISHED TELLING his story then brought his chin to his chest and sobbed. The entire group sat in silence. Even Jan had tears on her face. Megan had no words. She moved over in front of Terrence and reached out with her trembling hands. She sat in front of him and gently placed her hands underneath his hands and squeezed them with a soft feeling of understanding.

Megan tried to imagine what he looked like years ago. She looked up at his face and tried to imagine the boyish grin he must have had. Somehow, the pattern of his life all came together. It made sense. Terrence had so much life potential but spent most of it trying to numb himself over the guilt he felt. He believed that if he had done just one thing differently, his life could have been changed. Perhaps he could have taken the bullet. But he didn't.

Meg could hardly speak; the words came out in a muffled whisper, "I'll bet . . . I'll bet . . ." She cried again and made no attempt to stop the tears. She couldn't stop shaking. "I'll bet you were . . . the world's greatest brother. I'm so sorry."

No one in the room could make eye contact. The emotions overtook each person.

When the final round went around, each member commented on their sadness. Shaw was looking forward to hearing from Jan. For the first time, she showed emotion and connection; she actually cried, she actually thought about someone else's feelings. She's finally turned the corner.

Jan looked up at her turn and said, "I just want to say that I was upset today because I finally wanted to bring something to group, and we never got around to *my* issues."

"I lost it," said Megan. She sat down in her office with Shaw. Her hands came to her face as she leaned over.

"What's going on, Meg?"

"I lost it, I cried, I lost control. I've lost my ability to lead this group. Damn, Shaw what's wrong with me? I wasn't just crying for Terrence. I was crying for me too, and I lost control."

"So I'm a failure too?"

"I never said that Shaw"

"I've cried in group, but when I'm emotional, it's okay. When you cry you fail? Something's going on, Meg, and after last week, you never even answered me when I asked you about the other group members saying, 'They didn't know you.' Something's going on, and you won't even talk to me. They don't feel connected to you, and I've got to tell you now, Meg. I'm your best friend for God's sake, and you don't even want to talk to me."

Megan tried to balance her mixed emotions. She loved Shaw but felt angry and upset at the same time. "I don't know what you're talking about." Her jaw and hands alternated between clenches. She felt angry at herself, and it was starting to surface toward her best friend. She looked up and made eye contact with him. "I connect to others, Shaw. For heaven's sake I've seen hundreds of people in therapy!"

"Listen to yourself, Meg – *in therapy*. Therapy is your professional job. It's your job! Look at us, you're one of the best friends I've ever had in my life, but when you're upset – do you come to me? Do you go to anyone? When was the last time you hugged someone when you were upset? You give clients therapeutic empathy, but you won't let anyone understand you. You're able to take all the intellectual risks, but no personal risks, you can't be open with me even once! What the hell is going on?!"

Meg's head swirled with emotions – hearing this from a friend hurts. She had a lifetime of training in philosophical and theoretical insight, but personal insight was painful.

"Dammit, Shaw, I'm not your client, don't 'therapize' me!" She stood up, grabbed her bag, and walked out.

36

August 19, 1968

MAGS, SANNERS, AND Danny spent the night talking and crying. Mags initiated plans to cover Mickey's route. They would split it three ways and deliver it as long as they had to. They also mowed his lawn the next day. There would be family visiting after the funeral. It should look good.

Going back to Bud's was out of the question – it would be painful. They couldn't stand to go without their friend, and life would never be the same even if he did show up. The boys' lives were being transformed. *You shouldn't have to grow up this quick. It's not fair. These things aren't supposed to happen to kids. These things aren't supposed to happen to us.* The boys had been delivering tragic headlines for years. They never imagined that one day their lives would be in one: **Denver Fireman and Son Killed in Holdup.** Each of them spilled tears on their papers that morning.

The four of them finally got together after the funeral. Not a word was spoken about *the* day. They never spoke of *the* day again. Whatever was accomplished that day, whatever was wonderful about that day was wiped out. The conversations around Mickey were awkward. *What's there to talk about? What should we say?*

The funeral was a dramatic and overwhelming display of respect as fellow firemen from all over the city of Denver were lined up in their uniforms. They started a fund for Marilyn, and the donations were enormous.

37

Tying Flies

SHAW BEGAN CALLING Meg's office early in the morning. After the third call, her secretary said she had gone home for the day. Shaw finished his classes and cancelled his late-afternoon office hours.

Shaw tried to balance the pizza and the twelve-pack of soda. He had been knocking at Meg's door for five minutes. He wandered around to the back of her apartment and saw her standing on the grass whipping her fly rod back and forth over her head. She glanced over her shoulder and saw him coming. She continued to practice her casts as he sat down on the grass. He watched her grace back and forth, back and forth. "Meg, I have a big favor to ask. Could you teach me to tie flies?"

Meg kept casting and didn't look at him. A minute went by as she continued to cast. Shaw noticed a lone tear streaming down her cheek. She finally stopped and carefully laid the rod down. Sitting down on her heels, she fell over to her back. Shaw sat watching her as she lay on the grass and stared at the sky. A minute went by, and Shaw walked over to her. He extended a hand and helped her up. She picked up her fly rod, then walked over and picked up the soda in the same hand.

Shaw picked up the pizza and walked next to her on the way to her apartment. Meg gently reached with her free hand and edged her fingers into his. She softly held his hand as they walked toward her apartment. "I'd be happy to teach you how to tie flies."

They sat in silence eating the pizza for the next fifteen minutes. Shaw finally spoke, "I'm sorry I lectured you in your office yesterday."

"You're okay, Shaw, what are friends for?" She didn't look up.

He smiled and sipped his soda. "You're okay too, Meg." Shaw was always ready to break Megan up with humor. Today was not one of those days. After finishing his last bite, he wiped his hands and leaned back on the couch in silence. Megan walked over and sat in front of him on the coffee table.

"All I could think of yesterday was how Terrence was robbed of his childhood. That's not the way life is supposed to be. I've felt guilty all day. I didn't sleep at all last night. There's something I need to tell you. You know, yesterday when you said you didn't know me?" Her voice fluttered as she swallowed and continued. "Well, you don't know me, and I feel guilty about that." She reached out and took his hands. "Do you remember when I told you that I broke these fingers playing basketball? I never told you what really happened . . ."

Megan looked in the mirror and adjusted her dress; she was ready to go home. Even though she had just turned sixteen, she didn't have her driver's license yet. She would have to go when her friends were ready.

The junior prom was winding down, and she was tired. Life had been difficult over the past four years. Her father died when she was twelve, and her mother had gone into a shell. In the past year, her mother began dating, and a month ago her boyfriend had moved into their apartment. Megan and her little sister, Ally, had been the glue in the family ever since. Her mother worked nights as a secretary for a food-delivery service and began to distance herself from everyone. The boyfriends she had been seeing were often met in bars and were inadequate at filling the empty spot in her heart.

Her job was to coordinate the early-morning hours of deliveries. Her new boyfriend drank heavily but was gone most of the time. In the past month, he would come home after a night at the bar and would often be alone with the girls.

Ally was two years younger and nearly looked like her twin. When the new boyfriend began making passes at the girls, they passed them off as compliments at first but soon were feeling uneasy. Ally asked Megan to not go out at night, but on this night she was thrilled for big sister. It was the first time she had ever gone to a high school dance, and the two were giddy. Ally helped her pick out her dress, fix her hair, and make sure everything was right. There were no worries about the new boyfriend because he never came before midnight.

"Do you guys want to come in?" Megan looked back in the car. "Come on, guys, my mom's not home." Her two girlfriends confided that they had to be home early too, so she turned and walked to the door. She had a big grin on her face and couldn't wait to tell Ally. Four boys asked her to dance!

Megan opened the front door and noticed all the lights were out. "Ally?" she said in a soft voice.

She turned on the hall light. "Ally?" Again, no answer. She then heard crying, whimpering, from down the hall. Her heart pounded out of control. Her legs felt like they weighed a ton. She tried to run, but everything was in slow motion. She opened Ally's bedroom door and heard a scream. "Megan, help me!" Ally was pinned beneath a large figure.

He turned and yelled at Megan, "Get the hell out of here!"

Megan reached for Ally's softball bat leaning next to the dresser. In a blur and in a fit of rage, she swung wildly at him. With each swing, she let out a scream. No words came out, only rage. The first blow struck him squarely on his back. The second missed, and hit her sister's leg. He stood up and started toward her. "Stop it. You little bitch!" The third swing caught him in the face. He then grabbed the bat and tried to hit her. Megan wrestled with the bat and fought with every ounce of strength in her body. The bat came loose, and the two fell to the floor. As she swung to hit him, he grabbed her fingers and bent them back with a snap, breaking two of them. His large hand went to her throat and began squeezing the life breath out of her. Megan could feel herself passing out. Suddenly a muffled crunch echoed through the room, the fingers loosened around her throat, and he fell limp on top of her. She wrestled her way out from under him and saw Ally standing over him with the bat in her hands. Ally's crazed eyes were locked in a gaze on him as the end of the bat quivered in the air.

The figure continued to move on the ground. Megan ran for the nightstand and pulled out her father's pistol. The girls stood over him and waited. After trying to get up, he passed out facedown on the floor.

"Come on!" screamed Megan. She grabbed one leg and tried to drag him, but he was too heavy. "Come on! Help me!"

Megan had lost her senses. Her emotions had now escalated to hysteria, and she was focused on one goal – she had to get him out of the house. Ally reached down and grabbed the other leg. His pants hung halfway off his legs, and the sight repulsed Megan. *Just get him out.*

The girls finally got him to the doorway when he started to wake up. Megan was locked in a violent trance as she fiercely kicked him until he was out the doorway. Ally slammed the door, and Megan fumbled frantically to lock the deadbolt.

Megan sprinted back to the bedroom and picked up the bat and gun. Ally curled in a ball in front of the door, and Megan sat down next to her.

Megan could see Ally shaking. Instinctively, she reached out to comfort her younger sister. *I should have stayed. I should have been here. I never should have left you alone with this monster. It's all my fault.*

Megan pulled her close with her arm while holding the gun in the other hand. In her mental state of numbness, Megan was confused. She couldn't understand why her fingers would not grip the gun. She looked at her mangled fingers and laid the gun down by her side. Ally sat mesmerized, crying and pleading at the same time, "Don't tell Mom, don't tell Mom, whatever you do don't tell Mom."

Megan sat next to her and tried to pick up the gun again. A smash at the screen door made them both jump. Megan held Ally tighter.

He was waking from his drunken stupor. "Let me in!" He smashed the door again. Megan reached up to the door and checked the lock again. He yelled again and slammed the screen door. The glass shattered, causing them both to jump again.

For the next few minutes, they sat shivering in silence. They heard his truck start as he drove away.

"That's how my fingers were broken. It was the worst night of my life. Ally and I were young and afraid. For the next hour, all she could do was beg me to not tell Mom. I helped her bathe and put on new clothes. I held her all night long. We were both in shock – Ally felt she had done something wrong. He came home that night drunk out of his mind and started fondling her. She went to her room and locked the door. The more he drank, the angrier he grew. Eventually he kicked the door open and raped her. We never even saw him again. I had to make up a story about my fingers and the broken window to Mom. We were just innocent girls, but Ally was my baby sister. It hurt more than anything I've ever known. She made me promise not to tell. I was too stupid to know better. After that, she was never the same. She never wore a smile again.

"Shaw, you once asked me about my sister, and I told you she died in a car wreck when she was sixteen. She didn't. I was away at college my freshman year, and I got a call. When my Mom came home at seven in the morning one day, she found Ally in the bathroom. She slit her wrists. That bastard killed my baby sister. It took her years to die."

Megan's head fell to her chest. She closed her eyes and began to sob. She tried to breathe, cry, and talk at the same time. Shaw could feel her pain in every word.

"For the years that followed, I wished that I had died fighting him. I should have stayed home that night." Megan opened her eyes and glanced down at her bent fingers. They were a lifelong reminder of that horrible night.

"I knew something was going on with me in this group. Terrence's slit wrists and losing his brother, he was robbed of his childhood."

Megan moved next to Shaw on the couch and put her head on his shoulder. "Hold me, Shaw," she whispered. "Oh God, it still hurts so bad."

The two sat on the couch and cried together until she fell asleep in his arms. Shaw gently moved from her side and lay her head on a pillow. He pulled a blanket over her and sat on a chair and stared at her. He pulled his hands to his face and started crying again. At that point, he understood more about Megan than he ever had before. She closed herself off for years with a style of relating that said, *I'm unworthy of other's love, no one could possibly love me.*

The parallels to Terrence's life were now clear. Both became fiercely independent, one immersed in academics, another in alcohol – both numb to the pain. Guilt kept them from connecting to others. They both played their scenes over in their minds throughout their lives saying, *I should have been there.*

Shaw stood up from the chair and walked around her apartment. He had sat for two hours staring at his best friend. Shaw glanced at the clock – it was past midnight. He looked at her pictures, and they brought a smile to his face. When he saw the picture with the fly in his cheek, he chuckled. Over in the corner he saw her fly-tying kit. He moved it over to the coffee table and opened the book – *Beginner's Guide to Tying Flies.*

Shaw sat down and opened the pages. He then reached into the box and pulled out a few of the items. He attached his a blank hook to the small vice and began to tie his first fly. *Let's see . . . Step one . . . Hmm . . .*

A few hours later, he shook his fingers. Three of them now had Band-Aids on their tips, the rest had glue stuck to them, and two fingers on his left hand were stuck together. He overlooked one detail in tying flies – you're supposed to clamp the hook with the barb pointing down, not up. Every time he stabbed his fingers with the fishhook, he kept wondering if his "ow . . . ow . . . ow!" might wake her up. Megan slept quietly.

Finally, Shaw sat back and beamed. He finished tying his first fly. He laughed when he noticed that it didn't look anything like the pictures in the book. It sprouted from the hook in several directions. No fish in its right mind would mistake it for the real thing. Shaw chuckled out loud, imagining for the first time in the history of the nature kingdom, a school of fish laughing hysterically when they saw it. It was twice the size of anything he had ever seen Megan use. It was the Sasquatch of flies, plain ugly, but he was proud of it.

Shaw wrote a note, placed it on the coffee table, and laid the fly on top of it. He walked over to her, bent over, and softly kissed her on the cheek. He then stood up, wiped a lone tear from the corner of his eye, and walked out the door.

Dear Meg, I don't think I'll ever be able to find the words to tell you what you mean to me. If I could wave a magic wand and make the world perfect for you, I would. But I think you are perfect just the way you are, and you've been the perfect friend in my life. We all have shadows that haunt us, and I feel like the luckiest person on earth to be the one you trust with yours. You are the spark in my life that makes me keep wanting to do the work I do and to try to be there for others. You are the glow in a world that is often dimly lit. Thanks for always being there for me. I promise I'll go fishing with you this weekend if you'll have me along. Love, Shaw.

38

Lessons

"HAVE ANY OF you ever noticed how we tend to act a little different depending on who we are interacting with? Do you act the same around your parents as you do in class or with your best friend?" Megan waited and looked around at her class. "Somebody give me an example."

"I tend to be more argumentative around my parents," said a woman in her thirties.

"Ahh . . . ," said Megan. "So they tend to bring out *that* side of you, good, other examples?"

"When I'm in a meeting with other teachers, I become quiet. I tend to get nervous if I speak," said a male teacher in his twenties. "When I'm with my students, I'm okay, I'm confident, but then around my colleagues I doubt myself."

"Ahh . . . another good example. Help me out with this . . ." She waited and looked around.

The woman spoke again. "I feel more in control in my class."

"Yes, great stuff, did everyone hear what Joan said? Control. My experience with groups has enabled me to understand how we often present ourselves differently when we are under pressure than in other situations in life – and it's because of our fears. We fear losing control, exposing ourselves too much, and we fear other's evaluations of us. What happens is we develop roles. Some of this role is really you, and the other part of this role is behaving how you believe the other person or persons expect you to act. There is a part of you that is consistent, such as your mood or your outlook.

Are you typically a negative or positive person? These things remain fairly constant, but your style of relating depends on whom you are relating with."

"In group, we have the same thing, but sometimes our role is in flux. We change according to the paths we cross with other people. Think about the different groups you interact with in everyday life – with your friends, are you the humorist? Or with your family, a peacemaker? Or in class, the logical thinker? I've facilitated dozens and dozens of groups, and I am fairly consistent in how I relate. However, at times my path of emotions may take a diversion. In other words, have you ever felt odd, upset, or sad, or happy after you interacted with someone?"

Megan waited a moment, then continued, "I had a woman once tell me in counseling that she hadn't seen her mother in some time and then went to visit her. This woman had a severe drinking problem just like her mother. Her mother was dying of liver cancer, and when she saw her she said, 'That was it for me. I never drank again. I was done. I saw myself in that mirror and I knew that one day the woman in the hospital bed would be me.' Now, here was this woman moving along in her life along this path." Megan drew a line on the chalkboard. "And here was her mother on this path, and their lives flowed together in a unique way that shifted one person's course of life. It's remarkable. Sometimes we end up meeting someone, knowing someone, or relating to someone and *bang*! Our life changes, sometimes we don't even have enough insight to figure it out at the time. We have to keep our eyes open for these diversions in the flow of our lives. Sometimes the diversion makes us stronger and sometimes weaker.

"Group, to me is like taking all of these people who are seeking similar things, such as insight to our fears, understanding of our pain, a desire for strength in relationships, and diverting all of their paths together. What happens is sometimes clear to us, and sometimes it's a mystery. Sometimes our lessons are not even realized until long after the interaction.

"Even though the stages of group are predictable, what makes us emerge as different people is the creation of your new self as a result of your interactions with others.

"I never had a group I didn't learn something from. Sometimes they are little things and sometimes they can be big. We also have to realize that we, as leaders, are fragile. But it's okay to be fragile. In fact, we need to give ourselves permission to be fragile. As group facilitators we can't be afraid to face our own sensitive flaws."

"We don't facilitate groups for own issues, but sometimes our personal issues emerge when our life flows into theirs." Megan stopped and looked up. She was wandering into her own thoughts. She couldn't stop thinking about how her life's tears, and her life story had merged with Terrence's. Their lives had flowed together.

"*We* may emerge completely different people too."

39

Fall 1968

THE YEAR CAME to a close for Mickey, Danny, Mags, and Sanners. Local events seemed to blend into obscurity as the *Times* focused on bigger national events. A week after the holdup, for three days in late August, the world watched the Democratic convention in Chicago as the clash between the protesters and the police escalated into an eventual melee. Nightsticks flew, hundreds of arrests were made, and the paddy wagons filled with bloody demonstrators. During the convention week in a far away land called Viet Nam, a war continued to rage.

The boys continued to deliver the headlines reflecting the tumultuous year. The first week of September saw a picture of a woman carrying a protest sign stating *Welcome to the Cattle Auction,* as the women's liberation movement protested the Miss America Pageant in Atlanta. High heels and bras were pitched into a receptacle called a *Freedom Trash Can,* as women vowed the next generation would never be bound by such degrading items.

Major League baseball closed out its season in October as the Tigers beat the Cardinals in the World Series. A month later Nixon was elected president over Humphrey and Wallace. *Apollo 8* circled the moon in late December, and the world kept changing. For the boys, they made their arrival in high school. Danny went to homecoming with Jean and continued to date her. His confidence grew.

Sanners found his place in football and made the varsity squad. Mags went out for football as an offensive lineman. In one of the first practices while running drills, a cocky senior was determined to initiate the sophomores – he knocked Mags senseless.

It was the biggest mistake of that poor senior's high school career. On the next drill, Sanners knocked the senior out cold. His helmet went rolling. *You don't do that to a friend of Sanners.* It earned him a role in the starting lineup.

Eventually, Mags quit and became the equipment manager. He was so meticulous in his organization that the coaches started to treat him like an assistant coach. Soon he had inventoried and repaired equipment, and organized the entire athletic department in such a manner that he was indispensable. By December, he found unique ways to bid for athletic equipment, and now the coaches were inviting him to all of their meetings. He found his niche too. He discovered he loved sporting goods as much as he loved sports.

Mickey never went out for football. He became a recluse and even drifted away from Danny. That fall at a "woodsy" party near the Platte River, he also discovered the powerful numbing effects of alcohol. It soon became habit and the perfect way to forget the world and not feel anything.

Mickey began to ask people to call him by his given name – Terrence. Most kids at the high school called him Terry. Mickey was an image of the past. Mickey died last summer.

40

Session 9
Disclosing

Personal Journal

I think Megan is okay. Actually, I think the whole thing is okay. I'm so glad I did this.

"WHEN WE STARTED this group, Shaw and I explained that our roles as group leaders would also include some membership. Things that happen in group often affect us. Our goal whenever we start this process is not to come to group to work on our own issues, but we aren't afraid to understand when they do. Last week was one of the toughest group sessions I ever had, and I couldn't sleep for several nights that followed. When I was eighteen years old, my sister committed suicide." Meg's voice choked slightly then she continued. "When Terrence shared his past, it really touched something inside of me. It made me learn more about myself than I ever imagined, and I want to thank the group not only for how you've dealt with things in your own life while you've been here, but also for taking me to another place in my life."

Megan knew it would be inappropriate for a therapist to try to capitalize on any therapeutic process for the sake of their own issues. She also knew that it was helpful to use brief self-disclosure to allow clients or group members to know *how* a therapist can have empathy for their issues. For that reason, her self-disclosure was brief and to the point.

Megan sighed with relief as though a burden had been lifted. "Any other old business?"

Daniel spoke up, "I appreciate you sharing that, Meg." For the first time in group, he felt comfortable with her. Their eyes locked as he smiled.

The rest of the group time was spent talking about how events can shape one's life. Many of the members were reaching out to each other mostly as an extension of Terrence's emotion from the week before. They explored issues of intimacy and how alcohol had interfered with facing their fears. No matter how much you love someone, when you numb the bridge between yourself and another human being, you destroy your connection.

"Things are winding down, and everyone is pulling back as I expected," said Shaw. He plopped down in Megan's office to review the week's progress. Groups had a tendency to go through predictable stages. This group wasn't any different. The group struggled with issues of being social early, then control. Each group has different levels of conflicts depending on how much trust they give over to the other members, and this group was no different.

Shaw and Meg knew that toward the end of a group, the members' behaviors would begin to reflect life itself. When they have the feeling that a relationship is going to end, they naturally pull back and tend to avoid going deeper into emotions.

Most therapists referred to the final stage as termination. Meg always hated that term; to her, it seemed like something out of an Arnold Schwarzenegger movie: "We will now terminate our clients." She preferred to refer to it as the closure stage.

"My hope is that the group has learned new ways to relate to those who provide protection for them, you know, a healthy dependency," said Meg.

"Hmmm, sounds like you've done a lot of thinking about those kinds of things, Meg."

Meg smiled and said with a slight laugh, "Are you therapizing me again, Shaw?"

"What are friends for?"

41

Papers

DANIEL SHUT OFF the alarm clock. Five in the morning. He mumbled to himself and wandered to the kitchen where he turned on the coffee maker. His son, Marcus, was off at camp and his papers needed to be delivered. Tuesday papers. They will be light. It doesn't matter; they will be delivered from the seat of his Ford.

He picked up the bundles and brought them to the garage. Daniel stared at Marcus's paper bike. It was a new one that he saved for all summer. He looked at his older bike, both of them with canvas bags straddling the front bars. Daniel cut the wire bundle and stopped. He put the cutters on his workbench, walked out to his car and drove away.

Terrence rolled over. *What the hell was that? A dream?* He glanced at his alarm clock. Five fifteen in the morning. He rolled over and closed his eyes. This time he jumped. Something was swishing against his window. *What the hell? I'm two stories up, what the hell was that?*

Terrence sat up and looked around his small room at the Shiler Center. He stood up and moved cautiously toward the window. *Swooosh! Swooosh! Is that a tree branch brushing against my window? No . . . there's no trees outside . . .* He peeked from between the curtains and noticed a figure beneath his window. He reached out and unlocked the window and slid it open. At about the same time he saw the figure throw a handful of dirt at the window, and then he realized it was Daniel.

"What the hell are you doing?" He whispered as loud as he could.

"Get your clothes on and get down here. Come on . . ." he motioned with his hand. "I'm parked out front. Hustle up!"

Terrence followed his orders, dressed, and quietly walked past the front desk to the parking area.

"What's up, man?"

Daniel opened the car door and stepped in. "Get in. Let's go."

After Daniel told him he would help deliver Marcus's route, he started to feel a little giddy. He hadn't thrown a paper in years.

Daniel and Terrence efficiently folded and banded seventy-five papers, and their fingers began to show the residue of the black newsprint. The smell of the morning, the feel of the paper, and the sounds of a quiet neighborhood triggered memories. Good memories.

Terrence picked up an armful of papers and walked through the front of the garage toward the car. "Hey, pal, not today." Daniel walked over and pulled out a bike. "We're going the old-fashioned way."

Terrence laughed, and it made Daniel smile. He hadn't heard the "Mickey" laugh in years. It made him feel warm. It made an empty part of his life feel whole, and he suspected it was doing the same for Terrence.

Loading only half of a route on each of the two bikes was cake. Each of them took thirty-seven papers and left one at the house.

"Are you ready?" asked Daniel.

"You bet!" A huge grin crossed Terrence's face.

Daniel placed a foot on the pedal and pushed as he glided to the end of the driveway. He hadn't ridden a paper bike in years. He glanced over his shoulder to see Terrence following. The bags wobbled from side to side as he remembered the kind of athletic talent it took to guide a loaded paper bike. *It's like gently controlling the rudders on a plane. If you overcompensate . . .* Terrence hit the curb, and the front tire whipped to the side. The bags hit the tires, and his forward motion stopped.

Daniel stopped to watch the papers come flying out of the front of Terrence's bags. His body flew over the top of the handle bars, and he did a forward roll. He quickly jumped to his feet to see Daniel already in hysterical laughter.

Daniel tried to stop laughing but couldn't. As they leaned their bikes against the car, they reloaded Terrence's bags. Daniel was still out of control. "That was the funniest damn thing I've ever seen in my life!"

They eventually reloaded the papers and began delivering the route. A short time later, Daniel had a nearly identical experience of dumping of his papers as he tried to evade a stray dog that decided to nip at his heels. Terrence couldn't stop laughing this time.

It was only a matter of time before the tossing of the papers, the cool morning air, and the predawn sun aroused feelings and memories.

"Remember how Sanners was always late . . .

"Remember how Mags used to set two alarm clocks . . .

"Remember the door cop?!" Terrence reached down to hold his belly and nearly lost control of the bike.

Daniel and Terrence felt young, full of life, and full of enjoyment for a time of innocence in a carefree world. The memories rolled for the next half hour . . .

Jean . . . Whatever happened to her? I saw her at the reunion. Gawd she was wearing a blue gown. She's still a knockout . . . She married a DA in Aurora . . .

When did Lisa go to the Peace Corp? I never knew that . . .

Remember the heist?

I heard Eggs died of cancer . . . He was a great guy . . . a great man . . .

Did you see the strip mall they put up where Bud's used to be?

Remember the Y? They tore it down . . . It was the scene of the infamous public stiffy . . . Ya, it still happens to me . . .

The two laughed together as they hadn't for decades. In many ways, it made Daniel feel melancholy. *What happened to all that love we had for each other? Why did we let it slip away?*

When they got back to the house, they both stood straddling their bikes. It was as though they wanted to ride them forever. They stood in a moment of silence before Daniel said, "Hey, Mickey, remember the catch? That was the best damn catch I ever saw in my life." He smiled and gently shook his head in awe of the memory. He then stopped and looked up, realizing what he just said. For a fleeting moment, he wished he could pull the words back into his mouth. They had never spoken of *the day. Oh shit, I shouldn't have said anything. Why did I call him Mickey? Oh shit* . . . He hadn't called him Mickey since 1968; it just slipped out.

Terrence stared ahead; then a smile came over his face. "Hey, it wasn't me that saved the game. It was that tremendous relief pitching. That was a helluva game, wasn't it?" He rolled his bike over and leaned it against the garage wall. When he turned around, he had tears in his eyes, but the smile was still there. He walked toward Daniel, then reached out as the two embraced. Terrence's voice trembled. "Thanks, Danny," he said in a half whisper.

Daniel held him tight and said, "Thanks, Mickey."

42

Closure

Final Journal

We were the last generation of American men to grow up in a world without Internet, video games, cell phones, terrorist invasions, or cable TV. We didn't have character education, attention deficit disorders, or social skills curriculum. We made money delivering papers, mowing lawns, and cashing in soda bottles. It was a time when one sport hovered above all others, and it was played with a bat and a ball. Expertise didn't come from cable sport channels; it was found on the back of baseball cards. We may have been the last generation to actually read those cards – before carefully placing them in the spokes of our bicycles. We learned all about life on the vast sandlots which now are nearly extinct.

Autumn is on its way. I was unsure for so many years whether I ever wanted to go back. In the summer of 1968, I learned lessons that changed my life. During those sun-filled months, I found love for the first time and felt the joy of a first kiss. Golden sunbeams, the greenest grass I ever played on, and the carefree relationships allowed me to drink in deep breaths of air.

It was the last true summer of freedom before high school. We delivered the Rocky Mountain Times *newspaper in the predawn hours. We spent our days in confident moments playing baseball or in awkward moments with girls at the local pool. Nighttime found us lying on our sleeping bags and staring at the heavens above Denver. Our future and our dreams were shared with the stars that twinkled in perfect harmony with the sounds of crickets.*

For the first time, I understand the moment of passage. Today I am Daniel, but I can crisply recall the feeling of being Danny. My best friend, Michael Terrence Hannigan, I'm sure looks likewise in his mirror as Mickey again. The world was right in one glorious summer when Danny, Mickey, Mags, and Sanners rode through the streets of Denver in the predawn hours and delivered newspapers. We were comrades in mischief, determination, and purpose. Life is good when you have friends consumed in the same three things day after day: paper routes, girls, and baseball. What else could anyone ever hope for in life?

With all our love, potential, and spirit, I wonder still how a deranged force could wander into our path and steal everything life had to offer. I may never understand, but I am glad I returned to 1968. I am reminded of a true brotherhood. Yes, it was a brotherhood of the times.

But this is it. The final entry of the summer. I'm so happy to feel like I have a friend back. I once thought all this group stuff and counseling was crap. I think I understand it better now. I also feel kind of strange; in some small way, it's like I look at my family differently. I look at Monica differently. I look at life differently. It's so strange how two summers can come together.

I've learned that our lives are filled with unexpected events. How we deal with them can determine our sanity. There's so many unexpected things that can happen to us. What tomorrow may bring will always be a mystery. Finding love in what we have and in what we have left can often be our most difficult task but also the most rewarding. I think a lot about how our potential can go out the door at any minute. We have to rely on ourselves to understand it, but we need others to survive it. It was the death of hope in the summer of 1968 that hurt the worse. We just didn't know how to revive it, and we drifted apart.

Group, for me, was a like a small, wonderful miracle that allowed us to drift back together. I also realize that when we take one risk that seems big at the time, it can change our lives forever. The summer of 1968 changed all of us forever. I went off in a direction with more confidence than I ever had in life. Mickey lost his faith in life that summer. I will always feel indebted to Mickey. I feel bad that I wasn't there to repay him throughout his tough times. I just didn't know how. Now I do. It doesn't take any special skill. It just takes a brotherhood, in our case – a brotherhood of the Times. I'm glad he chose me to be with him again this summer. I'll be there for him for the rest of his life.

MEGAN HAD SEEN enough groups to know that in the final stages of a group, the ability to share is easy, but the desire to share is not as great. Group members don't want to start something that they can't finish. Megan saw the end of groups as a metaphor for one's life. When a relationship is ending, we need to say good-bye. To prevent any uneasiness in the final session of group, Megan had told them the previous week that in the final session, they would dispense with the usual old and new business routine. She informed them that they would have a closing activity and finish out with statements that would come from their homework.

"Tonight we will start with an activity that involves the pennies that Shaw is handing out. Each of you will have two pennies. You can do whatever you like with them. They are symbolic . . ."

"I don't like this activity," chimed in Jan. "I've done it before, and I don't think it's good for a group." Jan's nervousness was obvious to the whole group. Her greatest fear was that she would get no pennies. She was fearful of what may happen.

"As usual, Jan, we have the option to pass, but I would think that would be unfortunate because it can be a very insightful experience." Megan continued, "As I said, the pennies are symbolic. We've all given something to the group, but in particular, maybe because someone shared something you related to, or if someone gave you something to think about, or related to your struggle, you may have gained something valuable or unique from them. You may choose to give one of your pennies to that person or both of them if you like. You can add an explanation if you like or just give it away. The only rules are that you only get these two pennies, you can't go digging through your pockets for more, and you can't give one to your support partner. You can give them all the pennies you want to later. Since Shaw and I don't have support partners. We can do whatever the heck we like with ours." The group laughed. "The pennies can also be kept to yourself, you don't have to give them away. I realize that this can be a tough assignment because you have to make a choice. This also means that some may end up with more than what they started with and some with none. This is certainly not a reflection on popularity, or being liked. It has to do with whom you connected to in the group. We're going to go around until we are finished, so we will make a couple of rounds, don't feel pressured to make a decision on the first round, you can pass if you like."

Megan took the lead and demonstrated. "I'll start. I would like to give one of my pennies to Terrence for his courage in bringing such a tough part of his life to the group. You inspired me." She held his gaze for a moment, then scooted over and handed him the penny. She signaled to her left, and the group began. Rose connected to Gerri and Lisa during several sessions and decided to give one to Lisa with a smile, a gentle pat on Lisa's hand, and no explanation. The group continued around; Gerri, Tony, Doris, most were giving one away and commenting on their stories, struggles, and emotions.

Jan hesitated, then made a predictable move. "I am placing my two pennies right here in the middle because I really wish I had eleven pennies to give to each of you because I gained something from each of you. So, I'm giving my pennies to everyone."

Cop out, no risk, thought Shaw.

Daniel sat up straight, cleared his throat, and smiled. He looked directly at Megan. "I would like to give this penny to my favorite ass." The room erupted in laughter. He moved over and handed Megan a penny, then held up his hands. "Really, in all seriousness, stop laughing, Tony. I didn't mean it *that* way." The group laughed again. "I want you to have one of my pennies because I never trusted you until the end, and then I learned all about your heart, and I appreciate that, thanks, oh, and I'm sorry for calling you an ass."

Megan smirked, "That's okay, Daniel, I understand."

"I want to give one to Meg." Shaw winked at her and reached across to hand her one of his pennies. He had done this activity on numerous occasions and had never given one to Meg. Surprisingly, he felt himself starting to choke up. His lip quivered, and his eyes welled with tears. "I've learned a lot about our friendship during this group" – he stopped and sniffed through his smile – "and that's been very special to me."

Donald gave one to Tony. "You've inspired me in this group."

Terrence handed one to Megan. "I've never looked in the mirror and said to myself, 'You were a great brother.' When you said that to me, it helped me to forgive myself." His statement was somewhat open-ended, but the group knew what he meant. For his entire life, he had never forgiven himself. He always felt responsible for his relationships ending. For the first time since his youth, he felt energy. He sat down and beamed with delight. It was a smile no one in the group had seen before. Daniel smiled in his direction – he could see a boyish Mickey bubbling to the surface.

Lisa held a penny to her chest. "I really need to give one to myself. This is important to me."

Earl indicated he would pass this round.

As the group made their final round, some kept their pennies, and some gave them away. There was no tension in the group except with Jan. No one mentioned her name, and she was growing more nervous by the second. When it came back around to Earl, he gave one to Megan, then said, "I would like to give my last penny to Jan, and I hope you find happiness." Megan noted that Earl was observant and felt a little sorry for Jan. Jan was jubilant and about to burst inside. She was thinking, *I got a penny! I got a penny! I got a penny!*

"I told you to write down one thing you learned from group. And I told you to write them down before you would come here this week and drop them in my box in the office. These were submitted anonymously with the agreement that I would type them out and give them to the group for our final session. Shaw and I scrambled them in random order and also threw ours in. Here they are." She began to pass out the sheets. "Let's take a minute to read them to yourself."

I learned that if I pull away too much from those that really care about me, I can't see how I am affecting others.

I realized how much I love my best friend.

I learned that if I put up a guard and my only way to think about life is through shame, then I will never have the opportunity to grow.

I learned that there are a lot of people with troubles like me, and I don't feel so all alone.

I found out that my biggest risk in life is to reach out.

I finally experienced care; I pushed it away before. It made me learn that it's okay to let it in.

I learned that some people run groups the way they want to and that it doesn't matter if sometimes others get hurt during them.

I learned that it's okay to not keep trying to be brave by myself.

Life is something that flows through us. I learned that if I can go with the flow and not fight it, I will be stronger.

I discovered that I need to always work hard for what I really want in life.

I learned that I need to nurture my relationships rather than poison them.

The hole in my heart is finally gone. I learned that nightmares go away when you let the daydreams come in.

"All right, folks, to repeat something I just read. I don't know whose it was, but I agree that 'it's okay to not keep trying to be brave by ourselves.'" She looked at the group and saw Tony blush and smile. It was probably his. "So, if you need us, if you need others, stop by. If not here, then somewhere else. It's okay to reach out. Let's keep our life goals going. Shaw and I brought some refreshments, and I might add that Shaw baked that cake, so let's dig in."

The group milled about chatting and saying their good-byes. The conversation was lively. Some hugged, and others shook hands. A couple of members continued to covertly give away other pennies in gestures of good will. Daniel was talking baseball with Earl. Rose had to make sure she got a hug from Meg and Shaw. At one point, Lisa and Gerri had an arm around each other's waists. This was a group they could be open with. Shaw kept reaching down and pinching his waist as he contemplated, *Should I have two or three pieces of cake? What the hell, I'll have one more and a salad tomorrow.*

After the group, Megan and Shaw hugged. "Shall we write up our final case notes?" asked Shaw.

"Sure," said Megan

Terrence knew he would be leaving the treatment center in a few days. He felt apprehensive but confident he would keep his life together. He also knew he would spend a lot more time with Daniel, and the thought of it made him feel stronger.

Daniel mentioned to Terrence that he wanted to take him for a drive after their last session. They loaded up in his car and drove toward south Denver.

When Daniel pulled into Ruby Hill Park, he noticed a van parked at the top of the hill. As they drove closer he recognized the logo on the side: MAGS SPORT SHOPS.

In the spring of their sophomore year in high school, Mags's interest in sporting goods continued to grow, and eventually he knew it would become his life's work.

Sanners's home life grew more intense. Eventually he went the way of his older brother and lashed out at his father. He came home from school one day and saw the bruises on his mother's face. He went into a fit of rage and hospitalized his father with three punches resulting in a broken jaw. When an ambulance arrived, they called the police. The police took Vic Sanners into custody and put him in a jail cell. His huge body made him look twenty years old, and they treated him as though he was an adult by throwing him into a jail cell with other adults.

Mr. Magliano found out and immediately went to the police station. He went into an uncharacteristic rage and eventually had Sanners released to his custody. Mags had never seen his father so mad in his life. It frightened him but also confirmed his faith that his father was concerned about his best friend.

Denver Social Services eventually agreed that it was in the child's best interest to be removed from the home. At dinner that night, Sanners began to cry at the thought of having to leave the Magliano household. Mr. and Mrs. Magliano asked him where he wanted to live. Vic was hesitant to tell them for fear he would be a burden to their family. They assured him that he would never be a burden – he would be family as long as he chose to stay.

Mr. Magliano petitioned the court to be his legal guardian and was granted full custody. Mags and Sanners finished the last two years of high school as roommates.

Sanners found a sport that was perfectly suited for him – wrestling. In his senior year, he went to the state finals in the heavyweight division. Mags screamed so loud that he nearly passed out. Sanners was behind 7-2 when he threw his opponent on his back and pinned him with fifteen seconds left. His teammates, the Maglianos, and the huge crowd erupted at the come-from-behind win. Mags told Sanners it was the greatest day in his life.

After high school, Mags went to Denver Community College with a dream to start his own sporting goods business. He earned an associates degree in small business management in two years. Mr. Magliano took out a second mortgage on his home and Mags Sports Shops were born. The same year, Thomas Magliano married Jennifer. They stayed true to each other throughout high school. Eventually they had five children.

In frames behind the counter of his first store, he had several old sports photos. He also had a 1968 Nolan Ryan-Jerry Koosman baseball card in a frame. The card was torn in half with a half-inch gap between the two pieces. If it weren't for the tear in the card, it would be worth a great deal. Collectors are willing to pay thousands for a Nolan Ryan rookie card today. Under it was a small sign Not for Sale. It was worth millions to Mags. It held the memory of the day Sanners had ripped the card in two – and the day they won the league. Eventually Mags opened two more stores and was in the process of opening a fourth.

Sanners accepted a scholarship to Rangely Junior College for wrestling. He was twice a Junior College All-American and then went on to Colorado State College in Boulder to become an NCAA All-American as well. Eventually, both wrestling programs went the way of most college wrestling teams in the country. They were cut by administrators trying to trim budgets.

Vic Sanners started out as a health teacher, then earned a master's degree, and became a school counselor. After two years as a counselor, he started on a doctorate at Northern State University and finished it four years later.

Dr. Vic Sanners found his life's passion by specializing in violence prevention for youths. He eventually published several research articles in professional journals on abusive parenting and was regarded as one of the top experts in his field. Meg and Shaw heard him speak once at a conference in downtown Denver. Vic Sanners never married but had been living with another psychologist for the past eight years. He met her while working out at a health club.

Danny and Terrence both played baseball in high school with Danny improving year-to-year and Terrence disintegrating. Over time, Danny became a close friend of Chet Anderson after the two played in summer high school leagues together. Eventually they were roommates at Northern State University, and Danny shared the story of "the heist" with him. Whenever he felt like trash talking with his roommate, he brought up the heist and the fact that he got him for the final out of their childhood game.

Terrence went to the same college and joined a fraternity. The alcohol that poured at the frat parties served to only make his abusive drinking worse. Danny and Terrence remained friends and occasionally saw each other. One night Danny was awakened from his dorm room to respond to an emergency at Terrence's frat house. Terrence was backed into the corner of his room in a drunken stupor and threatening for the first time to cut his wrists. Danny talked him down and got him into bed to sleep it off. He had plenty of experience from his days at home with his brother Aaron.

Danny met Monica while he was teaching and later started their family after establishing their careers. Terrence married shortly after college and divorced three years later. Fortunately no children were involved. Eventually he met Maggie, and they started their roller-coaster marriage with Terrence attempting to give up his alcohol on several occasions, each time meeting futility.

Daniel pulled the car behind the MAGS SPORTS SHOPS van, and the two got out of the car. He called Thomas and Vic earlier in the week to have them meet at the park. Terrence grinned as he saw Mags's portly body waddle over to them. Dr. Sanners's body hadn't changed much either – he still lifted weights nearly every day. The four men exchanged embraces, then sat on a picnic bench, watched the sun set over the Denver skyline, and revived old memories. It was the first time the four had been together at the same time since 1968. For the first time, they talked about the memories – the good memories.

43

A New Group

MEGAN SCANNED THE new group – five new couples. She observed their body language – they were nervous. "Speak only for yourself, stay in the moment, try not to ask questions, and keep a confidential journal. Shaw and I will facilitate the group, but we will not be responsible for its content. This will be up to you." She scanned her head from side to side to make eye contact with everyone, then smiled.